<u>Did I Read This Already?</u>
Place your initials or unique symbol in
square as a reminder to you that you have
read this title.

The Calico & Cowboys Romance Collection

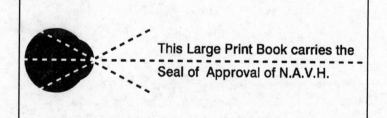

This Large Print Book carries the
Seal of Approval of N.A.V.H.

THE CALICO & COWBOYS ROMANCE COLLECTION

8 NOVELLAS FROM THE OLD WEST CELEBRATE THE LIGHTHEARTED SIDE OF LOVE

MARY CONNEALY

THORNDIKE PRESS

A part of Gale, a Cengage Company

Farmington Hills, Mich • San Francisco • New York • Waterville, Maine
Meriden, Conn • Mason, Ohio • Chicago

Pub 31

The Advent Bride © 2014 by Mary Connealy.
A Bride Rides Herd © 2015 by Mary Connealy.
His Surprise Family © 2016 by Mary Connealy.
Homestead on the Range © 2015 by Mary Connealy.
Sophie's Other Daughter © 2014 by Mary Connealy.
The Sweetwater Bride © 2016 by Mary Connealy.
Texas Tea © 2015 by Mary Connealy.
Hope for Christmas © 2014 by Mary Connealy.
Unless otherwise noted, all scripture quotations are taken from the King James Version of the Bible.
Thorndike Press, a part of Gale, a Cengage Company.

LIBRARY OF CONGRESS CIP DATA ON FILE.
CATALOGUING IN PUBLICATION FOR THIS BOOK
IS AVAILABLE FROM THE LIBRARY OF CONGRESS

ISBN-13: 978-1-4328-4625-1 (hardcover)
ISBN-10: 1-4328-4625-6 (hardcover)

Published in 2018 by arrangement with Barbour Publishing, Inc.

Printed in the United States of America
1 2 3 4 5 6 7 22 21 20 19 18

This book is dedicated to
Steven Curtis Chapman,
who sang a really encouraging song,
"Love Take Me Over," at a time I really
needed encouragement. Thank you to all
the wonderful, blessed artists in
contemporary Christian music.

CONTENTS

■ ■ ■ ■

THE ADVENT BRIDE

■ ■ ■ ■

CHAPTER 1

Lone Tree, Nebraska
Monday, November 29, 1875

Being a teacher was turning out to be a little like having the flu.

Simon O'Keeffe. Her heart broke for him at the same time her stomach twisted with dread for herself. The churning innards this boy caused in her made a case of influenza fun and games.

The small form on the front steps of the Lone Tree schoolhouse huddled against the cold. Shivering herself, she wondered how long seven-year-old Simon had been sitting with his back pressed against the building to get out of the wind.

On these smooth, treeless highlands the wind blew nearly all the time. No matter where a person sought shelter outside, there was no escape from the Nebraska cold.

Just as there was no escape from Simon.

Picking up her pace and shoving her dread down deep, she hurried to the door, produced the key her position as schoolmarm had granted her, and said, "Let's get inside, Simon. You must be freezing."

And what was his worthless father thinking to let him get to school so early?

Simon's eyes, sullen and far too smart, lifted to hers.

"Did you walk to school?" Melanie tried to sound pleasant. But it didn't matter. Simon would take it wrong. The cantankerous little guy had a gift for it. She swung the door open and waved her hand to shoo him in.

The spark of rebellion in his eyes clashed with his trembling. He wanted to defy her — Simon always wanted to defy her — but he was just too cold.

"My pa ain't gonna leave me to walk to school in this cold, Miss Douglas." Simon was offended on his father's behalf.

"So he drove you in?" Melanie should just quit talking. Nothing she said would make Simon respond well, the poor little holy terror.

"We live in town now . . . leastways we're living here for the winter."

And that explained Simon's presence. He'd started the school year, then he'd stayed home to help with harvest — or maybe his pa had just been too busy to get the boy out the door. And before harvest was over, the weather turned bitter cold. The five-mile walk was too hard, and apparently his pa wouldn't drive him.

The day Simon had stopped coming to school, her life as the teacher had improved dramatically. That didn't mean the rest of her life wasn't miserable, but at least school had been good. And now here came her little arch enemy back to school. It was all she could do to suppress a groan.

Closing the door, Melanie rushed to set her books on her desk in the frigid room. She headed straight for the potbellied stove to get a fire going.

Gathering an armful of logs, she pulled open the creaking door and knelt to stuff kindling into the stove. She added shredded bits of bark and touched a match to it. A crash startled her. She knocked her head into the cast iron.

Whirling around, expecting the worst . . . she got it.

Simon.

Glaring at her.

Around his scruffy boots lay a pile of books that had previously sat in a tidy pile on her desk.

Dear God, I'm already weary, and it's just gone seven in the morning, with nearly two hours until the other children show up. She was on her knees. What better to do than pray?

The prayer helped her fight back her temper. After seeing no harm was done — not counting the new bump on her forehead —

she turned and went back to stoking the fire.

Melanie swung the little iron door shut and twisted the flat knob that kept the fire inside. "Come on over and get warm, Simon." Kneeling by the slowly warming stove put heart into her. Her room at Mrs. Rathbone's was miserable. She spent every night in a mostly unheated attic.

Simon came close, he must have been freezing to move next to her.

The little boy's dark curls were too long. He was dressed in near rags. Was his father poor? Maybe a widower didn't notice worn-out knees and threadbare cuffs. And it didn't cost a thing to get a haircut, not if Henry O'Keeffe did the cutting himself. Water was certainly free, but the boy had black curves under his ragged fingernails and dirt on his neck.

Pieces of cooked egg stuck on the front of Simon's shirt, too. Sloppy as that was, it gave Melanie some encouragement to know the boy had been served a hot breakfast.

The crackling fire was heartening, and the boy was close enough to get warm. She reached out her hands to garner those first precious waves of heat.

"Soon, I'll have to get to work, Simon. But you can stay here, just sit by the stove and keep warm."

A scowl twisted his face. What had she said now?

"It ain't my pa's doing that I was out there. He told me to go to school at schooltime. I'm the one that got the time wrong."

Leave a seven-year-old to get himself to school. Henry O'Keeffe had a lot to answer for.

"Well, I hope you weren't waiting long. I'm usually here by seven, so you can come on over early if you want." The twisting stomach came back. She didn't want this little imp here from early morning on.

But she'd just invited the most unruly little boy in town to share her peaceful time at the school. Just the thought of dealing with him for more hours than absolutely necessary reminded Melanie of influenza again. Her stomach twisted with dismay.

But what could be done? The boy couldn't sit out in the cold.

God had no words of wisdom for her except the plain truth. She was stuck with Simon O'Keeffe. She'd have to make the best of it and help the boy any way she could.

CHAPTER 2

"Class dismissed." Melanie clasped the *McGuffey Reader* in both hands and did her best to keep her face serene while she strangled the book. It had to be better than strangling a seven-year-old.

Every child in the place erupted from their seats and ran for the nails where their coats hung.

"Simon." Melanie's voice cut through the clatter. Simon stood, belligerent. He held his desktop in his hands.

The three boys older than Simon laughed and shoved each other. There had been none of this roughhousing last week. They'd been acting up all day, reacting to Simon's bold defiance. She'd lost all control of the older boys. Four older girls giggled. Two little boys just a year older than Simon slid looks of pity his way. They all scrambled for their coats and lunch pails.

It hadn't helped that she'd started practice today for a Christmas program, scheduled for Christmas Eve, here at the school. Melanie had been warned that the entire town, not just parents, would be attending.

"Yes, Miss Douglas?"

Do not render evil for evil.

Why, that was right there in the Bible. Was disassembling a desk evil? Normally Melanie would have said no, but this was Simon.

"You will stay after school until you've put that desk back together." Melanie hadn't even known the desks could be taken apart. They'd always seemed very sturdy to her. But she'd underestimated her little foe.

"I can finish it tomorrow. Pa will worry about me." Simon stood, holding that desktop, the little rat trying to wriggle his way out of this trap. The boy was apparently bored to death with school. Studying would've made the day go faster, but that was too much to ask.

"When you don't arrive home on time, he'll come hunting for you, and this is the first place he'll check."

"But he said he might be late."

"How late?" Melanie clamped her mouth shut.

Simon's eyes blazed. The boy was always ready to take offense on his father's behalf.

Melanie had to stop saying a single word Simon could take as a criticism of his pa and address her concerns directly to Henry. But she wasn't letting Simon leave for a possibly cold house with no father at home. Simon's after-school time was, as of this moment, lasting until his pa turned up to fetch him.

"Get on with repairing the desk. Then you can bring your books close to the stove, and we'll study until you've made up for the schooltime you wasted taking your desk apart."

Simon glared at her, but he turned back to the desk. Melanie opened her book to study for tomorrow's lesson. The two of them got along very well, as long as the whole room was between them and neither spoke.

"It's done. Can I go now?"

Melanie lifted her head. She'd gotten lost in her reading. One of the older children, Lisa Manchon, was in an advanced arithmetic book. The girl was restless, ready to be done with school and, at fifteen years old, find a husband and get on with a life of her own.

Her folks, though, wouldn't hear of such a thing, or perhaps there were no offers. For whatever reason, Lisa was kept in school. Melanie worked hard to keep her interested in her work.

"No, you *may* not go." Melanie stressed the correct grammar. "Bring your reader to the stove, and we'll go over tomorrow's lesson together."

November days were short in Nebraska, and the sun was low in the sky. Obviously Henry was not yet home, or he'd have come to find his son. Melanie carried her heavy desk chair to the stove and stood, brows arched, waiting for Simon to come join her.

It helped that it was cold.

As they worked, Simon proved, as he always did when he bothered to try, that he was one of the brightest children in the school.

The school door slammed open.

"Simon is missing!" In charged a tall man wrapped up in a thick coat with a scarf and Stetson, gloves and heavy boots.

Henry O'Keeffe — here at last.

He skidded to a halt. His light blue eyes flashed like cold fire — at her. Then he looked more warmly at his son. "Simon, I told you to go home after school."

"Pa, she wouldn't —" The little tattletale.

"Your son," Melanie cut through their talk, "had to stay after school for misbehaving, Mr. O'Keeffe." Unlike her unruly young student, she had no trouble taking full responsibility for her actions.

She rose from her chair by the fire. "Is it a long way home?" It was approaching dusk. She didn't want Simon out alone in the cold, dark town.

"No, just a couple of blocks. What did he —"

"Simon, get your coat on, then, and head for home. I need to have a talk with your father." She noticed that Henry carried a rifle. Did he always have it with him, or was

19

he armed to hunt for his missing son?

"Miss Douglas," Simon began, clearly upset with her.

"Is that all right with you, Mr. O'Keeffe? Will your son be safe walking home alone?" Melanie wouldn't press the point if Henry wasn't comfortable with it.

"Of course. There's nothing in this town more dangerous than a tumbleweed, and even they are frozen to the ground these days. I need to get supper. It's getting late."

"Let Simon head for home, then. I promise to be brief. You're right, it is getting late." She arched a brow at him and saw the man get the message.

"Run on home, Simon. I'll be two minutes behind you."

Simon took a long, hard look at Melanie, almost as if he wanted to stay and protect his pa.

"We won't be long, Simon." Melanie tilted her head toward the door. With a huff, Simon dragged on his coat and left the building.

Melanie knew then he was really worried because the door didn't even slam.

CHAPTER 3

Why did all the pretty women want to yell at him?

Hank turned from watching Simon leave, then dropped his voice, not putting it past Simon to listen in.

"What's the problem, Miss Douglas?" Those snapping green eyes jolted him. He'd felt the jolt before, every time he'd gotten close to her in fact. And that surprised him because since Greta had died, no woman, no matter how pretty, had drawn so much as a whisper of reaction, let alone a jolt.

He'd gotten used to the idea that his heart had died with his wife. Melanie made him question that, but of course, all she wanted to do was yell at him. He braced himself to take the criticism. He deserved it.

"Mr. O'Keeffe, your son is a very bright boy. It's possible he's the smartest youngster in this school."

That wasn't what he expected to hear. Had she kept him here to compliment Simon?

Maybe she wanted to pass Simon into a higher class? He *was* a bright boy. Hank felt his chest swell with pride, and he started to relax.

"But he is disrupting the whole school. We have to do something, between the two of us, to get him to behave."

Hank's gut twisted. It was fear. He tried to make himself admit it. But that effort was overridden by a need to fight anyone who spoke ill of his boy.

"You're saying you can't keep order in school?" Simon was all he had. Hank knew he didn't give the young'un enough attention, but a man had to feed his child, and that meant work, long hours of work.

"I was doing fine until today." Miss Douglas's voice rose, and she plunked her fists on her trim waist.

Hank looked at those pretty pink lips, pursed in annoyance. He'd never had much luck with women. He still had trouble believing Greta had married him. She'd seemed to like him, too, and it hadn't even been hard.

Now, when he needed to handle a woman right, calm her down, soothe her ruffled feathers, all he could think of was snapping at her.

He clamped his mouth shut until he could speak calmly. "What do you want from me, Miss Douglas? You want me to threaten him? Tell him if he gets a thrashing at school he'll get one at home?"

Hank didn't thrash Simon. Maybe he should. Maybe sparing the rod was wrong, but the hurt in the boy since his ma died had made it impossible for Hank to deal him out more pain.

"I don't thrash my students, Mr. O'Keeffe. I have never found it necessary, and I don't intend to start now. What I want is —"

The schoolhouse door slammed open. "Hank, come quick; a fight broke out in the saloon."

Mr. Garland at the general store stuck his face in the room then vanished. Hank took one step.

A slap on his arm stopped him. Miss Douglas had a grip that'd shame a burr.

"I'm not done talking to you yet." She'd stumbled along for a couple of feet but she held on doggedly.

"We're done talking. I have to go. My Simon is a good boy. You just need to learn to manage him better." He pried her little claws from his sleeve and managed to pull his coat open. "Let loose. You heard Ian. There's a fight."

"Why do you have to go just because there's a fight at the saloon?"

"I have to stop it."

"But why?"

His coat finally flapped all the way open, and he impatiently shoved it back even

23

farther so she could see his chest.

And see the star pinned right above his heart. "Because just today I started a job as the town sheriff. That was the only way I could find a house in town. Now, if you can't handle one little boy, just say so and I'll get him a job running errands at the general store. Schoolin's a waste of time anyway for a bright boy like my Simon. Most likely the reason you can't handle him is he's smarter than you." A tiny smile curved his lips. "I got a suspicion he's smarter than me."

Then he turned and ran after Ian.

Chapter 4

About once a minute, while she closed up the school, put on her wrap, gathered up her books, locked the building, walked to Mrs. Rathbone's, and let herself in the back door, Melanie caught herself shaking her head.

"He's smarter than you."

There was no doubt in her mind that Simon was very bright. Was Mr. O'Keeffe right? Was it her fault?

"My Simon is a good boy. You just need to learn to manage him better."

Was it all about managing rather than discipline? She shook her head again. Not in denial, though there might be a bit of that, but to clear her head so she could think.

How long would Henry be dealing with that saloon fight? Simon was home, and he'd be expecting his father. Had Henry thought of that?

"You're finally here, Melanie?"

That cold, disapproving voice drove all thoughts of the O'Keeffe family from

25

her head.

"Yes, Mrs. Rathbone." As if the old battle-ax ever had a thing to do with her. Melanie hadn't even gotten the back door closed before the woman started her complaining. Mrs. Rathbone had made it clear as glass that Melanie was to always use the back door, never the front — that was for invited guests, not schoolmarms living on charity.

"I've eaten without you."

Melanie walked through the back entry and through the kitchen, where she saw a plate, uncovered, sitting on the table, without a doubt cold and caked in congealed grease.

She walked down a short hall that opened onto an elegant dining room and on into a front sitting room. Mrs. Rathbone called it the parlor. She sat alone before a crackling fire, needlework in hand. She glanced up from the bit of lace she was tatting, peering over the top of her glasses, scowling.

"Good evening, Mrs. Rathbone."

The older woman sniffed. "A fine thing, a woman cavorting until all hours. The school board would not approve."

Always Magda Rathbone seemed on the verge of throwing Melanie to the wolves, ruining her career, and blackening her name with the whole town if she was forced to tell the truth of how poorly Melanie behaved.

Melanie happened to think she behaved with the restraint of a nun — a muzzled nun

— a muzzled nun wearing a straitjacket. But no matter how carefully she spoke and how utterly alone she remained in the upper room, Mrs. Rathbone found fault.

"One of my students was left at school. His father is the new sheriff in town, and he was delayed. I minded the boy until his father could come."

"Hank O'Keeffe." Another sniff. "Everyone knows that boy of his is a terror, and as for Mr. O'Keeffe, he's got a lot of nerve being a lawman when he himself should be taken up on charges for the way he neglected his wife."

Melanie froze. What was this about Henry's wife?

"She'd still be alive if that man hadn't been so hard on her."

What sort of demands? Was she expected to work on the homestead? Or was there a darker meaning. Had Henry abused his wife? And was he now abusing his son?

"Go to your room now. I prefer quiet in the evening. Disturbances give me a headache."

Sent to her room like a naughty child. *I'll show you a disturbance, you old battle-ax.* Melanie had a wild urge to start dancing around the room, singing at the top of her lungs. Disturbance? She'd show Simon a thing or two about disturbances.

Melanie, of course, did nothing of the sort. "Good night, Mrs. Rathbone."

"One more thing."

27

Melanie froze. She knew what was coming, the same thing that came every Monday, after Melanie had worked hard cleaning Mrs. Rathbone's house all weekend to earn her keep.

"Yes, ma'am?" What had the woman found to criticize now?

"I distinctly told you I wanted the library dusted this weekend. It's as filthy as ever."

The library. Two or three thousand books at least. And from what Melanie could see, judging by the undisturbed dust, Mrs. Rathbone had never read a one of them.

"I'll get to it, ma'am, but Sunday you specifically stopped me from dusting to clean out the cellar. There weren't enough hours this weekend to do both."

"You'd have gotten far more done if you hadn't spent a half a day idling."

"I spend half a day in church." Melanie squared her shoulders. She would never give in on this, even if it meant being cast into the streets in the bitter cold. "I will always spend Sunday morning attending services. I've made that clear, ma'am. In fact, the Lord's Day should be for rest. But I worked all afternoon and evening on the cellar."

Melanie clamped her mouth shut. Defending herself just stirred up the old harpy. And Melanie knew how miserably unhappy Mrs. Rathbone was. Her constant unkindness was rooted in her lonely life — a friendless existence shaped by her cruel tongue, a heart hardened to God, and her condemnation of anyone and everyone.

The people in Lone Tree endured Mrs. Rathbone, in part because of her wealth that she sprinkled onto the needs of the town, not generously, but she gave enough so that no one wanted to out-and-out offend her. Instead they avoided her and spoke ill of her behind her back.

It was a poor situation.

Melanie did her best to do as she was asked, even though the school board had said nothing about Melanie having to work as a housekeeper to earn her room. She suspected the board had no idea what was going on.

But it was a small town, most houses one or two rooms. There was nowhere else for Melanie to stay. She remembered what Mr. O'Keeffe had said about needing to take the job of sheriff to get a house. She had little doubt there were no empty houses in the raw little Nebraska town.

"I don't appreciate your tone. Get on to your room."

Because no *tone* could possibly come out of Melanie's mouth at this moment that would be appreciated, she went back to the kitchen, picked up the plate of food, and walked up the back staircase.

Melanie worked like a slave for Mrs. Rathbone at the same time being told she lived on charity. Each step she took upstairs wore on her as if the weight of the world rested on her shoulders.

The narrow stairs had a door at the bottom and top. Both were to be kept firmly closed, which also kept out any heat.

In Melanie's room, a chimney went up through the roof. It was the only source of heat — a chimney bearing warmth from two floors down.

It wasn't a small room; the attic stretched nearly the whole length of the house before the roof sloped. But Mrs. Rathbone had stored years of junk up there. There was barely room for Melanie's bed and a small basket with her clothing. She had to walk downstairs for a basin of water and bring it back up to bathe or wash out her clothing.

She spoke the most heartfelt prayer of her life, asking God to control her temper with Mrs. Rathbone and with Simon and, while she was at it, with Henry. She prayed for strength sufficient for the day.

The prayers struck deep. Her impatience with Simon was sinful. It was easier to admit this now, with the boy away from her. While she was dealing with him, she felt justified in her anger.

Continuing to pray, she ate the unappetizing chicken — though it looked like it might have been good an hour ago. She swallowed cold mashed potatoes coated in congealed gravy. She was hungry enough she forced herself to eat every crumb of a piece of dried-out bread. She reached in her heart for true thankfulness for this food.

Only four days after Thanksgiving — a meal she'd cooked and served to Mrs. Rathbone, who had then told her to eat upstairs in her room. But Melanie knew she had plenty to be thankful for: first and foremost, a heavenly Father who loved her even if she was otherwise alone in the world.

She set her empty plate aside with a quick prayer of thanks that she wasn't hungry. She'd known hunger, and this was most definitely better. Turning her prayers to Simon, she remembered Henry's words: *"My Simon is a good boy. You just need to learn to manage him better."*

She begged God for wisdom to figure that out. If it was about managing Simon, then how would she do it?

Changing quickly into her nightgown in the chilly room, Melanie took her hair down and brushed it out, speaking silently to God all the while.

In the midst of her prayer, she remembered that moment earlier when she'd wondered about Simon going home alone tonight. She should have gone with him and stayed with him until his father arrived.

She worried enough about the trouble that little boy could get into alone that she was tempted to go make sure he was all right, though his father had to be home by now.

Her worry deepened along with her prayers as she set the hair combs and pins aside. Then her eyes fell on a large wooden box sitting on one of the many chests jumbled into the room. Strange that she'd never noticed it before, because right now it drew her eye so powerfully the dull wood seemed to nearly glow.

It was an odd little thing. Crudely made, the wood in a strange pattern, like a patchwork of little squares as if it had been put together with scraps of wood. About ten inches tall and as much deep and wide, a little cube. Four pairs of drawers were in the front, each with a little wooden knob. It wasn't particularly pretty, but there was something about it.

Her eyes went from the box to the combs and pins. They would fit in there perfectly. She should ask Mrs. Rathbone before she used the grouchy woman's things, but those little drawers seemed to almost beckon her.

With a shrug, Melanie decided she'd ask Mrs. Rathbone about the box in the morning, but for now, on impulse, she pulled open a drawer, which was much narrower and not as deep as she expected. Staring at the strangely undersized drawer, Melanie wondered at it for a moment then slipped her hair things inside.

A whisper of pleasure that made no sense eased the worst of her exhaustion and helped her realize the waste of energy worrying about Simon was at this late hour. Her chance to help was when Henry got called away. Now she was just letting sin gnaw at her mind and rob her of her peace.

The prayers and somehow the little box replaced her worry with a calm that could only come from God.

Prayer she understood, but why would a box do such a thing?

CHAPTER 5

Melanie asked about the box the next morning. Mrs. Rathbone snorted with contempt.

"I remember that shabby thing. It belonged to my husband's grandmother. His mother's mother. He adored that strange old lady and wouldn't part with any of her old keepsakes. That's what most everything is up in the attic. She was covered in wrinkles and dressed in the same old faded clothes, even though there was money for better. Those rags are probably still up in that attic, too. *Mamó* Cullen — that's what he called her — *Mamó,* what kind of name is that?"

An Irish word, most likely for mother or grandmother?

"She was ancient and blind by the time I came into the family and a completely selfish old woman. She seemed to be well into her dotage to me. The old crone seemed to never speak except to tell stories of the 'old country.' She always called Ireland 'the old country.' She was an embarrassment with her lower-class accent. I could hardly understand her. I hadn't met her before my marriage, or I might have had second thoughts."

Mrs. Rathbone waved a dismissive hand. "You can have that old box. I remember it well. My husband refused to part with it after his mother died. I'm not up to climbing all those stairs anymore. I'd forgotten it was up there, or I'd have thrown it away by now. Now as to dusting the library . . ."

Melanie listened politely while Magda found fault. Being given the box lifted her spirits, and her prayers last night combined with her renewed determination to be thankful got her through breakfast and the packing of her meager lunch. The packing was done under Magda's watchful eye, lest Melanie become greedy and take two slices of bread.

Setting out for the short, cold walk to school before seven, Melanie feared Simon would be sitting there in the cold. He wasn't, but he appeared minutes later and came straight for the stove Melanie had burning.

The plucky thankfulness was sorely tested for the next eight hours. Simon started a fist fight, then two other boys ended up in a fight all their own. He tripped one of the older girls walking past his desk. The whole classroom erupted in laughter. During arithmetic he used his slate to draw a picture of a dog biting a man in the backside and passed it

35

around the room to the wriggling delight of the other boys.

And through it all, the heightened noise and constant distraction, Simon hadn't learned a thing. And that was the worst of it. Neither Simon nor the other children were doing much work.

"My Simon is a good boy. You just need to learn to manage him better."

Manage him.

But how?

When the children were let out at twelve for lunch, they all ran home, except for Simon.

Her heart sank at the sight of him fetching a lunch pail and bringing it back to his desk. She'd planned for the noon hour to be spent in prayer that God would help her through the afternoon.

After eating his lunch far too quickly, Simon ran around the room — it was too cold to go outside. He complained and asked questions and just generally was as much trouble on his own as he was in the group. Instead of being able to sit in silence and listen for the still, small voice of God, she'd sent up short, desperate prayers for patience and wisdom — with no time to listen for God's answer.

He tore a page out of another child's reading book, broke a slate, spilled ink — and then he lifted the flat wooden top of his desk into the air and dropped it with a clap so loud Melanie squeaked and jumped out of her chair.

Her temper snapped. "Simon, why are you so careless?"

A sullen glare was his only answer.

Maybe if she threw him outside and told him to run in circles around the schoolhouse to burn off some energy . . .

"Hyah!" Simon dropped to his knees and shoved the desktop forward. He swung one arm wide like he was lashing an imaginary horse's rump and made a sound that was probably supposed to be a cracking whip.

Fighting to sound like it was a simple question, rather than the dearest dream of her heart, she asked, "Wouldn't you rather go home to eat?"

"Pa rides out to the homestead every day to do chores. We've got cattle out there. He can't get there, do his work, and get back in time to make a meal, so he packs a sandwich and milk for me."

The little boy had a better lunch than she did.

"Get off the floor and get to work putting your desk back together."

Simon stopped. "It was wobbly. I didn't take it apart on purpose."

He most certainly had.

"You have to stop taking things apart. Even if they're wobbly." It sounded like begging —

37

and maybe that about described it. She was at her wit's end.

"It came apart on its own. I'll put it back together." His begrudging tone made it sound like she'd just told him his "horse" desktop had a broken leg and had to be shot.

"You took another desk apart, and you didn't get it put back together well. Which is why I moved you. Now this one will be wobbly, too, if you reassemble it poorly. I'll be out of desks by Friday."

"I'm going to get to work putting this back together right away."

"Is there a chance you can improve on yesterday's task?" Melanie heard the scold in her voice and fought to keep it under control.

Simon sat up straight. His eyes lit up.

Melanie nearly quaked with fear.

"I'll bet doing it a second time will help me improve. Once I'm done with this one, I'll work on the one from last night. This is good practice for me."

What did he mean "practice"? "Are you thinking of doing this sort of thing for a career, Simon?"

That was a form of teaching, she supposed.

"Yep. Pa's already given me a knife to whittle with, and I've carved a toy soldier."

The thought of Simon with a sharp knife nearly wrung a gasp out of her.

"I'm going to keep at it until I've got an army." He was so enthused. "Then Pa's gonna show me how to build a toy-sized barn and a corral. He said pretty soon I'll be helping him build big buildings. We need a chicken coop come spring."

This excited him. "That is fine to learn a skill, but you're supposed to be studying reading, writing, and arithmetic while you're here at school. You shouldn't have time to practice your building skills."

Simon's face went sullen again. All the brightness and enthusiasm went out like a fire doused in cold water.

"Just get on with the desk, Simon. Maybe we can figure out a way you can work on your building skills after you're done with your studies." She tried to sound perky, but all she could imagine in her future was one disaster after another.

Then a thought struck her. "Say, Simon, is your pa a good carpenter?"

"Yep, he built our sod house, and it's the best one all around."

The best house made of dirt. What a thrill.

"And he built a sod barn."

"Will the chicken coop be made of sod, too?"

Simon shrugged. "I reckon. Where would he get wood? There ain't no trees around. They didn't name this town Lone Tree for nothing."

Melanie thought of the majestic cottonwood that stood just outside of town. Alone.

But the folks in town were planting trees. They'd tilled up the ground around the tree so seedlings had a fighting chance to sprout. Now little trees poked up every spring and were quickly transplanted. There were hundreds of slender saplings scattered around, but they were a long way from trees.

"Let's see if you can do a better job repairing this desk than you did last night. It will be a test of your skills. And please don't take anything else apart."

"But it was *wobbly.* It needed me to fix it."

Melanie decided then and there to impose on Mr. O'Keeffe and his admirable carpentry skills to keep the building standing — if working with sod translated to working with desks. What his son took apart, Mr. O'Keeffe could just reassemble.

And she'd start tonight because she wasn't going to let Simon go home to an empty house, no matter how late she had to stay at school. She'd felt the Lord telling her not to do that again.

Judging by last night, she could be here very late.

And wasn't Mrs. Rathbone going to have something to say about that?

CHAPTER 6

"Miss Douglas, Simon would be fine at home alone."

Melanie arched a brow at Henry O'Keeffe as she rose from beside the stove, where she'd been working on a desk, with Simon beside her. "He will stay here at school every day until you come for him. The only way to stop him from staying late is for you to get here at a reasonable hour."

She brushed at her skirt, and Hank suspected she had no idea what a mess she really was. Her blond curls were about half escaped from the tidy bun she usually wore. Her hands were filthy. Her nose was smudged with grease or maybe ash. Something black was smeared here and there. She didn't seem aware of it, or she'd have given up on smoothing her dress: that wasn't the worst of her problems.

Hank's temper flared, but he knew himself well. The temper was just a mask for guilt. Simon had spent too much time alone in his young life. The schoolmarm was right.

"I can try and find someone around town who will let him come to their house after school. I know it's not fair to ask you to stay here with him. I apologize that you got stuck —"

"Mr. O'Keeffe," she cut him off.

Then she gave him a green-eyed glare he couldn't understand — except it was pretty clear she wanted him to stop talking.

There was a crash that drew both of their attention. Simon had just tipped over a bucket of coal, and black dust puffed up in the air around him.

"It is fine for him to be here. I enjoy his company." Her face twisted when she spoke as if she'd swallowed something sour. So she must not want him to say she was stuck with Simon. Which she most certainly was. Where did the woman get a notion that speaking the truth was a bad idea?

"Simon, clean up that coal and stay by the stove where it's warm. Miss Douglas and I need to speak privately for a moment." He clamped one hand on her wrist and towed her to the far corner of the room, which wasn't all that far in the one-room building.

She came right along, so maybe she had a few things to say, too. All complaints, he was sure.

"Mr. O'Keeffe —"

"Call me Hank, for heaven's sake." Hank

enjoyed cutting her off this time. "It takes too long to say Mr. O'Keeffe every time."

"That would be improper."

She might be right, because Hank didn't know one thing about being proper. Dropping his voice to a whisper, he leaned close and said, "I'm sorry about this, but I work long hours and I see no way to run my farm and keep this job without working so long. And this job supplies us with a house in town — which we need because our sod house is too cold to live in through the winter."

She tugged against his hold and startled him. He hadn't realized he'd hung on. "You need to figure something out. Simon is running wild. He's undisciplined, and I think a lot of what he gets up to is a poorly chosen method of getting someone, anyone, to pay attention to him."

"He's just a curious boy."

A clatter turned them both to look at Simon, who had stepped well away from the coal bucket and was tossing in the little black rocks one at a time. A cloud of black dust rose higher with every moment, coating Simon and the room in soot.

To get her to look at him so he could finish and get out of there, Hank gently caught her upper arm and turned her back to face him. "Things are hard when a man loses his wife and a boy loses his ma. I know we aren't getting by as well as we could, but that's just going to be part of Simon's growing-up years. Short of —" Hank dropped his voice low. "Short of letting someone else raise him, I don't know what else to do. And I won't give him up. I love my son, and his place is with me."

"Clearly, what you need to do, Mr. O'Keeffe —"

"Hank."

"No, Mr. O'Keeffe."

"No, Hank. Everyone here calls me that. Men and women both. Nebraska is a mighty friendly place, and you sound unfriendly when you call me Mr. O'Keeffe."

"Not unfriendly, proper."

"Call me Hank, or I'm going to start letting Simon sleep at school." Hank had to keep from laughing at her look of horror.

"Fine, Hank then. But —"

"He can stay then? Until I get done with work each night?" She'd offered. Her offer was laced with sarcasm and completely insincere, but it was too late to take it back now. Hank knew he was supposed to promise to get here on time, but he couldn't do any better than he had been doing, and besides, making those green eyes flash was the most fun he'd had in a long time.

She didn't disappoint him. Burning green arrows shot him right in the chest. He got that same jolt he always got from her, and it occurred to him that he'd never had any idea what his wife had been thinking. Greta had always been a complete mystery.

Just thinking about it drew all the misery of living without her around him and all the fun went out of teasing Miss Douglas, who had never invited him to call her Melanie. Hank decided not to let that stop him. And if it annoyed her, all the better, because he needed her to stay away from him. He'd never again put himself in a position to face pain like he had when Greta died birthing their second child.

With that memory of pain, suddenly he couldn't wait to get away from the green-eyed schoolmarm and her fault-finding ways.

"Let's go, Simon. We've kept Melanie here late enough."

Her gasp followed him as he rushed to get Simon, who was now in desperate need of a bath. They were gone before the bickering with Melanie could start up again.

"Late again?"

You are a master of the obvious. "Good evening, Mrs. Rathbone. It's been a long day."

She waited. Maybe tonight would be the night Mrs. Rathbone would be agreeable. Or at least send her to bed with her supper and not a single word of criticism.

"If I told anyone on the school board that you're out at such a late hour, you'd be dismissed immediately. You are supposed to be a young lady of exemplary morals."

Melanie wasn't sure what the point was of that comment. She almost expected Magda to start blackmailing her.

"Split your thirty-dollar-a-month salary with me, or I will tell the school board about your sinfully late hours."

They wouldn't fire her. But Magda might kick her out of the house. Melanie wondered if the school board would object to her sleeping at the school. She was tempted to hunt them up and ask, but she knew it was improper for her to live alone, and sleeping at the school would certainly be alone. Unless, of course, Hank got any later and Melanie started sleeping there with Simon. A woman and her — sort of — child could stay alone together.

If she walked away, Magda would call her back, upset at her impertinence. If she defended herself, Magda would only speak louder and become more critical. If she sat down to have a long, reasonable chat with the old bat, Magda would take offense at the familiarity of a woman living on charity thinking to sit with her as an equal.

Melanie suddenly couldn't stand it anymore, and she opened her mouth to tell the awful old woman to go ahead and report her. Melanie would sleep outside through a Nebraska winter before she'd take any more of this.

46

Then out of nowhere came her memory of that box. And with it came peace. Calm. How odd. She was able, without any trouble, to stand and take the harsh words Mrs. Rathbone handed out, and when the inevitable "go to your room" moment came, it was as easy as if the poor old lady had just politely said good night.

"I'll see you in the morning, ma'am." Melanie turned away to the sound of an inelegant snort of disgust.

She picked up her supper, even colder than last night, and walked up to her room. The moment she entered, her eyes went to that box. What was it about that box that seemed an answer to prayer?

Even though that made no sense, Melanie knew it was true. She'd prayed for patience and that box had . . . had . . . glowed at her.

She ate quickly and removed the pins and combs from her hair, eager to put them away. Lifting the box from the trunk where it sat, Melanie sat on her bed, the closest the room had to a chair, and held the box in her lap.

Mamó Cullen. Melanie pictured an old Irish lady, wrinkled and full of charming stories of the old country. Was it possible Mamó Cullen hadn't been that thrilled with her new granddaughter-in-law and had, in fact, been unkind?

With a wry smile, Melanie knew that was entirely possible. She studied the odd box.

The outside of it was full of seams, little squares of wood, some longer slats, and a few decorative brass knobs that didn't move when she tugged on them. There was nothing beautiful about it, but it was very old, and that alone made it charming.

Melanie slipped her pins and combs into the top drawer on the left. Then, on impulse and because she really didn't want to put it down, Melanie pulled the little drawer all the way out and set it aside. Why was the drawer so small? She looked into the space where the drawer had been and saw solid wood. Then she pulled out the seven other drawers that went down the front of the box, each with a little brass knob just like those that didn't do anything. Each drawer was under-sized. But this box wasn't heavy enough to be solid wood through and through.

Reaching in she touched the back of one drawer — playing with it, tipping the box sideways, holding it up to the lantern light so she could see the back, she touched and then pressed and thought the back gave just a bit. Not solid wood.

There had to be something in that unaccounted for space. She worked over the box for nearly an hour when she heard a little click and the back of one drawer slid sideways just a fraction of an inch. For a moment she thought she'd broken something, but looking in, she decided it wasn't broken, that piece

48

was meant to move.

Finally she got it to slide farther, and that was accidental, too. She must have gripped something in just the right way, because the back of that drawer tipped forward, and Melanie could see it was on little hinges that showed when the cunning slat of wood fell flat. Something was in there.

Reaching, Melanie realized her fingertips trembled. She pulled a small scrap out, old, yellowed with age. A bit of cloth, no, a delicate handkerchief, very fine and nearly a foot square when she brushed it flat.

It was embroidered in each corner with a piece of the Nativity scene. Mary, Joseph, and the baby Jesus in one corner. Two shepherds — one with a shepherd's crook and the other with a lamb around his neck — filled the next corner. Three wise men and a camel were in the third corner. In the fourth, in beautiful flowing script, stood the words *Peace on Earth.*

The delicate stitches made each small picture a work of art. It was the most beautiful thing she'd ever seen.

Now that she knew how to open the one back, Melanie set to work on another and found it didn't work. The back had to come out, but not in the same way as the first. An idea sparked to life as surely as a match touched to a kerosene wick. An idea she knew was straight from God.

There would be something in each of these drawers. Almost certainly there would.

And finding them would be an activity to keep her . . . or better yet, an overactive little boy . . . occupied for hours.

A little boy who loved carpentry.

With a sudden smile, she set the box aside and went to her reticule and found a copper penny and put it in the hidden space. She closed it up, packed the box in her satchel and made plans to lure her unmanageable little student into a quest.

As she lay down, she realized the next day was December 1. The beginning of the Christmas month. One of the first days in the season of Advent.

How many more drawers were there?

She'd have to find them before he did, and — judging by the size of the one drawer she'd found — she'd have to seek out tiny gifts to put in each.

Maybe Melanie could do more than bribe her little rapscallion into good behavior. Maybe with this Advent box, she could begin a journey to Bethlehem, to the Christ child, to a new, happier time for a sad and neglected little boy.

That was a lot to ask of an old, homely wooden box, but she couldn't help but believe that God was guiding her, and He would use her to guide Simon.

They'd do it together. One secret drawer at a time.

CHAPTER 7

Wednesday, December 1
The Fourth Day of Advent

Hank felt a chill slide up his spine that had nothing to do with the cold December evening. His son, sitting right next to Melanie Douglas, their heads bent over . . . something. Hank wasn't sure what.

Just as he stepped in, they looked at each other and shared the friendliest smile. It terrified him.

Melanie looked up, but he could tell she was reluctant. Whatever they were looking for had them both lassoed tight.

Her eyes focused on him, and that jolt hit. "Come on in, Hank."

Then she gave him that same friendly smile she'd shared with Simon. Up to now, she'd never been real friendly to him. This was the first time she'd called him Hank without an argument. The pleasure of it curved up his lips. They smiled at each other for too long, and Hank forgot all about his chilly backbone.

"You got here just in time, Pa." Simon sounded happier than he had since before Greta died.

"Just in time for what?" Hank decided then and there that whatever Melanie had done to make his boy this happy, he was going to encourage it.

"Look at this, Pa." Simon held up some dark thing about the size of a man's head. "I found a secret drawer."

Hank came toward the teacher's desk, trying to see what his son had.

Finally, when he got up close, he saw a stack of small wooden objects beside Simon. The knobs on them helped Hank figure out what he was looking at.

"Those are drawers you took out of this thing?"

"Yep, it's an Advent box, Pa."

"An Advent box? I've never heard of that."

"I just named it that because there are more drawers, maybe enough to last until Christmas. Simon will search for one each day after school." Melanie turned to Simon, and with mock severity waggled her finger under his nose. "If his school work is done."

Hank knew how curious Simon was and how much he liked working with his hands. He'd taken to whittling like he was born to it.

"And there was a present in the drawer I found, Pa." Simon held up a penny. "Miss

Douglas said it's a Christmas present for me. This box is full of secret drawers. And I have to stop disrupting class, too. Then I can spend the after-school time searching for another secret drawer."

Hank met those green eyes again. He was the one who'd challenged her to manage his son better. And she had come up with the perfect way.

"Can I see the box?" Hank grinned, unable to stop it. He wanted to search for hidden drawers, too. Melanie could probably make him behave and study with this box.

Simon and Melanie shared a conspiratorial smile.

Simon snapped something inside what looked like the opening for one of the drawers. "You try and find it, Pa."

Hank took the box before he noticed it was full dark. "I want to, but we've got to go home. We'll be late for supper as it is."

"Maybe you could try and get here a bit earlier tomorrow night, Hank." The asperity caught his attention; then he saw the sparkle of amusement in her eyes.

It widened his grin. "Maybe I can think of a way to get here. I wouldn't mind helping with the hunt." His hands tightened on the box, and he was surprised at how badly he wanted to sit down and search or maybe run off with the box and spend the evening with it.

Melanie snatched it from his hand. "I see that look. Simon had it, too. No, you may not take the box. The only way for Simon to spend time with it is to study and behave. And the only way for you to spend time with it, Hank, is to get here earlier. The rest of the time, this box is mine alone."

She tucked the box into a satchel that stood open on the desktop. "Well, it is time to close up for the day, gentlemen. I will see you early tomorrow morning, Simon. And you, Hank, I'll see perhaps late tomorrow afternoon."

Hank tugged on the brim of his Stetson. She had him caught just like a spider with a web. He'd work faster tomorrow, and he'd be here closer to school closing than he had been. And spend a bit of time with his son.

CHAPTER 8

Thursday, December 2
The Fifth Day of Advent

Melanie woke up exhausted the next morning. She'd stayed up terribly late last night. It took forever to find the rest of the drawers, and she had to do it before Simon did.

She'd managed to finagle each of the backs of the eight drawers open — none of them worked the same way — and she hoped the bright little boy didn't find a drawer she hadn't, because there'd be no gift.

With a smile she knew if he found an empty drawer, he'd just have to keep searching for the day anyway, and the gift wasn't the thing. It was the search. If he found a drawer she hadn't, he'd probably crow with delight at having bested her.

Then she had to produce a small gift to put in each one. She had no opportunity to buy anything. She had to be at school by 7:00 a.m. to beat her little friend's arrival and stay until nearly six at night waiting for Hank to come for him.

She had to come up with a few tiny gifts before Saturday, when finally she'd have a chance to go to the general store.

She looked among her own meager things — she hadn't left the orphanage for this job with many possessions.

Two things for Thursday and Friday. A little red pin, circular with a white cross painted on it. She'd earned this for perfect Sunday school attendance. She could find only one more thing small enough. A tiny, silver angel that she'd had all her life. At the orphanage, she'd been told it was sewn into the hem of the little dress she'd been wearing when she was found left in a basket on a church doorstep.

The kind ladies who'd raised her kept it until she was old enough to care for it. It was her most treasured possession. Praying for a generous spirit, she thought of that unruly and loveable little Simon and smiled. It was easy to tuck the angel into the drawer.

If she thought of anything else to put in, and he didn't find this first, she might retrieve it. But where better to place an angel than in an Advent box?

As she left, with Mrs. Rathbone's nagging still ringing in her ears, she wondered if she should tell the old woman about the secret drawers. There was no question that Mrs. Rathbone had given her the box, but maybe if she knew about the hidden drawers, she'd want it back. After the first piece of embroidery, Melanie had found nothing in those drawers, and if she did, she would most certainly give anything she found to her landlady.

She'd spread the handkerchief on a flat surface to be a doily, and it felt as if she'd decorated for Christmas.

Melanie didn't ask. Simon was too excited about the box. What if Magda decided she did want it? Then what would happen to Simon and his behavior?

Melanie decided she'd wait until after Christmas to show Magda the hidden drawers. Though Melanie found herself loving the little chest, she'd return it to Magda if the woman wanted it.

Monday, December 13
The Sixteenth Day of Advent
"Have you found a new one yet?" Hank found himself nearly running during the day to get all his chores done. And he could have stayed longer at the farm and walked a patrol around the town to make sure everyone knew the sheriff was on duty. But he loved helping Simon and Melanie play with that box.

And each hidden space was harder to find. He had a feeling the hard part was just beginning.

"Hi, Pa." Simon lit up. "I've been hunting

58

awhile, but we've found all the easy ones."

"The easy ones?" Hank laughed as he hung up his coat and hat.

At the sight of his son's cheerful welcome, Hank kept a smile on his face, but honestly he wanted to kick his own backside. How many times had he been too busy to make sure his son was happy?

"Those hidden spaces in the backs of the drawers weren't easy."

Simon laughed, and Melanie's sweet, musical laughter joined in. She was so pretty. Hank pulled a chair up to the desk on Simon's right while Melanie sat on the boy's left. He'd brought the chairs over the third day they'd worked together; before that there'd only been Melanie's teacher's chair in the schoolhouse.

Simon turned the box so the side with the drawers lay facedown on the table. "The whole back half is still not open, Pa. The drawers and spaces behind 'em don't come close to taking up all the space." Simon held the box up so it was between them, his eyes intent as he examined the back.

"These thin slats of wood must open." Hank wanted to grab the box and push and slide those slats. Instead, he let his son work on it. Hank quietly pointed here and there, making suggestions.

"Try sliding two at a time. Remember that one hidden compartment that only opened when all the other compartments were closed and the drawers were back in place, except for the one we were working on?" Melanie reached for the box, checked herself, and pulled her hand back. Hank laughed quietly and looked up at her.

"Hard to be patient, huh?"

She laughed.

"Thanks for letting me find them." Simon looked up. Hanks's son's blue eyes gleamed as bright as a guiding star.

"Get back to work." Hank jabbed a finger at the box, but he smiled all the way from his heart. A heart that'd felt more dead than alive for the last two years. "It ain't easy to be so generous."

Melanie laughed. Simon joined in then bent his head back to the box, still chuckling. The boy focused intently on the job — but with a smile on his face.

Melanie brushed a yellow curl off her cheek and tucked it behind her ear in a move so graceful Hank could've sworn he heard music. She rested a hand on Simon's head with an amazingly motherly gesture. Hank looked up and met Melanie's green gaze. She quietly snickered and smoothed Simon's unruly black curls.

Her laughter, the affectionate touch, the change in his boy, the few inches that separated them — all hit Hank in a different way than the usual jolt.

Something so deep, so strong.

He cared about her, and not in a way that had anything to do with a good teacher who'd found a way to manage an unruly student. The feeling had nothing to do with Simon at all.

He cared about her. He knew he could love her.

Their eyes held. The moment stretched. Hank felt himself lean closer. With Simon here, he couldn't think of kissing her, but — he was thinking of kissing her.

He was drawn to her warmth and heat. She leaned his direction, just an inch, two inches, three. He lifted his hand to rest it on top of hers, still caressing Simon's hair.

When he touched that soft, smooth skin, he remembered Greta. They'd been this close, with Simon between them, as she died, their unborn child forever trapped inside her.

He'd touched her just this way. Simon, her hand, his. And felt the life go out of her. Seen the moment her eyes had lost vitality. Her hand had slid from Simon to the bed, and all Hank's love couldn't hold her. As she lay dying in childbirth, he felt as if his love had killed her.

Pain like he'd never known swept over him. He'd barely survived losing her. In a lot of ways he hadn't survived — neither had Simon. They'd stayed alive, but there was no life in either of them, no joy, no family, no love.

And now here he was touching another woman. He would *never* put himself through that much pain again.

Only a fool risked that. He didn't know what went across his face, but right there, with Simon so intent on the Advent box that they might as well have been alone, her spark of laughter died. Her hand slid from between Hank's hand and Simon's head, just as Greta's had.

She looked down and brushed some bit of nothing off her dress and cleared her throat. "I need to spend a little time getting tomorrow's lesson together."

"No, Miss Douglas." Simon looked up from the box, wheedling. "Stay and help."

"Let me get a few things done for the Christmas program practice for tomorrow. I ask you to do your work before you can work on the Advent box, so it's only fair I behave by the same rules." Melanie reached, froze, then almost as if she couldn't stop herself she brushed Simon's dark, over-long hair off his forehead. His curls flopped back right where they had been.

"I'll come back as soon as I'm finished." She smiled at Simon, too decent to let the boy see she needed to get away. "In the meantime, you and your pa work together."

He'd hurt her to protect himself. A shameful thing for a man to do.

Simon let her go without an argument. And Simon hadn't done anything without an argument in two years. His tears had dried after Greta's funeral and he'd started causing trouble. And Hank had found enough work so that he could avoid dealing with his troublesome son.

Only since Melanie had Hank been able to see a ray of hope that his son might stop being such an angry youngster. So, he'd thank her for it and thank God for bringing such a good teacher into town, but he would not let any feelings for her take root.

She moved away, and he focused on this strange box-full-of-secrets. As he studied it, he wondered if he was like this box. Full of hidden places.

Guarded, impossible to open unless someone worked really hard.

Hank decided he liked it that way. He would open enough to let his son in, but no more. And just as well, because what woman would work so hard for the doubtful pleasure of finding all the private places in Hank's heart, especially if he hurt them when they got close?

With regret, but feeling far less afraid, he went back to working with Simon. They were at it for a long time, completely lost in testing each and every piece of wood in every way they could think of. Then while he held a small slat of wood that sprung back into place whenever they let it go, Simon tipped the box on its side and they heard a faint click. Hank's eyes rose and met his son's.

"Did you hear that, Pa?" Simon almost vibrated with excitement.

It hit Hank hard that Simon had been sitting still, working hard, showing great patience for a long time. Hank had, too. He remembered how hard it'd been for him to stay in his desk when he was a sprout. One of these days he ought to tell Simon he was a pretty normal child. In looks Hank and Simon were a match, but it appeared that they were a match inside as well.

For now, Hank smiled at his boy; then the two of them turned back to the box. Simon went right back to his diligent work, but it only took a couple of seconds for him to slide one of the thin boards on the back. It slid all the way out and revealed a skinny compartment, as tall as the box but less than an inch deep. And inside the little space was —

"Miss Douglas, it's a tin soldier." Simon's voice shook with excitement. He'd been whittling, and he'd made a little soldier. Hank knew the boy had plans to build his own army. Now he could add this little tin man to it. The soldier shone in the lantern light, and that's when Hank realized it had gotten dark. Every day was shorter as they closed in on the first day of winter.

"Miss Douglas, come and see." Simon lifted up the toy. Hank realized, not for the first time, that Simon didn't understand where these toys came from. The boy thought they were just there, maybe miraculously, put there by God as Christmas gifts.

Melanie hadn't taken credit for the gifts herself.

She came close, her attention all on Simon, and smiled at the intricately shaped toy. "That's beautiful. Didn't you say you were whittling a toy soldier?"

"Yep and now I've got two. By the time I'm done, I'm going to have a big enough army to protect everyone."

Hank wanted that, too, a way to protect everyone.

But first Hank had failed his wife. Then by neglect, he'd failed his son. Now he was busy protecting himself from another broken heart.

Did that mean for once he was doing right by protecting himself? He looked at Melanie, who'd never spared him a glance, and wondered if instead it meant he was failing again.

CHAPTER 9

"And don't think I won't talk to the school board!"

Melanie could usually remain calm, but the way Hank had looked at her tonight — as if he wanted her as far away from himself as possible — had shredded her normal calm. She'd prayed almost desperately while she tried to find something to do to keep busy until Hank and Simon left.

In the end, she'd rewritten some of the lines of the play, sewn hems in two costumes, worked on some decorations she wanted the children to finish, and read through the highest level arithmetic book she had, a book she was familiar with and understood completely.

Through it all, she prayed.

Memories of the years at the orphanage haunted her and seemed tied to that look in Hank's blue eyes. She'd always borne this heavy feeling there was something wrong with a little girl who had no parents, an older child who was never adopted, a young woman who'd never found a man to love her.

She didn't have those thoughts so much anymore. Living alone in an attic and working all day with children, she was too busy or too alone to be rejected.

Until now. By Hank.

"I know you're spending time in that schoolhouse — alone with a man. There's talk all over town."

Melanie had to dig deep to find the calm needed to keep from snapping back at Magda's verbal assault. Every day it was harder to turn the other cheek, to return good for Mrs. Rathbone's evil. And today — thanks to Hank — holding her tongue was harder than ever.

"Simon is there, Mrs. Rathbone. We're certainly not spending time alone, and Hank, uh, that is Mr. O'Keeffe is often occupied with his work as sheriff. I won't send a little boy home to an empty house. I'm trying to get Simon more interested in schoolwork and less interested in causing trouble. And he's doing very well. Often when Hank gets there, Simon is in the middle of something. . . ." *Trying to open hidden compartments in the box you gave me, which I should tell you about. But I don't dare, for fear you'll take it from me.* "I hope a few more nights" — twelve: there were twelve more days until Christmas — "and Simon won't need extra help anymore."

The Advent box in her satchel seemed to

weigh more with each passing moment. Melanie felt heat climbing up her neck, and she knew she had to get upstairs before she said something that got her thrown out of this house — the only available home for her in town.

"One word from me to the parson and the doctor and Mr. Weber at the general store," Magda rattled off the names of the men on the school board, "and I can blacken your name to the point you'll be fired." Mrs. Rathbone waggled a finger from her chair by the warm fire.

"And it's a wonder I can breathe with the dust you kicked up cleaning the library last weekend."

"I'll dust the rest of the house this weekend, ma'am." Prayer. Melanie clung to prayer.

God, don't let me shame myself with my foolish temper. I need this home. Surround me with protection from this enemy.

"I won't have a woman of questionable character in my home. No Christian woman should have to put up with it."

Melanie knew it was either run or say something absolutely dreadful. Terrible, sinful words burned in her throat, and it wasn't even Mrs. Rathbone's fault. All of her need to rage could be laid right at the feet of Hank O'Keeffe because of his withdrawal from her.

She chose to run. "Good night, Mrs. Rathbone."

Grabbing her plate, ignoring Mrs. Rathbone's insistent demand to come back, she rushed up those cold stairs. Every day the weather was worse. Melanie had been able to see her breath in the room when she got dressed that morning.

Today was Monday, and the weekend had allowed Melanie to find a few more drawers in the box, but she knew the strange object still held some unaccounted-for space. She'd become nearly obsessed with finding them all. She'd bought enough tiny toys and candy to last until Christmas; whether the hidden compartments would last that long, she didn't know.

Of course, she only had to find enough drawers to keep Simon busy on school days. A smile crossed her lips as she remembered Simon sidling up to her at church to plead for a look at the box right then.

The little pill was as eager as she was.

Melanie gained her room, set her plate on the bed, drew the Advent box out of her satchel, and set it on the trunk. She studied it and felt led to pray as she ate her cold meal.

The entire center of the box was still unexplored. The little drawers on the front and back were accounted for . . . by her. Simon still had a while to go finding them.

The meal was decent enough, if a girl had spent her entire life in an orphanage with a meager budget. She finished it quickly and picked up the box. She'd been listening for that click as Simon and Hank worked.

She'd spent all weekend finding it herself.

Now which of the many little seams between wooden slats and tiles was the one that needed to be tipped just so, pressed just so . . . Often two things moved at the same time . . .

At last, because she'd learned tipping the box made a difference, Melanie finally pushed the right boards with the box tilted at the perfect angle, and the whole box popped. A seam appeared right down the middle, separating the front with the visible drawers from the back with the other compartments they'd found. Hinged on one side, she found more little tiles and slats of wood. But a grin broke across her face. She was learning how this strange box worked. There were little nooks and crannies to be found all over in this new section.

Not easy, because nothing about the Advent box was easy. But findable. She could do it. Simon could do it. And very possibly, just based on the small sizes of the drawers they'd found up until now, there might be enough spaces to last until Christmas.

After that, she'd tell Mrs. Rathbone about the little drawers, and if the contentious old lady agreed to let Melanie keep it, she'd give it to Simon as a Christmas gift.

The discovery of the new stash of drawers

helped set aside the hurt from Hank. Well, not set it aside really, just accept it. More pain in a life that had dosed her with a lot of it. Nothing new, not even a surprise.

She got ready for bed with a prayer of thanks in her heart.

CHAPTER 10

Tuesday, December 14
The Seventeenth Day of Advent

They found several slender lengths of wood painted bright red.

"What's this, Miss Douglas?"

Hank looked at Melanie, who was busy writing, always working on her Christmas play. Or so she said.

With a sweet, sad smile that made Hank's heart ache — because he'd put that sadness there — she shook her head. "I don't know. What do you think it could be?"

She did a very good job of acting mystified.

It had been left to Hank to notice the little slots that fit together to form an outlined A-frame building.

Wednesday, December 15
The Eighteenth Day of Advent

"It looks like a little ball of yarn, Pa." Simon's brow furrowed as if he had no idea what to make of a knotted up ball of yarn.

Hank noticed Melanie lean a bit toward them from where she sat by the potbellied stove, with a pair of knitting needles and a ball of white yarn.

"Look closer, son. It's got a little red nose and two blue knots for eyes. And these little sticks are legs. It's a lamb."

Simon had brought the strange little A-frame sticks with him, and suddenly Hank knew what it was.

"The sheep goes in the barn, only it's a stable, like the stable in Bethlehem."

Melanie eased back in her chair without comment and went back to her knitting.

Thursday, December 16
The Nineteenth Day of Advent

"It's a star." Simon's voice rang with excitement. He knew now what was coming. The stable, the sheep, the star.

Hank watched as Simon examined it. The star was sewn with felt and just the tiniest bit padded like a tiny star-shaped pillow. It was stitched onto a button, the whole thing painted bright yellow. Melanie had made this with her own hands, just like the sheep.

A loop of thread on the button was perfect to hang the star on a little notch on the stable. Hank hadn't noticed that notch until just now.

What else had she made? There had to be an entire Nativity scene coming. Each of the few pieces were clever. But how did she make the people? She should have come to him. But of course he'd made it impossible.

He looked over, and her gaze met his. He got his jolt for the day. Then she looked back at the piece of white fabric she was cross-stitching. She wasn't even pretending to be busy with schoolwork anymore.

Friday, December 17
The Twentieth Day of Advent
Simon squealed over the tiny piece of carved wood. It was Mary, the mother of Jesus. Hank knew then what she'd done. He'd seen these figures in the general store and had never given them a second thought. For one thing their price was a bit dear. But Melanie had bought the set, and now they'd be introduced to the Holy Family one at a time.

Family. Hank rested his eyes on Melanie. Her head bent over her work. How he'd loved having a real family.

Monday, December 20
The Twenty-third Day of Advent
A little donkey.

"Donkey's are stubborn things, ain't they, Pa?"

"It's *aren't,* Simon, not *ain't.* You must use proper grammar." Melanie's voice drew Hank's attention, as if he wasn't already paying too much attention to her.

"They are stubborn, Simon," she said. "Almost as stubborn as men."

Melanie's lips quirked in a smile. A real smile. He detected no sadness. But the smile was gone, and she didn't look up.

He needed to find a way to make her look up. He needed his daily dose of her pretty eyes.

Tuesday, December 21
The Twenty-fourth Day of Advent
"Was Joseph Jesus' father, or was God?" Simon studied the little bit of wood, perfectly painted, about as tall as his little finger.

"Well, God was Jesus' real Father, but Joseph was like the father God gave Him here on earth."

"Like Mike Andrews has a new pa? I hear Mike call him a stepfather, but he acts just like a regular pa."

"I don't know if Joseph is exactly Jesus' stepfather, because that's what you get when your own pa is dead, and Jesus' heavenly Father was with Him in spirit."

"Is Ma with us in spirit, Pa?"

Hank looked down at Simon and saw only curiosity. No hurt. He probably could barely remember Greta. Hank's thoughts faltered because, for a few seconds, he couldn't picture her. Couldn't bring her face to mind. Then it came back to him, Greta's face. But he pictured her as his young bride. Happy, working hard, a good cook, a pretty woman with a nice singing voice and a tendency to nag. She was usually right, so Hank didn't hold that against her.

He realized that he'd always before pictured her as she was when she was dying. In pain, ashen white, bleeding. But now the good memories came flooding in and replaced the bad. He felt a part of his heart heal.

And he looked at Melanie, who for once didn't have her eyes fixed on her work. She watched Simon with concern and kindness. Maybe afraid Hank would say some bone-headed thing that made Simon feel bad.

"She is indeed, Simon. But that isn't exactly how it was with Jesus being God's Son." Hank told Simon the Christmas story in a way that was more real than the usual reading from the Bible. Precious as those words were, talking with his son, discussing a heavenly Father, a stepfather, a mother who'd died, the story of Jesus was more real to Hank than it had ever been. And he owed that to Melanie.

He looked up at her as he talked, and for once she smiled at him as she had before he'd driven her away from the desk and the Advent box.

She'd never by so much as a tone in her voice punished Hank for his harsh rejection.

"Melanie, come over and see what we found." Hank didn't betray himself, but Melanie looked up, and her eyes flashed.

"What is it?" She knew good and well what it was. She'd put it there.

"Come and see, Miss Douglas." Simon sounded excited, and Hank knew that however unhappy Melanie might be with him, she'd not deny Simon her attention.

Rising with great reluctance, she set aside her needlework and came to the desk to see Simon hold up the tiny angel. Hank had no idea where she'd gotten this.

But he couldn't ask without letting Simon know she'd put it in there. He was willing to believe this box was just for him, maybe the gifts put there by God. Hank wasn't sure just what his son thought about this box, only that he loved it, was fascinated by it, and that as he'd opened the secret drawers, he'd also opened his heart. Hank had regained his son's love. And he'd have never done it without the generous schoolmarm.

"It's an angel, Melanie." Hank didn't take it from Simon; he'd have had a tug-of-war. But he lifted Simon's hand and turned it a bit so the angel shone in the lantern light. This drawer had taken hours to find. Hank couldn't believe how well Simon had learned to concentrate and stick with a task.

Rising from his chair, he stepped around his son so he was just a little bit closer to Melanie. "An angel put in this box by an angel."

Melanie looked past Hank to Simon. But his son was busy finding the perfect place for the angel in his nearly complete Nativity set.

Hank touched her arm and gained her full attention. "Thank you, Melanie. And I'm sorry I've made it so you" — he dropped his voice to a whisper — "couldn't help. So sorry. God bless you for letting Simon and me take this journey to Christmas together. But I'd like it if you joined us. I let fear and my grief push you away, but I've found my way past it now. I have you to thank for it, and if you'll forgive me, please help us, these last two days before Christmas, search for the last drawers."

Melanie looked scared, like a woman might who'd been hurt too many times. But she nodded. "I'd like that. Thank you."

Thursday, December 23
The Twenty-sixth Day of Advent
When they opened the next little cranny, Simon said, "It's a baby Jesus."

He reached his chubby little fingers into the ridiculously well-hidden spot and pulled out a tiny baby in a manger. Hank wasn't too surprised. His eyes went to the little Nativity scene set up on Melanie's desk. Simon brought them every day and set them up before he started hunting.

"Pa, it's just like when Jesus was born." Simon looked up and smiled. All of the pain his boy had carried for two years seemed to be gone. Hank was at fault that the boy had been so unhappy. He'd blamed it on Greta's death, but spending this time with Simon had shown Hank the truth.

And it was because of Melanie's wisdom that they'd come so far, taken a journey just as the Holy Family had.

Smiling, uncritical, Simon asked. "But what's left now? Finding the baby Jesus should have happened Christmas Day."

Hank didn't know. Had Melanie hoped they wouldn't find Jesus until tomorrow? Christmas day was Saturday. But the Nativity was completed. What else could there be?

And though she'd joined them in their search today, after he'd asked her to forgive him, she hadn't steered them. They found whatever they found. So, it's possible this wasn't the order she'd hoped the compartments would be opened in.

He looked at her, and she was watching Simon, smiling. Not a flicker of alarm that they'd found the wrong drawer.

"Let's go ahead and put Jesus in by Mary and Joseph." Melanie and Simon turned to arrange all the little figures.

While they did it, Hank, his hands moving

idly on the box did something and a new drawer popped open. A drawer Hank could see had nothing in it. The oddest little slit in the wood. She hadn't found it yet. He knew if she had there'd be some bit of a thing in there.

But this drawer, well, Hank knew exactly what belonged in this one. He took a second to study the cunning little space before he snapped it shut.

And then he made his plan while Melanie and Simon talked about the first Christmas.

Thursday, December 24
The Twenty-seventh Day of Advent

Melanie lined the children up to sing their final song. They were so bursting with Christmas cheer it had been hard to get them to do their parts, but in the end, with a few funny mix-ups, they'd done a wonderful job.

When the school finally was almost emptied out, she smiled at the two who remained. She'd asked Magda's permission to keep the box, even opened a few of the little drawers. Magda had waved it off as if it smelled bad.

"Simon, can you come here, please?" As always, Simon came rushing up, eager to search. But tonight there was to be no search.

She reached under her desk to get her satchel. "It's gone." She straightened to see Hank holding the box.

"I wanted to look at it closer." He handed

it to Melanie.

"We've found all the drawers, but I do have one final gift for you."

She extended the Advent box to him. "This is for you and your pa." Her eyes raised to Hank.

"It's mine?" Simon gasped then grabbed the box and hugged it, his face beaming with joy.

"Yes, merry Christmas."

Hank stood beside her, both of them facing Simon.

The sweet little boy set the box down. "I'm going to open every little compartment just for the fun of it."

"Simon, it's too late. We can't —"

"Let him work on it for a while, Melanie."

Melanie saw a look pass between the two and wondered at it.

The warmth of Hank's voice drew her eyes from the boy to the man. Hank rested one strong hand on Melanie's arm. Smiling, knowing he wanted space between them and Simon so they could talk, she let him pull her over to the stove. All of ten feet away from the distracted child.

"Melanie —" Hank rested both hands on her upper arms. His blue gaze locked on hers, and it drew her in just as his hands drew her closer.

"Y–yes?" She hoped that yesterday had changed things between them. But she was a woman who had learned so long ago not to hope.

"Melanie, it's taken me too long. I've been stubborn, and mostly I've been afraid. But I'm not afraid anymore."

His voice charmed her. His hands, so strong, could protect her from the whole world. Oh yes, she wanted to hope.

His head lowered. His lips touched hers.

The first kiss of her life. The sweetest kiss she could imagine.

"Melanie, that box has one more secret to tell."

"What?"

Then he kissed her again, and she didn't care much about that box, no matter how it had taken them on a journey to find each other.

"There!" A harsh voice shocked Melanie out of the romantic daze, and she jerked her head toward the schoolhouse door.

"I demand she be fired." Mrs. Rathbone stormed into the schoolhouse with the parson, the doctor, and Mr. Weber right behind her.

Parson Howard arched a brow. "Hank, what's going on?"

"That's a stupid question, Parson." Doc Cross smiled at Melanie.

Mr. Weber alone looked shocked. "I can see how upsetting this is to you, Magda. Of course, we can't keep a young lady who'd behave so scandalously working here."

"What?" Melanie needed a job.

"And she won't sleep another night under my roof."

Gasping, Melanie said, "It's snowing out and bitter cold. And you'd throw me out of your home?"

"And what's more, she's a thief."

"Thief?" Melanie cried. "I am not a thief."

"What about that box?" Mrs. Rathbone jabbed a finger at the box just as Simon came up beside her, holding it, its many hidden drawers now wide open.

"But you told me I could have it. I asked again this morning."

"You did no such thing. You're a thief and a liar. Mr. Weber, Hank can't be trusted to do the sheriff's job. Please take over."

The fear that swept through Melanie nearly choked her. Mrs. Rathbone was just spiteful enough to demand Melanie be arrested.

Simon stormed right up to Mrs. Rathbone.

"No, Simon, come back." Melanie remembered in a flash all the changes that had come over Simon in the last month. But now he nearly quaked with anger. If he believed Melanie had lied and stolen — for heaven's sake, stolen a gift for him — would it undo all the good Melanie had done?

He shoved the box right at Mrs. Rathbone's ample belly. "Here, take the box. Miss Douglas isn't a thief. But if you want it back, you can have it."

Magda caught the box by reflex then gave it a distasteful look. Melanie knew the old bat didn't want that box. She just wanted to cause trouble. Walking in on a kiss was one good way to accomplish her goal. Had the woman agreed Melanie could have that box with the plan of accusing her of theft? Or had the woman just seen it in the schoolhouse and seized on another accusation.

With one quick move, Hank snatched the box out of Magda's hands.

Mrs. Rathbone squawked like an angry rooster.

"You can have it back in just a minute." Hank looked at the three men standing a step behind her. "And you can all just stay right here for a while longer. I think I can clear all this up."

"I'd appreciate it if you would," Doc Cross said with weary amusement that didn't match the emotional temperature of this upsetting meeting. "And be quick about it. My wife is holding supper."

Hank turned with the box and brought it to Melanie. He let go of it with one hand and touched Simon's shoulder. "Stay right here with me, Son. This is from both of us."

"You can't give her that box as a gift; it's mine." Magda was still storming around.

"I won't give her the box." Hank manipulated two boards while holding the box nearly on its side and the slot tipped open.

"Reach in. Today it was my turn to bring a gift for you."

Melanie saw the sincerity in his eyes and slowly reached in the tiny dark gap he'd opened. She grasped something and pulled it out. "A ring."

Nodding, Hank said, "A wedding ring. Marry me, Melanie. You have no home to go to, so we can marry and you'll come home with me."

Her stomach sank as she heard the practical reasons she should marry. And a lonely child who'd never been loved couldn't help noticing he hadn't said the one thing she wanted above all to hear. "Th–that isn't a good reason to get married."

"Then just marry me because I love you."

She gasped in delight. Hank leaned down and caught that gasp with his kiss. He pulled back. "Say yes, Melanie, marry me. Then let's finish this Advent journey we've been on. Let's end it at our home."

Hank's hand left her arm to rest on Simon's head. The little boy grinned up at her in what looked like glee. "Marry us, Miss Douglas. We love you."

Melanie couldn't stop the grin that spread across her face, though so many looked on and she'd been accused of terrible things.

"Yes, I'll marry you." She looked at sweet Simon. Then her eyes lifted to meet Hank's gaze. She couldn't look away. "I'll marry you for one reason only, Hank. Because I love you, too."

Hank turned to face the four people who'd witnessed his proposal. He handed the now-empty box back to Mrs. Rathbone. "You can have that, ma'am."

Magda looked at it with a scowl. "Oh, just keep the ugly old thing." She slammed it onto a desktop and walked out in a huff.

"Parson, as long as you're here, will you say some vows and give us your blessing?" Hank asked. "And, Doc, Mr. Weber, will you be witnesses?"

Both men grinned. Doc Cross said, "Make it quick, Parson, my wife is a fine cook."

They said their vows, and Melanie received the finest gift of all. The gift of being an Advent bride.

Hank slid the ring on Melanie's finger at just the right time. Simon hugged the Advent box tight. Then the three of them walked home.

Just as Mary and Joseph on that long-ago Christmas had completed their Advent journey, now Melanie, Hank, and Simon completed theirs: a journey that brought them to Christmas, to family, to love.

■ ■ ■ ■

A Bride
Rides Herd

■ ■ ■ ■

CHAPTER 1

Montana
July 23, 1894
Matt heard the scream and whirled in his saddle.

A fast-moving creek barreled down the mountainside, and the scream came from that direction. Another scream, louder, higher up, from someone else.

Matt vaulted from his gelding and sprinted toward the water.

He cleared the heavy stand of ponderosa pines in time to hear another scream and see someone drowning, swept along by the current at breathtaking speed.

The creek was narrow, but it plunged down a mountainside. So did whoever was drowning.

Matt saw a spot just ahead littered with stones. Branches snarled up, damming the creek and making it deeper without slowing it down.

Whoever had fallen in would be smashed

to bits on this barrier, and if they somehow got swept past it, there was a waterfall a few dozen yards ahead.

He leaped up on the boulder closest to the bank and slipped. His boots weren't made for rock climbing.

There was no time to shed them.

"Grab my hand!"

The youngster, because Matt saw now it was a child careening down the rapids, turned to look at him then went under. Matt assumed this wasn't deep water, how could it be when it was rushing downhill, but it was deep enough for a child to submerge. He caught himself holding his own breath as if he'd gone under. He stepped across the stones, picking his way.

Ready.

He'd have one chance to grab this child, a girl, he saw long blond braids, and then he'd never see her again.

Heart pounding, Matt dropped to his knees and extended his arms to the limit. The child raced toward him. A tree just upstream of the rocks bent low enough . . . Matt was going to lose sight of the little one for a few crucial seconds right before he had to make his grab.

Then the child vanished behind the branches.

Matt braced himself to not let go and not get swept off the rocks.

The tree suddenly bowed until the branch

looked ready to snap. Then it whipped up and the child went flying into the air, kicking her legs hard, and she swung to the shore, landing neatly.

Another scream. A second child.

Now Matt barely had time to gather his thoughts and get ready when the tree bowed again, snapped up, and another little girl went sailing upward, swung, and landed right where the first had.

Matt sprang to his feet as the two laughed hysterically.

One, slightly smaller than the other, said, "Let's go again!"

His knees almost buckled, and he jumped across the rocks to get out of the water. He didn't want to finish this off by falling in.

Then he really saw them.

White-blond hair, skinny, wild — Matt had a gut-wrenching suspicion. "Are you by any chance named Reeves?"

The two spun to look at him, ready to run, he thought. Good self-preservation instincts. To stop them he said, "I'm your Uncle Matt. Mark Reeves is my brother."

The older child edged back, but her eyes were full of fascination. "We've got lots of uncles. You aren't one of them."

Imagining them running upstream and casting themselves into the water again, Matt said, "I haven't ever been to visit before. Can you take me to your pa and ma?"

"Nope." The older one seemed to do the talking for both. Matt had heard about Mark's three daughters.

"You're Annie, right?" Matt said. That earned their full attention. He then turned to the littler girl. "And you're Susie."

Both girls' eyes went round with amazement. "You know our names?"

"Sure I do. Mark, your pa, writes home about you a lot." Well, about once per child and those letters came from his wife, Emma. "And I know you've got a little baby sister named Lilly. Let's go home."

He had to get them away from this wild stretch of water and tell Mark what he'd caught his children doing. Even as he trembled in fear he thought of all the crazy stunts he and his brothers, including Mark — especially Mark — had gotten up to over the years.

But that was different, they were boys.

Little girls were supposed to stay to the house and be quiet and sweet. Like his ma.

"We'll take you to our house, but we can't take you to Pa." Annie reached out and took his hand. She looked to be about six, though Matt knew nothing of girls and could only guess. Susie took Matt's other hand. The sweetest, softest hands he'd ever felt. Matt realized right then that he loved his little nieces with his whole heart.

"I have to bring my horse." He tugged on

their hands, and they came along happily. Susie even skipped a few steps. Matt couldn't stop himself from smiling.

They were beautiful little girls. He'd never met Mark's wife, Emma, but she must be a pretty thing.

They found Matt's horse, grazing where he'd ground hitched it, and Annie ran forward to grab the reins, then led the horse back to Matt and took his hand again.

They headed off in the direction Matt had planned to ride.

"What do you mean you can't take me to your pa?" It hit him that maybe something had happened. Matt had been roving for a long time. For all he knew his brother could be long dead and buried.

"He's on a cattle drive."

Matt's panic ended before it had fully begun. "So we'll go see your ma then."

"Nope." Annie gave him a look like he was stupid, but if her ma and pa were both gone then —

"Annie! Susie, where are you?" A voice that sounded like a woman being gnawed on by wolves cut through the clear mountain air.

"That's Aunt Betsy. She screams a lot." Annie shrugged one shoulder as if to say her aunt's ways were a complete mystery.

"It sounds like she's worried about you." As well she should be. "I'd better answer her," Matt said quietly then he shouted,

93

"They're over here."

Pounding footsteps came at him through the dense woods. Aunt Betsy sounded like she weighed three hundred pounds.

Then a beautiful woman with hair and eyes so dark she couldn't possibly be related to these girls, charged into view. Not three hundred pounds. Not. Even. Close. She had a white-haired baby on her slender hip, and the tyke was clinging for dear life.

She skidded to a stop when she saw Matt, and, faster than a man could blink, she drew a gun, cocked it, and said in a dark, dangerous voice, "Get away from those children."

Matt raised his hands, stunned at the dead serious look in Aunt Betsy's sparking black eyes. Trouble was, the girls had a firm grip. When he raised his hands, they clung and he lifted them right off the ground. They started squealing, and the fire in Aunt Betsy's eyes seemed to take their glee for alarm.

Quick before she pulled the trigger, he said, "I'm Mark's brother, come to visit. I found the girls, and they were showing me the way home. You must be Aunt Betsy."

Betsy kept her gun level and cocked. "You have the look of your brother, I'll give you that."

Matt had the impression that Betsy was inclined to shoot first and sort things out later — which Matt conceded spoke well of her protective instincts. But that didn't mean he wanted to be full of bullet holes out of respect for her vigilance.

"He knew our names, Aunt Betsy," Annie-the-Talker said. "Even Lilly's."

Then Matt remembered the tone of pure panic in Aunt Betsy's voice and the speed at which she'd come running. He knew something that would distract her. "I found them riding the creek down the mountainside. Looks like they're old hands at it."

Those black eyes went so wide with fear, Matt could see white all the way around her dark pupils.

"Girls, I told you to stay out of that creek." Her eyes, formerly trained on him, now looked at the soaking-wet girls. "Your ma and pa told you clear as day it was dangerous." Betsy lowered the gun, looking mighty defeated.

Matt suspected that if she was in charge of these two, and with a baby on her hip besides, well . . . after knowing his nieces for around ten minutes, he felt some sympathy for pretty Aunt Betsy.

"Let's go back to the house, girls." It looked like his life was out of jeopardy from poor Aunt Betsy, but he wanted to be farther from that rushing, rocky creek.

Betsy's lip quivered and she nodded, shoving her gun into a pocket in her skirt that looked like it'd been sewn for just that purpose, as the gun fit perfectly. She came toward him, her shoulders slumped.

Lilly, who looked too young to walk, bounced on Betsy's hip and giggled then reached out her arms to Matt and said, "Papa."

Matt had been holding babies since before he was even close to old enough. He saw the launch coming, and Betsy must be an old hand, too, because she didn't let Lilly hurl herself to the ground.

Matt took the baby without dropping his horse's reins, and earned a grin with four teeth. Nine months old at the most. "Howdy, Lilly. I'm your Uncle Matt." He tickled her under her chin.

Betsy took Susie's hand and tried to take Annie's. The older girl dodged and caught hold of Matt's arm. He quit tickling and let himself be guided through woods so dense no sunlight reached the ground. There was no trail Matt could see, but the girls seemed familiar with the woods, pretty surprising when this was an area forbidden to them.

Well, Ma had done her share of "forbidding" with Matt and his brothers. And she'd had poor luck earning their obedience — though he wasn't sure she ever realized it.

The woods thinned out and Matt saw the house and was surprised by his pang of envy.

CHAPTER 2

Betsy saw the house and was all too familiar with the pang of terror.

Emma was going to kill her if she came home and found both girls had died or run off or been kidnapped by roving outlaws. Oh, there were a hundred ways to come to grief in the West. And that was if you were careful. These girls didn't show one speck of caution . . . which meant there were a thousand ways to die.

"Nice house," Matt said, sounding almost reverent. Polite, too, and smart enough. His horse looked like it was well cared for. He wore a gun as if he knew how to use it.

Betsy decided then and there to do some kidnapping herself. Matt Reeves wasn't going anywhere until his brother came home.

"I'll have the noon meal ready in an hour, Matt. Turn your horse into the corral and come on in."

She wondered if she should pick her moment and hide his horse or depend on her feminine wiles to get him to stay.

Not that she had any feminine wiles. Ma hadn't been of much use when it came to teaching such things. Belle Harden was more the type to advise her daughters on how to run men off. Betsy was a hand at it, and she had Pa and Ma to help . . . even when she didn't want help.

And that's how she'd ended up a near spinster. Eighteen years old and not a beau to be found.

She was too busy most of the time to care, but a girl had a few daydreams.

"I'll be right in." Matt, the gullible fool, handed Lilly over. The baby screamed and cried and threw herself at Matt.

Well, Betsy had been handling babies from her first memory, so Lilly didn't manage to cast herself onto the ground, but it was a near thing.

Susie escaped while Betsy wrestled Lilly. Then Matt plucked the baby out of her arms, Susie took Annie's hand, and the four of them . . . five counting the horse, left Betsy behind.

She started to yell warnings to Matt but figured anything she warned him of would just give the girls inspiration.

She was abandoning those girls to a stranger, and she dreaded it. Not because of danger to the girls. Nope. She was purely afraid Matt was going to come to his senses and run off.

Heading for the house to make the best meal she could manage, she wondered just what the man was made of. Those girls would soon reveal his every weakness.

Matt snatched Annie out from under the restless hooves of his horse just as Susie climbed to the top of the pen that held a snorting, pawing mama longhorn.

Faster than he ever had in his life, Matt stripped the leather from his horse, with a baby in his arms, then went to turn his gelding loose in a stall that stank of dirty straw.

What was going on here? Who was tending this barn?

He shooed the horse out into the corral, while juggling all three girls. Doing the minimum while saving the girls' lives at every turn, he was an hour getting to the most basic chores.

More attention should be paid to the barn, and the stalls needed forking and his horse needed hay. Then he thought of pitching some of the lush hay filling the mow in Mark's barn down for his horse, and imagined taking all three girls up there. He ran for the house with them before he lost one permanently. Betsy could watch them while he did chores.

He shoved them inside, thinking to slam

the door and run. Then he smelled sizzling steaks.

His favorite.

"Dinner's ready." Betsy was just about the most beautiful girl Matt had ever seen. Not that he'd seen many girls. Not that many wandering in the mountains, and that's where Matt had been for the last few years.

But she was the prettiest, bar none. And while he was at it, staring at that thick curling black hair and those big shining eyes and her tempting pink lips, he decided she was the most beautiful woman ever, including all the ones he'd never seen.

There couldn't be one more beautiful.

Maybe her lips were tempting because she was talking about food and he was just plain starving. Especially starving for a meal cooked by a woman's hand.

He'd eaten a lot of roasted rabbit, quail, and trout. It was tasty, but some variety was tempting indeed.

He should go back out and clean out that stall and turn his horse into it and water and hay him, then hit the trail and give Mark a week or two to come home.

She pulled lightly browned biscuits out of a cast-iron oven and moved a halfway-to-done pie to the center.

Pie and biscuits.

Matt wasn't going anywhere. He was as surely caught as one of those trout he'd eaten.

It was every man for himself. His gelding was going to have to survive on its own.

He'd brought the girls back alive.

She admitted to being surprised.

Well, that wasn't exactly true. She'd expected the man to keep the girls alive or she'd have never let him leave with them. That he'd stayed away so long and managed to get the saddle and bridle off his horse and get the critter turned out to pasture *and* kept the girls alive.

That was the impressive part.

No notion if the man was any good with ranch chores beyond turning his horse loose, but the barn wasn't on fire and that was good enough for Betsy. She had to admit her standards had dropped through the floor since about four days ago when Mark's last hired man had quit and left her to run the place alone. The nasty, selfish varmint.

Mark had left four behind. One had quit because Susie dropped his boots in the water trough. A second had taken to the trail after Annie accidentally let the bull loose, which knocked over the outhouse while he was in it, wearing nothing but long red underwear and those, down around his ankles.

Betsy hadn't seen it, but the final hired man had told her, laughing until he cried.

Then Lilly had wet clean through her diaper while toddling a bit too close to the last cowpoke's lunch pail. He'd grabbed a handful of mane and lit out for California.

Wimps.

Now she had another man in her clutches. She smiled and fluttered her eyelashes. She'd seen her ma give her pa a similar look, and usually Belle got what she wanted when she did it. Of course Ma wasn't pretending, she really did look at Silas in a way that warmed Betsy's heart and made her curious about love.

Now, Betsy had to fake it, but she tried to make it look natural and Matt came on in, sniffing the air. Paying the fluttering lashes no mind but apparently fascinated by the smell of a baking pie.

Fine enough. Betsy would use anything that worked.

"The steaks are ready to take off the fire. I've got fried potatoes ready, and the pie will come out of the oven about the time we're done eating." She fluttered again, just for practice. It was the first meal she'd cooked since she'd taken over. They'd been living on biscuits and milk, and sometimes jerky and water. The family on the trail drive were eating better than she was.

Matt happened to look at her right at that moment. He quit sniffing. He gave her a smile that was like the August sun coming out after a January blizzard. The man must love pie.

Annie picked that moment to jump on a chair and climb onto the table. Matt snatched her just as she prepared to fall face-first onto the platter of hot biscuits.

He made a quick move that settled Lilly in a high chair, then grabbed Susie as she stumbled and tripped right toward the burning-hot stove.

"Emma is going to be so sorry she left these little imps with me when she comes home and finds them all maimed." Betsy's lower lip trembled. She hadn't cried a tear in her life until this week.

"Where are the hands?" Matt sat Susie at the table, and as the four-year-old started to stand, Matt slapped a biscuit in her hands and said, "Sit still, or I'm taking that back."

Susie stayed in place.

Hah! As if that would last.

"I want a biscuit, too!" Annie yowled. Both girls tallied unequal treatment more closely than a miner watches his gold.

"Sit up to the table, then." Matt set a biscuit in front of another chair, broke a third one up and put it in front of Lilly as Annie clambered into her chair, and the room went silent.

He looked back at Betsy, who felt her lashes flutter without giving it one thought.

"The hands? It looks like they're behind on the chores."

"The last one quit on Monday."

Matt flinched. "It's Saturday. How long has Mark been gone?"

"Two weeks, and they'll probably be at least three more before they get back."

"Strange time of year for a cattle drive. We drive in October in Texas."

"Fall comes early here and Emma doesn't like cutting it close. She's mindful of the high mountain gaps filling in with an early snow. They normally go later than July, but this is the first one she's gone on for years. She's either been round with a baby or had one mighty young. She loves a cattle drive though. I convinced her to go and let me watch the girls."

Betsy's lashes fluttered again, completely of their own accord. Matt had come closer, and the girls were feasting. Betsy dropped her voice to a whisper and added, "The stupidest thing I've ever done. I'm not taking good care of the girls. And I'm not taking any care at all of the ranch."

"And the hands all quit?"

Nodding, Betsy said, "Mark left a skeleton crew, four men, plenty to watch what's left of the herd and do daily chores, but two days after he left the steadiest hand broke his arm diving to save Annie when she fell out of the haymow. I'd let her get out of my sight and she'd climbed up there, and Hank saw her in time to catch her."

"Is he here, just laid up?"

Shaking her head, Betsy said, "He saved Annie, but he rammed his head into the barn wall, besides breaking his arm. He was knocked out cold as a mountain peak. They had to take him to Divide to the doctor, and when they got back they said the doctor wants him to stay in bed until he stops seeing two of everything. I don't know when he'll be back.

"Then the other three quit one at a time. I think if any of them but Travis had been last, they'd have stuck it out rather than abandon me. But Travis was always the least useful of Mark's cowpokes. He gloated when he told me he quit. Then when he rode off and left me he looked back and laughed. The man works with cattle and horses all day. A leaky diaper makes him quit?"

"Betsy, you need help."

She waited for him to say the obvious. He was silent.

Stupid, useless, fluttering lashes.

Not wanting to beg unless she absolutely had to, she rested one open hand on his chest and leaned close so the girls wouldn't start talking and scare him off.

"I need you." She spoke barely above a whisper.

His eyes focused on her words. Or rather her lips, but that was the same thing. He said nothing.

Inching closer, because the situation was

dire, she whispered, "So will you help me, Matt? Will you stay? You're going to want to see your brother, aren't you?"

Matt was nodding, watching her. He seemed dazed.

Betsy smiled, and his eyes almost crossed. She gave him a friendly pat on the chest then stepped back, just as his hand whipped out and pulled her close. She bumped right into his chest.

Then as if the impact woke him up, he let her go and took a step back.

Betsy reconsidered the power of fluttering lashes as she whirled to the stove and started scooping up food.

A chair scraped and she glanced back to see Matt sink into it. He looked stunned. She could well imagine. What had happened? She felt like time had stopped and the world had turned soft and beautiful and very private.

Matt felt like he'd been hit with an ax handle.

It took a bit to gather his thoughts, and by then he was eating and no speech was required. When the meal was finished all three girls looked as if their eyelids were drooping. Nap time. Matt knew all about nap time. How he'd hated it for himself.

How he'd loved it for all his whirlwind little brothers.

"For the next two hours we will have peace," Betsy said. "Then it all begins again until night."

"Will you be all right then, in here, while I go fork out the stalls and do a few other chores?"

Betsy, who had ignored him completely while they ate, suddenly looked at him again. Her eyes, so dark brown he could barely see where the pupils began, gleamed with relief and pleasure. "You're really staying then?"

He couldn't do much else. "Yep. Uh . . . you won't let the girls in the creek again, will you?"

Betsy's smile flashed as bright as her eyes. "I handle them fairly well except when I try and do the chores. I just don't have enough hands and eyes. And apparently not enough sense. If you'll do the chores, I can take care of the girls."

Matt nodded and pushed back his chair. "I'll get to it, then."

He took his Stetson off an antler used as a hook and clamped it on his head and pretty much ran outside.

He'd be fine . . . unless he wanted to eat again. Then things could get confusing.

CHAPTER 3

Someone pounded the door with the side of their fist. Betsy rose from the chair, the first time she'd been off her feet all day. But whoever was here sounded urgent.

She rushed to the door, flung it open to find Matt, water dripping off his head, right onto Annie, who grinned and revealed a missing tooth.

Betsy was pretty sure the child had all her teeth just an hour ago when she went up to bed.

"How did you get outside?"

Annie jerked one shoulder. Betsy had sounded ferocious, and yet Annie didn't even quit smiling.

"I went out. It's easy." Then she pointed to her mouth. "I lost a tooth, Aunt Betsy."

"And you lost one of your children." Matt looked furious. His face was red enough the water drenching him might turn to steam at any time.

"I sat with them until they fell asleep. I

promise you, I did."

"I believe you." Matt spoke between clenched teeth. He clearly wasn't happy with how this week was going.

Betsy was cooking the best food she could manage, and that was pretty good. Anything to keep from running him off.

"What happened?" Betsy knew that was a stupid question.

"Escaped child. Water trough. Nearly died." Matt growled more than spoke. "Same as every day."

"That's just so true it's almost heartbreaking," Betsy said. "Come in and get changed."

"I'll change in the barn."

"You're freezing. That trough is fed with water from a mountain spring. Run and fetch a change of clothes while I heat up some coffee."

Matt closed his eyes and dragged a deep breath in through blue lips. Betsy appreciated that he was fighting for calm. He'd been sleeping in the bunkhouse all week, and he was doing a fine job of running the ranch . . . for a man without help. She'd tried to help a few times with all three girls at her side. What else could she do but bring them?

"No! Don't even think about helping me." He seemed to rein himself in when he realized he was shouting. More calmly, he said, "I would appreciate something warm. I'll be right back."

He stood Annie on the floor rather than shove her into Betsy's arms. Which Betsy appreciated. She would have gotten soaked.

Matt stomped away dripping.

Betsy thought she showed great restraint by not snickering . . . until after he was out of earshot.

"Bye-bye, Aunt Betsy." Annie had shed her dress and was on her way out the back door, stark naked. Betsy quit laughing and made a dash to catch the little imp.

CHAPTER 4

"Another fine meal, Betsy." Matt leaned back from the supper table and patted his stomach — which Betsy couldn't help but notice was flat and hard as a board — even though he put an alarming amount of food away every time she fed him.

All three girls were either asleep or the next thing to it. Matt had moved the baby's tin plate, or she'd be snoring with her face resting in gravy.

"I'll help you get them settled."

"I'm not tired!" Annie wailed. Then her head nodded, and jerked back up. Susie gave up, crossed her arms on the table, and laid down her weary head.

"Thank you, I'd appreciate it."

Betsy and Matt had learned to work as a decent team. Matt changed diapers with easy skill. Betsy had the two older girls in their pajamas and tucked in bed by the time Matt had pulled the sleeping gown on Lilly and brought her in. All three girls slept in one room. Mark and Emma shared another. There was a large kitchen with space for a stove and table and sink and some cupboards on one side and a fireplace with a pair of rocking chairs on the other.

It was a tightly built, well-tended home, and when all three girls fell asleep instantly after they laid down, Betsy followed Matt out to those rockers and sank down beside him.

It had become their habit to talk for a few minutes at the end of the day, while they waited to make sure the girls wouldn't stage a prison break.

Matt had nailed the window shut in their bedroom as well as the front door and every other window in the house. The back door was the only way out, so to get out, the girls had to come past Betsy.

The summer nights were cool up here in the mountains, and Matt always laid a fire and started it burning before they ate the evening meal.

By the time the girls were tucked in, it felt good to sit before it for a few minutes. Both of them sighed, such an identical sound that they looked up, and Betsy smiled, then Matt laughed.

She said, "I don't know how Emma does it. I'm sure it helps to have practice, but I spend all day either cooking for them or chasing after them. Lilly can't walk yet, but she crawls so fast and pulls herself up on everything.

She scaled a chair and then the kitchen table this morning. She was sitting right on top of the butter dish playing with a butcher knife by the time I got to her."

Betsy shuddered to think of the danger.

Matt shook his head. He took a look at the butcher knife, now hanging from a nail high on the wall, and grinned. "Good spot for it."

"The nail was there. And there's a hole in the knife handle. I suspect that's where Emma keeps it. I just forget all the ways these wily children can find to harm themselves." They shared a look of terror, then both of them laughed.

"How are things outside? Have you cleaned up the mess I made?"

"You couldn't possibly do the outside chores and tend those girls. It wasn't a mess you made, it was you making the right choice and caring for those girls. That's a job that takes all day every day."

Betsy's heart swelled a bit at the kind words. "I think we've almost found everything they can use to kill themselves."

There was an extended silence, broken only by the creak of the rockers. Finally, Matt said, "You're an optimist, aren't you, Betsy?"

They both broke down and laughed hard. It was the closest to a sane adult moment they'd had since they'd met.

"So you've got a herd of little brothers, is that right?" Betsy asked.

"Yep, and one little sister. She's seven years old and that's the last baby Ma had, but Ma is getting up into her forties now. Time for her to slow down with the babies."

Smiling, Betsy said, "I remember all those years I was growing up, Mark telling tales of his family full of boys. Then when your ma had a baby girl, he was so stunned, we thought he'd ride all the way to Texas just to check and make sure they were right."

"I did it."

"What?" Betsy turned away from gazing in the flames to stare at him.

"I went to check. I was in Oregon when I got word, and I rode all the way home. It was just such a shock. I was slow getting there, and Hope was near a year old. And Ma had taken control of the family."

Betsy felt her brow wrinkle. "Taken control how?"

"She made everyone settle down so her baby girl wouldn't be raised in a madhouse. It was a great home to be a growing boy in. A lot of the things we got up to remind me of how Mark's girls act. But the unruly ways of my brothers drove us all away from home at a young age, looking for some peace. Now, well, I thought long and hard about staying down there. My older brothers Abe and Ike are both living near my folks, and I've got several nieces and nephews growing up there. I may wander back down thataway in the end.

I've just never quite got the wanderlust out of my blood."

"Where all have you been?" Betsy sounded wistful to her own ears. "I've never been beyond the state of Montana. In fact, I've barely traveled from here to Divide and Helena. Ma likes to keep us close to home. She doesn't even think her daughters should show themselves in town."

"Why not?"

Betsy shrugged. "Just a habit. The trails are better, and there's a train spur from Divide to Helena now. We can get there in half a day. But when we first settled here we were mighty cut off, and there were a lot of wild men around. Ma didn't like them knowing she had a passel of girls living out in this remote area."

"Well, I've been to near every state in the Union west of the Mississippi. I've never gone back East — except once. I don't know much about city living, but I can survive in the wilderness with a knife and a rifle, don't need any money nor a job. But it's a lonely life. I grew up surrounded by a crowd. I don't last too long on my own before I start longing to hear another voice. I've turned my hand to most every job a man can do. Mining in New Mexico. Lumberjacking in Idaho. I've scouted for the cavalry in Arizona and driven a stagecoach in Colorado. I went to sea in California and sailed all the way around the southern tip of South America. I even landed in New York City, but it was so huge and dirty, I stepped onshore and signed on to a boat sailing back only an hour later. I've seen the Grand Canyon and worked a dozen ranches from Texas to North Dakota. I was even a sheriff in Kansas for a while. I've loved my wandering ways. I reckon I need to settle down one of these days, but it's never stopped being fun to live such a free life."

They talked and rocked late into the night. Betsy knew the morning would come early, with hungry livestock and hungrier girls. But she found herself almost desperate for the quiet adult conversation. It was too sweet to end.

A log split and sent a wash of sparks out of the fireplace. They both jumped up, and Betsy realized how low the fire had burned.

"How long have we been sitting here?" She felt as if the outside world had intruded on something very personal.

Neither of them had a pocket watch, nor was there a clock in the house, but it had to have been more than an hour.

"I reckon I've talked until your ears are aching." Matt gave her his friendly smile that reminded Betsy so much of Emma's husband.

They stood, and Matt stepped to the fireplace. "It's a cool night. I'll build up the fire before I go."

"No, it's a tight house. We'll be fine. Thank you." Betsy stood just as Matt turned from the hearth and nearly bumped into her. Matt caught her by the arms to keep from stumbling then was still. His eyes wandered around her face. She felt it like a caress.

He asked, "How did you end up with such shining black curls? Mark told me Emma's hair is whiter than his, and the girls are all so blond."

"Ma married and was widowed. We have different fathers, and Ma says I take after him in looks. My real name at birth was Betsy Santoni; my pa was Italian. But he died when I was a baby, and Ma married Silas. He's the only man I've ever known as my father, and he's a good one and I'm proud to carry his name. My ma said my own pa was pretty worthless."

Matt smiled. "I don't know what kind of man he was, but he must have been good looking to have a daughter as beautiful as you."

Betsy felt something awaken deep in her chest. Something she hadn't known was sleeping. Something she hadn't known was there.

"Thank you." She wondered if she was blushing. She had skin that tanned deeply, and she wasn't given to blushes.

Matt lifted a hand and drew one finger across her cheeks. They must've turned red . . . Why else would he touch her?

"Don't tell me you haven't heard that

before. The men in Montana aren't all blind."

Betsy shrugged. "Ma and Pa don't let men come around much."

Matt grinned. "How'd Mark ever get past them?"

"There was trouble and Mark was the right man to help, and somehow, when the trouble passed, he and Emma were planning a wedding. It was fun watching Ma and Pa try'n run him off. And your cousin Charlie was with him, and he ended up married to my sister Sarah."

"I'll have to see Charlie while I'm here, too." Matt's hand opened and rested on her cheek. Quietly, he said, "I don't want to talk about my family anymore."

He leaned down and kissed her.

Her first kiss.

It was his first kiss.

Matt wasn't sure how in the world Betsy Harden had ended up in his arms, but he wasn't going to waste time wondering because it was the best thing that had ever happened to him.

He slid his arms around her waist, his only thought to get closer. He drew her hard against him.

"Matt." She turned her head to break the kiss. Her hands came up to press against his chest. "Wait. Stop."

Her words shocked him into using his head

for the first time in a while. He dropped her, only realizing as she slid away that he'd lifted her off her feet.

He stepped back and slammed into the fireplace, which sent him stumbling forward, and somehow, she was right back in his arms. His lips descended, and hers rose to meet him.

The next time they stopped his hands were sunk deep in the dark silk of her hair. He carefully unwound all those lush curls, lingering, kissing her eyes and her blushing cheeks.

She hadn't said "wait" the second time. In fact, her arms were wound tight around his neck. It all added up to her liking this kiss just as much as he did.

This time she stepped back then turned away and breathed deep. "Um . . . you'd better go."

"I want to talk about what just happened here, Betsy. I want it to happen again. I want to have the right to kiss you."

She looked over her shoulder. Her lips were swollen from their kiss. Her hair had tumbled from its bun and flowed wild around her shoulders. She had a little dimple in her chin and her cheekbones were high, her nose strong in a feminine way. He wanted to get to know every bit of her as well as he knew her face.

"What are you saying, Matt? Are you saying you want to court me?"

That wasn't what he was saying. He wanted to marry her and carry her to the bedroom right this minute. And as a man who knew almost nothing about women, he thought he had a great idea of how to proceed.

But courting?

That cleared his thoughts. "Uh, courting. How does a man even court a woman when he's living with her, eating with her, and raising three children with her? That sounds more like two people who have been married for years." Except of course in one very important way.

His thoughts honestly shocked him a bit because he'd always kept to manly places like the mountaintops and the sea, mining camps and remote ranches. He'd never so much as spent time alone with a woman, not once. Never long enough to consider rounding her up and claiming her.

"Well, nothing like this can happen again as long as we're here alone. It's sinful."

Matt thought it might well be sinful except his intentions, passionate though they were, were completely honorable.

"So you go on now, and when Mark and Emma get back we can talk more about such things as" — kissing, holding, loving? Which would she say? — "courting. Until then, this is improper and a bad example to the girls."

Who were fast asleep and wouldn't know a thing about it.

Matt figured he'd had the only run of luck he was going to get tonight, so he nodded, not agreeing one whit that he needed his big brother around to tell him how to behave, and headed for the door. "I'll see you in the morning for breakfast then, Betsy."

He plucked his Stetson off the hook then turned back to see her watching him, one hand gently touching her lips. Only a will of iron kept him from crossing the room and gathering her right back into his arms.

"Good night." He clamped his hat on his head to keep his hands busy.

"Good night, Matt. I'll see you at breakfast."

CHAPTER 5

Matt might've just gone whole hog pursuing Betsy Harden if it weren't for those girls, and about a thousand head of cows.

The thunder and lightning in the night had kept Matt from sleep, along with thoughts of beautiful Betsy. As the storm came, Matt felt like he was in the middle of it. Up this high, the clouds sometimes went across the lower slopes of the mountains, below a man. But not this time. The storm was all around him, and sleeping in the bunkhouse, he felt like he was in the middle of a plunging lifeboat at sea.

When the worst passed, he made a dash for the house, worried about Betsy handling the girls. He'd just slammed the door open when the thunder started again. Only it sounded wrong enough that he turned to see hundreds of cattle charging right for him.

He swung the door shut just as a thousand-pound bull leaped up on the porch and ripped the railing away. The animal hit the house so hard it rocked.

A scream behind Matt turned him around to see Annie running for a window, as if she needed to escape. The window was nailed shut and shuttered, but Matt dashed forward and nabbed the little lunatic just as a longhorn rammed its head through, shattering glass and sending shards of wood blasting through the room.

Matt jumped to the side and dropped to the floor, ducking under those horns as fast as he could without crushing Annie. He felt a few sharp slashes, but he missed the worst of it. Then a bellow whipped his head around, and he saw the animal that had busted the window get bunted so hard he came right through, into the room.

Betsy rushed out with a shrieking Susie in her arms. She yelled and grabbed for the broom by the fireplace. She brandished it as the panicked yearling skidded on the split-log floor then fell, jumped to its feet, whirled, and leaped out the same window it'd come in.

The door shuddered under an impact. Matt, still holding Annie, threw his back flat against it. He didn't think he could hold back a charging bull, but if the animal hit the door a glancing blow and Matt kept the door in place, the cattle might not storm inside.

The thundering hooves were deafening.

A wail from the bedroom had a nearly

stunned Betsy turning around and rushing in to get Lilly. "Annie, come here to me," Betsy called.

Matt lowered the little girl to the floor. Matt's arms must have seemed like a haven because she turned and jumped back at him.

He hoisted her up, hoping a cow didn't run through the door and crush them both.

Betsy came back, Susie on one hip, Lilly on the other. The noise went on and on.

"The lightning must have spooked them." Betsy spoke loud enough to be heard.

Nodding, Matt started thinking beyond survival moment by moment. "How am I going to round them all up?"

"You can't do it alone. We'll have to ride after them."

"We?" Matt looked at how full her hands were. His, too. "We can't take three babies out to herd cattle."

"We can and we will. I don't see as we have much choice. Hopefully they'll calm down and stay mostly together. But if not we'll be combing them out of the trees for ten miles. You can't do that alone."

Matt tried his best to think of something else, but, "You're right. I can't do it by myself. We'll have to let the girls ride with us."

"Emma has a pack she wears so she can strap the baby on her back."

"So one of us wears Lilly?"

"Sure, didn't your ma have something like that?"

"Nope, when we took the wagon to town, the baby sat on her lap until a new one came along, then he joined the brothers in the wagon box."

"Well, we can't hope to herd cattle with a wagon, so we have to ride."

"Listen."

Betsy's eyes lit up. "It's over."

"Almost. They'll tear along for a while, but they'll tire out and calm down."

With a comically arched brow, Betsy said, "That sounds a little like the children."

"A little." Matt grinned as he patted Annie on the back. "The girls never do seem to quite calm down."

They shared a smile, their arms full of children until the last of the thundering hooves faded in the distance.

Betsy realized what else had faded. "The rain and thunder are over."

Nodding, Matt said, "We can't wait until sunrise; who knows how far they'll wander by then. Let's get saddled up."

CHAPTER ·6

"When Emma asked me to watch her children while she went on the drive I was just plain tickled." The leather of the saddles creaked as they rode along the trail left by the rampaging herd.

Betsy kept up easily, though Matt set a fast pace. They were hoping to catch the cattle before they'd spread far and wide.

Matt had Annie riding in front of him. The little girl's head lolled over Matt's supporting arm. She was deep asleep, as were her sisters.

"I wanted to spend time with my sweet nieces." Betsy gave Susie's tummy a gentle pat. She rode in front and Lilly was on her back.

Matt had wrangled with her, wanting the heavier load, but Betsy had persuaded him that if there was any hard riding — and there would be — he'd have to do it. Betsy let him think he was the better rider, and maybe he was, but she'd done her share in the saddle and could carry her share of the load.

"And of course the chores would all be done by the hands."

"Those men oughta be horsewhipped for abandoning you."

Nodding, Betsy went on as they rode in the dark. The storm had passed, and the trail, churned up by the cattle, was muddy enough they rode off to the side to avoid the mud as best they could. When the trees got too thick, they were forced to wade through the only existing trail, but when they found open meadows, they could get away from the deep mud. And in those openings, they could see the sky awash in starlight.

If they hadn't been facing hours of grueling work, it might've been nice.

If they hadn't been toting three children, it might've been romantic.

If letting all of Emma's cattle run off wasn't financially ruinous, it might've been fun.

"I thought of it as an adventure. And an honor, honestly. Emma never leaves the girls. She's a fierce, protective mama. So I knew it was a high compliment. Also the cattle drive to Helena is a long, treacherous journey. Even though someone from my family drives cattle every year it's never easy. So Emma must have wanted to get away, have a break from the ranch. I was determined to prove to her she'd done right by trusting me."

"You've kept them alive; no one could dare hope for more."

"So far I've kept them alive. She's not home yet."

Matt smiled, and Betsy realized she could see his face. The gray light of encroaching dawn was pushing back the night. "It was a different kind of adventure than I expected."

"Yep, less like fun and more like a constant battle for survival for all five of us."

Betsy smiled back and spoke the simple truth. "I don't know what I'd have done without you, Matt. I'd have had to abandon all care for the cattle. Which is bad enough without this stampede."

"I'm glad I got here when I did. Betsy, I think, um . . . that is . . . don't you think . . ." The bellow just ahead turned them to face a longhorn bull as he stepped out of a clump of aspen trees, pawing the earth, its ten-foot spread of horns lowered.

"Whoa!" Matt pulled his horse to a stop so suddenly, his gelding reared.

"Go right." Betsy issued the order with a snap then wheeled her horse to the left and raced into the trees. She glanced back to see Matt vanish into the woods on the opposite side of the trail, giving only a moment's thought to the fact that he'd obeyed her so quickly. She'd probably ordered him to do something he was already doing and about to shout at her.

They made a pretty good team.

Betsy put distance between her and that

wiry white-and-tan beast, giving the old mossy horn time to calm down as she picked her way through a forest so dense she had no business in it. No trail anywhere. Underbrush between the trees grew until it was almost impenetrable. Bending low to duck branches, letting her horse pick his way through, she headed forward, hoping to get behind the bull and maybe drive him back toward Emma's ranch.

If they could get him moving in the right direction, he would probably just follow his instincts for home. The other cattle might even realize the bull, their natural leader, was gone and follow him.

The practical ranch woman in her doubted it would be that easy.

She thought she'd gone far enough when she heard the lash of a whip. Matt had carried one he'd found in the barn, so he must be working the bull. She headed back for the trail to find the longhorn headed for home, trotting.

Matt heard her emerge from the woods and turned, his alert look telling her that bull had given him all he wanted to handle.

As he rode up, he smiled. "Let's see if we can turn a few more back without getting gored."

"How many cattle were in the herd closest to the house?" Mark and Emma had the cattle spread into several grassy stretches of the high mountains.

"Probably two hundred. I looked before we rode out, and about half are still there. They probably ran a bit to the west and let the thick woods stop them and turn them back. I'd say we're looking for at least a hundred head of cattle."

"So one down, ninety-nine to go?" Betsy sighed. "It's going to be a long day."

The sun peaked over the horizon now, though they were in thick shade. It was finally full light.

"It seemed like a lot more than that when they were crashing around the house last night," Betsy said as they rode on in the direction the cattle had run.

"Well, one bull jumping into the house is a lot." Matt shook his head. "I can't believe there was a longhorn in Mark's house."

Betsy smiled then chuckled. "Emma is going to want us to do some explaining about that."

A small clearing in the woods opened to a couple dozen of the runaway cows. These were docile and their bellies full, so they cooperated nicely and headed down the trail the way they'd come.

"I hope they keep moving, because I'm not going to follow them all the way home." Matt and Betsy sat side by side to watch them disappear down the trail for home.

"You know what else I hope?" Betsy asked.

"What?" Matt reined his horse around and they moved on, following a clear trail that led farther into the woods.

"I hope we catch up with these cows pretty quickly, because I want to get everything in neat order before Emma gets home, or she'll never let me babysit again."

"You mean you want to?" Matt sounded horrified, and Betsy turned, annoyed. He was smiling, laughing at her, and she couldn't help laughing at herself.

The laughter and the sunlight helped wake Susie and Annie up. Lilly slept on as they chased cattle. They got another dozen straggling along the forest path headed back. Then another dozen, then another.

"Another thing I hope . . ." Betsy said when they'd finished with that clearing. Probably seventy-five cows now bound for home.

"What's that?" Matt asked as the woods surrounded them again. Tracks went on even farther from home.

"I hope we find the rest of the cows soon, because if I want to keep this secret we're running out of time." The woods thinned sooner this time, and Betsy saw a few cows ahead. Most likely not all of them, but Betsy decided they'd call this good and give up. They needed to gather what they had and count them, then they could comb the woods for the rest of them over the next few days.

Lilly cried from the pack on Betsy's back.

131

"We've got to stop. She needs a dry diaper, and I have some food for all the girls. We're all due to stretch our legs for a bit." Betsy swung down and Matt was just a second slower. Then he stood Annie up on legs that wobbled from riding so long. He led the horses a safe distance away and staked the critters out to graze.

When he came back, he said, "What do you mean by running out of time? We've got as long as it takes."

"I mean we're getting too close to Ma's place."

"Your ma? I thought she went on the cattle drive." Mark led Annie to where Betsy had set out apples and jerky and biscuits. She'd packed well. He could see she'd figured to be all day with this. She changed Lilly's diaper with quick, well-practiced skill.

He doled out the food, and Annie and Susie ate like they were starving, which they most certainly were not.

Betsy sat on the rock with a small cup of milk she'd poured from a canteen and began giving Lilly sips. Matt broke up a biscuit and gave Lilly bites between drinks. He sat beside Betsy, mighty close, since the rock wasn't overly large. He liked the feel of her pressed up to his side.

"Where'd you get an idea like that?"

"I reckon I got it because you were over at Mark's alone. When the last hand ran off, why didn't you load the girls in the wagon and take them to your ma's house to get help?"

Betsy shrugged one shoulder. "It's because my ma raised me and my sisters mostly alone and ran the ranch, too, after the husbands died."

"The husbands? You mean Emma's pa and yours?"

"And one more. Your cousin Charlie is married to my sister Sarah, and she's got a different pa than Emma and I do. She'd buried three husbands before Silas. They were all a worthless lot when they were alive. So she did it all herself.

"I felt like I should be able to handle the girls and the cattle for a few weeks at least. I wanted to prove I could handle whatever trouble I faced. It's because I didn't want to go home, crying for help. And it's worse now than then."

Matt frowned as he slid one arm around Betsy. He was a little hurt. He'd been helping her. "Why's it worse now?"

"Because Ma's not going to like it one bit when she finds out you've been at Emma's with me without an adult chaperone. In fact, she might consider that you've been dishonorable."

"She won't be harsh with you, will she?" Matt was angry at the thought of Belle Harden being wrathful with her daughter. He felt protective. He pulled her closer, the baby still between them but not keeping them far apart.

"I won't let you come to any harm, Betsy." He leaned down and kissed her.

"I'm not worried about me coming to harm, for heaven's sake." She went to push him away and darned if her arm — that wasn't holding Lilly — didn't circle his neck instead and pull him closer.

"You're not? Then what's the matter?" He didn't really care, not right now. He was too busy kissing this beautiful woman. And enjoying just how enthusiastically she kissed him back.

Betsy broke the kiss but only held herself away a fraction of an inch. "I'm afraid Ma might shoot you on sight."

A chill rushed down his spine at her dead-serious tone. Before he could ask her if she was as serious as she seemed, a crash from the far end of the trail turned his attention. Longhorns plunged out of the woods. The noise was so sudden and startling, that the girls all rushed to Matt's side, and he pulled Betsy close and put an arm around both girls.

Cows kept coming and coming. Probably nearly every one of the unaccounted-for cattle lost in the stampede.

Smiling he looked down and said, "They're all back! We're done with our roundup." He leaned down and kissed her deeply and joyfully.

The sharp crack of a rifle cocking broke the kiss, and he turned to look right down the barrel of a Winchester.

"Get your hands off my daughter."

Chapter 7

A woman rode straight toward him, her rifle drawn and leveled.

The woman's eyes flashed with golden streaks that a man might mistake for lightning.

Right behind her a man rode, also armed. He was as mad as the bull that'd almost taken them.

Belle and Silas Harden. They didn't look one speck like Betsy, and yet there wasn't a doubt in his mind.

Matt let go of Betsy fast and stepped well away from her. He hoped he lived to tell Mark about how he'd met his in-laws.

The woman's eyes shifted between him and Betsy. Matt figured she didn't miss a thing.

Then he only saw Betsy's back. "Ma, you can't shoot him, he's Mark's brother."

"That ain't enough to save a man who's got his hands on my daughter."

Betsy's head tilted a bit. "It is if he's got my permission."

The pistol sagged, and Belle Harden didn't look like the kind of woman who ever got careless with a weapon. Then with abrupt, angry motions, she reholstered it. He noticed Silas still had his in hand but pointed in the air.

"He came to visit Mark right after the last hand quit. He saved the girls' lives when they got away from me."

"And why didn't you come to me when that happened?" Belle swung off her horse and ground hitched it. Matt noticed the horse stayed right there, a well-trained critter.

Betsy suddenly broke from where she stood, guarding Matt . . . which had been humiliating, but at the same time he really appreciated it. Leaving Annie and Susie behind, Betsy, with Lilly on her hip, threw an arm around her mother and started crying.

Matt started praying.

He spent a few moments recommitting his soul to the Lord and making sure his spiritual affairs were in order. Because one wrong word from Betsy and he'd be standing at the pearly gates.

Belle didn't shoot, but Silas dismounted and stalked straight for Matt, who scooped both girls up in his arms and said, "Grandpa's here, girls. Let's give Grandpa a hug, shall we?"

Both girls yelled with glee. Silas looked frustrated as the girls flung themselves out of

Matt's arms and into his. Hard to beat up a man while little girls are hugging you. The look Silas gave him told Matt he was well aware of what Matt was up to. But Silas couldn't resist the little girls and quit trying to burn a hole through Matt with his eyes.

Finally believing he might survive, Matt realized more people were flooding into the canyon. It looked like Belle had found the stray cows and sent up an alarm.

Betsy was babbling something to Belle. It sounded like she was just telling about the cowhands and the trouble. He definitely heard the words, "girls drown" and "Matt came and saved them both."

Which probably wasn't true. The cute little monsters had been fine.

A beautiful redhead rode in, and right behind her was Matt's cousin, Charlie. Charlie would save him. Or Matt would get Charlie killed.

Whichever happened, it was nice to see a familiar face.

A little redheaded boy on Charlie's lap, who looked a lot like the pretty redhead, gave Matt hope. Belle wouldn't shoot her son-in-law's brother, would she?

Matt kept up his praying just to be on the safe side.

Charlie saw him and rode straight over. He dismounted and almost ran, not that easy while wearing cowboy boots and carrying a toddler, and he threw his free arm around Matt and pounded him hard on the back, laughing.

He pulled away not knowing he was now a human shield.

"Which one are you?"

Matt had heard that question hundreds of times in his life. It was a fact, he and his many older and younger brothers bore a mighty strong resemblance to one another.

"I'm Matt."

Nodding, Charlie said, "You look so much like Mark I was trying to figure out how he could be here and in Helena at the same time."

"I'm so much better looking than Mark it ain't even funny."

Charlie started laughing. "And is it true that your ma had a girl?"

"Yep. Pa's thirteenth child was finally a girl."

"Twelve sons?" Belle exclaimed. "And your ma didn't lose her mind or take after your pa with a skillet?"

Betsy turned to Matt. "Ma's always been fond of her girls."

Belle was now holding Lilly, which made her seem far less dangerous.

Silas came up beside Belle. "You're fond of your sons, too, aren't you, honey?"

"That I am, Silas. Right fond of the sons we've made." Belle gave Silas such a warm look Matt was almost dazed.

A young man caught up with Belle and stood beside her, grinning. "I've taught you how good it can be to have a boy, haven't I, Ma? Me and my four brothers?"

"This is my little brother, Tanner." Betsy pointed to another barely grown boy. "And that's Si. The rest of the boys went on the cattle drive with Mark."

Tanner was as tall as Silas and had his ma's hazel eyes, and skin that was as tan as an Indian. Si was probably Silas Jr. He took after his pa, though both the parents were brown haired, so the resemblance between them was strong in general coloring.

Charlie shook his head. "It was all we could do to stop Mark from riding for Texas when he got word about a baby sister. He figured a terrible mistake had been made, and if it hadn't, he was scared for his little brothers."

"Most of us got home to see if it was true. Ike's moved home permanently and married Laura McClellen."

"I hadn't heard that." Charlie's eyes lit up. He looked at Belle. "Laura McClellen is Mandy Linscott's baby sister."

"Sophie McClellen ended up with a Reeves in her family, too?" Belle looked glum.

The pretty redhead plucked her little boy out of Charlie's arms.

"Why is my sister crying? Betsy never cries." Less friendly than Charlie by a country mile. Matt remembered her name was Sarah. Betsy had mentioned her plenty of times since he'd gotten here.

Charlie looked from Matt to Sarah to Betsy. His brow lowered with worry, and he rested a hand affectionately on Sarah's back. "We found Mark's cattle coming onto our property. Figured the storm stampeded them. I sent word there was trouble, which brought Belle and Silas and a passel of others. How long have you been living with Betsy?" Charlie choked over that and cleared his throat and said, "I mean, uh . . . how long have you been sleeping together at Mark's place . . . no, I mean —"

Matt kicked Charlie in the ankle, and he didn't even care that everyone saw it. "Stop talking before you get me killed."

There was a long silence. Charlie looked to be thinking of what to say and discarding many possible choices. Finally, he raised his hands as if surrendering and said rather weakly, "Welcome to Montana, Matt."

If this was how a man got welcomed to Montana, it was no wonder the state was mostly empty.

"Let's get these cattle home, then we'll settle this." Silas took charge, which seemed mighty brave for some reason. It stood to reason the man of the family would take charge, and yet there was something about Belle that said no one took charge of her,

141

ever. Matt would bet she wasn't a tractable kind of wife. Love and honor, sure, if she deemed a man worthy.

Obey . . . most likely she'd only do that if she was ordered to do something she planned to do anyway.

But Silas looked like a man who knew ranching, which Belle most likely respected, so her going along with him, well, if a body wanted to call that obedient they were welcome to do so.

A couple of the hands went on ahead. The rest of the hands, along with Betsy's two little brothers, hazed the critters in the clearing toward the trail and fell in behind them.

The cattle were tired from a long run, and their bellies were full of lush grass. It had turned them into purely docile critters.

The Harden family — and Matt — brought up the rear. They were on the way to Mark's in a matter of minutes.

But the trail was barely wide enough to ride two abreast, and Belle led the family group with Betsy at her side and Lilly strapped on her back. Betsy had Susie in front of her.

Silas was next, riding side by side with Sarah. Silas had Annie.

Matt found himself at the end of the line with Charlie, and Charlie's son riding on his pa's lap. The riding arrangements didn't suit Matt at all. He needed to talk to Betsy, and he knew about decent behavior, so he needed to set things right by having a talk with Betsy's pa about his intentions . . . even though he hadn't exactly had time to figure out what his intentions were.

As they rode, Matt thought that no two girls ever looked less like their ma than black-haired, black-eyed Betsy and green-eyed redheaded Sarah.

Matt leaned close to Charlie and whispered, "Do you have any control over your wife?"

Charlie grinned. "Not mostly."

"Can you get her back here so I can have a talk with Betsy's pa?"

Charlie's eyes went wide. Fear, plain and simple. "I've done that before. It ain't an easy talk." Then Charlie, who'd always been Matt's favorite cousin, said, "Welcome to the family."

Much like his welcome to Montana. Charlie was just full of interesting ways to greet a man. And then he proved to have another one. He looked down at his boy, whose name Matt hadn't even asked yet, and patted the tyke affectionately on the tummy.

"Sarah," he spoke so his voice carried to his wife, "I haven't fed the baby in a while. You have some biscuits we could feed him, don't you?"

Sarah went from ignoring Matt and talking quietly with her pa to looking down at her son with concerned maternal eyes.

She dropped back, and Matt didn't waste a

moment urging his horse ahead to take Sarah's place. He saw Charlie grab his wife's reins when she tried to block Matt. Then Matt was there and Silas turned the coldest blue eyes on Matt he'd ever seen.

Well, Matt was no boy, nor was he a coward. He'd spent time kissing Betsy, and as an honorable man, who wanted leave to kiss Betsy any time he wanted, he didn't hesitate to do what was right.

CHAPTER 8

"Elizabeth Harden, what were you thinking?" Belle set a brisk pace, and Betsy had the sense her ma was trying to leave Matt in the dust.

Since Matt was riding along with Charlie, who knew the way, Betsy didn't figure they'd lose him.

Every time her ma called her Elizabeth, it sent a chill down Betsy's spine, because trouble always followed.

Well, Betsy was past the age of getting a hiding, and Ma had never been one to hand out her punishments in that harsh way.

But on the other hand, there was never any doubt that making Ma mad was going to be followed with long, deep regrets.

"Why didn't you just load up the girls and come home? We'd have helped." Then Ma's expression changed from anger to something else. Something soft and sad, as if she was hurt. Her pain was a lot harder to take than anger.

"Have I ever acted as if you can't come to

me for help, Betsy? You know I'll always come a-runnin' if you need me. I haven't acted as if you can't, have I?"

"No, Ma." Betsy reached across and gave her ma's arm a squeeze. "It's because I knew you'd come that I didn't ask. I wanted to prove I was up to handling everything. I've heard the stories of you taking care of our whole ranch with no man. I felt like a failure because I wasn't up to it. I kept meaning to just come for you, but then I'd think I could just get through one more day, prove to myself . . . and you and Pa, that you'd raised me right."

"Betsy, you're as smart and hardworking as the day is long. You don't have to prove a single thing to me because I've seen plenty of proof over the years."

Letting go of her ma's arm, Betsy smiled, but inside she couldn't help feeling the twist of failure. "But you did it, Ma. Why couldn't I? Because I was sure enough failing at it. And if Matt hadn't come . . ." She thought of that fast-moving creek, and a cold chill raised goose bumps on her arms. "Matt saved the girls' lives, Ma. They'd slipped away while I did chores, thinking they were napping. If he hadn't been there . . ." Shaking her head she couldn't control a shudder.

"But you shouldn't have been kissing a man you'd only met days ago."

A long silence followed. Betsy glanced back

and saw that Matt was now riding alongside Pa and Sarah had dropped back and was fussing with her baby. Betsy said a quick prayer to God to protect Matt from Pa.

Leaning close to Ma, she spoke so her voice wouldn't be heard. "How long did you know Pa before you kissed him the first time?"

Another long silence. Then Ma said, "Don't try and change the subject. I've told you before that a man can't be trusted. You know better'n to —"

"How long, Ma?" Betsy knew her ma real well, and she knew when a question was being dodged.

"Anthony, your pa, came around for weeks before I —"

"I'm talking about Silas, and what's more, you know it. He's the only man I call Pa."

Ma glared at Betsy, who'd been raised to be tough, even with her own mother.

Betsy arched her brows and stared right back, maybe not so ferociously as Ma, but then Betsy wasn't half trying.

Finally Ma looked away. "When we first kissed isn't the point. We'd known each other through a long, hard cattle drive. I knew the kind of man he was. I respected —"

"That fast, huh?" Betsy smiled then snickered. "Why, Belle Tanner Harden, you scamp. I think the two of us need to compare our history and just see which of us is better behaved around men."

Ma's eyes narrowed, then after a few seconds she rolled them toward heaven and said, "Our first kiss came too fast."

"I'm sure mine and Matt's did, too. But it was only a kiss. He treated me with honor; he worked hard outside, slept in the bunkhouse every night, and helped with the girls as well. He's got a passel of little brothers, and he's as good with children as I am, maybe better because by his own admission he was as much of a scamp as Mark growing up."

"No one can be as much of a scamp as Mark." Ma didn't admit it often, but Betsy knew she was right fond of her son-in-law, and Emma was still very much in love with her husband.

"That's true. But Matt seemed to keep ahead of the girls as if he'd seen it all before."

Ma glanced back then looked quickly away. "You're sounding like you're pretty serious about this young man. Just because he's Mark's brother doesn't mean you really know him. You need time to learn if he's an honest, God-fearing man who will be dependable over the years."

"I agree. I like him real well, but I'm going to spend time getting to know him better. I can promise you I'm not going to be rushed into anything with a near stranger."

"Belle." Pa had closed the distance between himself and Ma.

"Yes, Silas?" Ma looked as if she wanted to keep pestering Betsy.

"Matt just asked for Betsy's hand in marriage. He wants to ride straight into Divide and have the wedding today."

CHAPTER 9

Betsy started coughing.

They emerged from the woods with only a wide pasture ahead of them before they reached Mark's house.

Matt rode past Silas and brought his horse right up beside Betsy — on the side away from Belle. He patted her on the back until she recovered.

"I wanted to talk with you about it first, honey." He gave Silas a narrow-eyed look for being so blunt. His soon-to-be father-in-law . . . if Matt handled all this right . . . looked completely unrepentant.

Now here he was with Silas and Belle watching his every move, and Charlie and Sarah close enough to have heard everything — and riding in closer. And Betsy looking like she wanted to make a run for it.

"Give your horse to your pa and let's walk together the rest of the way."

"You're not going anywhere alone with my daughter," Belle snapped.

Matt knew good and well that before this was over he was going everywhere with Betsy Harden. He let that thought keep him from growling.

Instead he dismounted and plucked Betsy off her horse. "Watch us. Listen to me talk then, Belle. But Betsy deserves to hear some nice words about how wonderful I think she is. And she needs to hear . . ." Matt looked away from Belle and talked to pretty Betsy.

". . . you need to hear that I want the right to kiss you anytime I choose. I want to spend my life with you, Betsy. You're the prettiest woman I've ever seen. The prettiest I've ever imagined."

Matt realized that the crowd was gone. They were probably disgusted, but maybe they also had a little shame. For whatever reason, the family had ridden on for the ranch house, Charlie leading both Matt's and Betsy's horses.

"But that's not why I want to join my life with you. I can see your goodness, and I respect your toughness and your fine heart and sharp mind. I would be the luckiest man in the world to have you marry me. You're the kind of woman a man would want to have by his side to weather life's storms like last night, and to enjoy during the good times."

Betsy honestly wanted to say yes, but he'd yet to say the one thing that would matter,

151

and what's more, he couldn't say it. They'd been through a hard spell together. She'd seen how he handled trouble. But that wasn't enough for her. She wanted what she saw pass between Ma and Pa. Between Mark and Emma, Charlie and Sarah.

"I know you're a practical woman, Betsy. So I've given you practical reasons why you should marry me. But the real reason I'm asking is, I've fallen in love with you. Now, I don't reckon —"

Betsy threw herself into his arms and kissed him before he could say something that would make a hash out of the beautiful words. Matt's arms came around her waist; he lifted her straight off her feet. Then he whirled her in a circle and broke the kiss to laugh out loud with joy.

When the celebration ended, Matt eased her away from him. "I'm taking that for a yes, but I'd like to hear the words."

"Yes, I'll marry you, Matt. And I'll consider myself the luckiest woman on earth."

They were speaking again for a while, then Betsy pulled away and said, "Let's go on and catch up with the others."

Her family had to have settled the cattle in by now. So they'd be waiting at Emma's house.

Nodding, Matt looked at her for too long, and Betsy had never felt so wanted, so loved. Not in a man and woman kind of way.

"Let's go." He slid his arm around her waist and they walked toward the ranch house, a hundred yards away.

Chapter 10

Five riders approached the cabin as Matt neared it. His spirits rose — and that was sayin' something because they were already sky-high. One of those riders was his brother.

"Mark's home. That must be Emma at his side."

"Yep, we made it. We kept all three girls alive."

Matt chuckled, then outright laughed, and Betsy laughed along with him until the two were nearly limp.

They were calming down when they reached the house. Mark had gone inside, but he came running out looking around. His eyes landed on Matt.

"Matt!" His big brother rushed to him, and they grabbed each other. Matt was shocked at how nice it was to see someone from his own family. He had one terrible moment when a burn of tears washed over his eyes. He fought them off and hung on to Mark, pounding his back and laughing.

Mark finally backed up and dashed his wrist across his eyes, but Matt saw what just might have been tears. He'd have tormented Mark about it if that wouldn't have made him a hypocrite.

"It is good to see someone from home, little brother." Then Mark turned to Betsy. "And I was inside long enough to hear my brother was asking you to marry him."

The smile that broke out on Mark's face helped Matt to make some decisions on the spot. The main one being he'd find a way to stay in this area, because he'd been considering taking Betsy on his wandering with him while they hunted for a place to settle. Maybe taking her home to Texas. But having Betsy's family nearby, and Matt having his brother and cousin, was too tempting to resist.

Betsy's smile was as wide as Mark's. "Yep, we're getting married."

"We didn't talk about when." Matt took Betsy's hand. "But I'd like to see to it right away."

He met Betsy's eyes, and she nodded. "As soon as we can hunt up a parson."

Matt took her hand and threaded his fingers between hers. "That suits me just fine."

"I now pronounce you man and wife." Parson Red Dawson smiled as he closed his prayer book. "You may kiss the bride."

Matt turned to Betsy, humbled and thrilled

to have gotten such a treasure for a wife. The kiss was quick and sweet, a completely appropriate kiss for two people standing before a throng of family and friends.

They faced the gathering, then Matt took Betsy's hand and hooked it through his elbow and they marched down the aisle formed by their wedding guests.

He was outside and surrounded by well-wishers when he saw a familiar face. "Mandy McClellen?"

"Matt!" Mandy took both his hands, smiling so big it was blinding. "Have you been home lately? Have you seen Laura since she married Ike?"

The two chattered together a long while. Matt loved seeing another face from home. Since Matt had been home recently, Mandy was full of questions about her sister Beth, not to mention her other sister Laura who'd married Matt and Mark's brother Ike. Mandy quizzed him until he'd told everything he knew.

Then a tall blond man dragged Mandy's hands away from Matt.

"Oh Matt. My husband, Tom Linscott. Tom, this is Mark Reeves's brother. He's got another brother, Ike, married to my little sister Laura. You remember when I got word Laura was married?"

Matt saw clear as day that Tom Linscott hadn't liked another man holding his wife's

hands. But he must have trusted his wife —
he'd have been a fool not to. Mandy was the
most upright fussbudget Matt had ever
known. Mark especially had lived to torment
her when they were kids — and Matt had
helped all he could.

Belle joined them, her hazel eyes serious,
stern, worried. Well, Matt would ease her
worries by being the best husband a woman
ever had. But it would take time to prove all
that to Belle.

"We've all brought potluck," Belle said. "We
can have a feast."

Silas was behind his wife. "I've got a stretch
of land for you, Matt. It's a nice high valley
that will be close to Charlie and Mark and
close up the distance between us and our
Lindsay. I've a mind to own every inch of the
trail to Helena before I'm done. And with all
our boys," Silas slid his arm behind Belle's
waist and smiled down at her, "I think we
can do it, don't you, honey?"

Since Matt was determined to make his
wife happy and living next to Mark suited
him, he nodded as Silas Harden arranged his
life.

Charlie came up as soon as there was a
break in the hand shaking and back slapping.
"I've got a line shack near my place. I sent
my men out there to make sure it's clean and
stocked with food and to set it up so you can
have privacy."

A wave of dizziness came over Matt thinking of the wedding night ahead.

Mark was right behind Charlie. "Trust me, Matt, you don't want to stay overnight at your in-laws' house on your wedding night."

Matt had himself a wife, and he wanted to be with her, as a man was with a wife.

"I'll tell Betsy. I didn't figure I was ever gonna be alone with her." Frowning, he added, "It sounds like Silas is going to tell me where to live and build me a house and give me some cattle. He doesn't have to do that. I have some money saved up, and I'm not afraid of hard work."

"He did that for me," Mark said. "It was like standing in front of an avalanche. I tried to tell him I could take care of my own wife, but he wouldn't hear of not helping me get set up. The whole Harden clan is crazy to protect their daughters. Belle's first husband left her to do everything on her own. I guess this is their way of not letting that happen to their girls. And it made Emma happy, as well as making our first years together much more comfortable."

Matt looked at Charlie. "You and Sarah, too?"

Charlie nodded, "Yep, 'tweren't no stopping him. And when I protested I was a little bit afraid Belle was going to shoot me, so I just gave them what they wanted."

"Anyway, the land he's speaking of is a

158

beautiful place. And not too far from here."

They'd gotten married at Mark's place.

Mark slapped Matt's shoulder. "I'm glad to have some more family close by. Charlie and I have been treated real well by the Hardens, but to watch them all be a close family makes me lonely for more of my own brothers. I'd love to see Ma and Pa, too. I might do it now that you're close. Emma and I could ride to Texas, catch a train part of the way, and leave the girls here with you and Betsy."

"That's not going to happen, Mark." Betsy's horrified voice turned them to face her. "You take them with you if you want to go to Texas."

"I can't. Ma and Pa are snowed in during the winter, and there's too much work during the summer."

"They're not snowed in anymore. Ma made Pa dynamite the opening so it's wider. They come and go all winter long now."

Mark gasped. "How'd she get him to do that?"

"There've been a lot of changes since that baby girl was born."

"I'd heard there were, but I never dreamed they'd blasted the canyon entrance."

"Yep, the little brothers never miss school either."

"They must hate that."

"Not really. Ma brought order to the whole house, and the boys behave well at school, too. It's shocking at first, but you get used to it. But even if you couldn't go in the winter, we wouldn't watch your young'uns." Matt went to his wife and slid his arm around her waist. "Your daughters are more than we can handle, Mark. You take 'em with you, or you don't go."

Emma said quietly, "I noticed the bars on the windows." She glanced at Mark and smiled. "Why didn't we think of that?"

"Besides," Matt went on, "Ma will want to see her grandchildren." Matt looked down at Betsy, who was smiling at him, probably grateful that he was saving her from Mark's daughters.

Nope, he sure as shootin' didn't want to spend his wedding night with his in-laws.

"Let's go saddle up, wife. Charlie has cleaned up a line shack for us. We can commence to having our honeymoon as soon as we get there." Just saying it out loud made Matt's head spin. He urged Betsy toward the horses.

"Pa wants to help build us a house, but he'll wait until tomorrow." Betsy smiled and leaned against him then she lifted her right hand to show him the satchel she carried. "Tonight we're on our own, and I'm ready to go."

EPILOGUE

The peace of a new beginning washed over him as they said their good-byes and walked toward their horses together.

The line shack wasn't far, but far enough. When they came to the front door, Matt dropped the satchel and swept Betsy up into his arms.

"I've heard of a tradition, Mrs. Reeves. It's supposed to bring good luck to a marriage if the groom carries the bride over the threshold of their first home."

Betsy gave him a teasing smile and reached down to open the door of the tiny one room cabin. "Good luck brought by such means smacks of superstition, Mr. Reeves. And I don't hold with such things."

"Neither do I, Betsy darlin'. But your ma gave me such an evil look when I told her we were leaving the party, I think I can use all the luck I can get. And the protecting hand of God, too."

Betsy laughed. "Carry me in, then, and you

can carry me into our home, too, when Pa gets it built."

"That will be my pleasure. Any excuse to hold you close." Matt walked inside, and Betsy gasped.

"Did Charlie do this?" The room was filled with wildflowers, and the scent of them made the little cabin homey and welcoming. A pot of stew simmered on the stove, adding to the pleasant aroma.

"He said he sent some of his hired men over to bring bedding and food. I'm betting your sister thought of the flowers. That ain't Charlie's style."

Betsy laughed.

Matt stood Betsy on her feet and closed the door, shutting out the world.

"I have myself a wife who is tough and smart and sweet and kind. The prettiest woman I've ever imagined. I can't wait to get on with being a husband who is worthy of you."

"You know, Matt, even though I spent most of the last week inside, I really am used to helping outside. I know horses and cattle. I understand mountain grazing and treacherous trails. I'm going to be a partner to you in this ranch."

"So I've got me a bride who rides herd, huh?"

"You do, indeed."

Matt kissed her soundly and got on with

being a husband in the most wonderful way
of all.

■ ■ ■ ■

HIS SURPRISE
FAMILY

■ ■ ■ ■

CHAPTER 1

Helena, Montana
1898

Silas Harden's life began when the train arrived . . . and the train was late.

He pulled a watch out of his pocket and stopped his jiggling knee.

It was about the tenth time for both.

A whistle screamed. He jumped. He looked around quick, embarrassed. No one seemed to notice he was acting like the lone chicken in a fox den.

His heart sped up as he finally saw the big iron monster chuffing around a far curve, here at last.

It carried his bride. Well, bride-to-be.

He couldn't wait to meet her.

Ever since his brother Tanner had married last year Si had lost his best friend and had an itch to do grown-up things. His folks, Silas and Belle Harden, had helped him build a cabin and go out on his own, but no woman appeared in the mountain peaks where he lived. Tanner had gotten the only one hiding up there.

It'd be another fifteen minutes before the train got here. The straightaway after it came around the last curve was two miles long. He was afraid he'd start hopping up and down or running down the tracks toward the train. So he pulled Meghan's most recent letter out of his pocket to keep himself busy, and noticed his hands trembling.

Thank the Good Lord Ma and Pa aren't here.

He'd never seen his pa, nor even his ma, tremble. This was the lowest he'd ever sunk. To be nervous, shaking, heart pounding. And all over a woman.

Of course marrying a woman you'd ordered from a catalogue was likely to make a man worry. In fact, it was a hair-brained thing to do, but they'd been writing a while. Meghan was smart and funny and most of all a woman of strong faith. He couldn't say he exactly was in love with her, but he intended to turn his attention to that as soon as she got onto solid ground.

The train whistled again but he still had plenty of time to read the letter one more time.

Dear Silas, I can't wait to be your wife.

Si had to admit he felt a little bit light-headed every time he read that.

I will endeavor to be a good wife to you in every way that you desire.

A man really could be forgiven for reading . . . things . . . into that.

I've lived in a very cramped boarding house since my parents died. Even a small house will be a wonderful thing.

Meghan's words made him feel like a hero in an old book, someone fighting dragons, or rescuing princesses.

I will work with all my might to make a nice home for you. And I promise you will never regret marrying me.

He wasn't going to let her work with all her might, for heaven's sakes. He wanted to care for her, protect her. Yes there was a lot of work, but there would be time to be quiet and together, too.

I wish we could have exchanged photographs. But instead I will imagine you in my mind as I travel to Helena, Montana. I can't believe I'll ride so far.

The train whistled again. He jerked his head up, as if he hadn't heard every chug of the engine, every turn of the wheel as it came nearer. The first squeak of the brake.

Steam shot out. The brakes squealed louder. Finally the train rattled to a stop.

Time ticked by as if he held his pocket watch to his ear.

Finally, she stepped out. It had to be her. His little Irish mail-order bride. Red hair that looked to be making an escape from her green and white flowered bonnet, fair skin with a scattering of freckles, no more than five and a half feet tall if that. A dress from the same fabric as her hat. She looked just as she'd described herself.

She scanned the small crowd waiting for the train.

She was here.

His life was about to begin.

Meghan McCray stepped out of the train, her satchel in hand. Two children stepped behind her, followed by a third, carrying her trunk.

Once the trunk was settled on the train station platform, she thanked them and the children ran off and around a corner.

Then she turned to face Silas Harden. The man who would save her. She sent prayers heavenward, for the blessing of it, and for him to care about her, and for him to forgive her.

Eventually.

He rushed right up to her. It had to be him.

Tall, dark-haired, more handsome than she'd ever dared hope. Shining blue eyes that looked nervous and happy. She thought that was a good sign. Not some hard-eyed, bold man who expected to rule her and be thanked all day every day for every crumb of bread she ate.

Though she would have gladly married a man like that, too. Well, perhaps not *gladly,* but her choices were very limited.

"You're Meghan McCray?" He reached both hands out and she dropped her satchel and raised hers so they touched for the first time. A pleasant shiver went down her backbone. He had the hands of a hard-working man, and his voice rang with kindness.

Her eyes burned but she fought back tears. She wasn't much of a crier in the normal way of things, but there was nothing normal about marrying a man on the same day you met him.

"Aye, that's me. And I'm thinkin' you're Silas Harden?"

A smile bloomed on his lips. "I am indeed. I like your voice. The accent. It's pretty."

"It's called a brogue. An Irish brogue. Ma and Da brought me to America when I was but ten years old, so I've not been here long."

"I . . . uh . . . are you hungry? I thought . . . thought . . . we'd just go ahead and have the wedding this afternoon, if that's agreeable to you? But if you're hungry we can eat first."

171

She realized then that Silas was very young. She guessed, just a few years past twenty. And no more experienced than she at such things as holding hands and weddings.

Her stomach rumbled with hunger, her knees were weak from too many missed meals. Eating first was almost too tempting to deny. But she wanted to get married quickly, so she agreed. "Today would be fine. And would we have time to get to your home today?"

"I had hoped so, but the train is late. We'd be riding well into the dark and the trail is treacherous in places. I saw to my chores, in case I was delayed, so we could stay in town tonight."

She felt her cheeks heat up at the very thought of the night. But she realized she'd been holding Silas's hands the whole time and it was much to her liking. She could also face the night.

"Let's get married, then."

"And supper afterward. The hotel we'll stay in has a nice dining room."

She managed to gain enough possession of herself to look up at him. "I will confess to being very hungry. Supper after the wedding sounds good."

She left other confessions for later. Did she admit what she'd done right after the wedding, or wait until morning?

It made her nervous to think that she was

hoping by morning things would have moved past the point of an annulment.

"Let's go." He took her hand and smiled sideways at her. "You're beautiful, Meghan. I have a little sister with red hair and you remind me of her some. I can't wait for you to meet my family. But I wonder if you might want to wash up a bit before the wedding."

"I have grime on me from the train ride, don't I?" She suppressed any thought of repeating those words about family back to him.

Silas looked past her and said, "Ben, can you take that trunk and satchel over to the Cattleman's Hotel?"

She glanced back and saw a man standing near the station who nodded. Silas must know him, or perhaps knew he was a man who did such work.

Silas flipped a coin toward the man and Meghan nearly gasped to see such careless treatment of money. When had she ever had even a penny to spare?

He led her to a water trough and after an uncertain moment, he handed her his handkerchief to wash her face. She was sure it barely cut through the worst of the soot that had built up over the days.

She straightened from her scrubbing and Si took the kerchief and dabbed at a couple of places she'd missed, then wrung it out and carried it in one hand while with the other he took hers again.

"Let's go and change your name to Harden."

That part she was eager to do. She'd never cared much for her pa, and that included carrying his name.

They emerged from the church and he was watching her so close he saw the second tears filled her eyes, an unusual shade of blueish green. Her red hair emphasized the greenish side. He turned Meghan to face him and ran one thumb gently across her cheeks, to wipe away a single tear that had spilled.

"What's wrong Meghan? Are you sorry we got married?" Si hadn't been around women much, except his ma and sisters and they, that is his sisters, were more likely to come after him with a fist than cry. Ma was more the slap-on-the-back-of-the-head type.

"Should we have waited?" he went on, desperate to stop the tears. "We could have courted a while. I'd have had to go home, but I could have found a place for you to stay. I never meant to . . ."

She reached up and covered his mouth with her fingertips. "Please, don't. Don't apologize. It's just my emotions getting the better of me. I suppose it seems foolish to you, but right now I'm crying because I'm so happy and honored that a fine man would marry a lass like me. Thank you, Silas. Thank you."

Her voice broke into sobs and she flung her arms around his neck and buried her face in his shirt.

He wrapped his arms around her waist and held her close. The tears were worrisome but the words were as if he were doing her a kindness, when it was just the opposite. This beautiful woman traveling all this way to marry him was the finest thing anyone had ever done for him, to him, with him. The right word failed as he felt her, alive and warm and soft, clinging.

Bursting with energy, he swooped her up in both arms and carried her down the boardwalk to the top of the steps on the corner. He bounced to the ground, then crossed the street to the Cattleman's Hotel.

Smiling fit to bust, he walked straight into the hotel, managing the door knob without once loosening his grip on her.

He walked on into the dining room, which was mostly empty, but about three tables had folks eating. He'd never seen a one of them before.

He gave them a huge grin he couldn't control and said, "We just got married. She says she's crying because she's so happy and honored I married her. I feel just the same about her, even more."

The people smiled and started clapping. Now his smile about split his face.

A gray-haired woman, Mrs. Garvey, came

in from the kitchen, probably drawn by the commotion. She ran the place while her husband ran the hotel. She must've heard his announcement because she shoo-ed him toward a table and said, "Dinner is on the house for newlyweds."

"Ma'am, that is kind and generous of you, and God bless you for it. But I want dearly to buy my wife our first meal as a married couple. Would your feelings be hurt if I insisted on paying?"

She rested a motherly hand on Meghan's red head. "That would be fine, but let me finish your meal with a dessert. I've made a cake and we can call it a wedding cake if you'd like."

"Thank you, Ma'am." He looked around the room. "Thank you all. It was only us at the wedding and you've made it more of a celebration. And if she ever finishes with her tears, I'm sure she'll thank you all, too."

He got some wide smiles and a few chuckles for that.

She snuffled, the crying seemed to have tapered off. He sat down with her in his arms and dug a handkerchief out of his pocket. It was still damp from washing her face. Mrs. Garvey noticed his dilemma and pulled a handkerchief out of the wrist of her dress.

"Give her this." She thrust it into his hands.

As she lifted her head he handed it to her, which made her take her hand away from his neck. One of her hands, the other still clung like a burr.

She mopped up her face a bit and finally needed two hands to blow her nose. Two cups of coffee were brought to the table by Maud Garvey.

Meghan lifted her chin, her nose glowing red, her eyes puffy, some of her red curls stuck to her sogged up face. "I'm sorry to have carried on so."

She said this to Maud, who set down the coffee.

The woman clasped both hands on Meghan's. "A wedding is a big event. It's right to shed a tear or two. Now, come to your own chair." Mrs. Garvey drew Meghan out of Si's lap and settled her across the table.

Meghan offered her the kerchief. "Thank you so much."

"Nonsense, I've plenty of them. Take it as a wedding gift."

Meghan nodded and dabbed at her nose some more.

Si missed holding her, but it would've been hard to eat with her on his lap. Not that he hadn't intended to try if she wanted to stay close.

"Is this your restaurant?" Meghan asked.

"My husband owns the hotel, and I run the kitchen and dining room. I'm Maud Garvey." She leaned very close to Meghan and whispered, "I'm here if you need . . . anything . . .

anyone to speak to about a . ... a wedding night."

Si heard it but couldn't think what Meghan might need. Maybe another handkerchief? She'd gone through two mighty quick.

"Thank you so much for everything." Meghan clasped Maud's hand and gave her a tremulous smile. "But I will trust my new husband in this."

Maud, who Si had met a few times — his family always ate at the Cattleman's when they came to Helena to sell the herd — squeezed Meghan's hand and bustled away to the kitchen.

Silas wanted to ask what that was all about but he was afraid of her answer. He realized he was afraid of most everything right now. Especially anything to do with the upcoming wedding night.

Chapter 2

"The meal was delicious, Silas."

He watched her eat the fried chicken, potatoes and gravy off her plate until it was clean. He braced himself to stop her if she began gnawing on bones. Then she gobbled down the dessert brought to the table, in such a way that he wondered if he should get her a second serving. Was she still hungry? He noticed how skinny her wrists and hands were, and her cheeks had a hollow look. He suspected she hadn't eaten well for a while.

It was going to be his pleasure to fatten her up. He should have fed her before the wedding and again afterward. With a sigh that sounded like pure contentment, she patted her lips with her napkin. Before she'd been eating like a cowpoke at the end of a long, hard cattle drive, but now she acted like a delicate lady. He hoped she was tough enough for a Rocky Mountain winter. He was prepared to do whatever he had to do to help her handle things. And he needed to take her to meet Ma, but not right away. He wanted to get to know her better himself. And while he did that, he'd find out what skills she had, whether she was plucky enough to meet any task head on, or the type to hide from hard work.

He'd really never met a woman like that. He'd heard of such but he'd never known one, so he hoped it was just a wild rumor that women could be like that.

"Are, are you . . . you ready?" He cleared his throat, then cleared it again. "Umm . . . that is ready to h–head up–upstairs?"

He watched her, afraid she might make a break for it. He was a little worried he might, too.

Instead of running, she stood and reached out a hand, trembling slightly, but her eyes met him dead on and he rose, tucked her hand through his elbow in a way that felt very formal, very officially married, and they left the dining room and headed for the hotel stairs.

Si had never slept here before, in fact he'd never slept in a hotel. When they brought the cattle in, they made camp outside of town and slept on the ground.

Any trips they made to the little town of Divide, the nearest town to their home, was made in a single day.

But it seemed right for a wedding night.

He took his first step up those stairs, on his

way to being a fully married man, when a hallway door slammed open and Mrs. Garvey came out with a small boy slapping at her, while she kept a firm grip on his ear.

"You will not steal from my kitchen, young man. If you'd asked I'd have given you a bite to eat. Now, instead, we're going to see the sheriff."

"Ouch, let go. I'll leave. It's hungry I am." Then the little boy twisted away, glanced over to Si, where he stood with Meghan and yelled, "Help Meghan! Make her stop."

Meghan gave Si a desperate look. He didn't blame her, this was one of the children who had carried her trunk. Now the boy wanted her, a stranger he'd met on a train, to save him from his own sins.

Meghan tore her hand free of Si's elbow. "You let my brother go."

"Your . . . your . . . your . . . brother?" Si stumbled and almost fell down the stairs. Good thing he was on the bottom step.

Meghan ran to the boy and pulled him into her arms.

Maud arched a brow and looked straight at Si. "You're responsible for this young thief?"

Si was speechless, so that gave him a lot of time to think. Except his brain seemed to freeze up. He looked at Meghan, hugging and fussing over the young man, who had curly red hair and a most unusual shade of blueish-green eyes.

This little boy was without a shadow of a doubt related to his brand-spankin' new wife.

She'd never said a word in her letters, or since she climbed down off that train about having a family. And she'd sure as certain never said a thing about bringing family along.

And if she had family with her, they'd also be hungry. He remembered how she'd eaten, so eagerly. And a growing boy would only eat more. Si said the only thing he could think of. The only thing he was sure of. With his stomach sinking, he answered Maud. "Yep, I am responsible for him."

Even if he'd never heard of him and never known he existed until right now.

Which switched on a lantern light in his head.

Three boys had gotten off the train right behind her. All red heads, all helping her, all quick to run off.

He suspected they were waiting for her to give Si the news that he'd married a woman with a family to care for.

"Where are the other two?"

That drew Meghan's attention away from the boy. She looked at him, her eyes wide, like a frightened deer, frozen, ready to run.

Then she straightened away from the boy and said, "I suspect they're nearby, Silas. I brought my three brothers along with me to Montana. I–I was waiting for the right moment to tell you."

"She said we're to live with you on your ranch." The little boy didn't seem to notice Silas' tightly clamped jaw.

"Tell 'em to get in here." Then he spoke to the confused Mrs. Garvey. "It looks like we need three more dinners, Mrs. Garvey, if it suits you. I wouldn't blame you for refusing to feed us. I'm willing to pay for whatever this boy stole, too. Add it to the bill for our dinner and do you have another room to rent?" Si hesitated, not sure if he had enough money. His folks had filled his cupboards and his root cellar, and they'd left him a hundred head of cattle, besides a couple of milk cows, chickens and a litter of pigs just past suckling age.

But any money he had was earned here and there. And he just realized he had a whole lot more supplies he needed to buy.

Mrs. Garvey was a soft-hearted woman. "Don't worry about the piece of cake he took. Consider it as more of your free wedding dessert, but Si, we're out of rooms. You and your wife have rented the last one we have available."

So now he had three boys sleeping on the floor of his room with him and his wife?

It didn't matter. He'd realized clear as day that he didn't know his new wife well enough for any wedding night hijinks.

"We'll make up pallets on the floor then. I

promise you I'll make the boy work off what he owes when I get them all home."

They can start by helping me build a couple more rooms onto my cabin.

The boy pulled away from Meghan, ran for the back door and slammed it open. "Shay, Liam, come in for supper."

He heard what sounded like banshees shrieking in the back of the hotel — joyful banshees. Then thundering footsteps.

She'd said three brothers. Now two came sprinting back and ran right into the dining room. Meghan gave Si one more terrified look, then hurried after them.

"I'll send up extra blankets and pillows." Maud went along after Meghan, probably worried about the breakables.

A third boy came in, not joyful, though he was mighty thin and probably as hungry as the rest of the family. But this one was more man than boy.

Silas looked at him and saw the sullen eyes and withdrawn attitude.

"We're eating supper, you're welcome to join us."

"I'm Liam. I know what my sister did, told you a lot of blarney to trick you into marrying her and taking in the lads and me. We aren't your job. I'm going to take the little boyos and find work here in Helena."

The thing the kid didn't say, maybe he didn't even know was, he'd go find work and

184

take the boys, and Meghan would blame Si and hate him forever. If she even stayed with him.

Well, Si had made his vows before God and man. As angry as he was at Meghan, he knew he had one chance of a wife in his life and Meghan was it.

"I appreciate the offer. How old are you?"

"I'm fifteen just this summer. But I've been working to support my family. I'll do a man's work. Meghan's cared for us since our folks died, Ma of a fever, and Pa soon after from the drink. I can take the lads myself now. It's my turn."

"You're all coming home with me. If you want a job, I'll give you one. There's plenty of work for all three of you boys."

Liam held Si's gaze. Si had to admit he was impressed with the boy. He knew how hard it was to be taken care of when you saw yourself as a man.

And yes, Meghan was a little liar. In fact he suspected he'd do well to never trust a word she said. But she was also desperate.

"Come home with us, Liam. Give life on my ranch some time. If you don't like it and don't feel like you're doing enough work to deserve a roof and a meal, or the work doesn't suit you, then I'll bring you back to town and we can hunt up work for you."

Liam's steady eyes wavered. Si hoped he gave in because the boy was coming home with him if he had to tie him up and haul him to the ranch, draped over a saddle.

"You promise I can come back to town if I want?"

"Yep, and if you find something and can get settled, the boys can come with you then if they wish." Si hadn't tried to raise any children single-handedly but he'd been doing a hard day's work long before he turned fifteen. "But don't ask me to abandon three youngsters on the streets of Helena. I won't do it and your sister would hate me if I did. That's not gonna make for much of a marriage."

That made the corners of Liam's mouth curl for just a moment before he went back to looking sullen. "I reckon I can ride out with you. And I won't give you cause to think I'm a lay-about."

Si nodded. "Good, that's settled. Now let's go have some of Mrs. Garvey's fried chicken."

A mighty hungry look crossed the boy's face. Si felt guilty for having such a lengthy talk with him. The boy moved past him, unable to move slow. They went inside the dining room as Meghan tucked a napkin under the youngest boy's chin. Mrs. Garvey bustled in with three plates heaped with food.

Si was all of a sudden worried about how long his flock would last. And if Meghan knew how to fetch around a chicken dinner.

He really needed to take her to meet his

ma, except now he was worried about it. Would Ma see her as a sneak and a liar? Or would she take Meghan under her wing like she did to most everyone she met?

There was no reason to take that ride to Ma and Pa's anytime soon.

CHAPTER 3

Meghan jerked awake when a hand pressed over her mouth. Her eyes went wide with terror. She knew their neighborhood was dangerous. She'd always feared . . .

Then her eyes focused on Silas.

He released the hold on her mouth and put his index finger to his lips to indicate she should be quiet. Eight-year-old Lock was asleep in the bed with her. She knew Shay, twelve, was asleep on the floor by Liam. Si had been bedded down there, too.

It looked like the man wanted to have a talk and she knew there was no avoiding it. She should bless him for waiting until the lads were asleep so their talk could be in private.

The seething beneath his generosity had not gone unnoticed by her. He fed the lads, saw they had decent beds, gave up the soft bed to her and never spoke a word of complaint.

But she'd seen the cold in his expression. It

hadn't been there before the boys had turned up.

She wondered if they were going outside so he could tell her good-bye and good luck. He was going home without any of them.

She followed him, barefoot, out the door.

He closed the door and walked to the stairs and down. When they were in the entrance to the hotel they were finally out of earshot of the boys.

He turned to her and said, "Talk."

It was about exactly what she'd expected him to say, though she'd expected more words, and more yelling, perhaps a slap across her face as her da had handed out to all of them, her ma included.

Instead he just glared.

"What is there to say?" Her voice threatened to break, but this was all her fault and she would not add tears to sway him toward kindness.

Unless she couldn't control them.

He tilted his head sideways, crossed his arms, kept his eyes straight on her, and remained silent.

Squaring her shoulders, she braced herself for all his fussing, but she would lie no more.

"My ma died four years ago. Da passed shortly after. We've been living on the edge of starvation ever since. I cleaned rooms at a hotel and waited tables and cooked in the kitchen. All of it barely enough to keep a roof over our heads and a meager bite in our bellies."

Now she was sounding like a weakling. "A year ago Liam quit school, which I desperately did not want him to do. I thought his only way to a better life was by giving himself time to learn."

Something flickered across Silas' expression that she didn't understand. He didn't share his thoughts with her. "Go on."

"I hated that he quit his studies. But the worst of it was, he took a job in a meat packing plant. I watched him grow thinner and angrier as he brought home pennies in pay for long, harsh days of work. I knew it was ruining him but he refused to quit. And Shay found out the plant would hire children as young as eight. He quit school and headed to the plant."

She paused for a moment, remembering the desperate need to save her brothers. "There is nothing wrong with hard work. But —" She cleared her throat. "Anyway, I'd heard of mail-order brides. I even knew a few who'd done it. Being poor Irish, what that means is, they'd just go away. Get on a train and never be heard from again. I wasn't close to any family who had a daughter go off like that, but to go away from the place we lived sounded like a dream come true. All four of us in a rooming house in a space little bigger than where we're sleeping tonight."

She saw Silas look at the door but he remained silent.

"So I did it. I knew no one would respond to a woman with three brothers in tow. So I wrote a letter to the catalogue with no mention of my brothers, but I intended to take them with me from the start. I've been clinging to pennies from the moment I contacted the catalogue, so I could pay their way. Then, instead of the sleeper car you'd paid for, I sat in the passenger car to pinch out the last bit of their fare and include a bit for food. I explained to the lads I was getting married, but they thought they were welcome. I told them the truth just before we climbed down off the train."

With a deep, shuddering breath that shook her whole body, she said what she had to if she wanted to be an honorable woman. "We can annul the marriage. I'll not protest, Silas. No matter what work is to be found in Helena, I will give the first of it to you. I'll pay you back for my fare."

She lifted her eyes, though her head was weighted down with guilt, and looked at his blue eyes. "But if you keep us, if you let us move to your ranch, we will all work hard and consider it a blessing. We will not ask for clothes or an over amount of food. I will be a dutiful wife, meet your needs, sew your clothes, cook your food, do whatever chores you feel are needed. I won't be a nagging wife, nor ask for a penny for myself. The Mc-Cray's know how to work. That certainly includes me." Her mind skittered over the jobs for growing boys in Helena.

It was a bustling town of over ten thousand people, tiny by the standards of Omaha, but Helena had gold and there had been a fortune made in it. She'd found free moments to go to a library and read all she could about Helena. One magazine told her there were fifty millionaires living in the city. There were grand buildings, or so she'd read. But she'd gone from the train station to a small church, then to a nice but by no means lavish hotel. She'd seen no sign of any wealth but Silas, paying for a meal for four people, five including himself, and even asking to rent a second room, seemed to be a man of riches.

"I know I've ruined your chance to find a different wife as things stand now. But you haven't found such a one as that, have you? Or you wouldn't have begun writing to me."

After a long, deep breath, she said, "I will abide by your wishes, Silas. Whatever they are."

Silas said nothing. He looked at her a long time and his eyes burned. He was furious, so furious she braced herself.

"All I can think of right now is I married a liar, a woman I can't trust." He stared at the floor then and continued to speak with controlled rage. "But I'm a God fearing man, and I took my vows before Him. There'll be no annulment. Go on back to your room. I'll sleep elsewhere. We leave for home as soon as the General Store opens. They have my order for supplies, but I'll need a few more things it seems."

She opened her mouth to tell him no, to tell him not to get anything more. But he turned and charged out the door. She had no idea where he'd sleep. And she knew it was a bad sign that she was glad her husband had chosen to walk away from her on their wedding night.

Meghan woke up in the dim light of first dawn. She looked at the clock ticking away on her bedside table.

She'd worn her one and only dress to bed. It was heavily soiled from long hours on the train. Her brothers were in like condition. She owned a nightgown but hadn't thought it fitting to change with Silas in the room, then after their talk she'd not noticed what she was wearing.

Now she'd present herself to her angry husband in pathetic filth.

"Lads, let's be up and away. Silas is hoping to be on the road early." As if that was the most of what he'd said. Squaring her shoulders, she had the boys out of the room and heading downstairs before they'd quit rubbing the sleep out of their eyes.

The boys thundered down the stairs. Meghan hurried after. She wanted to move in a more lady-like way. She'd been raised in poverty and had always been something of a hoyden. And nothing in her life had trained her for much in the way of polished manners. But she wanted to impress Silas to the extent possible.

But he wasn't here right now and she was afraid the boyos would rush out into the street and she might lose track of them.

She was thundering herself when the hotel door swung open and Silas walked in. "Let's eat breakfast boys, and be on the road."

Shay shouted and jumped. Liam hunched his shoulders as if he didn't want any favors from anyone. Lock ran straight at Silas and leapt into his arms. Silas caught him and Meghan saw his smile. Then his eyes lifted to her and that smile shrunk away like a woolen dress in boiling hot water.

He stood Lock on his feet, the lads all three turned and raced for the food. Then Silas scowled at her and waited.

"I can go tend the packing of the horses." She tried to look serene when she wanted to drop to her knees and beg him to not hate her. Another part, the side with a temper that went with her red hair, wanted to grab him by the collar and yell at him that her brothers were good boys and he was lucky to have such fine young men want to live with him.

She controlled all of that.

But maybe not all that well because suddenly he bent down until his nose practically touched hers. "I saw the surprised look on your face when I said we'd eat breakfast. Do you think I'm going to starve you? It's nice to know what kind of man you think you've married."

"No, I didn't think that." Meghan rested her hands on his arm. Her temper faded and she returned to feeling guilty. "I expected to head out quickly. A bite of food on the trail would have been fine. I'd have gladly agreed to that to save money and time, even if it was only myself going with you. The cost of the dining room is dear."

"Go on in. I woke up the owner of the General Store so he could get my order together. I've got time to eat because my order is a sizable one and . . . and," Silas stopped talking long enough Meghan wondered what he was thinking about.

Then he went on. "The man loading my string of packhorses said he'd be at least a half hour."

She had no idea what to do about any of his anger or her lies, so she turned and went into the dining room. She was just as hungry as her brothers. They'd been eating like birds for years.

CHAPTER 4

About two seconds after he'd brought up the horses, Si found out that none of them knew a lick about riding.

They were decent animals, easy to ride, but Si wasn't familiar with them because he'd bought them this morning, along with two extra pack horses and he'd more than doubled his order at the store. It'd taken his last cent. And he'd brought extra money along. He'd hoped to buy things for his new wife and impress her that she'd chosen a prosperous man.

Instead he bought a lot of cans of vegetables and piles of fabric because they were all dressed in rags.

Pa and Ma had set their children up well when each had gone out on his or her own. They'd treated Si like a partner in the ranch and it was true that he'd worked long days alongside his folks to run the Circle H.

It was a good thing because he was going to need every bit his folks had given him and he'd need to earn plenty on his own, to take care of everyone.

The going was slow, with his four green-horns as companions. And his route was long because he didn't take the most direct way home. It went through his sister Lindsay's property. In fact, he'd skirted her place on the way to Helena so she wouldn't ask why he was heading to town. And he'd planned to take the same long way home. He wanted to be married a while and settled in with his wife, before the family found out.

So it hadn't changed his plans much except he had a child riding in front of him and another behind him. Meghan and Liam rode their own horses but after a few miles he'd tied the horses on a line behind his own. Now all anyone had to do was hang on which Liam and Meghan did in grim silence, but the two boys with him, Shay in back and Lockley in front, never stopped hammering him with questions.

Si led a string of eight horses because of the pack animals, too. Nothing about this trip was gonna be fast.

They rode through the canyon entrance to his ranch just as the sun was setting. And the days were long.

He took one look at his humble cabin. It had three rooms. A main room, a kitchen and a bedroom. He had running water into the kitchen and drains to take the water away. They'd built a nice entry way on the back doorway to stop the wind, along with a modest barn and a nice corral behind the house.

"Silas," Meghan sounded almost reverent, "it's a fine home you have."

It was a jolt to look at his little cabin and think someone envied him. It told him a lot about how she'd lived up until now and he felt a pang of sympathy for her, even a moment of understanding how a decent woman might find herself lying to get away from a terrible situation, especially if she was fighting for children she loved who were suffering.

She rode up almost even with him. Her gaze swept the valley he'd claimed and he realized she wasn't talking about the house.

It *was* a beautiful place, lush grassland, jutting rock breaking it up but not often enough to bother his herd or himself. A cool breeze swept down from the mountain peaks that surrounded his home and ruffled through the tall grass as if the hand of God caressed this beautiful, sky-high corner of His Creation.

What caught the eye first was a waterfall that gushed out of the heights and splashed into a pond that emptied into a flowing stream. His cabin was close enough to it he could run a pipe to bring water into his house.

The tidy cabin was small, but Pa was a fine

builder and Si knew the way of it, too. And it looked perfect set just to the far end of the pond. Beyond the pond and stream, thick woods he'd yet to explore lined the back of his cabin.

It was a sight so beautiful that alone had convinced Si to stay here. Silas had seen where that stream became another waterfall falling to a lower valley. Pa had bought that valley to and he'd gotten it for pennies an acre because no one knew what was up here besides rugged mountains. Ma and Pa had given it to him as part of his earnings for a lifetime of hard work.

"It's grand, Silas," Lockley looked back over his shoulder to smile. "And all this grass is yours and the cattle, too? You have so many. And more horses than all these we rode home?"

The boy sounded awestruck. Silas thought of his parents' large house, many bedrooms, the wrap-around porch and well-made furniture. He'd been seeing the modesty of his home. But he remembered Meghan saying their hotel room was the size of the home she and the boys had lived in. This wasn't huge but it was three or four times larger than that.

On the ride home he'd been planning the two bedrooms he needed to add. Then the house would start to fit them. He itched to start chopping down trees right now, but he needed to go hunting first. He had a lot of mouths to feed.

With a kick, he set his horse to moving and Meghan, followed by Liam, fell into line behind him, both of them still tied one behind the other. They had no notion how to guide a horse.

When he reached the house, he dismounted, which wasn't easy with two boys to get to the ground.

He helped Meghan down and caught Liam as he dismounted on his own. His foot had gone through the stirrup and the boy was going to end with his backside on the ground. Liam glared and didn't speak a word of thanks for being saved.

"We'll unpack the horses first, then I'll show you where things go." He looked at Meghan for that. "You can store supplies away while I put up the horses."

Si wasn't much of a talker and suddenly he was tired of hearing himself. He went to the first pack horse and set to work.

The supplies vanished as fast as he untied them. All four of the McCrays were eager workers. He followed Shay in, carrying the last of the load to find a mountain stacked in the center of his house.

"Uh, I might have gone too far with the supplies but I wasn't sure when we'd get back to town."

"Is there a root cellar or some such place to store things?" Meghan had her hands twisted together in a way that looked too much like begging. As in begging him to let her work herself to death probably.

She seemed like a decent person, if only every word out of her mouth when they'd been writing and after they'd met hadn't been a lie. Si was having a whole lot of trouble believing anything she said now.

"There's a trap door under that rug." He nodded at a hand woven rug near the kitchen wall. "Move the rug and you'll see a ring to pull up and open the cellar. There's a ladder and most everything that doesn't fit in these few cupboards up here can go down there."

He felt awkward asking but decided he might as well. "Do you cook, Meghan? Can you make a rising of bread and slice up a ham and fry it? You'll have to work over the fireplace."

"I can make bread and fry a ham. I can cook a good many things. We lived in a rooming house so I had to prepare our meals, meager though they were."

"That sounds good. Hunt through the supplies and in the cupboards and cellars, there are potatoes and, well, use anything you find. I'm ahead with the wood chopping so we won't need to do that for a week or two. And it's warm enough we won't need a fire other than at meals, so that'll save on wood. It's a one bedroom house and Meghan, you can have it." And Silas felt his cheeks heating up and realized with horror he must be blushing. He talked fast so he could get out of here, desperate to make it clear he didn't expect any wifely things from Meghan, although he had until he'd met her brothers. Now he expected exactly nothing. "Lockley can share the bed with you and the boys will use bedrolls on the floor of your room. I'll sleep out here."

Liam's eyes narrowed as talk of sleeping arrangements came up. Si didn't blame him for not liking that but it had to be said. She must be wondering.

"A wife's place is with her husband." Meghan wasn't going to let it stand as he'd said. "I'll not be shutting the door to you. I know my duty." She sounded brave but she had her hands clenched together into one large fist, right at her waist, and Si could see her white knuckles from across the room separated by a mountain of supplies and three young boys.

"I'd say that's true if we'd married under more normal circumstances." He cleared his throat and tried to ignore his hot cheeks. "But we're still strangers and I think it's fitting that we get . . . get to know each other more before we sh–share a room." *And a bed.*

Silas turned and started for the door at top speed, which was a half-wit idea because the door was about two steps away and he had a few more things that he had to say.

"I'll bring in wood and get a fire started." He grabbed the door knob then forced himself to look between the two older boys. "Liam and Shay you can come with me to see where I've stacked it and carry it in. Bringing in wood can be your job. I'll show you how my fireplace works. Then I'll leave you to the unpacking. I'll tend the horses, and go hunting for food, best do it right now while the light holds."

Silas couldn't remember another day in his life when he'd said so many words. He decided to quit talking and get to work. He walked out of the house without saying anything more and if the boys didn't tag along, he'd just do it himself.

He'd figured on adding two bedrooms to the house but now he wondered if a second house wasn't a better choice. He could live quietly a few hundred feet to the south.

As he walked away he felt like he was making a prison break.

The minute Silas left, Meghan quit her blushing. It was driven back by pure anger. She plunked her fists on her hips and turned to her little brothers. "All right boyos, we are having a talk."

"He had no business speaking of such to you, Meghan." Liam squared off in front of her. It wasn't the first time she'd noticed he was looking down an inch to meet her eyes.

Maybe two inches. Her brother was bigger than she was. "And not in front of little lads, for a fact."

Meghan might be small but she felt ten feet tall she was so angry. "And just when was he supposed to talk to me alone, Liam McCray? You'll notice there hasn't been any privacy since the minute Lock was caught thievin'."

She glared at another little red-headed boy, who got busy studying his toes. She might've given his backside a swat if she didn't feel so terrible that he'd been hungry.

"Now you'll not be interrupting me again while I talk." She glared at them and they kept quiet. "Silas Harden had all of us sprung on him, and he's being as nice as can be hoped for. So, we are going to do everything we can to make sure he never regrets agreeing to this marriage."

At least no more than he regretted it right now.

"We are going to be nice to him." She glared straight at Liam. "We are going to work so hard he'll never know how he got along without us. We are going to cook and clean and labor on the ranch. If we have to ride horses then we'll learn and be glad of the chance. If he is unhappy we're here, we're going to accept that and remain polite and cheerful and hard-working regardless of our feelings. And when that gets too hard for you, remember we're standing on land we get to live on. Remember that waterfall and this big house and all the supplies we have to stow away, much of it food. Food, lads. All the food we can eat. Every time you want to sass Silas or be rude or angry at him, you think of that dark little room we lived in with little heat and less food and you hold your tongue and treat this kind man right, because we are going to live here. I'm bettin' he wouldn't throw us out, not after his Christian words about his vows to God, but do not give him reasons to despise us and want us gone."

Liam drew in a long breath and that sullen look that had over-taken him right after he'd gone to work fell over his face.

Meghan couldn't stop herself from going to her mostly grown little brother and fling her arms around him. She said to him alone. "Please don't ruin this chance for us, Liam. Please dig deep and find it in yourself to be grateful and to work and learn at Silas' side. Please, please. I am begging you."

Liam's arms hung at his sides but when Meghan begged, suddenly he hugged her tight. "Don't beg, Meghan. And don't you dare be tellin' one more lie. Yes, I'll do me best. Aye and it's a fine thing to be standin' in such a large home and on our own land, at least the land that's become yours through marriage. I'll work at your side, and at your husband's side, to make a life for us. You have my solemn word."

Meghan would have burst into tears if Liam wouldn't have been horrified. She held onto her feelings and stepped back from her brother. "Lockley, let's get these supplies packed away, and get a supper on. Liam and Shay, go quick to help haul wood in for Silas and spare him the chore."

CHAPTER 5

Silas was late to dinner but how was he supposed to go in there and face that pack of strangers?

If the light hadn't been failing he'd've started chopping down trees to add rooms onto the house. As it was, he probably had to go in. They seemed like the type to start searching if he didn't.

He swung off his black stallion, a descendant of Tom Linscott's thoroughbred, and dragged the deer down. He made quick work of hanging and gutting it. He'd see to the butchering tomorrow.

He put up his horse and paused to listen to the howl of a wolf. They weren't close but his herd was spread around and that eerie echoing sound was a reminder to keep a close eye on his cattle. He waited long minutes listening. Finally the howl faded and he knew he'd been stalling. He trudged toward the house. Unable to think of one single other thing to do.

There was a lantern burning, so unless they'd all gone to bed with the light still on, he figured he was going to have to talk to someone.

He swung the door open and all four of them looked up from where they sat on the floor, each with a plate of food on their lap.

It occurred to him he didn't have enough chairs. But he did have two. "So, since you couldn't all have a chair you decided none of you would take one?"

Meghan smiled and stood with such spryness it made Si, who was twenty-four, feel kinda old. He really knew nothing about his wife. Well, he was in no hurry to find things out.

"I'll start building chairs tomorrow." Then he thought about his empty stomach. "It smells good. And I see you've stored away the supplies. Thanks for doing that."

Meghan nodded, "It's pleased I am to run your household, Silas."

She rushed to the stove and dished him up a plate of ham and mashed potatoes. He washed up and she waited on him while the boys ate like a pack of wolves.

They'd waited supper on him for a long time. And he knew they were hungry, probably had been for years. They'd finally given up and grabbed some food, and sat on the floor in his house without enough chairs.

All sudden-like he knew while he was avoiding them, they'd been patiently waiting for him. So now he was hurting a hungry child. That made him a mighty big polecat.

He needed to apologize more, but what he really needed to do was accept what he had gotten into. "I went hunting. I didn't buy any fresh meat. I always go fetch a deer or elk or whatever I'm hungry for when the meat runs low."

He looked directly at Liam . . . forced himself to look. "Tomorrow, you want to learn how to skin and cut up a deer?"

Liam's eyes went wide. He swallowed hard. "O–okay. I-uh . . . I worked in a meat packing plant you know. I've worked on jobs like that. If you show me how it's done with a deer I can have that be my job."

"That's right, you did. Good, thanks. You were there, too, Shay is that right?"

"Yup."

"Good, you can help, too. You're old enough to learn." He looked between each of his new family members. They seemed strangely co-operative.

"By the time I was your age, Lock, I was riding horseback alone. I could already rope a calf and with a good cowpony I could throw it, but I still needed help hog-tying it. And I went hunting with Pa and my brothers all the time."

"You shot a gun? At eight years old?" Meghan asked, then clapped her hand over her mouth as if she was afraid to speak.

"I was a decent shot, and I'd had a bunch of practice with still targets, but I was just learning to shoot a bird in flight or a running animal."

Meghan nodded and didn't speak again.

Since it was so quiet, Silas kept on talking. "You all need riding lessons, and we'll get to that tomorrow, too. And as long as I'm building chairs you boys can tag along and I'll show you how to gather the right wood for it and make a good solid chair. Liam and Shay are old enough to take up the furniture building for me. And if the chair doesn't teach you, you'll learn while we're adding a couple of rooms onto the house."

Every one of them gasped out loud.

Si thought he'd mentioned that before but clearly he had not.

Meghan looked a bit overwhelmed but she nodded.

"You made ham. It looks delicious."

Meghan whispered, "You don't need to build onto the house for us."

Her little brothers all nodded.

In fact they all looked scared, even Liam.

He wondered if it was something he said. He dug into the meal to avoid adding to their fright.

CHAPTER 6

Si was swarmed with four of the hardest workers a man had ever seen.

Liam cut up that deer like he'd done it a thousand times before.

Which he had at the meat packing plant.

Shay was the best at horse riding. He took over most of the tending of the horses by the end of the first week of the McCray's living with him. Lock, the little wild man did exactly as he was told and did it quick. He had a way of watching Si and jumping in as fast as if wolves were baying at his heels.

And Meghan was a wonder. She was baking bread, tending the chickens and milking the cow — although she'd needed some training with that. The house almost sparkled it was so clean and she'd been sewing up a storm of clothes for her little brothers. At first she'd balked, not wanting to cost him anything, but Si was starting to figure out his new family now and he made it an order.

Every one of them was more obedient than

a well-trained hound.

Si had a real modest garden and Meghan jumped in and killed every weed as if it were an invading army.

They were unfailingly polite, quiet, careful to obey, they asked for nothing for themselves and they worked like he was laying a whip across their backs.

It was driving Si mad.

Today, day seven of his married life — which had led to nothing resembling marriage, more like he'd hired a maid, a cook and a bunch of cowhands — he was done with it.

Si had seen what a marriage was supposed to be. His ma and pa loved each other and they worked hard side by side.

Somehow he had the working part all arranged but he had none of the love.

It made him ache inside that nothing was growing between himself and his wife, nor between himself and her little brothers.

In fact he suspected these four were hiding something, or afraid of something. But of what? All he could think of was they had trouble on their back trail and they'd all lied about that, too. They hoped no trouble was coming but feared it was.

Had Meghan really come west because of poverty or was she running from something?

At breakfast on the seventh day of his sham of a marriage, he said, "We've chopped down enough trees so today we are gonna start building on two bedrooms."

All four of them . . . each sitting on a chair now . . . turned to him with a snap worthy of a cavalry private in the presence of a general.

"Just tell us what you're wanting of us, Silas." Meghan might as well have saluted.

"It's good we are to help." Liam, who wouldn't even speak without growling on the first day here, was sharp as a first lieutenant.

Shay sat up and folded his hands on the table, maybe in prayer that he could obey Si perfectly.

Lockley's eyes went wide. "Adding onto the house is a fine idea, Silas, but you don't have to do that for us. We're happy to sleep four to a room. In fact you should have the bedroom and we can sleep —"

"Enough!" Si slammed his fork down with a sharp click. "I want to know what is going on around here."

"What?" Meghan leapt from her chair. Then she turned to Liam. "What did you do?"

"I didn't do a thing, Meg. I've been as helpful as I know how."

"Shay?" Meghan looked to be planning to question the whole family.

"Now I figured it out." Si cut her off. "It's you." He jabbed his pointer finger right at his red-headed pill of a wife. "What did you tell these boys to make them all scared of every word they say?"

Meghan had her hands clenched. A sure sign she was upset. Too upset to think clearly enough to lie for once. "I just told them that if they didn't behave and we didn't work hard to earn our keep you might just take us back to Helena and make us find our own roof."

There was a dead silence before Si managed to say, "You just told them I'd throw them out? *Just,* Meghan? You've been scaring them into obedience by thinking I'd abandon you all, leave you homeless to starve on the street?"

"Well," her voice sounded mighty weak, "I never said we'd starve. I have hopes of finding work."

Si slapped his hand flat on his face. He prayed for patience and common sense and the right words — because he was sure as certain the words he was thinking were the wrong ones.

She had no idea what she'd done but it'd made Silas so angry it looked to be blowing out the lamp in his brain.

It was all she could do to not rush to her brothers and hug them. Brace them against the coming fury. Except she was afraid that was the worst thing she could do.

"You," Silas jabbed a finger straight at Meghan, "have a lot of nerve not trusting me." Now he pointed that finger right at himself. "I'm not the one who came into this marriage bearing a wagonload of lies."

"Silas, I'm sorry. I —"

"And that's another thing." He cut her off.

She had no idea what that meant. "What's another thing?"

"My name is not *Silas.*"

There was a stretch of silence. Meghan could think of only one thing to say. "Yes it is."

His face turned so red she was worried for him. Could a man's hair ignite?

"No it's not, and if we'd had one calm conversation this whole week you'd know it."

Many things flooded through her mind, all very reasonable, like for example, him signing his letters Silas. But instead of listing something so obvious, she asked, "What is your name then?"

She braced herself for it to be something very strange.

"It's Si."

She looked at her brothers, who were all looking at each other.

"A nickname then is it?"

"We didn't know," Shay said. "We'll call you anything you want, you've but to ask."

Si slammed his hand flat on the table and it sounded like an explosion. "So now I'm scaring you again, and you'll hurry to do as I bid before I cast you out in the streets of Helena to survive or die on your own, is that it?"

It honestly was pretty much it. What Meghan didn't understand was why being polite and hard-working made him so mad.

Meghan felt her temper simmer. Most of it had been pounded out of her by years of exhaustion and hunger. But here she was rested and her belly full and she was right back to the fiery young girl she'd been.

"Silas, just calmly explain what we're doing wrong and we'll change. It's not right that you're so angry with us when all we've been is good to you."

That seemed to ignite his temper yet again. Meghan had seen her da slap her ma many times. She knew little about marriage outside her family so she assumed such things went on everywhere. So she was prepared to take that from Silas. But it didn't suit her. And if he laid a hand in anger on her little brothers —

"I do not want you to fear me." His hands clenched into one large fist on the table. He dropped his head down as if he prayed, but then he spoke and it sounded as if he spoke through clenched teeth. Not a prayerful countenance. So she feared him all the more.

When he raised his head, instead of anger she saw hurt. "I want a family. Yes, I want us all working together but because we want to, not because you're scared into it. After a week together haven't any of you even begun to like me? Don't you see anything of what kind of man I am? I'm far and away more upset by this than I was to find out my wife brought her brothers along."

He relaxed his hands and stood from the table. Every one of the four of them stepped back. Lock even hid behind her skirts.

Nodding, Silas . . . no Si . . . said, "That's it then, I reckon. You're to be servants and hired men and I'm to be the boss. In that case I believe I'll go sleep in the barn. We'll get rooms added onto your house — and then I'll build one for myself. If I order you to help me, I reckon you'll do it. And until then, the barn is tight. No heat, but it's summer. I'll get the other house built before the winter wind blows."

He turned and walked out into the growing dusk. He didn't even slam the door. Instead it shut with a quiet click that somehow made it all the more final.

CHAPTER 7

Meghan sank down onto one of the chairs. Her brothers leaned back in their seats. The head of the table was empty with Silas . . . Si gone.

"What are we to do now, Meg?" Lock asked.

After a long quiet moment, Meghan answered, "I might not be the one to answer your questions, Lock. It seems like I've handled my new husband all wrong."

"I am more at fault, Meg," Liam spoke up. "I offered to stay behind in town with the lads that first night before we'd even come home. I said I could find work and we'd be none of his concern."

"And he didn't agree to that?" Meghan would've thought Silas . . . Si would have thanked Liam and helped him find a room and a job.

"Tis a good chance I insulted him, judging by how he's acting now."

Meghan shrugged her shoulders helplessly.

"It seems like a generous offer to me, but, well . . ." her voice faded as she considered it.

"We've been helpful, Meg, but we haven't spent a second trying to get to know him." Shay propped his chin on his fists, sounding glum. "He's right. I've been scared of him. Working hard because I was afraid he'd kick me out."

"We can still work hard," Lock chimed in. "Sure and that's no sin. But we need to add Si to our family."

"He lives alone out here. And we've got each other." Meghan shook her head, "But how do we add him?"

Liam stood from the table and walked to the front door. "I think I'll start by apologizing to him and being friendlier to the man who's put a roof over my head and given more food than I've ever had?"

Which told Meghan something else. "Liam's right, each one of us needs to apologize for our own behavior, me most of all."

With a quick tug, Liam headed outside, closed the door and was gone.

She stood and brushed a hand over Lock's head. He'd had a haircut and he was wearing new clothes she'd sewn with needle, thread and cloth provided by the man she'd warned might throw them out. She'd warned her brothers, as good as threatened them and turned them against Si.

Plenty of apologizing ahead for her, and she owed Si every word of it.

CHAPTER 8

"Wash up the dishes, lads and to bed with you." Nervously she rose from the supper table.

"Si, will you come outside for a walk with me?" She cleared her throat nervously, met his eyes and added, "Please?"

He went along with her, braced for the fourth apology of the day. The boys had done a good job. What's more, he thought they meant it. He thought they wanted to be friends and trusted him to mean it when he said they had a home.

As their feet crushed quietly on the grass out front of the house, he wondered if they might just be pretending. Just giving him what he wanted with no honesty behind it. With the boys he could stand it and with their friendlier behavior he hoped they really could start to know each other better.

But his wife, well that was a little different. In truth it made him a little sick to think she was going to give him some apology that included being friendlier. Maybe it'd include wifely things.

He didn't want that when he didn't trust her to mean a word she said.

"We're far enough the boyos won't be hearin' us, Si."

"Let's keep walking while we talk." Si didn't want to look her in the eye. She was too pretty and he wasn't going to let that sway him. Instead he just wanted to hear her words. He wasn't going to decide anything tonight about her.

He'd wait and let her prove herself. He suppressed a flinch when he thought that was just what she'd been doing. Behaving with care until he proved himself.

That was different. He wasn't the liar in this marriage.

"Si." She glanced sideways at him.

He noticed so he must be looking at her a little.

"I've been practicing calling you Si in my head all afternoon."

That almost made him smile. He had to admit he'd never told her to call him Si. But that was mainly because they'd never had a real talk.

"This week, it's poorly how we've acted toward you."

Grudgingly he admitted, "You've all worked hard, you've done a lot to fit in here, Meghan. I have no complaints about that."

"Our hearts were in the wrong place and that was my doin'." She hooked her left arm around his right elbow. It wasn't the first time she'd touched him, but it hadn't happened often. It felt good.

"I've told you about me and the lads being orphaned, and you can tell we've been in a bad way. I've told you how desperate we were and that's what led me to lie. But there's more I didn't even realize until today, when you were hurt by our fear."

"Meghan, I would never throw you out. For heaven's sakes, I —"

"Hush now, Si. I know. From the first moment you fed my brothers, I knew you were a fine and decent man. A better, more honorable person than I am. But even with that plain as the nose on my face, it was easy to doubt you — not fair but easy. M–my da was a frightening man."

"Liam said he died from the drink."

"He told you that?" Meghan stopped short and looked sideways at him, startled.

With a tug, Si got her going again. They'd reached the barn and now walked alongside a corral fence. There was still plenty of sun on the long summer day. Si wanted to be out of sight of the house in case any yelling went on. He didn't want the boys to see him and their sister snarling at each other. The house had been left behind but he thought how voices carried and he walked on.

"Liam has never spoken of it before." Meghan now clutched his right arm with both her hands as if she needed to hang on. "In fact he's never spoken of Da after he died and, if the youngsters did, he cut them off. It's become a family habit to pretend we never had a father."

Si thought of his own pa and what a fine man he was. He was such a big part of the family and such a team with Ma. How could a person even talk without including him? It was hard to believe there were pas that were bad to their children.

Si admitted he'd lived a sheltered life.

"Liam mentioned it just that once. Your pa wasn't much help when it came to — to anything. Raising children. Putting food on the table."

Shaking her head, Meghan said, "Da worked when he wasn't ailing, but we never saw a penny of that. Ma worked from my earliest memory. She was a sly one. She stopped for food on her way home from her work cleaning in a hotel. So there was little money for Da to take to the pub."

"I hear affection for your ma." Silas was relieved she had at least one decent parent.

"Aye and that's the truth, though I wondered why she picked a man like my da. She'd work, and I'd watched the wee ones. She took in laundry. Liam and I would work on that chore, but Da liked quiet when he had a head sore from the drink. And his temper wasn't easy at those times. Then after Ma died, Da folded up soon enough. The lads were in school by then so I could find work and the men I worked for were cheese paring and quick with a fist if the work wasn't done. Then when Liam, and later Shay, went to work, well, no whip was laid across their back but they were treated little better than slaves. So I've come to expect the worst from more men than just my da."

She turned to face Si and took both his hands, then looked him square in the eye. "And I expected the worst from you, too, even after I saw your kindness. It wasn't anything you did, Silas. Uh — Si. It was all my own fear. I believed after my lies I deserved no better than to be cast out, and my brothers with me. I apologize for that."

Then was a stretch of silence as Si tried to decide how to respond.

Maybe the silence was too long, because Meghan filled it with more words. "We need to trust each other, and I tell you now that I do. I will trust you to mean what you say. And I will promise to never lie again. What's more . . . I want to begin to know you better as a wife should know her husband."

Si froze on that one, afraid of what came next. Something he should resist, but as he stood here holding her hands he was afraid it might be hard.

"I'd like to find time every day to take a bit of a walk with you. Get away from the lads and talk, get to know each other. I know nothing about you. You've mentioned family but I've never asked about them. Can we do that? I know building rooms on will make for long hard days, so if you're too tired —"

Si pulled one hand free and used it to cover her mouth. "You couldn't have asked for anything that pleased me more, Meghan. It's exactly what I'd have asked of you if I'd spoken first. Now, you said you were you born in Ireland and traveled to America. Do I remember that right or were you born here?"

Meghan's brow furrowed. "What has that to do with our talk?"

"Nothing, but it does have to do with getting to know each other."

With that she smiled and returned to his side, holding his arm. They walked on, sharing their lives with each other until the sun began to set and they turned to head back to the house.

As the dusk drifted to darkness, Si turned to her once again while they were still out of sight of the house. This time he took both her hands.

"I want to be married to you in all ways, Meghan, but —"

"No one calls me Meghan."

That startled him. "They don't?"

"Call me Meg."

With a smile that turned into a chuckle, Si said, "We're making real progress, Meg. One week of marriage and we already know each other's names."

Meg smiled, too, and the smile turned into a laugh. Si leaned close to her and slid an arm around her back and their laughter went on until he was holding her close.

The laughter ended but the embrace went on. The silence of the evening was broken only by the gentle breeze and the distant song of the nightingale.

Si eased back without letting her go. "I said I want to be married to you in all ways, but some of those ways must wait until we know each other better."

Meg agreed without pulling away from him. "Maybe if the rooms take a couple of weeks to build, by the time we have our own, we might feel close enough to share it."

Very careful to not be overly forward, Si leaned down and touched his lips to hers. He felt their breath mingle. He pulled away before he forgot how and their eyes met.

Somehow, though their kiss had only seemed to last a second, her arms had come around his neck. Somehow his hands were buried deep in her flame red hair. Perhaps the kiss had lasted longer than he'd thought.

"Why don't you see if you can't get your building project done a wee bit faster than two weeks, husband."

He kissed her again, but pulled away and turned toward the house, her holding his arm again. "I'll do just that, Meg."

Honestly they really only needed one extra room. They didn't need to wait until the whole addition was done.

CHAPTER 9

"You always make me carry the heavy side." Lock tossed the slender sapling aside and crossed his arms, glaring at Shay.

Shay tossed his end down and charged toward his brother, hands fisted.

Meghan dashed from the shallow trench they were digging. She got there in time to jump between her little brothers and keep them separated.

"Now you two settle yourselves. I'll not have you going at each other."

She looked at Si. "You should have waited another week or so to encourage these whelps to be themselves."

Si scratched his head, shoving his Stetson back a bit. "Because this is how they usually act?"

They threw themselves at each other again and she grabbed them by the shoulders.

"Aye." She looked between the two boys. "If you're not up to handling this job you, Shay, can go fetch eggs and feed the chickens, then the pigs. I left those chores until after breakfast, now you can do it."

"That's woman's work!" Shay pulled away from Meghan but she held on. She'd had practice.

"All the better. And when you're done with the women's work there are barn stalls that need the straw pitched and replaced with clean."

She turned to her little brother. "Lock, you peel the potatoes for our midday meal. I left a pile of them on the table. Then I'll set you to washing clothes. You can build up the fire and heat the water and wash three days of work clothes."

Lock howled, "No!"

She didn't blame him, building up a fire and working over simmering water on a hot summer day was no fun. But Lock started this. "Those are your choices. And you've shown no interest in continuing to work together on the house."

Lock and Shay glowered at each other.

"Fine." Lock gave first, as she'd known he'd do. Mostly because this was his fault and Lock had a good sense of right and wrong to go with his short temper.

"Before you two go, that tree looks as even as the tolling of a church bell. Stacking the smaller ones is a much easier job than what Liam and Si are doing. Uncle Si chopped down trees that were even to make a good tight room. To say one end is heavier is to insult your new brother."

Quietly, Si muttered, "Uncle Si?"

Lock looked sheepish. "I didn't mean no insult."

Shay shrugged one shoulder and kicked the toe of his boot into the ground. "Sorry."

Meghan noticed he didn't say it as he would have yesterday. Today he was cranky and childish rather than obedient and scared. Si might start wishing they'd go back to being afraid of him.

"I'll keep working on the new rooms, if it's all right, Uncle Si." Shay sounded a tad more sincere than he had while apologizing.

"Ask your sister." Si went back to digging. He was out working them all and well Meghan knew it.

"You can stay with it until the next cross word about one of those logs."

The two boys picked up the log and carried it on to the stack Si had told them to make. These slender logs would be split and used for the roof. Si and Liam were preparing the building site to set the heavier logs into place, forming the room base.

Meghan got back to work and they made some progress over the next half hour. She did her best to ignore the racket.

"My hand!" Lock started jumping and shouting.

"Stop being a little crybaby," Shay shouted back.

The bickering never ended but the lads worked on.

Meghan could think of no way to keep the peace, and her little brothers were very creative. There were no more cross words about the logs being uneven, but as soon as she forbade something, the boys would be into something else. They squabbled over minding Si, all the while racing each other to be his helper. They shoved and kicked and shouted. But continued working with a good will.

There was a wrestling match at noon over who got the biggest biscuit.

Shay tripped Lock as he headed out the door to work.

The two young lads were behaving like . . . two young lads.

For all their ruckus, Liam was the worst.

He hadn't spoken a friendly word all day. Back to his sullen, resentful self — the boy he'd turned into after he went to work at that meat packing plant.

He worked hard, but he refused to respond to any friendly comment Si made. The stubborn boyo obeyed without response or a smile.

He did answer when Si said Liam could have his own room. In a biting voice, he said, "No, my brothers and I will share and you and my sister will each have a room of your own."

Meghan had a feeling that wasn't Si's plan, at all.

Liam must have suspected it as well. The way he said it sounded more like an order than a suggestion. Meghan might even go so far as to say he had a threatening tone.

Meghan decided Liam was a problem for Si to solve. She had her hands full controlling Shay and Lock.

The afternoon was no better but the room did begin to go up. The corners were square and solid. Si built in a dividing wall to split the addition in two, and he put in one tight window in each room. Meghan heard him showing Liam the job, talking in detail and letting the grumpy Liam do some of the work himself. By the end of the day they were nearly done with the walls.

"Let's have a bit of supper, Meg, and we can get more work in before we lose the light."

"I'm tired," Lock hollered.

Shay scowled at Si. "You're going to make us work until dark?" He turned and ran inside.

"They're just fussy from the hard work, Si. They'll be ready to go back at it after a meal, and they'll sleep well tonight."

"I'm sure you're both tired, too." Si said to Meghan and Liam with a smile that looked like he had to scrounge it up. "I'm used to working on my own. And the first day on a new job makes you weary, man, woman and child. We've got a lot done. I'll just come out alone after we eat and make sure things are safe to leave overnight. We can pick up on this tomorrow."

"Sure and you're callin' me lazy, is that it Harden? After all the work I've done today, you think I'll quit on you, too?" No 'Uncle Si' for Liam it seemed.

Si's eyelids closed, and Meghan had heard of a person counting to ten before they spoke. But whatever trick Si used, after a bit he opened his eyes and seemed calm. She couldn't remember her da ever fighting to control his temper.

"Get on with the meal, Meg. The boys can help or rest, whatever you choose. Liam, I'll be glad for a second set of hands. If we work together 'til dark, we can get to the top of the walls before supper, then maybe we can frame the roof before we're done for the night, that'll steady it. We'll finish by tomorrow night, then cut open doors into the main house and be done but for some finishing work."

Si went back to work and Liam slouched as he followed.

Meghan said a quick prayer of thanks for Si. And she wondered when he'd start in shouting.

CHAPTER 10

Si and Meg went for their nightly walk even though Si could barely keep his eyes open.

"I don't know how long I'll wait before I start banging heads together," Meghan said as soon as they were out of ear shot.

Si took her hand and squeezed it just enough to draw her full attention. He smiled. "I'll admit I wanted to start in layin' down the law today a few times, but while I watched them eat supper so hungry they acted as if their belly-button was rubbin' on their backbone, then come right back out to work, even with their fussin', I had a thought."

She loved the strength of his hand. She loved that he hadn't unleashed a temper on her brothers.

She loved *him.*

She stumbled at the thought and pitched forward. Si's strong hand held her and pulled her close. He kissed her. There was to be a kiss every night she hoped.

He broke the kiss then brushed his lips on

her cheek, then her forehead, then each eye and hugged her close.

"Quit distracting me, wife." When he smiled his teeth shined in the dark like a gleaming lantern leading her home. "I've got a lot of manly wisdom to share tonight."

She laughed, and slid an arm around his waist. He rested his across her shoulders and they walked on.

"Have your brothers always been like this? The two little ones squabbling, Liam so angry?"

"I — I, yes, I guess."

"I had a passel of brothers, Meg, and the young'uns don't worry me much. They act a lot like I did with my brothers and they work hard the whole time their mouths are going. But Liam's anger had me worried, until while I said my prayers at supper, the Lord whispered me an idea. And when I get an idea popping into my head out of nowhere during a prayer I always pay real close attention."

She hugged his waist. "What is this idea, husband?"

"Well for one thing, yes, we cleared up the boys being scared of me." He pinched her side and gave her a mock frown.

"We certainly did, there wasn't a lick of fear today, more's the pity."

"I think the boys are feeling safe. That's why they are showing us how they really feel. For Lock and Shay that's not a problem because they're just acting like boys, healthy, fearless, well-fed, reckless, impatient boys."

That almost made Meghan stumble again, instead she whirled to face Si. Then she flung her arms around him and burst into tears.

Si hadn't meant for that to happen. "Meg, what did I say? I'm sorry."

With a quiet sob, she grabbed his head, pulled him down and kissed the livin' daylights out of him.

Apologizing didn't seem so important after all. He returned the kiss and then he lifted her off her feet and kissed deeper, harder, not even sure what had set her off but mighty glad it had.

Then he figured he'd better ask, because Meg liked to talk and he was never sure what she was going to say.

He lowered her back to the ground and pulled her away just a few inches. "What's going on in that female head of yours, Mrs. Harden?"

She giggled through the tears and said in a broken voice. "My brothers, the little ones, when you said they were well-fed, I realized you're right. I don't even know what two normal little boys act like. Yes they used to bicker more, but they've gotten quieter as the years passed, and then Shay went to work. Since then our whole family has been nearly silent. We did no talking beyond the words needed to survive."

She kissed him again, but ended it far too soon. "You've given that to me, Si. More than your name, more than a roof over my head and food in my belly, you've given those boys back. Because of you, they're the way boys should be."

The moon made her eyes glow. Her lips were swollen from being kissed long and hard. Her hair had come free of the knot she wore on top of her head. She was the most beautiful woman he'd ever seen.

"You've given me everything and now yes, I've given the work of my back, but I want to give you much more, all I have to give."

"You don't have to give me one thing, Meg."

Resting one hand on his cheek she whispered, "Can I give you —"

"Meg, Lock's gone!" Shay was out of sight, but the door slammed and his feet pounded as he came charging outside so fast, screaming so loud, Si expected to see that his hair had caught on fire.

Si looked at Meg, who shook her head and growled. "I had more to say to you."

"And I want to hear every word. But we'd have to move fast to hide from him."

At that moment, Shay came far enough toward the barn they could see him.

No flames.

Meg laughed. "If only we could."

"What's got you so upset, lad? Lock must've

run out to use the privy. No need to be so upset."

They headed toward Shay, the mood broken, Si none too happy about it. But things were better. They had come a long way in a short time, and he liked the direction they were heading.

He took her hand and she flashed him a smile in the moonlight and squeezed his hand tight.

He liked it very much.

"Meg, Uncle Si, come quick!"

Meghan moved faster, not worried but wanting to settle Shay before the lad was so worked up he was beyond all chance of going back to sleep.

Meghan opened her mouth to question him and Shay said, "I saw Lock go out. He didn't go in the outhouse, he went behind it. He never came back. I went out back and hollered but he didn't answer."

Meghan exchanged a quick glance with Si. Lock might be up to mischief but there were thick woods behind the privy and Lock might get himself in trouble. They picked up their pace. Shay, still running toward them, skidded and crashed into Meghan so hard only Si's quick hands kept her from being tackled to the ground.

Liam stepped out of the house, his clothes pulled on hastily. Sure as certain, he'd heard all the fuss. Shay was in his nightshirt.

"Shay, run in and pull on your boots. You can't go barefoot into the woods."

Her brother gave her a furious look, but veered off toward the house. "Don't go into the woods and leave me behind."

"We won't, Shay, trust me." Si kept moving.

Meghan's heart almost twisted with fear as she realized how much trouble a little boy could come to lost in these woods. And then the fear steadied as she thought of her husband and how much she did trust him. How glad she was that he was with her right now.

CHAPTER 11

Si knew how boys could vanish then re-appear. He and his brothers had been known to get up to trouble now and then back when he was younger.

But he'd never had a speck of trouble with his new set of brothers. Of course they'd just turned into their wildest selves today. He reckoned he could expect plenty of surprises.

He picked up his pace until he was jogging toward the woods behind the privy.

"Lock, where'd you get to?" Si's shout was met with a silence so profound his ears echoed.

The dew had come on the grass, and Lock's footprints were easy to read even in the moonlight. The boy headed straight for the woods. That wasn't enough to bother Si, a boy'd sometimes rather slip into the woods than use an outhouse.

"Lock, answer me."

There was only silence.

"Everyone stop!" Si's voice cracked like a whip.

Liam and Meg obeyed instantly.

"What's wrong, Si?" Meg stood only inches from him.

"I see his tracks. If he's not answering I'm afraid it means he can't. I need to track him and that means you need to hang back so you don't destroy any sign."

A wolf howled. Not far enough away to suit Si.

"Liam, run to the house and fetch the rifle and a lantern, quick."

He hadn't needed to add 'quick', Liam was already sprinting to the cabin.

He came back, rifle in hand, with Shay who'd made quick work of pulling on his clothes.

"You three stay close together, and a few yards behind me. It's gonna be black as pitch once we step more than a few paces into those trees." What Si didn't say was with only lantern light, finding any tracks would be next to impossible.

The wolf howled again. That brute was coming. But it wasn't close enough to've gotten Lock. So where was the boy?

Si lit the lantern and studied the trees. Based on the tracks in the grass he could see right where the boy went in — but what would he find beyond that? For the first time since he'd moved Si was less than thrilled with his new home. He realized he didn't know these woods. He had no idea what of the hills and dales, the gorges and even the pit holes. The Rockies had everything a man could want when it came to danger.

He turned to Meghan and the boys. His family, he realized as he held the lantern high, trying to think of something smart to say, helpful, wise. He was too worried to come up with much.

"I'm going to go slow. I haven't explored these woods yet. We could find a drop off."

Meghan gasped.

Si moved on, sorry he'd scared her. "Or who knows what. I don't want you getting past me, nor fanning out behind me because we're not sure what we're facing in there. Stay close."

Nothing more came to him to say. He stepped into the woods, rifle in his right hand, lantern in the other. He noticed a broken off branch that Lock must've pushed through and went into the woods there. Once there he examined every step and plant, every blade of grass. He saw a scuffed pile of leaves. A heavier branch, swung low, had a tuft of red hair caught under its bark.

Each step he took was painstaking. Once he stopped and called out. "Lock. Answer me if you can."

Only silence. Then a howl, now two wolves talking to each other.

Si said, "Stay quiet and listen. If Lock fell he might've knocked himself out but he could come around, moan or rustle some leaves. Pay close attention."

They went on. What could that scamp have been up to? Had something lured him into the woods.

Or someone?

Si hadn't thought beyond Lock getting himself into trouble, but now Si's imagination was going wild. He forced himself to focus on the thick woods, the trees pressed closer as they went in farther. He found a thread here and there. A broken branch of a scrawny scrub bush. Inching forward, Si felt time passing. The wolves howled nearer.

One of his feet went out from under him. Si grabbed at the trunk of a massive oak tree and swung out over nothing.

"Look out!" His grip was slipping, the tree was too far around for him to get a good hold.

Then hands were on his shirt and his belt, pulling. All three of his companions tugging at him. They helped him scramble for a better hold on a scrub oak, and pull himself back to solid ground. He realized he no longer held either the lantern or his rifle.

Suddenly a match flared to life and the lantern was lit. "I saved it before the kerosene poured out," Liam said, sounding proud but shaky.

"And here's your rifle, Si." Meghan held it

firm in her hand. Shay was still clinging to Si's shirt, holding on for all he was worth.

Si realized what he'd found. "Give me the lantern. This could be what happened to Lock. He might've fallen."

Liam handed it over quick. Si dropped to his knees and held the lantern out over the edge. The light didn't reach the bottom of whatever this was.

"If Lock fell down there we have no idea how far it is, but we've got to go down." He looked at his family. They'd saved him. They were courageous and quick thinking.

"Liam, go back to the barn and get all the rope you can find. Meg, you stay right here and don't move an inch." Si heard Liam running before he could continue his orders. "Shay there are two more lanterns in the cabin. One in the bedroom and —"

"I know where they are." Shay raced away.

"Meg take this lantern. I want you near the edge, but be careful, it might be the type that will cave off, so stay back a bit."

"I am here." The lantern was raised high and it bathed her in a circle of warm, glowing light. "I won't budge an inch."

There was a long silence broken only by the brush of the summer breeze and the unearthly howl of a wolf, no, two wolves. Si listened. He thought maybe three now and they were moving.

"How far can he have fallen, Si. What if he's —"

"Don't add trouble on top of trouble, Meg. We'll do what we need to do to find Lock, nothing less."

He heard a muffled sound from her and was afraid she was crying. He was no great admirer of tears but he understood these.

Then Liam was back. Shay was soon behind him.

"I'll light a lantern and lower it over the ledge with the rope until we see what's down there." Si was fast at work.

Shay had the third lantern going and all four of them knelt as close to the drop off as they could get. The lantern descended for far too long and finally reached bottom. The circle of light it cast showed Lock, lying face down, unconscious.

"He's there. Oh, Si, what if —" Meghan cut off her words.

"Let me tie off this rope and get down there." Si had the rope fastened around the tree as fast as he could talk. "I'll get him hooked up and we'll haul him back up in no time." Si refused to think what he'd do if the boy was badly hurt, or worse. He hung the strap of his rifle over his shoulder and swung over nothingness. He scampered hand-over-hand down to where the lantern cast it's yellow glow.

Dropping to the ground, he rushed to

Lock's side, the boy lay unmoving.

Kneeling, Si carefully rolled Lock onto his back. A mean gash bled at his temple and a goose-egg-sized bump was raising up beneath the cut. Si glanced around and saw a small rock right where Lock would have landed. Otherwise the ground was soft and the drop was no more than twenty feet, not enough to do terrible harm unless a boy landed just wrong.

Si saw the boy's chest rise and fall evenly. There was a firm, steady heartbeat beneath Si's hand. Lock groaned and his hands flopped around and pushed at Si. There was strength in the shove and that was encouraging.

Looking up to where two lanterns gleamed many feet overhead, Si said, "He's alive!"

Meghan cried out with relief. Si heard quick talk pass between all three of those up on high but he couldn't make out their words.

"He's been knocked cold but he just groaned and he's moving. Give me a minute to see if he'll wake up before I let you haul him up."

Just as Si said he wanted more time, a wolf howled only a few yards away.

Chapter 12

Meghan heard the wolf howl and a chill raced up her spine that made her leap to her feet and grab the rope.

"I'm going down."

Liam caught her arm. "No, Si will hurry now. He heard it. He'll tie off the rope and we'll haul Lock up. Look down there."

Meghan bent forward. Then she realized they were going to be pulling up Lock and leaving Si behind until another rope could be lowered.

Quick, efficient moves from below told her Si was doing just that.

"If we had a gun we could protect him."

"He's got a gun, Meg." Shay said. "He'll protect himself."

Just like he was protecting all of them.

"Pull him up." The shout from below rang like a shot starting a race.

Meghan, Liam and Shay pulled their little brother hand over hand up, as fast as they could. He was light-weight and it was no job to bring him along, but Meghan feared her grip might slip and send her brother tumbling back down. Hanging on for dear life, they had him in hand within seconds.

Meghan untied Si's sturdy knots as quick as a Kilkenny's cat.

Liam tossed the rope back over the edge. "Grab hold, Si!" Liam shouted.

A vicious snarl cut through the night, followed by the roar of a gunshot.

Si heard the wolves but he couldn't see them. He'd gotten one with the first shot and they'd vanished. Now all he could do was aim into the night. He heard Liam's shout and backed toward the rope. He kept his gun aimed at the darkness.

He caught hold. A wolf leapt out of the black. Silas fired and fired again.

The wolf fell with a thud and skidded to a stop near Si's feet. He kept his eyes roving left to right just outside the circle of light.

Motion surrounded him on three sides . . . black against black, ghostly, so quick and silent he couldn't be sure of hitting one of these big beasts. He couldn't climb with one hand, and he didn't dare ease off his aim.

Wolves didn't travel in a pack in the summer. Why were they here? He counted four and he'd killed one and at least wounded a second. But why were they here?

Then he knew. They'd been drawn by the

smell of blood. Once together they fell immediately into the actions of a pack.

Again he reached behind him and caught the rope. But if he could just get up a ways he'd be out of the reach of crushing jaws.

Waiting, biding his time, he watched for any motion in the swallowing dark.

He practiced in his head what to do.

He couldn't climb with one hand gripping the rifle.

With a quick, sure tug, he could hang the gun over his shoulder.

He moved to do it but the second the rifle was lowered, a wolf leapt into the lantern light.

Si whipped his gun up and fired but the wolf was gone. With three shots fired Si suddenly wasn't sure how fully loaded his gun had been. He'd gone hunting earlier in the week. But in his distraction with his new family and all he had to do, to live with them, had he forgotten the simple act of checking his gun over and reloading it? He just couldn't remember.

Climbing up was his only option. Meghan with all her brothers' strength couldn't pull him up, he was too heavy. Meg, Liam and Shay together weren't up to that chore.

"How much rope did you bring?" Meghan looked at Liam, who dodged into the dark and came back with a big armload of it. He'd stripped every piece of rope out of the barn.

Meghan grabbed at it and found an end. "I'm going to fashion a loop. Si can just drop it over his head and we'll pull him up."

"I don't think we can do it, Meg. He's too heavy."

Meghan froze, trying to convince herself they had the strength.

Into the quiet, Shay said, "How about if we had a horse pull him up?"

Liam and Meghan turned toward Shay. Liam said, "I'll be right back."

He vanished into the night so quick Meghan couldn't help remembering tall tales from the old country about the magical Little People.

"I'll tie a loop."

"Let me do it, Meg. Si showed me how he drops a loop over a calf, and I've been practicing the sliding knot."

Shay grabbed the rope and went to work. That left Meghan with nothing to do but worry about Lock, worry about Si and pray for all of them.

A rifle blast from below made Meghan drop to her knees and lean as far out as she dared.

All she could see was Si standing in that pool of light. Then a memory surfaced. She'd witnessed a house fire her first winter in Omaha. Many stood watching, but not too close because the flames drove everybody back.

Hoof beats sounded. Liam would be here

in only moments.

"Si, can you use the kerosene from the lantern to make a semi-circle of fire to keep the wolves back. Liam is bringing the horse and I'm lowering a rope with a noose you can drop over your head and under your arms. We can pull you up even with your rifle aimed."

It was an idea born in desperation.

A perfect idea! He was ashamed for not thinking of it himself.

A horse had the muscle he needed, of course! Tying that rope off in a loop would've been risky to do down here. He was too busy wolf hunting to even think of it.

But Meg up there had nothing but time.

"I'll splash out the kerosene and light it. You get the rope dropped in place. Tell me when the horse is ready to pull."

He surrounded himself with an arc of kerosene with the cliff at his back, as he ignited the fluid, flames rushed down that curve, growing, crackling with the sound only fire can make.

The arc of fire cast more light and wolves darted into the black, staying farther from him.

He wondered how long the fire would last before it consumed the kerosene.

The rope dropped right in front of his eyes and for a second all he could see was a noose and hope he didn't end up hanging himself. Then, with the wolves kept back, he dragged the rope over his head and under his arms.

"I'm ready," he called straight up, gun still aimed. "Pull me up anytime."

All he had to do was get up higher than the wolves would jump. Then he'd sling the rifle over his shoulder and help clamber up the rest of the way.

The rope went tight just as a wolf leapt through a spot where the flames were dying. His aim was thrown off and the wolf gave a terrible snarl, jumped at Si's rising body and sunk it's teeth into his boot.

The tough leather kept the wolf from getting a chunk of Si, but the added weight pulled so hard the rope creaked and the noose threatened to slide right off his body. Si swung the rifle like a club and whacked the wolf in the snout just as another one jumped like a fish looking to hook himself.

The second wolf missed.

The first yelped and released its fanged grip. Si lifted smooth and fast. Waiting for his chance to twist around and get his hands on the rope to climb, he never found such a moment.

It seemed the horse was heading for the barn at a gallop because Si zipped up that cliff slick as a sleet covered mountain slope.

He whipped over the edge and kept going.

"Liam, stop! He's up."

Si dragged along another dozen feet while Liam yelled, "Whoa!"

Finally the horse stopped and Si skidded forward a bit longer over scrub brush and saplings, then he began rolling. He stopped face down against a spruce tree and felt like he'd lost a fight with a porcupine.

Then he remembered Lock. No time to moan and groan.

Hands were on him. Meghan's for sure. Probably Shay's. Then the rope was slack. Liam either backed the horse up or released it from where he'd fastened it to the saddle.

Then Si was free. There were a jumble of concerned voices, Meghan's sweetest of them all. Si climbed to his feet.

"Where's Lock? Is he all right?"

"No, he's still unconscious. I checked him when he first came up, then we turned to trying to fetch you up here with the rest of us."

Patting her back, Si said, "Where is he? I don't see him."

Meghan led the way but Shay dashed forward, then around her. Si found Lock laid out flat near an oak trunk.

"Let's get him inside." Si lifted the boy and headed for the house. Hoping he came around soon and with no worse damage than a headache.

He led the way to the cabin and reached it just as Liam came from the barn.

"I left the horse inside and brought in the

other three from the corral. I didn't know if those wolves could find their way up here or not."

"Good thinking, Liam." Si carried Lock straight into their one and only bedroom, and settled the boy on the bed. Meghan followed with the lantern, then left it, dashed out and came back in with another one.

Si made a quick check for other wounds. He ran his hands up and down the boy's limbs and pressed his ribs. "No broken bones I can see."

Meghan came in again, this time with a basin of water. "Let me clean up that gash on his head and see how deep it is, Si."

He stepped aside and let her in to work.

"It's not deep. I won't even try to set stitches. He's just knocked cold. He needs time to come out of it and then a couple of easy days. I hope that's all because I don't know any more doctoring than this."

Meghan looked at Si. Their gaze held. It was like a prayer shared silently.

A wave of pure exhaustion washed over Si and he wondered what time it was. He looked at Shay and Liam, they'd had at most an hour's sleep. "I know how worried you boys are about Lock but do either of you think you could sleep? Morning comes early. Meg and I will sit up with him. If we need help, we'll call for you."

Liam had a flash of that sullen look, like he

255

wasn't going to leave his brother to anyone other than himself. But it didn't last. He'd stepped in like a man tonight, and Si had treated him like one. There was no place here for a boyish temper.

"Shay, let's go. Meg and Si, you each take an hour, then call me. I'll take part of the shift so we can all get some sleep."

"Thanks, Liam, I'd appreciate that." Si nodded. Liam met his eye and was satisfied with what he saw.

With only a word or two of protest, Shay followed Liam out to rest on the bedrolls Si and Liam usually slept on by the fire.

Meghan rested one hand on Si's back, then turned back to fussing over Lock. "You might as well catch an hour of sleep, Si. I couldn't close my eyes for the next hour, for the visions of Lock bleeding and the wolves tearing at you and . . . and . . ." Her voice broke. She reached for the water basin and began rinsing out a cloth.

Si settled strong hands on her shoulders and turned her to face him. Her cheeks were soaked with tears. "You saved him. You saved my little brother."

Strong slender arms, wrapped around his waist and she buried her face against his chest. Sobs shook her whole body.

With patience that surprised him, he held her close and let her cry out all her fear. When the worst of the storm had passed, he rested his cheek against the top of her red curls and whispered, "And you saved me, Meg. You and Liam and Shay saved me as surely as you helped me save Lock. You were quick thinking, you never wavered, and you saved your tears for when we had time for them."

The sob was broken by a shaky laugh. Then finally silence. And still she hung on.

From behind them, they heard a moan. They sprung apart and turn to Lock. He tossed his head and moaned in pain. Meghan reached the bedside one step ahead of Si.

Lock's eyes flickered open and he looked at Si and Meghan, side by side, watching over him.

"What happened?"

Si grinned, "You fell and got knocked clean out, boy. We were worried about you. Let me go get Liam, we thought we'd be taking shifts all night watching over you."

A quick step to the door and Si hollered, "Come on back in boys. Lock's awake."

By the time everyone had a turn looking at those wide open eyes, Lock was looking like he was wrung out.

Meghan adjusted the cold cloth on his forehead. "Go on back to sleep now. I'll share the bed with you like every night and we can all get some rest." She looked over at Si.

"Sounds like a fine idea. I'm pure tuckered out from worrying about you, young'un."

Also for fighting for his life against a pack of wolves but why bother the child with that part of this story.

The whole family turned in for the night.

Si was startled awake when his front door swung open. Full daylight shone from behind a pair of broad shoulders.

Si sprung to his feet, but the invasion wasn't a bad one. He knew that by the time he was standing upright.

"What're you doin' sleeping the day away, Si?"

"Pa! It's good to see you."

"And who's this with you?"

Si had forgotten everything for a few seconds. Now, as Liam rose, it came back. Three little brothers-in-law who called him Uncle Si.

And a wife.

Meg barreled into the room right then. Lock slower but awake, on his feet and unbroken.

"It's a story best told over coffee and eggs, I reckon."

Ma stepped into the cabin next.

Which was the perfect opportunity for introductions. "The explanation can wait a bit but Ma, Pa, I'd like to introduce Meghan Harden. My wife."

Ma gasped but quietly, still for her that was a big reaction.

"And Meg's little brothers, Liam, here beside me." Si clapped Liam on the shoulder and hoped the hard fight for their lives last night had created a bond. At least enough Liam wouldn't jerk his shoulder away. He didn't.

"And Shay is next. That's Meg and the one with the bandage on his head is the youngest, Lock."

Suddenly Si was so happy to see his parents he felt a wave of something wash over him that made him think of crying. Of course a man didn't cry so it couldn't be that, but it was an outlandish feeling for a fact.

Pa swung the door shut. Ma went straight for Meg and took both her hands.

"My son didn't do anything foolish to get a wife so fast did he? The sheriff isn't forming a posse or anything like that?"

Si knew Ma was referring to his big brother Tanner kidnapping his wife. Si had done nothing of the sort.

"No, it was honored I was to marry Si." Meg's pretty Irish lilt sounded like a happy bit of music for a summer day. "Your son is a wonderful man. He took me and my brothers in. Our marriage has been a pure blessing. Did you see we're building on to the cabin? I told him it wasn't necessary but he's so generous. Sure and he's taken on a terrible burden and never shirked. You've raised a fine man, Mrs. Harden."

"Call me Ma. And Silas Pa."

Meg's eyes went to Si. Who saw her confusion. "No, she doesn't want you to call *me* pa. My pa's name is Silas Harden same as mine, that's why I always ask folks to call me Si, to help keep the confusion to a minimum."

Meg smiled and nodded. "I'm afraid we're slow moving this morning. We had a hard night. Lock fell over a cliff we didn't even know was in the woods behind the house. Si had to lower himself down and we hauled Lock up, knocked cold as an Omaha winter. Then a wolf pack set upon Si and he fought them off while we got the horse. The wolves were too close to —"

It was with some true fascination that Si listened to Meg draw him out to be the mightiest of heroes as she told her story.

His folks enjoyed the telling, and he knew they were thinking highly of him.

He wondered how long they could keep that going.

"I even slept in my clothes because I spent most of the night watching over Lock. If you'll give me a minute to straighten my hair and wash the sleep out of my eyes, I'll get breakfast on."

"You go on in and take a few minutes, Meghan," Ma said. "I'll start breakfast."

"It's Meg if you don't mind, M–ma." Meg's voice wobbled and she squeezed Ma's hands tight. "It's hard to use the name, my own ma's been dead these many years, and my da gone a while. It gives me great pleasure to call you such, and I'm honored you'd allow it. Thank you."

Meg nodded her head quickly, then turned and dashed out of the room. Since the boys were all dressed, too, as was Silas, there wasn't much getting ready for them.

"I'll take the boys out and fetch eggs and milk the cow."

"There are plenty of eggs here, Si. Leave the chores and all of you help get breakfast on the table. I can get to know my new . . . uh . . ." Ma stared at them. "If you're Meg's brothers, then you're Si's brothers-in-law, and that's mighty close to being a brother so I guess. . . . that makes you my sons."

Ma glanced at Pa and smiled. He rolled his eyes.

"So all of you call me Ma, too. Let's get breakfast on."

The supplies were plentiful and Ma and Pa did a good job of getting the boys to talk, better'n Si ever did. But their talk was only of kindness. There was no mention of the lies and anger that had marked their efforts to be a family.

Meg was back in a trice and she set to working by Ma's side with a good spirit.

Ma had a close look at the cut on Lock's head. The boy stood so close, he at one point just plain rested his head on Ma's belly while she checked his wound. She asked a few questions and he called her Ma when he answered. The little one was as lonely for a ma as any child would be.

By the time breakfast was done Ma and Pa had as good as adopted all four of the Mc-Crays. Pa had ordered them to change their names to Harden, and they agreed without hesitation. They didn't appear to have much affection for their name nor the pa who'd given it to them.

The menfolk went outside to do chores and Si had a nervous feeling about leaving his wife behind with his ma. Would they join forces against him? Would Meg tell ma all about the lies and how gullible Si had been? Or would she lie about the lies? That might make everything worse if the truth really came out that he'd been made a fool of.

Pa clapped him on the back and, with a start, Si realized he'd stopped walking and turned to stare at the house.

"Leave 'em to get acquainted, son. We'll do up the chores quick and get started on the finishing work on your new rooms. I think you might need a third one spare bedroom and maybe a second fireplace."

Meghan and Ma had the house tidied. The men had helped some before they left. Ma asked about the boys' clothes and before long, Meghan had her sewing out and Ma was helping place stitches, and doing it at double the speed Meghan was capable of . . . which sped Meghan up, too, as she watched and learned.

They were going to finish a shirt long before Meghan had hoped.

Ma talked about running a house, and gave advice so unselfishly that Meghan was in love with the woman before she was done talking.

She realized there had been gently asked questions about her parents and the home they'd left. Meghan even heard herself admit she'd sneaked her brothers along and Si had taken them in just as surely as the Bible commanded.

Ma got very quiet as she heard of Meghan's scheming. Then Meghan didn't spare herself in the telling and she did her level best to talk about how generous Si had been to them all. And she told more details about Lock's fall and the wolf pack.

A hewing ax and clatter on the added rooms drew Ma's attention. "They must be working on the addition. My Silas is a fine builder and your Si is near his equal. The room that you added is well done but you maybe should have added three. Babes will come soon, that's the way of married life and you'll have trouble shoving all three of those boys in the same room. Liam is old enough to want a bit of space away from his brothers. I wonder if, by next spring Liam won't be wanting land of his own and a cabin on that land."

Ma laid aside her sewing and patted Meghan's hand. "Let's start dinner. The men will be in soon. Then this afternoon the two of us will help them. You are new to frontier life. It'll be fun to teach you all the tricks I know."

From Ma's smile, Meghan could only guess that teaching was one of Belle Harden's favorite things.

Si pushed back his chair after the evening meal and cleared his throat, strange to have his parents here at the table. He'd even made two more chairs today with Pa's help.

"Meg and I usually go for a walk after dinner. We are getting to know each other more every day and we . . . well . . . I didn't ask Meg so I hope it would be all right for us to continue that."

"After the dishes are done, Si." Meg pinked up a little.

He remembered the talk they'd had last night, before all the shouting started. He wanted to get his wife alone before she forgot any of it. And by that blush he thought she might be remembering it very well.

Meg reached for her plate.

"Now don't bother with the dishes, Meg." Ma stopped her with firm hands. "Let Silas and me work on them. The boys can help."

Si braced himself for the whining, but Ma's

hazel eyes skipped across each boy's face and not a one of them protested. Ma had that effect on people.

"You two head on out for your walk." Pa said with a smile. Well, it was more of a smirk.

Liam's eyes narrowed but he kept quiet.

Lock said, "I don't want to go to bed." No one had mentioned that but Lock could see the sun setting as well as any of them. He knew what came after they washed dishes.

Shay rolled his eyes as if his little brother was a pure nuisance, as if Shay hadn't been fighting for Lock's life last night right along with the rest of them.

"We'll talk about bedtime later, son." Pa rose and rested a hand on Lock's back.

"Yes, Pa." Lock responded to Pa's gentle touch and the word 'son' as if he was watching a miracle before his very eyes.

"We're done with the rooms, even got them divided. You and Shay and Liam can have one to share. Ma and I will have the next, and Si and Meg the third. Tomorrow I think we'll add on one more on the far side of the house. You'll be able to spread out."

Swallowing hard to stay silent, Si realized he should have told Pa more about how things were between him and Meg. But it didn't matter, he'd sleep on the floor in the main room like always. Pa might figure that out come morning but that didn't bother Si. Not much.

Then he looked at Meg, who had a gentle pink blush on her freckled cheeks.

He reached for her and helped her to her feet before any more could be said on the subject of sleeping arrangements.

They walked a few paces because Si didn't put it past those boys to eavesdrop. Ma might do it, too.

"Your parents are fine folks, Si. It's glad I am to have them come visit. Your da is a fine a builder. I can see where you learned such skills. And your ma taught me more in one afternoon than I've learned in my whole life, and she did it while making me feel like I was as smart as a whip, not an unskilled city woman. I love her."

"It's hard not to love Ma, unless you run afoul of her, then, well, it's best to just hightail it — head back east and never come back. But she mostly saves that for outlaws so I wasn't a bit worried she wouldn't take to you and your brothers."

Si took her hand and they walked on, enjoying the gentle breeze of summer. The house was growing. There were more beds to build and chests to hold clothing, a few things of that sort. But Ma and Pa were planning to stay a few days so Si knew it'd all be done, and be done right.

"I wish I could show you off to the rest of my family, Meg. I've got four big sisters, all married. The oldest, Lindsay, has a daughter close in age to Liam and a bunch younger. My big brother Tanner is married now and the family just keeps growing. There's a new baby every time we turn around it seems."

"We've been busy getting to know each other and settle in here." Meg sounded uneasy.

Si smiled at her. "It's a crowd and I don't blame you for worrying about such a big family all descending on us. But I think — that is . . ." Si cleared his throat for too long before he went on. "I think we should talk about Pa saying we need to share a room."

His hand tightened on hers and thought of the way Pa had pointed to a room on the far side of the house. Suddenly he knew that Pa intended that room, with a fireplace, for Si and Meg. A bit of space between them and the boys.

"I don't want you to feel rushed into that. I'll sleep out by the kitchen fireplace just as I have in the past. I'll find a chance tomorrow to explain to Pa that we're waiting to know each other better before we — we, uh, before well, we take another step into being married."

They were out of sight of the house now. Meg tugged on his hand and stopped, turning to face him. "You'll not shame me by sleeping on the floor in another room, Si. No, you're wrong about us not knowing each other well enough. It's been coming along as we've walked and talked this week but after last night, after you saved my brother and stood strong in the face of those attacking wolves —" Her voice broke and her chin dropped to her chest.

Si gently lifted it until she was looking up at him in the moonlight, her eyes sparkling with unshed tears. He couldn't resist bending down to kiss each eye and taste the salt of her kind-heartedness.

"And then you saved me right back, Meg. All of you up there on the cliff, thinking of ways to save me faster than I could think of them myself." That stretched a wide smile across his face and he added, "I'd say that makes us a good team, huh?"

Meg nodded, then out of the blue, she flung her arms around his waist and burrowed so tight to his chest that all he could do was hug her back, long and tight.

Against his shirt she said, "Si, I've fallen in love with you."

"Be–because you love my ma?" He wasn't sure if that suited him exactly.

"No, yes. Both. I almost told you last night before we ended up fighting off a pack of wolves. By the time we'd gotten everyone to safety, a warm glimmer of love had turned into a burning fire. Your parents today being so kind only fanned the flames."

She shifted her arms, wrapped them around his neck and pulled him down for another kiss, a deeper more passionate kiss. A kiss full of love.

Si didn't have the freedom to speak for long moments. He had feared he was doomed to live out his life with a hard working wife he couldn't trust. Now that fear melted away at her precious, sincere words.

Finally the kiss ended and he said, "Meg, I've fallen in love with you, too. I humbly thank you for giving me your heart, the most precious thing a woman has, I offer mine in return."

He bent low and gave her a kiss. He felt her love sent back to match. The kiss deepened and Si knew without a doubt that he didn't want to spend the night in a room with his parents only steps away. And he didn't want to wait for one single more moment to have his wife in private. It occurred to him that they were alone together right now.

He swung her up in his arms and she squeaked. "What are you about?"

She looked down at the ground as if she were afraid there were flood waters rising.

"I've got a strong yearning to spent time alone with you without my parents near to hand and any little brothers pestering me. Will you let me be with you as a man should be with the wife he loves, Meg?"

The kiss they shared said more than words, but when it ended, she gave him those words, too. He carried her to the barn and it's stalls of clean, fresh straw.

And he and Meghan made their marriage real in beauty and in truth.

■ ■ ■ ■

HOMESTEAD
ON THE RANGE

■ ■ ■ ■

Chapter 1

Lone Tree, Nebraska
1875

"Do you want a needle and a spool of thread, Mr. Samuelson?"

Elle glanced up at the question, asked to a man. Mere curiosity because needles and thread usually were sold to women.

She saw a man with eyes as wide as a scared horse. She could swear she saw white all the way around the blue center. Biting back a smile, she felt an urge to go help him. Or at least she could advise him to find his wife and let her take over such business.

Being neighborly, she walked to his side. The Lone Tree General Store was bustling on a Saturday morning, and a line had formed to buy supplies while Myrtle talked to Mr. Samuelson.

"Good morning, Myrtle." Elle had known Myrtle Garvey for years. The older woman helped her husband run the only general store in the small northeast Nebraska frontier town.

"Mornin', Elle." Myrtle's eyes sparked with her good nature, but it was a busy morning for her and Elle could tell the woman was fretting about Mr. Samuelson's questions. "Have you met Colin Samuelson? He just claimed a homestead out by yours. Wouldn't be surprised if you shared a property line."

Colin turned to Elle, as if looking away from the spool of black thread in Myrtle's hand was a pardon from a hanging.

"Welcome to Lone Tree, Mr. Samuelson." Elle nodded. "Myrtle, if you need to see to your customers, I can help with the thread selection."

"Mr. Samuelson, this is Eleanor Winter. She is just the one to help you." Myrtle set the notions down quickly and hurried to her front counter as if afraid Elle would change her mind.

Myrtle wove through her store, packed with shelves and barrels and people, leaving Elle to deal with the clearly overwhelmed Mr. Samuelson.

"I'd appreciate the help, Miss Winter." He doffed his wide-brimmed hat and smiled at her, the nicest smile. He seemed to really look at her in a way no man had in years. "I have fabric on my list, but it appears that there is more to a shirt than just fabric."

He had overly long dark curls under that

hat. The shirt he was wearing now was so threadbare it would shred in a high wind.

"It's Mrs. Winter. I assure you, I'm no Miss." Though many people thought it. She was short and slight. Her cheeks were quite round and her hair thin and blond and flyaway. She'd always looked younger than her age. She kept waiting to get old enough to count youthful looks as a blessing.

"I apologize, Mrs. Winter."

"That's fine. You do need these things, unless your wife didn't ask you to buy thread and needles and buttons because she already has them."

"I'm not married, and I just moved in with only the barest of supplies."

Elle hated to ask, but the condition of his shirt and his lack of knowledge about sewing forced her to. "Have you ever made a shirt before?"

Sadness seemed to dim the light in his vivid blue eyes. "Nope, my wife used to handle that for me. I'm afraid I'm near to useless."

"You're a widower?" Elle immediately felt such empathy for him. She reached out and rested her fingertips on his wrist. She felt the solid muscles flex under his poor shirt.

His eyes went to where she touched him as if a magnet had drawn them. She pulled away quickly, shocked at her boldness.

She cleared her throat then cleared it again and went on. "I'm a widow, and I remember well how much I had to learn when my husband died."

Five years now and the grief had faded until thinking of Jerome brought happy memories rather than tearing grief.

"Do you really have time to help me?" His smile was so genuine and so eager that it warmed something in Elle that had been cold for years. Exactly five years.

"I'm in no hurry." She was enjoying this visit immensely.

CHAPTER 2

Colin reached into the pocket of his pants — of course there was a hole big enough he could reach all the way through and scratch his thigh. Here he was talking with the prettiest woman he'd seen in an age, the first one he'd even noticed since Priscilla died. Her bright blue eyes matched her crisp blue-and-white gingham dress, while his clothing was nearly in rags. These were his good pants, too, and they were nearly worn through at the knees. He needed all new clothes, and he had no idea how he would get them.

He produced a piece of paper that unfolded, then unfolded again, and again. "My list. And there are more things on it I don't quite understand."

Elle covered her mouth, but a chuckle still escaped. The spark in those light blue eyes drew him. Shocking, when his thoughts had been for no one but Priscilla even with her gone now for a solid year. It felt like a betrayal of his love to notice how pretty Elle Winter was, but notice he did.

Colin shrugged one shoulder sheepishly. "Well, you did ask."

Elle let the laugh escape. Colin laughed, too, and the moment stretched. It was surprisingly pleasant.

"I'd be glad to help. Let me see your list."

She'd said yes. They spent the next half hour stacking things on the counter, off to the side, so they didn't interfere with the lady running the store. Neither of them talked much about themselves, just the list. He was busy worrying what to buy, and she was busy teasing him.

And they were both busy laughing.

Colin had done little laughing in the last year.

It turned out his land did abut hers.

"You should build right along the property line on the west side of your homestead. I'm right up against my own line on the east. My husband built there because there's an artesian well that has cold water pouring out year-round; even in winter it keeps running. It bubbles up right on the border of our land. You have as much right to that water as I do, and you wouldn't have to dig a well. It would be nice to have a close neighbor."

Colin's shoulders lifted. "I was worried about water. I've never dug a well before. I drove out to my land, picked a likely spot with no idea what I was doing, unloaded my

278

wagon and took off the canvas, then came straight to town for supplies. Yes, having a well already there sounds wonderful." He had a lot in front of him to settle a homestead. Most of what lay ahead of him came as a shock. "I'd just planned to hire someone to build a house and dig a well."

"Most folks are mighty busy trying to work their own homesteads. Chances are you can find help with your soddy, but you'll have to work hard alongside whoever steps in."

"A soddy?" Colin had just taken off from St. Louis, so tired of his home and the painful memories. He'd heard he could homestead, which would be so different from his city life there should be nothing to remind him of Priscilla. He'd made the decision in a rush and was just learning what it meant to "stake a claim" to land on Nebraska's vast prairie.

"Well, yes. That's the only building material, unless you ship in the wood for a board house, but that takes months."

"Shipped in?" Colin felt the shock of that to his toes. "It takes months? Why is that?"

"Well, there aren't trees anywhere around. We call this town Lone Tree for a reason." She gestured out the front window to the massive cottonwood that stood just outside of town. "The closest trees are along the Missouri River, straight east nearly twenty miles away, and even those we do have are heavily picked over, leaving only sparse and spindly trees. They don't make good log cabins. So the boards have to be shipped in to the nearest railhead then loaded into a wagon and hauled out here. You'll need to build a sod house to get you through the spring and summer. There is a bit of lumber to be had in town, enough to frame the house, but not enough for walls."

Colin ran one hand into his hair and knocked his hat off.

Elle caught it.

"I don't know how to build a sod house."

"I have a sod-busting plow you can borrow." Surely she'd just said that to torment him.

"I'm a doctor. I wanted property of my own. But I've never built a house. I'd planned to hire it done."

"A doctor? Lone Tree needs one desperately. And I think I can name a man or two who would be willing to help you."

She gave directions to the well and said a bit about his property lines, while Myrtle sent a hired boy out with box after box of supplies to his team standing in their traces out front.

Looking at the team reminded him he was taking too long with this. It had just been so nice to talk to a pretty woman. As much as she'd thrown a few surprises his way, he didn't want it to end. But it had to.

Or did it?

"I've had a wonderful time, Mrs. Winter. Uh . . ." His eyes locked on hers, his smile faded, and he was sorely afraid his face was heating up with a blush. Well, it was the plain truth he had no experience talking to women.

He forced out the words he had in mind. "Would you be interested in taking a . . . a . . . a . . ." He swallowed hard. "That is going on a . . . a . . . a, well, um . . . a drive with me sometime?"

Elle's eyes widened, and since Colin was looking right at her, quite intently, he noticed.

"I think that would be lovely, Mr. Samuelson."

"Call me Colin, please." He decided to get moving before she changed her mind. Then he noticed she had his hat. He reached for it and she handed it over, rather unsteadily. He finally managed to be the one surprising her.

"All right, Colin. And I'm Elle." She gestured toward the door. "I'm running late myself."

Walking with her, he reached past and opened the door. "I'll be a few days getting settled. How about Sunday, after services? Maybe I can see your home, Elle."

Nodding, Elle stepped out on the board-walk. "I'd like that. Thank you, Colin."

They turned and faced each other, and the world seemed to fade away. Colin didn't hear if horses or wagons passed. If anyone walked by them, he didn't notice. Only Elle was real.

"Ma! You're late!"

CHAPTER 3

Turning, she saw her four children running up, along with quite a few other young'uns she'd never seen before.

"I'm sorry." Honestly, what she was sorry for was the interruption, but she'd been a mother for a long time. She was used to it.

She noticed her son, Tim, whispering to a girl who seemed close to his age. The pair seemed awfully friendly for just having met.

Hers swarmed around her, and the three others yelled, "Pa."

As they ran up to Colin.

"Yours?"

Colin was staring at her children. "You have four children?" He sounded strange.

"Yes, and yours? I guess we didn't get that much talking done. You've got three?"

"Seven children," Colin said, sounding a bit faint. His eyes were wide open, and they jumped from child to child.

Tim, fifteen, taller than she was. Her only boy and the image of Jerome, with his shining brown curls that peeked out around the edges of his broad-brimmed hat. Mercifully he had none of Jerome's dark moods.

Martha, twelve, looked more like Elle every day and was nearing her in height. Petite and fair haired. The twins, Barbara and Betty, were identical and very small for six and a match for Martha and Elle. They'd been one year old when Jerome had died, and just surviving had been a struggle with two infants and all the work of running her homestead.

Elle quickly introduced them to Colin.

"We met at the church school party, Ma." Tim gave a raven-haired girl a long look. "We were coming to look for you. We found out we're living next door to each other."

The brunette, Sarah, had a full woman's height and was probably an inch taller than Elle. The girl had beautiful, bright green eyes and a wide smile, a complexion burned from the sun, and a few coiling ringlets that had escaped from a bun. "My name is Sarah, Mrs. Winters. Tim, this is my pa, Dr. Samuelson."

Sarah gave her father a bright smile, which he didn't notice because Colin was still looking from child to child to child.

Her son, Tim, was skinny, and he hadn't gotten his growing on yet, but he was a serious boy whose hard work at Elle's side had gotten her through the last five years. He extended a hand as if he were an adult.

"Nice to meet you, Doc Samuelson." Colin managed to shake, but there was something wrong with him.

Elle wasn't sure what, but there was a dazed expression, and his eyes were so wide, she could see white all around them. Like a frightened horse — much as he'd looked when she'd first noticed him.

Well, they could talk more after services on Sunday.

Sarah quickly introduced her two little brothers, who hadn't stood still for a second. Russell with chocolate-brown hair, who resembled Colin, and Frank as dark haired as Sarah.

"We need to be going, Mr. Samuelson." She realized she'd started calling him Colin in the store, but now, somehow, with the children at hand, that seemed overly familiar. "We will see you at services on Sunday and maybe before that if we're neighbors. In fact, if you'd like help settling in, come by our place. And I strongly hope you build close to us. It would be good to have neighbors."

She shooed her children into the wagon. Tim climbed up and took the reins.

Colin's children ran to climb into their wagon.

"Well, good-bye then."

Colin's hand whipped out and caught her wrist. He leaned very close to her and whispered, "About that ride."

He faltered, cleared his throat, and went on. "I won't be coming."

"What?" Elle probably had that frightened horse expression now.

"Elle, I really thought we got along well in that store but . . . but seven children between us?" Colin shook his head, tiny frantic moves surely hoping the children wouldn't notice. "That is just out of the question. I can't even take care of the ones I have."

He smiled weakly. "I'm sorry. Good-bye, Elle."

Elle's mouth gaped open, and she stood, shocked, as he turned and nearly threw himself up onto his high seat. All three of his children were there, Sarah holding the littlest boy, Frank, on her lap; Russell squashed between Colin and Sarah on a seat clearly built for two. But the back end was so full of supplies they had to fit.

It dawned on Elle that he'd bought so much because he had three children to feed and clothe.

He shook the reins and yelled at his horses to move with far too much enthusiasm. They took off. His children waved, and hers waved back. Stunned as she was, Elle managed to raise one hand.

Colin never looked back.

Finally, with his horses picking up speed with every step, Elle came out of her shock enough to be annoyed. Her children were too much for him, then? He liked her, but he didn't like her children, whom he'd only met for about two minutes? Annoyance grew into anger as she marched to her wagon and climbed up beside Tim.

Her son gave her such a sunny smile she forced herself to ignore her anger. "I liked the Samuelson family, Ma. I'm hoping we can all be good friends."

"They seemed nice." Elle managed a smile and said no more because it served no purpose to let her children know Colin Samuelson had been horrified by their very existence. How could she say, "Don't you dare be friends with them. At least not if their skunk of a father is anywhere around"?

Besides, she thought as she calmed a bit, seven children. Though she controlled it outwardly, inside she shook to think of all those children. That was an incredible number of children, and half grown . . . that seemed like more than if they'd come one at a time and started as tiny babies.

Of course Tim acted like most growing boys and was always starving, but add two more boys? And did Sarah give Tim a flirtatious look? How could brother and sister also have romantic notions about each other?

It was still annoying to have her children make a man run for the hills, but good heavens. She pictured her house and his lack of a house. Seven children! He was right. It was just as well not to start something that had no chance to go on.

That didn't stop her from wanting to kick Colin Samuelson in the backside.

CHAPTER 4

"Ma, we've got to go, fast." Tim came in with an unusually frantic look on his face.

"What's wrong?" Elle straightened away from the bread she was kneading.

"It's the Samuelsons, they need help."

"We just saw them at church yesterday." Tim and Sarah had talked, the rest of the children had played together. Elle hadn't gone near Colin, and he certainly hadn't come near her.

"I just saw Sarah. We've got to go, hurry."

"You saw Sarah? You mean you rode over there? Just now? I thought you were doing chores." As she said it, she realized the morning had been getting on. Tim had brought in milk and eggs, and he'd gone back out at least two hours ago. Her son was so mature and dependable she hadn't thought to notice his long absence and question what he was doing.

"Yes, and we have to stop him."

"Stop him from what?" Stop him from

moving away was her first thought. Moving away so he never had to be near Elle and all her children again.

"He's going to build his house right in a waterway. He's turning up the dirt for a foundation right now. Floodwater will run right through his house, but all he sees is a smooth place. Easy to build on. You know that old Logan Creek bottom."

"Why didn't you just tell him not to build there?"

Tim rolled his eyes. "I tried, but he hired two men from town." Tim named the two biggest layabouts in Lone Tree. "And they told the doctor to pay me no mind. He took their word over mine. But he'll listen to you. We've got to go fast because if he gets any further along in building, he'll decide moving the house is more trouble than it's worth."

"And it could flood and do them harm and destroy their supplies." Elle grabbed a towel and started wiping her hands, yanked her white bibbed apron off over her head, and tossed it over a chair. She had a dark yellow housedress on and her hair was in an unkempt knot on her head, but she wasn't going to take time to change when time was of the essence.

"Yes, and there hasn't been any flooding for a couple of years, so some grass has grown and it doesn't look like a bad spot. And the creek is close by and so deep and the water so low, I can see why he doesn't believe me that it could ever jump its banks."

"Why is he even building over there? I thought he was going to build close over here and use the artesian well." But Elle knew exactly why the moment she asked the question. To avoid her and, more so, her children.

"I wondered that, too." Tim gave her a strange look, like he was wondering how she'd managed to scare Colin to the far side of his claim.

"Hitch up the wagon. I'll get the girls."

Tim jerked his chin in satisfaction. In fact, he seemed more than satisfied, he seemed delighted. It wasn't the first time that Elle had wondered if he was sweet on Sarah. They were too young of course, but they were at the age when youngsters had thoughts of the future. And Elle had known Jerome from childhood, and they'd already planned a future together, in their childish way, by this age.

She abandoned her bread. The girls abandoned their cleaning. Tim abandoned his chores. All to save a man horrified by her children.

Colin Samuelson was a trial.

CHAPTER 5

"I've got the team hitched up, Lou, now how do I cut bricks of sod?" Colin was exhausted from the morning's work. Lou and Dutch had come out as planned, with sturdy timbers for a house frame. Then Colin, mostly by himself, had cut a trench in the dirt as a foundation, and his hired men helped seat the heaviest logs, then they'd settled in to give orders.

It had been hard, heavy work. Russell and Frank had pitched in with good spirits. Were long hours of hard labor the answer to controlling his overactive sons?

Of course Sarah was so grown up, Colin trusted her with everything. He worried sometimes his sweet girl was being forced to grow up too fast, but he couldn't figure out how to ask less of her, because he couldn't manage without her.

Colin had no idea in the world how to build a sod house, which put him completely at the mercy of these two men, and he wasn't a bit impressed with either of them.

They'd seemed decent and eager for work when he'd met them after church yesterday. Someone had mentioned them and told Colin where to look; neither man had been to services. The only two men in town who had time to hire out for work.

Colin now wondered if the reason they were available was because they were lazy slugs and none too bright.

Dutch, short and stout, probably just about Colin's age, rose from where he sat on the ground and ambled over. To point.

Colin listened with near desperate concentration as he held the two tall, curved handles of the plow the two men had brought with them. A sod-busting plow. Elle had mentioned having such a thing and being willing to share.

These two were charging Colin to rent it.

When Colin found his mind wandering to that pretty neighbor of his, he shook his head and focused hard on what Dutch was saying.

He had to hold on to the plow handles and slap the horses with the reins to make them go.

His horses were blooded stock and had never been hitched to a plow before. They kept looking behind them nervously. And the plow wasn't sunk into the ground. Did it just go down when the horses started moving forward? And how did he hold the plow with two hands and slap the horses on the back at the same time?

"Dutch, I —"

"It's just something you have to practice at, Dr. Samuelson, like any other skill, I reckon. You'll get onto it. Me 'n' Lou left some supplies we'll need in town. There wasn't room to bring them along with the plow and timbers. Can we have our pay for today now? We'll eat lunch in town."

"My daughter is making lunch, and I'm sure any supplies will wait until tomorrow. Surely I'll be all day cutting sod." All day? Try all year!

"Nope, we need them now, and it takes both of us. We'd prefer to eat at the diner in town."

Dutch held out his hand and waited. Colin knew with a sinking stomach that if he paid this man anything, he'd never be back, at least not until the money was gone. And while he might not be knowledgeable in the building of sod houses, he was far from a fool.

He released the heavy plow and reached into his pocket for two bits. He'd offered them two bits each for a day's work, which was a good wage for a hired man. He thrust the coin at Dutch.

"Here's for half a day for the two of you. I'll pay you for the afternoon's work at day's end."

Dutch hesitated. Something unpleasant,

even dangerous crossed the man's face. Colin braced himself in case the man swung a fist. It was one thing to hire a man who didn't work hard — it was another to have someone violent around the place.

Colin waited, praying nothing ugly would happen in front of the children. He didn't fool himself that in a fight with these two he'd escape unscathed.

With a grunt of disgust, Dutch reached out and snatched the coin and stormed off toward his horse. Lou caught up to him, the fastest he'd moved all morning.

As the men swung up on horseback, Colin called out, trying to sound casual, "I think I can handle this now. I won't be needing you anymore after this morning. Thanks for coming out."

Dutch threw a furious look over his shoulder but then faced forward, and the two rode off.

Most likely they weren't willing to protest being dismissed from a job they had no plans to return to anyway, but it was clear they'd hoped to ride off with two bits apiece.

They might have even come back to get it. Colin was glad now they wouldn't.

He turned to grab the plow again. He saw the heavy blade of the plowshare and the sod before him. The harnesses seemed twisted at several points, but Dutch had said they were okay. This couldn't be that hard.

"Sarah, you keep the boys back while I cut a row of sod." He asked too much of his daughter.

She caught the boys' hands, and they jumped and hollered, playing and laughing.

Smiling at his children, Colin turned back to the plow. Might as well get on with it. He let go of one handle and lifted the leathers to slap the horses.

A gunshot blasted at a distance, and he whirled around, afraid Dutch and Lou had returned to rob him.

Elle lowered the rifle she'd just fired into the air as soon as Colin turned to look.

After his first jump of surprise, he relaxed and dropped the reins he'd been about to slap on his horses' backs.

"We stopped him in time." Elle heaved a sigh of relief to Tim. "You got us here fast. Good driving. Thank God I had the rifle."

"You always carry it, Ma. It'd only be worth mentioning if you didn't."

Her son wasn't a big talker. Being surrounded by women seemed to have developed the most manly possible side of him.

Barbara and Betty both poked their heads between Elle and Tim.

"Why'd you shoot, Mama?" Barbara did most of the talking for the two of them. "It was loud."

Elle smiled down at her girls. "I wanted Mr.

Samuelson's attention, that's why."

Betty gave her an impish smile. "Okay."

Martha, from where she sat calmly in the back, said, "At least you weren't trying to kill him."

Her oldest daughter was always a bit sarcastic and used to caring for her little sisters. She was a child who was handy in a crisis, though Elle tried to avoid ever having a crisis by planning ahead.

Which only led to a crisis two or three times a week.

Brushing the flyaway white hair back on Barbara's forehead, Elle said, "Sit back, girls. We're almost there."

Colin came and helped Elle down from the high buckboard. He caught her around the waist as she jumped. It was a novelty not climbing down by herself. Tim was lifting the twins out of the back, and Martha had hopped out all by herself. The children ran straight for Colin's children, and the chattering and giggling began. It gave Elle a moment of privacy with Colin in the bevy of children.

"Why did you shoot the gun?" Colin's hands were solid and strong, and he didn't remove them from her waist with any great hurry.

"I — I — uh, well, you were about to whip your horses, and I had to stop you."

He let go with what looked like reluctance.

A furrow appeared on his smooth brow. "Why? I'm cutting sod to build a house."

Elle turned to the team and almost shuddered to think what would have happened if she'd been even a minute later.

"Tim, help me get these horses out of the harness."

Colin caught Elle's arm but with no force, his hands were very gentle. She could well imagine him having healing skills. "But why? We're all ready to go."

Closing her eyes for a second, Elle remembered how Jerome had acted if she'd ever corrected him. He wasn't nice about it. In fact, he could be rude and surly, sometimes for hours after she'd tried to tell him something was wrong. It had gotten to the point she'd just stopped talking to him in those instances, even though she'd always lived out in the country and Jerome had grown up in town.

But his irritation at being corrected, even when he was blatantly wrong, made it more trouble than just letting him learn from his own mistakes. Elle remembered now clearly why she'd done absolutely nothing to encourage a man since Jerome died. She'd found marriage to be a trying business.

Bracing herself for Colin to take offense, Elle knew she had no choice. She'd have even spoken up to Jerome. "The plow is sure to tip if the horses move it even an inch. And that sod-busting plow is heavy enough to pull the horses along with it when it falls. It could cut them, hock them even. You could hurt them enough they'd have to be put down."

Colin looked at his horses in shock. "Put down?" Colin rushed to their sides and began frantically unhitching them.

Relieved, Elle went to the far side to help. She could have showed him how to do it right, but what she had to do was convince him to move. Another chance of unleashing his temper.

Once the horses were led a safe distance from the plow, Elle had a chance to look at the camp the Samuelsons had set up, and shuddered.

It was chaos.

Clothing and food and household supplies were all scattered everywhere. A fire that was far too big to cook over smoldered, and it had to be hours after breakfast.

A big tarp — most likely it was the canvas they'd used for their covered wagon — draped over another mountain of . . . something.

Elle turned to watch Colin tie his team of beautiful brown Belgians to a tree in such a way that they couldn't graze. Did he not know they should be staked out differently? Or was he planning to get right back to work? Either was bad.

He dragged a broad-brimmed Stetson off his head and came up to her. "I hired two men to help me. They let me hitch the team up that way."

"I heard." Elle flinched. "That's why we hurried. Dutch and Lou are known men in Lone Tree. They aren't men you want around your children. They sneak a bit of liquor all day long, and they have foul mouths. And they aren't hard workers." Elle looked around. "Where are they?"

Quickly, Colin told her what happened. The children weren't paying attention; in fact, they'd all vanished over the creek bank. Her last glimpse of them was of Sarah and Tim talking rapidly. Yes, her quiet son was talking, and Elle was struck that the two youngsters didn't look like children. Tim was still lean, like any kid, and he had some height yet to gain, but he wasn't a child any longer. And Sarah, well, a girl of fourteen was full grown, and she had a woman's curves.

They probably needed to be carefully chaperoned, but then they were walking with five other children, better than a chaperone any day.

Tearing her eyes away from the shocking realization that her son was becoming a man, Elle turned to the other man she had to worry about. She cleared her throat. There was no way to say what needed saying except just plain speaking.

Quietly, so the children couldn't overhear, she said, "I understand that when you decided we shouldn't go riding together it was because of all our children. Honestly, I understand that. But there's no reason we have to avoid each other like we did yesterday at church."

Colin was tanned and strong and probably very intelligent, being a doctor and all. She was surprised when a flush darkened his cheeks. He rubbed the back of his neck.

"I'm sorry about that. Yes, I acted like a fool yesterday."

"And that's why you're getting ready to build a house all the way over on this side of the property, to stay away from me." She wasn't asking a question, she knew the truth.

"There's water here and a smooth place to build."

"It's smooth because you're building on a flood plain."

Colin jerked around and stared at the digging they'd done. "That's why it's so perfectly level?"

Elle nodded.

"But the creek is deep. Are you saying it can rain enough to jump its banks?"

He hadn't started growling yet, and she knew from the flush that she'd upset him. That was usually when Jerome got grouchy.

"Yes, it not only can, it does, almost every spring and often a time or two during the summer and fall. Your sod cabin would have been washed away before you'd been here a year. And the creek water is muddy most of the year. It would be fine if you had no choice, but you do have a choice, Colin — my artesian well. Come and build closer to me." Elle managed a small smile. "Seven children is overwhelming and no sod house could hold them, and my house certainly couldn't. I haven't set my cap for you, but I do think we . . . we could be friends, don't you?"

Shifting his eyes back to Elle, Colin stared for a few seconds too long. His blue gaze was intense. Elle had to force herself to remember she was proposing a friendship and absolutely nothing more.

"That really could have ended in me having to shoot my horses?" Colin shuddered.

"I know how to hitch up a sod-busting plow, Colin. Tim does, too." Elle didn't tell him Martha was also fully capable. And the twins couldn't do it alone, but they'd be a big help if asked. She thought that might be a bit too much for Colin to handle. "We would be glad to help you. This is even a mile farther from town. You're adding quite a bit to your drive to Lone Tree just to avoid me."

That jolted a smile out of him. "I'm sorry about that, Elle." Colin gave her another one of those deep looks. "It hasn't been that long since Priscilla died. It's just that no woman has so much as gotten my attention, not in the way you did. But I just can't imagine taking on seven children. I'm sorry, they seem like wonderful young'uns, but —"

Unable to stand hearing it, Elle reached up and touched Colin's mouth to stop the words. When she touched his lips, the heat of them made her draw back fast. "Let's not talk of it. We agree that we aren't a match for each other. As long as we remember that, we can be friends and neighbors. You can even leave the children home alone when you do your doctoring, knowing I can help if need be."

"I'm not leaving them home alone." Colin's expression darkened for the first time. She'd finally offended him. "Sarah does a good job."

If she wasn't mistaken, she saw a flash of worry. "You ask a lot of Sarah. I do the same with Tim. I'm sure she is perfectly able to watch the children. It's not a criticism, just an offer of help."

A shout from the depths of the creek drew both their attention. Then laughter followed, so Elle didn't go check.

"The truth is, I ask too much of her." Colin looked at the creek bank, treeless of course. "She's a good cook, and she chases after Russ and Frank all day, does the laundry and mending, though she's never done much of that. We lived in St. Louis, and I could hire someone for that. But we need new clothes, and she's told me to let her figure it out. She's such a good girl, and I depend on her.

Priscilla took her parents' deaths hard, and in her grief she took sick and didn't have the will to fight it off, I suppose. Sarah was already taking care of us a year ago."

"Jerome's been gone five years. Tim was nine when he died, and he had to grow up fast. All my children did, though maybe the twins less so because Martha did so much caring for them they might be confused who their mother is."

A smile slipped across Colin's face. "She'd have been what, eight?"

"Seven, actually."

"Mercy, I can't imagine how you got by. And seven years old? That's a mighty young mother."

"Well, I helped some." Elle smiled back. "We managed to stay alive, that was about it."

Their eyes met again, and Elle felt as if she were looking deep inside him. His pain was there, his worry, his kindness.

Silence stretched between them. A breeze hushed around them and the prairie grass bent and swayed, dancing as if God drew His fingers across it.

The day was warm. Early June was about the best time of the year out here. She was glad Colin was seeing Nebraska at its most beautiful.

Another shout from the creek broke the connection.

"So, do you mind moving closer to me, Colin?"

He took a step, erasing the space between them. A thrill of pleasure rushed through her before she laughed.

"No, I mean moving your house site closer to mine."

This time Colin laughed. They'd laughed together in the store.

"We'll be friends, Elle. Just friends. I'm barely surviving now with three children to care for and spend time with. I can't add anything to that."

Nodding, Elle ignored the pinch of disappointment. "That's fine. Let's get your supplies loaded and your team hitched. It looks like it will take at least a couple of trips, but it isn't far."

Colin turned to the creek and raised his voice. "Sarah, Russ, all of you kids, come up here. We need help."

The shouting fell silent, and Colin added, "We're moving across the claim to live nearer to the Winters."

A shout of joy tore loose from the depths of the creek, followed by laughter and pounding footsteps. The children rushed over the lip of the bank and began loading.

CHAPTER 6

Colin clutched his lower back as he straightened from setting down his last crate of supplies. They'd loaded and unloaded the wagon twice. He was within fifty feet of Elle's home, a pretty white clapboard building that made him almost sinfully envious. Her home would have fit inside his St. Louis house twice over, but they weren't in St. Louis, were they?

Elle buzzed around the campsite making orderly piles of his supplies. She wore a dress as yellow as goldenrod, and her smile gleamed nearly as bright as sunlight. She lifted and arranged and sorted, bending and reaching until she danced like the flowers waving amid the prairie grass. And everything she did was with a riveting feminine grace.

He really needed to get over being riveted.

It had been a poor excuse for an idea to move over here. She was too pretty and sweet. The pull he felt toward her was so strong it shocked him. And marrying her was out of the question. As a friend, though, he thought they could deal well with each other. He hoped, because he had no intention of marrying again, and that made the ideas that rippled through his head lacking in honor.

Even with the Winters's help, Colin and his family were looking at a long stretch sleeping outdoors. Just as they'd slept outdoors while the wagon train had made its way here. So far the children seemed to take it in stride. Colin, on the other hand, was heartily sick of sleeping on the ground.

All the children had worked with a good spirit, even his rambunctious boys seemed to tag after Tim and imitate his hard work. Elle had taken charge and done a good job of marshalling their youthful forces.

Once the wagon was empty, Elle got busy organizing. Tim hooked up the plow and started cutting the prairie sod. Sarah had talked quietly with Elle, then she'd taken all the children into the Winters's house to get an evening meal.

He could already imagine his home taking shape. Water burbled out of the artesian well, and the wind seemed a bit broken by a swell of land to the north.

Elle's property was a prime example of what could be made of this endless grassland with years of hard work. She had a few hundred sturdy little trees growing as straight as soldiers standing at attention, their leaves fluttering in the breeze. One row was of shorter trees, and he wondered if they were apple. It would make a fine windbreak . . . in about thirty years.

She had a barn, and a door sloping up out of the ground looked like a root cellar. A well-tilled garden stretched between the house and the cellar door. There were long lines of barbed wire stretching to the east, and a herd of cattle grazed placidly while calves frolicked in the tall grass.

She'd returned her team to a second corral with three more horses in it, including a foal so young it must have been born this spring. Chickens pecked and scratched in the shorter grass in a small pen behind her house. Beyond that were tidy rows of corn. Each plant was about a foot tall, and they stood in neat, precise rows, stretching away to the west. There was even a little sod house standing near the well — no doubt what they'd built when they first homesteaded. It was closed up tight, and Colin had no doubt that the ever-efficient Mrs. Winters was putting it to some extraordinarily brilliant use.

He needed to think about something other than Elle. "Where's the shovel? I can get started digging the foundation trenches."

Elle straightened from where she'd been folding a crate of clothes. She winced a bit. "You don't need trenches."

"What?" Colin thought of his blistered hands and sore back. "Dutch and Lou had

308

me spend all morning digging."

"I know. I saw. I'm sorry. I could have told you those two were worse than nothing. You could have saved yourself a lot of aching muscles, not to mention two bits if you'd unbent enough to talk to me yesterday in church."

She really was a snippy little thing. Colin appreciated that she didn't slip the word *stubborn* into her politely delivered news. Or for that matter, *stupid.*

"Your place is beautiful, Elle. You've done so much work. The house has a settled look to it. Did you build it before your husband died?"

"Yes, it had just gone up. We homesteaded right after the law was passed. We got married, moved out here. Jerome got the sod house up." Actually he'd had a lot of help, including from Elle. "And he went off to fight in the war. Tim was born five months after he left, and we were all alone in the soddy when he came."

Colin gasped. "You had your baby alone, not a doctor, or even a neighbor?"

Elle gave her head a sassy little tilt. "There were no neighbors for ten miles. Lone Tree wasn't even a settlement yet. It was winter, there was just no possible way for someone to come and help. It was frightening to be so alone, but everything was fine. And then I had a baby to care for and finally some company out here. Jerome didn't come home until Tim was two years old. Then Martha came along. We proved up on our claim and our crops started to yield, so we built the board house, then the twins were born. A year later Jerome was dead from something. We don't know what, just a terrible pain in his belly that lasted a week before he died."

"I've seen folks with an inflammation like that. It happens sometimes just out of nowhere. I'm sorry."

"It was awful at the time, so shocking. But the children kept me going and we learned to get on, and the truth is, Jerome was gone almost as much as he was here, with the war. Some days I can't quite remember what it was like when he was here."

"Priscilla has just been gone a year now. Maybe in five years it will be less of a gap in our lives." Priscilla had always been delicate. She'd gone to bed with each child on the doctor's orders, and she'd stayed in bed for months after the baby's birth. They'd had a nanny and a wet nurse for each baby, and a personal maid for Priscilla. Besides a housekeeper and a cook and a few downstairs maids. Colin had made a point of stopping in to spend time with Priscilla each night in her bedroom — they each had their own — or he'd have gone days without seeing her. He told Elle none of this. It felt disloyal to poor sweet Priscilla.

Elle saw Colin's eye look into the past. He was still in love with his wife. That was the kind of thing that only time could heal, and if he was deeply in love with his Priscilla even time might not set things right. It was as well that they hadn't taken that ride.

"Dinner!" A call from the house turned her around to see her Martha and Colin's Sarah stepping out of the house, chattering, each with a twin at their side. The boys stuck their heads out of the door then dodged between the girls and came sprinting toward their pa.

"They did that fast." Elle smiled at Colin, glad for the interruption. "Let's call it a good day's work and go eat."

Martha started clanking the triangle that hung from the porch roof. Tim stopped turning sod, unhooked the plow from the team, and came walking in behind the horses.

He hollered, "I'll let the horses have a bit of grain and a drink, but I can work another couple of hours after supper."

Elle started for the house, and Colin came behind her. "I should be doing that. He doesn't need to cut all my sod."

Smiling, Elle said, "If you were going to do it all the time I'd agree, but cutting sod is tricky and we only need to do it once to get your house built. Tim can get enough sod in a few days. We can start bringing in slabs after the evening meal. Tomorrow I'll help you get a frame up for the house. At least Dutch and Lou brought you the right supplies for that. Then we'll build while Tim cuts."

Colin nodded.

Elle hated his grief, but he didn't act hurt or offended by her taking charge. It would be foolish to when she knew what she was doing and he didn't, but that wouldn't stop most men.

They walked into the house side by side.

Chapter 7

"I think Sarah and Tim are sweet on each other," Elle whispered through the window gap they'd left in the wall of the soddy. After a week of hard work, the walls were up to the roof level.

Today they'd start the roof. Tomorrow was Sunday and they wouldn't work. But if things went well, Monday night Colin could sleep in his house.

"Sweet?" Colin's eyes went blank, as if she's spoken to him in Pawnee or something.

Nodding, Elle said, "Yes, they're always together. They whisper —"

"We're whispering and we're not sweet on each other."

There was no use responding to that. "I just thought you might have noticed."

Colin's brows slammed down. "My daughter is a child."

"No, she's not, Colin." Elle couldn't control a smile. "She's only three years younger than I was when I married Jerome — and I was already sweet on him when I was fourteen."

Elle looked left and right to make sure they were still alone. The children were carrying sod slabs, about three feet long and two wide, toward the house. Not the twins, they couldn't lift the slabs, but they tagged after the other children. Frank and Russ had to carry one together. Tim had cut enough of them to use for the roof, too. Elle didn't especially like the idea of a sod roof, it was too prone to leaking, but there were no choices. And Colin had ordered wood for a house, so this soddy would be a stable by the time winter winds blew.

"You're going to have to get used to the idea that your little girl is growing up."

A look crossed Colin's face. He seemed so stunned it made Elle's heart hurt for him. Poor guy. She was a little shocked herself, but she'd had a week to get used to the idea.

"I do not have to —"

"Ma, we're gonna need a little more wood to frame this door. You left too big a gap." Tim smiled at her.

She didn't bother to tell anyone she'd deliberately made it oversized so Colin's Belgians could get in. This soddy was going to be a stable before long.

Well, now she had to pay for that decision. "I can drive into town —"

"I'll go. And Sarah wants to ride along. We'll go straight in and back." Tim looked sideways at Sarah, and she smiled at him.

"Sarah needs to stay here." Colin's voice was gruff to the point of rudeness. "Someone's got to watch the youngsters."

Sarah's face fell at her father's tone. She quietly nodded. "That's fine, Pa. I'll stay. I guess I wanted a break from watching the little ones, and that's selfish of me. I'm sorry."

Tim threw Colin an angry look, then he turned and stormed toward Elle's house. He'd hitch up his own team to the Winters's wagon.

"You can take my team, Tim," Colin called after him.

"I handle mine better." Then Tim was out of earshot.

Colin looked back at his daughter, who was walking toward the children and their heavy task. Her shoulders were slumped.

"I'm sorry I spoke of her and Tim. You'd have let them go off together if I hadn't said anything, and she's a good, hardworking girl. She doesn't ask for much."

Colin turned to look at Elle. Helplessly, he said, "I don't know how to raise children."

"Your wife did everything? That's the usual way, I suppose."

"No, they had a nanny. Priscilla wasn't . . . wasn't well a good part of the time. I played with them, but I never taught them anything, I never disciplined them, I never was a real father to them. I was too busy with work. We lived in her parents' house in St. Louis, a grand old house. We lived with them during our marriage, and I loved her folks. Her father was so generous and welcoming. Her mother had the gift of making that house into a warm, welcoming home. They were so good to all of us."

Elle noticed he gave that credit to his in-laws. He didn't mention Priscilla making the house a home. That seemed strange.

"Then they passed away and we inherited it. Then Priscilla died. I felt like I'd stolen that house from Priscilla's family. There was no one, Priscilla was an only child. I couldn't stay there with every room a reminder of a family that was all gone. The children were so devastated when their grandparents died. The whole town of St. Louis seemed to be a reminder. I sold out and moved west before the ice broke on the Mississippi this spring."

He gave the small sod house a disgusted look. "I didn't think it through. I didn't know what I was getting into. I only knew I needed to get away from all that grief."

She was ridiculously hurt to have him give that sneering look to the house. Of course it was humble, it was made of sod for heaven's sake. But she'd been the one who directed the building. She'd worked until every muscle ached as she lay in bed at night, only to wake up and go right back to work. She'd neglected her own home, her garden, her livestock, giving all that a lick and a promise while she poured her time and energy into getting a roof over Colin's head before a rainstorm passed over.

And for all that work, he sneered. She was tempted to wrap a slab of sod around his neck and tell him to go cook his own supper.

CHAPTER 8

Elle and Colin sat in rocking chairs to eat.

Holding her plate in her lap was awkward, but Elle didn't know quite how else to manage it. Her table was full, and that included having the twins in one chair and Colin's boys in one.

The boys behaved fairly well. Instead of their usual constant wrestling, their focus was all on their food. They'd worked hard all day, and they were tired and starving.

Tim and Sarah sat one at the head of the table and one at the foot, which was so symbolic of their coming adulthood it twisted Elle's stomach.

Martha sat between the twins and Sarah so she and Tim could cut the girls' food. Russ and Frank sat across from the twins and Martha. Sarah and Tim helped the boys when it was called for.

Elle's kitchen was bursting at the seams. She liked her house and had always found it spacious, but the Samuelson family had filled it to the limit.

Which made it easier to rock beside Colin and not be annoyed with him. There wasn't room for them in the kitchen, though the rockers, set up in front of her fireplace, were situated so they could both watch the children.

"Sarah and Martha are fine cooks." Colin ate salt pork and sliced potatoes with a good appetite. Elle realized the chairs were a bit too close together. She hadn't moved them, but someone had, and she'd simply sat down and started eating, as hungry as everyone else.

They discussed the day and what lay ahead. As they finished eating and set their plates aside — the floor was the only place available — Elle asked, "Would you like to ride into church together tomorrow?"

Dear heavens, she'd asked him to go for a drive.

Colin didn't respond. Surely he didn't think she'd been flirting.

Then after what seemed much too long, he said, "Thank you, yes, we'd appreciate the ride." Colin turned to her. "You've done so much for us this week."

That tug she'd felt between them from the very first was there when he turned those blue eyes on her.

"I've been glad to help. We're looking forward to having neighbors."

Colin turned to the table full of children. "My boys watch Tim and copy him. And he's a better example of how a man should act than I am."

"No, he's not." Elle rested a hand on his forearm. He was so close it was simple. "The boys are just tagging after an older boy. It's just different than a father."

"And Martha and Sarah work so well together, it's like they've been friends for years." Colin rocked silently for a minute before he added, "I've asked so much of my daughter."

"Maybe." Elle patted his arm. "But it's made her into a mature young woman. It's done her no harm."

"Ma, we're going back to work." Tim stood from the table.

"We'll be right along." Elle quickly removed her hand from Colin's arm and smiled at her son. Then she saw him circle the table and meet Sarah. The two stood just within view through the doorway between her kitchen and the living room with the fireplace. They whispered together, then both gave Elle and Colin a sharp glance and looked away too fast. There was definitely something between those two.

Tim said something quietly to the table full of children, and they all stood like their chairs had been jolted by lightning.

Tim walked out with Colin's boys.

"We'll get on with the dishes." Martha sounded rather falsely chipper as she began clearing the table with Sarah and the twins.

In just seconds her kitchen table full of children was empty, and they'd all vanished from sight. She heard the clinking of dishes and utensils and girlish voices whispering. One of the boys — she thought Frank — shouted and laughed from outside.

She and Colin were alone.

His gaze turned to her. He reached across and rested his hand on her shoulder. "You have this crowd overflowing your kitchen. You've as good as built a house. You've taught Sarah more about mending and sewing in one week than I have in a year. And your shoulders, bearing so much weight, are relaxed. You don't seem to be tied up in knots, inside or out. And meanwhile I have both. Knots in my muscles, unaccustomed to this kind of heavy work, and knots in my belly from worrying about every decision I make with my young'uns."

His touch was so solid, his words so kind, that she set aside how he'd sneered at the soddy. His hand massaged her shoulders for a bit, then they stopped. Their gaze locked. He leaned closer, or maybe she did. Maybe both. His eyes flickered to her lips, and it was almost as warm as a touch.

His hand on her shoulder became a caress, and she liked it.

She blinked and reached to move his hand. "Colin, we agreed to be friends. You insisted, and you were right to do it. But there can't be moments like this between us if friendship is going to survive. Please, it was your decision, and I don't want to confuse things."

Colin straightened away from her. "You're right. I apologize." With a sigh he let his head rest on the tall back of the rocker.

It occurred to Elle that from the first minute they'd discovered how big their families were, they'd begun thinking in terms of how a marriage wouldn't work. Even though they were avoiding a romance, their thoughts had gone to a very serious relationship immediately.

As if a man and woman taking a ride inevitably led to *someone* and his children moving in.

They rocked in silence for a bit longer, enjoying this rare moment without the demands of the children. "They're going to start growing up and moving out before we know it. Right now they are the center of my life, but Tim could be on his own in a year or two. Martha not long after that if she marries young. The same for Sarah. Your boys and my twins have a few more years to wait, but it will go fast."

She gave Colin a rueful smile. "Maybe you can lean back close to me in about five years."

A startled laugh escaped Colin's lips, and

he nodded. "Yep, maybe I can."

He heaved himself to his feet and reached out a hand. She took it and let him help her stand. He said, "In the meantime I've got a house to build."

They got back to work.

CHAPTER 9

A crack of thunder jerked Colin awake. Thunder? He lurched to his feet in the roofless soddy and rushed toward the wagon where his children slept.

A bolt of lightning split the air. It hit the ground not a hundred yards away. The thunder sounded at the same moment as the flash of lightning.

And the children were sleeping in the wagon with the cover on it. The highest thing around, save the unfinished house.

Shouting, he raced toward them. "Wake up. Get out of the wagon!"

He was a doctor. He'd seen the damage lightning did to a human body. "Hurry. Sarah, Russ, Frank!"

Then Sarah poked her head out the back; the boys dove past her and raced to Colin's side. Sarah caught up just as another lightning bolt flashed. Another and another lit up the countryside like daylight. In the maniacal light, Colin saw something so ugly he wanted to drop to the ground and cover his head.

"It's a tornado!" he roared. The spinning funnel lit up in the raging storm. It was coming straight for them. He grabbed the boys by the hands. "Sarah, run! Come on."

But come on to where? Nothing was safe from one of these deadly storms. He saw Elle's house only a hundred feet away and sprinted for it.

"Tornado! Elle, Tim! Wake up!"

Out of the dark, Elle emerged, running toward them. She saw them and shouted over the roar, "Get in the cellar, now!"

Elle took Sarah's hand, turned, and ran. Colin followed, and the lightning showed Tim fighting the howling wind to hold the sloping door open. Martha scampered down with both twins in tow.

A lightning bolt exploded behind them, and Colin turned to see his wagon being blown apart. The whirling demon stormed right for the fire.

The first drop of cold rain hit the back of his neck. He kept moving. They had to survive this night first, then they'd worry about what they lost.

Colin herded everyone down the steps. He stayed above to get the door. He grabbed the handle and fought against the wind to hold it while everyone got down the stairs. Tim stayed with him and grabbed the edge of the door, dragging with all his weight.

Colin yelled over the storm to Tim. "Get down there!"

"I've got it. Go." Tim clung to the door.

A blast of thunder seemed to shake the whole earth. Colin grabbed Tim by the shirtfront with one hand while he wrestled with the door with the other. "Go. Now!"

Tim looked past Colin, and pure horror shone in his eyes. He let go of the door and dashed down the steps.

Getting around the door was a trick. Colin managed it barely and started down the steps, pulling the door closed behind him. Suddenly something tugged on him. He felt himself being lifted off the ground.

Then Elle was hanging from one leg, Tim from another — they threw all their weight against the power of the storm and dragged him down, the door slamming over his head. Elle reached past him and rammed home an iron bar to latch it.

"Get down," Elle shouted over the deafening noise of the raging storm. "Crouch in the farthest back corner. Keep your heads down, eyes closed."

Her children were already there. They were so clearly experienced at this madness. Colin's family rushed to huddle with the others. Elle sat down, her back to the cellar door, and she spread her arms wide to protect the children, as if she planned to hold her children against the force of this storm with her bare hands. Colin dropped down behind her. She felt his arms, also spread, but he was sheltering her. She wanted to scold him to get closer, to move up beside her rather than sit behind. Every inch they could get from that door could make a difference.

But his arm was so solid on her back. And his other arm was wrapped around Sarah, who held one of Elle's twins. Tim had both boys tucked behind him, crowded against the dirt wall in the back. Martha clung to the other twin. Everyone huddled together to protect the others.

The roar outside grew louder and more terrible with each passing moment. Time dragged on. Seconds passed like hours. Colin's strong arms seemed like a haven she'd never known. She shifted her body, and his arm tightened. Maybe to hold her in place, but it didn't feel like that. It felt like a hug.

And then the screaming storm lessened. Still loud, the worst of that deafening roar eased, replaced with thunder that shook the earth. Elle looked over her shoulder; lightning flared in a gap in the door.

"Is it over?" Colin asked.

"I think so. But sometimes there can be more than one tornado in a storm."

"There can?" Sarah sounded horrified.

"Yep," Elle said, patting the girl on the

shoulder. "We'll stay down awhile. Anyway, do you hear the rain? We'd get soaked walking to the house."

Colin groaned quietly. "The house. I wonder if I have one anymore."

"So do I." In the pitch dark, Elle said, "If we don't, well, there's plenty more sod where that came from."

Colin choked, then he coughed, and next he laughed. In the terror that had just passed, with all of them wound up tight as a pocket watch, his laugh set them all off. Soon they were laughing wildly. Elle knew it was reaction to the madness of the storm, but it felt good to let some of it go in laughter.

By the time the laughter died, Elle felt that the storm was easing enough she could at least get some light down here. And of course the cellar was well equipped.

"Let me light the lantern."

Colin's hand tightened on her shoulder. "You took the time to grab a lantern?"

"No, we keep one down here. I know right where it is, too, so I can find it and the matches in the pitch dark." Elle thought Colin's strong hand let loose of her shoulder rather reluctantly.

"So you're saying you plan for this? You've come down here before?" He sounded stunned.

"Yes, of course we plan for it. We have a storm cellar for just this reason. Tim was going to start digging yours as soon as the roof went on your soddy."

"I thought it was a root cellar."

"I keep potatoes and beets down here through the winter, and pumpkins and squash. I have canning jars, and it's cool, so in the summer we can keep milk down here, and butter and eggs and cheese. But its primary use is as a place to go during a tornado."

"People know about a storm like that, and they still live out here?"

Silence fell over the cellar. Elle stood and found the lantern. With moves she'd practiced out of necessity in the pitch dark, she found the matches and lit the wick. The flare of bright light lifted her spirits, and she set the lantern on a shelf built just for that and turned to look at her crowded shelter.

"Didn't anyone mention tornadoes when you were claiming a homestead, Colin? That seems like information they should share with you. It's not safe to let people build their homes without a warning about the occasional need to take shelter."

Colin slapped himself in the face and kept his hand there, covering his eyes. "Why do you stay here?"

Elle smiled. "The storms haven't gotten us yet, and no place is without its troubles. Some land floods, mountains are steep enough a child can roll right off a cliff. There are grizzlies in the Rockies, too, and mountain lions. We have blizzards, but down south they have such terrible heat it's all a body can do to survive the summer." Elle shrugged. "No place on earth is perfect, and I've decided my little corner of Nebraska is as close as I'm going to get."

Colin shook his head rather frantically. It reminded Elle of a dog she'd once seen shaking off water.

"Our wagon burned, Pa," Sarah said. "But it was mostly empty except for blankets. I hope the house is still there, and our supplies."

The howling of the wind had dropped until all was silent outside. The children asked fretful questions about the possible damage until Elle decided she couldn't hear rain pounding on the cellar door anymore.

"Let's stop worrying about what might be and go see for ourselves." Quietly she added, "There is loss in life, children. Colin and I are your parents, and we love you and will always do our very best to take care of you. But we don't have to tell you that terrible things happen. You've all known great loss already. Whatever we find when we go out there, we will go to work fixing. What we've lost can be replaced as long as we survived. God will carry us through. You all know that, don't you? He's with us, in all the storms of life. And that includes this one."

Her children stood. They'd been through this many times before and had learned to accept it. Colin's children were slower to get to their feet.

Rising beside her, Colin's deep voice seemed to fill the little cellar. "That's very wise, Elle. Thank you for remembering that. And thank you for saving us. We are very likely alive because you were prepared and you came for us when you should have run for cover. God bless you for that."

Elle went to the cellar door and threw the latch.

Colin came up beside her. "Let me get the door." He reached past her without waiting for her to step aside, and again they were close, pressed together. The sense of protection and strength almost made her light-headed.

Then Colin pushed the door wide and went on up the steps.

Dreading what she'd find, Elle followed him to see . . .

CHAPTER 10

"Both houses are still standing." Only the lightning, fading in the distance, made it possible to see.

Colin couldn't believe it. He froze in amazement.

Elle poked him in the spine, and he flipped the door all the way open and surged out of the cellar. His half-built soddy. Elle's house and barn. All still there.

"Put out the lantern, Martha," Elle called over her shoulder. She added, "I don't want to take it out of the cellar. I learned a hard lesson once when I took it to the house and we had a second storm come through and had to spend hours down there in complete darkness. It's hard to endure the storm without light."

"A second storm?" Colin tried to think where he could move to. Where were things perfect? Surely he could get closer than this.

The light behind them blinked out and left them in a night as dark as pitch.

"My wagon burned from that lightning bolt, but that's all. And there's even some of it still there, the rain must have put out the fire before it consumed everything." And the fire was long out. Colin couldn't see it, but if there'd been flames he would have.

All the children came barrelling out of the cellar. Except for the now-distant lightning that showed the storm racing onward to the east, it was a coal-black night. Not a star in the sky. There'd been a bright moon, but the sky was heavy with black clouds even after the storm.

Colin saw Elle flash a bright smile, her white teeth visible when precious else was.

The children started talking and laughing. Russ and Frank were wrestling, like always, and the twins giggled and caught hands together and spun in a circle.

The older children talked loudly, full of high spirits, like they'd just had a great adventure.

Elle and Colin had moved forward to let the youngsters out of the cellar, and they'd kept walking until they stood a bit apart. The ground was soaked, but the rain had passed.

Elle said, "You'd better sleep with me tonight."

Colin had most unfortunately been inhaling at just that moment, and his gasp made him start choking.

"Oh no." Elle looked behind her. "I meant

I'd like you to spend the night with me."

Colin started laughing.

"Hush up." Elle's extremely poorly worded invitation and her embarrassed order were too much, and the laughter almost bent him double. He knew it was simple joy at being alive.

She slapped him on the shoulder and in a harsh whisper, made things even worse, "Settle down or I'm not sharing my bed. Uh . . . I mean letting you sleep over. No! I mean . . ."

She was furious at him, but she was also overreacting, just as he was, from relief. She shoved him hard and hissed, "Your children are welcome, but you can sleep outside in the mud for all I care."

In the pitch dark, even with the voices of the children near, Colin could barely see a foot in front of him. It was pure delight, pure high spirits that made him wrap one arm around Elle's waist and haul her up against him.

"I accept your very tempting offer." He kissed the living daylights out of her.

She wacked him on the side of the head. She was so full of energy and life and strength. So sturdy. She struggled and fought back. Priscilla would have gone limp, maybe fainted, certainly pleaded for him to let her go. Of course he'd have never treated Priscilla like this. They'd had three children together and never spent a moment as passionately as this one right here, right now.

He'd never felt so vitally alive in his life.

And then her arms came hard around his neck, and she raised up on her tiptoes and kissed him back.

Ten seconds ago, he hadn't known what being vitally alive meant. He deepened the kiss and lifted her right off the ground.

Then her arms were gone. "Stop!" She wrested herself away and backed up so fast she stumbled.

Colin reached out and grabbed her to keep her on her feet. He absolutely knew they had to stop. He agreed with her completely. Then he reeled her back in and kissed her again.

The next time she stepped away she was more nimble, and he missed her when he tried to keep ahold.

Elle turned and stomped right into the midst of the children. Colin realized she was wearing a nightgown. Barefoot. He aimed directly for her like he was a magnet and she was true north. The children surrounded her, chattering, laughing, wrestling, dancing.

He felt as if he'd kissed Elle forever, but it must have only been moments.

And in her nightgown, too. There could hardly be anything more improper than that. And then a whole long list of more improper things cascaded through his mind, and he forgot to breathe.

"Now, let's all go inside." She clapped her hands and waved them a bit as if she were shooing a flock of chickens. "The Samuelsons will be sleeping with us tonight. Some of you children will have to sleep on the floor, but there's no help for it.

"We have church in the morning," she went on. "Then we may have to break the Sabbath and try to get a roof on their house so they have shelter by tomorrow night."

He saw nerves in every move of her hands. Her voice was a bit husky, and her words tumbled out too fast.

The children seemed thrilled with the invitation and acted as if they were throwing a party. They all turned toward the house and Elle was right behind them, trying to avoid even a second alone with him.

He didn't blame her because if they had been alone he wasn't sure how firm a grip he'd be able to cling to. All he could really think of was that pretty white nightgown and the bundle of strength and energy within.

CHAPTER 11

Elle had the twins in bed with her. Martha and Sarah were in the bedroom Martha usually shared with the twins. The Samuelson boys were together in Tim's room, which wasn't really a room: her house had a small attic that was really just space between the ceiling and the peaked roof. Tim couldn't stand upright, not even in the center, which was highest. But he'd declared it his room even before Jerome had died, and he willingly crawled up there to sleep, happy to have any space of his own in this two-bedroom house. The three boys would be lying side by side like strips of sod.

Colin was downstairs on some blankets in front of her fireplace. She could swear she heard him breathing.

The storm had come late in the night, and she'd resigned herself almost immediately to lying awake the rest of the night.

As she contemplated Colin and his noisy breathing, she realized it was good that they

337

were all jam-packed into her house. It helped her see just how impossible it was for their families to be together.

Every time her mind veered to that kiss, she pictured this house packed literally to the rafters with children.

And what if they had more? Elle had shown no sign of difficulty having babies. Clearly, Colin was also up to the job.

When that notion popped into her mind, she couldn't breathe for fighting off that tantalizing vision, having Colin's baby. Conceiving Colin's baby.

Maybe she needed to go outside and sleep in the mud. It might calm her down.

She lay there and listened to the clock downstairs tick away the minutes, wrangling with all that darted through her unruly mind. Finally the black night gave way to dark gray then finally dawn.

Her rooster crowed. She really needed to get up and go outside and assess any damage.

Footsteps downstairs told her Colin was up. Had he slept at all? Maybe he had. Maybe that kiss hadn't bothered him one speck. Or maybe he'd lain awake, tormented with regrets. Scared to death Elle would come downstairs expecting him to propose.

After the way he'd kissed her that would be the proper thing to do, but proper wasn't always right.

She forced herself to stay in bed. If she didn't and she went down there, she'd end up in his arms again.

Colin got out of the house the first possible minute. He knew that if Elle came down she'd end up in his arms again.

He hurried out to see what was left of his wagon and his house. He'd seen the walls still standing in the lightning, but he needed a closer look. Or at least he needed to get away from Elle. Sleeping on the hard floor, which was actually harder than the ground where he'd been sleeping, had been a strong reminder of why he couldn't think of marrying her.

Well, that wasn't true. He could think of it all right. And think and think and think.

He headed for the soddy first. There was no damage he could see on the outside. Then he stepped inside and it was like a haven, like the world closed around him, blocking certain pretty blond ladies out.

They'd stored most of their supplies in there once the walls were up, and covered them with heavy blankets and the wagon tarp. So, though things were wet, he hadn't lost anything.

Then he went to inspect his wagon, and his first action was to reach under the charred frame near the front on the left side. He found the metal box he'd fastened under there and made sure it was tightly closed. He wasn't worried about fire because the box contained only gold coins. His entire wealth. His St. Louis home and all its lavish furnishings and artwork, the building he owned that housed his doctor's office. Some other real estate and a stable full of thoroughbreds, to name the big things. He'd cashed in a lifetime of stock-market dabbling Priscilla's father had amassed, and it was considerable.

He'd left everything personal that would remind him of his life with Priscilla. Even the money was a reminder of her, and he intended to leave it to his children.

He could use it to build a grand house out here that had plenty of room for two good-sized families, but he didn't want to live in a house funded by Priscilla's family. He'd bought and paid for his doctor's office building himself. That money was his, and he'd worked hard for it. He'd used that money to pay for their journey west and had enough left to buy a humble home, possibly as nice as Elle's. But they'd just proved that both families wouldn't fit in hers.

He knew one thing, he liked being near her too much.

He had to get out of her house before he found them all crowded into that small home without room to breathe . . . and another baby on the way soon enough. Maybe he could make a bedroom out of the cellar.

"Colin, breakfast!" Elle called out the back door, but she didn't stand there and let him look at her. In fact, she kept her head down and swung the door shut as fast as she'd opened it.

He'd bet his whole box of gold she'd waited to call him until the children were up. Elle Winters didn't want to be alone with him any more than he wanted to be alone with her.

It was far too tempting.

CHAPTER 12

Elle was determined to stay as far away from Colin as she could. And he seemed to be in complete agreement. He sat in the back with the children on the ride to church, even though Tim offered to let him drive.

At church, they sat in two rows, just because they wouldn't fit in one, but Elle went in ahead of her four children. And one row behind, Colin went in after his.

If he looked at her she didn't know because she never took so much as one peek.

They rode home together, never speaking.

An almost frantic haste went into their building, even though Sarah complained of working on the Lord's Day and Tim insisted the Samuelsons sleeping in the Winters's house was fun.

There was no door yet and no windows, but it was a warm summer night and the roof was on. The Samuelsons slept at home.

The days took on a different shape than before. Colin started riding into town to run his doctor's practice.

Sarah stepped in and cared for her brothers, though Elle insisted they eat together. She hoped that took some of the weight off Sarah's slender shoulders.

The three Samuelson children spent a lot of time with Elle, and she welcomed them. Their lives were so much richer with some company. But once Colin came riding home, his children went to his home and he closed the door without a word to Elle. She could have invited him to supper, but she never did, knowing he'd turn her down if she asked.

Of course she nearly ran the other way when she saw him coming, so who was to know if he'd have been friendly, given a chance.

She thought not.

They'd gone on in that rather chilly fashion for two weeks. Tim and Sarah spent long hours together, doing chores and riding out to check the herd.

Elle worried about how close the two were growing, and then one day she looked out and saw Tim and Sarah talking in a way that seemed almost frantic. Sarah waved her hands around. Tim nodded. He didn't speak as much as Sarah but more than he ever did when Elle tried to talk to him.

The two took frequent furtive glances at the house. The sun must have been shining to reflect the windows rather than let the two see inside, because though they seemed worried about being seen, they kept talking.

Then Sarah clapped. A huge smile broke out on Tim's face, and he reached over to rest one hand on her shoulder.

They both nodded firmly, as if whatever they'd been discussing had been settled. It struck Elle as a very serious nod. As firm as any vow sworn between two adults.

And her children . . . she was counting Sarah among them for this purpose . . . were not adults, though they both looked it.

The two split up, and Elle went back to her housework, wondering what exactly they had just agreed to.

"Elle, wake up!" Colin, shouting. A fist hammered on the front door, and Elle leaped out of bed and ran.

She rushed down and flung the door open just as she realized she was meeting him in her nightgown . . . again.

"Sarah's gone. And I've got a note." He lifted up a small square of paper. "She's run off with Tim to elope."

"Elope! They're just children."

"It looks like they think they're mighty grown-up." Colin waved the note in her face.

Elle spun around and charged up her stairs. Martha had her head out of her bedroom door. Elle kept going up the slender flight of stairs to Tim's attic room. She only poked her head into the low-ceilinged place. "Tim, wake up."

No sound. There was enough moonlight coming from two small windows on each end of the house to tell her Tim wasn't there. A closer look revealed a square of paper on his pillow. She crawled forward, almost landing on her face when her nightgown caught under her knees and tripped her. She grabbed the note and scooted backward to the doorway. She rammed into Colin. He'd followed right behind her.

"Tim's gone. There's a note." Elle wondered what in the world she looked like crawling about, but Colin whirled and was gone down the stairs. He was beyond looking at her legs.

Elle rushed down the stairs. Martha was in the hallway with a lantern by this time. She held the light so Elle could read the note.

I ran off with Sarah. Tim.

"Well, he was to the point."

Colin stuck his note up close to the lantern; it covered an entire page with writing.

Elle's eyes scanned it, and she saw the words *ran off* and *please forgive me, Daddy, but I know what I'm doing . . .*

Elle quit trying to read sideways. She got the message. "We have to stop them."

Then she remembered the talk they'd been having just that day. "I saw them planning this."

345

Like a hungry wolf, Colin turned on her. He looked for all the world like he wanted someone to chew up. "And you didn't stop them?"

"We don't have time to talk. Where would they go?"

Colin looked into space. "They need a parson. There's one in Lone Tree, but Parson O'Flaugherty wouldn't perform a ceremony for them. He knows them. They can probably convince a stranger they're old enough to get married. But Parson wouldn't do it without talking to us."

Elle knew how things worked in the West. "He would if he believed they had a . . . a . . ." She glanced at Martha and couldn't say *baby on the way.*

Instead, she said, "We've got to go. Martha, you're in charge of the twins."

"If we're not back by morning, bring the boys over here." Colin gave the order as if Martha was as much his to boss around as she was Elle's. There was no time to object.

"I'll be dressed in two minutes." Elle rushed toward her room. "Colin, go hitch up —"

She skidded to a stop. "Is the wagon gone? Did they ride horses? Colin, check on that. We may need to saddle horses instead of taking the buckboard."

"We'll take horses anyway." Colin thundered down the stairs. "It's faster."

He was out the door, and Elle rushed into

her room, threw on her clothes, and headed out.

"We'll be back as soon as we can, Martha."

"Ma!" Martha's plaintive cry stopped Elle's headlong rush. She realized they'd been throwing orders at the girl without any explanation. Of course Martha was standing right there, so she knew what had happened.

Elle forced herself to stop and turn back. Martha came downstairs. Elle saw tears in her daughter's eyes.

Martha didn't stop, she rushed into Elle's arms and they held on tight.

Finally, Martha whispered, "Would it be so bad, Ma? If two people love each other, is it so bad to marry young?"

Forcing herself to hold on to the daughter right in front of her, Elle drew in a long breath. "Sarah is fourteen, honey. That's so young for marriage. And where will they live? Tim might find work, but most likely he'll have to come back home and bring Sarah with him."

"Then they can just move in here."

"But the only room Tim has is that attic, and Colin lives in a one-room soddy. That's not how a married couple lives, so crowded, no privacy."

"They can live in our old soddy."

"I've been storing tools in it for years. The roof leaks, and —"

"We'll fix the roof and clean it out, or we'll

build them a new one. Or Sarah's pa has ordered boards for a house. They can get by living in a crowd then move into Sarah's soddy when her pa gets the new house up." A strange tone came into Martha's voice. Elle was too frantic to understand it, but suddenly her daughter didn't sound all that upset when she said, "I like the idea of our families joining together. I thought at first you and Mr. Samuelson might be interested."

"No, honey. I mean, Mr. Samuelson is very nice, but we have seven children between us. And we live in these little houses. We wouldn't fit."

"If you loved each other you could find a way to fit, Ma." Martha sniffed, and Elle pulled back to see her daughter crying quietly. "Love always fits, Ma. Family always fits. I'd love to have Sarah in our family. She's the best friend I ever had."

"Sarah is a fine young woman, Martha. I'm not saying she wouldn't make Tim a good wife. They're just too young."

Martha pulled away and stormed up the stairs. "Don't worry about the five of us, Ma. We'll manage, just like Sarah and Tim will manage and just like you and Mr. Samuelson could manage if you wanted to."

Then her daughter was gone into the tiny room she shared with her twin sisters. Her door closed with a sharp slap.

For a second, Elle wasn't quite sure what

had just happened. In a childish sort of way, sweet little Martha had just given her quite a scolding.

"Elle, hurry up," Colin called from outside. "Your wagon is still there, they must've ridden."

Shaking her head to focus on what was important, Elle turned and rushed out of the house. Colin was on horseback with a second saddled horse close behind.

She was on horseback and they were galloping toward Lone Tree and still Martha's words haunted her. *"You and Mr. Samuelson could manage if you wanted to."*

Forcing herself to pay attention on the wild ride, she wondered how far they'd have to go to find those troublesome children. They couldn't be off together for even a single night or it would be too late and marriage would be the only choice.

CHAPTER 13

In the dead of night, Colin galloped into Lone Tree. He'd pushed his horse beyond reason, to find . . . nothing.

He reined in his horse in the dark town, and Elle caught up to him in just seconds.

They rode at a walk, side by side, their horses blowing hard.

"What do we do? There's not a light on anywhere."

Elle said, "I can't believe the parson would bless a union between them. But let's ride to the church and look."

The parson's house sat in darkness.

They swung off their horses in front of the silent church. "Let's go in. They might be hiding there, trying to decide what to do."

"There are no horses, Elle." Colin swung down despite his words. He was absolutely right. There wasn't a horse tied to a hitching post anywhere in town. The livery sat at the end of Lone Tree, doors closed, no lantern light.

Elle led the way into the church with Colin behind her. It was a small building. An altar that was a simple table. A Bible and a cross resting on top. No cloakrooms or closets. Nowhere for two reckless children to hide.

Colin came in behind her, and they stood, thinking. It occurred to Elle that they might have been better served to do more thinking earlier.

Moonlight streamed in the window, casting shadows in the building. "Let's look very carefully, in case they're ducked behind something."

There were rows of benches. With no better notion, Elle walked up along one wall while Colin went to the other wall and walked up front. They met before the altar.

"What do we do next, Elle?" Colin whispered in the dark.

She turned to face him, and he looked so devastated that despite his standoffish ways the last two weeks, she couldn't stop from reaching across and taking his hands.

The way he grabbed hold of her made her feel like she was saving a drowning man.

"The worst that can happen is they end up married." Elle thought of Martha. "And if they do get married, well, we'll figure something out. You're going to build a house, so they can live in your soddy when the house is done, or I can clean my soddy out. It needs repairs, but I reckon if we build one from the ground up, we can fix one."

"But my little girl." Colin raised his eyes to meet hers. "It's not your son, you know that, don't you? Tim is a fine young man, and I'd be proud to have him marry Sarah, but I can't help feeling like if I'd just been a better father —"

His voice broke, and Elle couldn't withhold comfort from him. She wrapped her arms around him, and his snapped around her waist and pulled her hard against him, his face buried in her shoulder.

"You're a fine father, Colin."

"No, I've made her do too much. Why wouldn't a girl acting like an adult decide she was grown-up enough to marry? Maybe she even agreed to elope to escape from me. From the life I've dropped on her young shoulders."

"I've done the same with Tim. Treated him as an adult almost from birth, long before Jerome died. Given him chores then left him the responsibility to carry them out." Elle's voice dropped to a whisper. "And what am I going to do without him?" She swallowed hard. "That may be the most selfish thing a mother ever said."

Her throat closed, and they stood in the holy place, holding each other. Elle let her mind go to God, to His will.

It helped ease her regrets. Finally she straightened to find her arms around Colin's neck. His around her waist. When she lifted her head, he did the same, and they looked into each other's eyes.

"God will see us through, Colin. If we stop the marriage, they will no doubt try again. If we don't stop it, then we'll . . . we'll . . ."

Martha's words came to her. *"Love always fits, Ma. Family always fits. You and Mr. Samuelson could manage if you wanted to."*

"Elle," Colin said quietly, reverently.

"What?"

"I failed my children."

"No you didn't, you —"

"Shh. Let me just —" Colin touched her mouth with his fingertips. "When Priscilla died —" He acted as if the words hurt. "She was so beautiful, so delicate. I shouldn't have wanted children with her, and certainly not three. But it seemed so natural that I did. I'm a doctor, but I just . . . I did stop . . . stop . . . going to her after Frank was born."

Frank was five years old. What a lonely sort of marriage.

"She spent nearly her entire pregnancy in bed, then after each one she was a year recovering. The children and I hardly knew her. She was like a shadow living in her room. We would visit her, but she never joined in our family after a child would come, and with the nursemaids and nanny, she didn't need to. Then she'd gather her strength and be up and about more. And then another baby would come."

Shaking his head, he said, "I was a fool."

"And a baby . . . is that what happened to finally break her health and lead to her death?"

"No, when her parents died it was like the last source of her strength went with them. Her mother particularly had taken diligent care of her all through our marriage. But when her mother died, Priscilla took to her bed in grief and never recovered. A fever was too much for her, and she died a year after her parents."

Elle thought of surviving Jerome's death. It had been shocking, and the weight of all that was left to her could have crushed her. But she just hadn't had time to curl up and die. Of course she hadn't adored Jerome like Colin did Priscilla.

He ran one finger along her lips then closed his fist like he was hanging on to the feel of her. "And here you are, so strong. Up to the task of raising your own children, doing so much for mine, helping me build a house, for heaven's sake. Even birthing Tim with no one there."

Shaking his head as if it was unthinkable, he looked at her, and she waited, wanting him to talk about his wife and how much he loved her and how much he admired that delicate feminine woman, and how lacking he found Elle. She wanted him to get on with breaking her heart so she could get on with living without him.

"Do you have any idea how much it hurts to have a woman give up on life when she's got a husband and children who need her? The children barely knew to mourn her because she'd spent so much time ailing. And as I doctor I knew . . ." His jaw clenched until she hoped he didn't break his teeth. "I knew it was mostly just nonsense. There was nothing really wrong with her. There are sound medical reasons why a woman needs to stay off her feet for some difficult pregnancies, none of those reasons applied to Priscilla."

Elle heard something in his voice that she hadn't before. She'd thought he was so sad over his wife's death, but that wasn't it. He was sad over her life. Over their marriage.

"And I've seen women who, after a child was born, need to be very carefully treated. Some of them seem emotionally devastated in a way no one understands. Some have done damage during the birthing that takes time to heal. Priscilla had nothing like that. She was simply a spoiled, selfish woman who wanted to be waited on hand and foot, and her mother indulged her to a ridiculous degree. Once her mother was gone and Priscilla no longer had that slavish devotion, she seemed to lose interest in life. And not a husband nor three beautiful children could hold her to this world."

Then he whispered, "Elle, I never thought I'd find a woman as strong and wise as you. As good a mother. As good a partner. You're wonderful. I've fought it every way I know how. I've avoided you because I couldn't see how our lives would mesh. But I'm through fighting it now." He pulled her close. "I've fallen in love with you." His lips descended on hers, and she was back in his arms.

From being ready to have her heart broken to his declaration of love was such a swoop, such a change in her thoughts, she was dizzy from it. She clung to him to keep from falling over in a heap.

When at last he lifted his head, she said, "We'll still have seven children, Colin. That problem remains."

He smiled. His handsome face and dark brown hair washed blue in the moonlight. "Somehow the children don't seem like a problem anymore, not if we work together to handle them. We'll find a place for them all to sleep."

"We can manage if we want to." Elle quoted Martha's words, but they were pure truth.

"And do you want to, Elle? Will you marry me?"

"Yes."

A shout spun them both around to see children pouring into the church. Seven children. Tim and Sarah were with them.

Frank shouted, "It's about time!"

They started to laugh, and before they knew it the entire church was in an uproar. Hugs and chatter and enough laughter to keep them happy even in a crowded house.

CHAPTER 14

When the racket died down, Colin looked at Tim, with Russ and Frank clinging to his legs and Sarah holding one of the twins while Martha had the other. Colin still wasn't sure how to tell those little girls apart.

"I thought you two ran off?"

"We did run off." Sarah giggled.

"B–but you were running off to *elope.*" Colin flexed his hand around Elle's waist, glad she was there for support.

"We never used the word elope." Tim rolled his eyes. "She's my sister."

Sarah gave Tim a firm nod. Tim smiled and went to a lantern hanging from a nail on the church wall and lit it. There were three others, and in moments the room was glowing in the firelight.

"Then where were you?"

"We took two horses and hid them behind the barn, then the two of us stayed in there until we heard you ride off."

"But why?" Elle sounded bewildered. Colin

knew exactly how that felt.

"Because," Martha spoke up, "we have been trying to get the two of you to just spend a bit of time together for the last two weeks."

"We knew you were in love." Sarah patted either Betty or Barbara on the shoulder and set her down. "But we also knew you weren't doing a thing about it."

"Martha is the one who came up with this plan. Sarah and I would've never thought of it." Tim sounded bewildered by the whole notion of him and Sarah together. Which Colin thought proved the boy was still really young.

"We knew you'd finally do something together when you went to search for us."

Elle narrowed her eyes at Martha. "You came up with the idea of staging an elopement?"

Martha grinned, and Colin was struck by how much the girl looked like her pretty ma, right down to the gleam of intelligence in her blue eyes.

"Martha decided a fake runaway marriage was the right way to manage you two." Sarah slung one arm around Martha. The two were a study. Sarah so dark and tall, Martha so fair and petite. Both beautiful girls. Colin was going to have his hands full for the next few years when men came courting.

"We were even real careful not to lie when we left a note. We never said anything about eloping, we said we were running away together. And that's just what we did."

"We didn't run far," Tim interjected.

"It wasn't my first plan." Martha grinned without an ounce of repentance. "But I couldn't figure out how to let the twins get lost on the prairie."

"Martha!" Elle shouted in horror.

"And the creek is running fast, so I thought about letting one of the boys get swept away by floodwaters, but that seemed risky."

"Swept away by floodwaters?" Colin slapped one hand on his face over his eyes as if he could see it in his imagination and couldn't stand it. "You could have died."

"Well, that's why we didn't do it." Martha sounded as if she were speaking to a pair of slow students.

Russ smirked. "We went to see if we could jump in the water and float away, but it looked mighty dangerous."

"You're just tormenting me now," Colin growled.

His son giggled and added, "The land where you'd dug the trench for our soddy is under water since the rain that came with that tornado."

"You boys aren't ever to go in that creek for any reason." Colin shuddered to think of the chances they'd nearly taken. And his first homesite was flooded? What a disaster that would have been. The Winters family had saved him from that.

"And now you and Ma finally admit you love each other, right? And you're ready to get married?" Martha crossed her arms. "We want a pa, and Sarah and her brothers want a ma. I expect you two would have figured that out in time, but we were tired of waiting."

Dead silence fell over the room. Colin noticed the church was overly crowded, and their homes would be worse. And he didn't care one speck. "Yep, we've admitted it." He turned to look at Elle.

She lifted both hands as if she was giving up, surrendering, which meant he'd caught her. "I do think I need help raising these children."

"I need more help than you." Colin reached for those hands, so strong, so competent. Rough with calluses and chapped from long hours of hard work. He'd never felt anything more perfect. "I love you, Elle. Will you marry me? Will you join your family with mine and help me take care of this crowd?"

The smile on her face grew with every word he uttered.

"I would be honored and thrilled to marry you, Colin. I love you, and I have no doubt we'll" — she turned to look at all the children and added with some spunk — "we'll find a way to manage."

The children sent up a cheer that shook

some dust out of the rafters. They rushed to Colin and Elle. The hugging and laughter was contagious. It was the happiest his children had been since Priscilla died. Maybe the happiest they'd ever been in their lives.

"What is going on in here?" Parson O'Flaugherty came in, dressed in an untucked white shirt and black pants. He was barefoot, and his thinning white hair stood nearly straight up on his head. His wife peeked over his shoulder from behind him.

Colin looked at Elle, who gave him a firm nod of her chin.

"We'd like to get married, Parson. Elle and I would like you to perform the ceremony right now."

The parson's brow furrowed as he looked from one joyous face to the next . . . which took him a fair amount of time, considering the crowd.

He cleared his throat. "You're sure about this?" He sounded wary, like he knew if they just took a bit of time they'd come to their senses.

Well, Colin had no intention of coming to his senses. "We're sure."

Elle said, "As sure as can be, Parson. And we'd like you to say the vows right now, please. We're all here. We might as well get on with the ceremony."

Colin reached out his hand, and she laid hers firmly in it. They shared a smile and turned to face the parson. He shrugged and came forward, tucking in his shirt.

He squeezed through them and took his place in the front of the church. His wife came up the side so she didn't need to make them all step back in the limited space.

"Tim, you and the boys come and stand at my side." Colin waved them over. "Is that all right, if I claim your son to stand up with me, Elle?"

"If I can have Sarah."

Sarah clapped her hands, and she and Martha lined up to Elle's left, the two older girls had their hands resting firmly on the shoulders of the twins between them.

Tim took Russ and Frank's hands, and the three of them lined up on Colin's right.

The parson didn't get a prayer book, he didn't open his Bible, he didn't even run home to put on his shoes. "Dearly beloved . . ."

CHAPTER 15

"My house came in," Colin said as he entered the bedroom he'd been sharing with Elle for the last two months. "I hired men to haul it out tomorrow and build it."

"Not Dutch and Lou?" Elle looked up, alarmed. She really wished he'd talk with her before he made plans.

"Nope, the men who delivered the wood said they were willing to put up the house. They claim to do it a lot, and they'll have the house done in a couple of weeks."

"Good, because we need the space."

Colin laughed. "That is so true. We can't keep letting the boys sleep alone in my soddy. It's just not a good idea to let Russ and Frank have that much freedom, nor is it good to make Tim shoulder so much responsibility.

The boys slept on pallets on the floor at Colin's house. The girls slept all four in the second bedroom in Elle's house.

"And I explained the situation, that the house wasn't really big enough. I should have ordered more lumber to be shipped, but it was already on the way and I didn't want to wait for more." He'd ordered the lumber before he'd faced up to getting married.

"I've figured out how we'll manage." That was starting to be one of Elle's favorite words. They'd found a way to manage meals together. They'd found they could manage seven children. They'd even figured out how to very discreetly manage intimacy in the night, which was no small trick in Elle's tiny house.

"How?"

"Your house is the same size as mine, isn't it?"

"Yep, I explained to the men who sell lumber I wanted one just like yours, and let them do the ordering."

"My house is close to the border of my land but not quite close enough to attach a second house. You have to live on your property to keep your claim. If we build your house on my land, it will reach just a few feet past the edge of your property line. You and I can sleep there."

"Is that legal?"

"Yep. I asked at the land office just this morning when I went into town for supplies."

Colin knew she'd been in. She'd come to the doctor's office, mercifully alone, and the two of them had eaten lunch together in the hotel in Lone Tree.

"The agent knows men who've done it," Elle went on. "Built a one-room soddy like yours, right on top of the property line, then slept on opposite walls to fulfill the homestead requirements. He said it's completely legal."

With a smile lighting up his face, Colin said, "My house is laid out just like yours, but if we attach them we can open up the kitchen and attach it to mine. It'll be big enough for a table that will hold us all. Then we can use the part that's a sitting room in your house for a bedroom in ours. I was thinking we'd have four bedrooms, but if we change the sitting room to a bedroom, we'll have five."

"If we use one wall of my house that will give us leftover lumber, and we can use it to add another bedroom on the main floor. I think we should get the boys down out of the attic, if they are willing. That's not a decent space up there. So still five bedrooms, but we'll store things in the attic instead of sleep there."

Colin came close and drew her into his arms. They were alone in the house because the children were doing chores while Elle got supper. He'd tracked her down in their room.

Elle enjoyed the moment. They'd had lunch and now this bit of time. It was always rare and wonderful to be alone together.

He whispered in her ear, "And that will give

us a bit more privacy than we have now."

"Hush." Elle looked past him. They were definitely alone.

And yes, they had the nights together, but right now they had one very thin wall between themselves and the girls. A bit more space would be welcome.

She decided she'd wait another month or two to tell him about the baby. Let him enjoy that feeling of privacy for a bit longer.

He bent his head, and she raised her lips to meet his kiss.

The kiss deepened and grew heated, and Elle could only think of just how wonderfully alone they were.

The back door crashed open. "Ma, Betty got stung by a bee. Ma, where are you?"

Martha hollering. Betty sobbing.

Elle broke the kiss and rested her forehead on his shoulder, laughing.

"Yes, Colin, I think a bit more privacy would be a blessing."

Colin laughed. "No more of a blessing than our crowd of children."

They smiled.

Colin took her hand, and together they headed down to manage — as they always did when they faced the challenges of seven children living in their little homestead on the range.

SOPHIE'S OTHER DAUGHTER

CHAPTER 1

Mosqueros, Texas
December 23, 1887

Laura McClellen rode her horse into the tunnel of doom.

When she'd told Beth she'd work for her — or rather when Pa lowered the boom — she'd never imagine she'd sink this low.

Visiting the Reeves.

Usually, she handled Pa perfectly but not this time.

As a rule, her pa never thought any man was good enough for her. But she'd turned down one he was mighty happy with and he said if she was determined to stay single it was fine but she needed to get a job.

Now she was nursing for Beth and Alex.

Laura didn't want to be a nurse. And yet here she was checking on Grace Reeves, due to have her child any day.

And why a woman who popped out babies as easily as Grace needed a doctor, Laura couldn't imagine. Beth said neither she nor

Alex had ever attended a birth in Reeves' Canyon and there'd been plenty of them.

The walls closed in around Laura as she entered the narrow canyon entrance. It was so tight it was hard to breathe. She shivered and it wasn't because of the early December cold. Daniel got a wagon through but it wasn't a big wagon.

And there was something about this place that caught the wind and held it . . . and if there was snow in the wind, the canyon filled up and melted mighty slow.

Daniel had carved a path out over the canyon wall. But it wasn't an easy climb. Even though most winters were fairly mild there was always the chance a cold snap and a heavy snow could seal the canyon. And Daniel reasoned it would be worse to be sealed out. Because of this, the Reeves family rarely appeared in Mosqueros during the winter. And it was especially rare in the years Grace had a baby on the way, that high mountain pass was hard enough when she wasn't great with child.

More than most anything in the world, Laura didn't want to end up spending the winter with the wild Reeves boys. She rode on anyway, knowing she was just looking for an excuse to bolt.

Then she was out of that smothering bottleneck and turned loose in a mad house.

Not that any of the madmen were in sight

right now.

She rode up to the house, which was a lot bigger than she remembered from her one and only visit here. Ma had mercifully learned to come visiting alone.

It stretched out so long she wondered if Daniel added on a room every time a child was born.

She tied her horse to the hitching post and knocked on the front door. A crash made her jump. Voices as loud and wild as a pack of wolves erupted and grew louder. She stepped back and it was a good thing because the door slammed open.

Here were the little lunatics now.

A little crowd of stair-step white-haired boys boiled out of the house, shouting and knocking against her as they rushed past her. She thought one of them shouted the word 'snow' but mainly it was just general screaming.

"Come in." Grace Reeves, sounding calm and chipper. Laura had never figured out how the woman managed to remain so pleasant when she was surrounded by pure bedlam.

Laura stepped inside to find Daniel rising from the table and lifting a little bald-headed boy, from a high chair.

"Laura, thanks for coming." Grace smiled.

Daniel frowned. "I asked for the doctor to come out."

"Beth and Alex are both busy. A family east

of town is down with a fever and they both needed to be there, so they sent me. They promised to come out as soon as possible. It will be a few days though."

Grace rested her hand on her rounded stomach and sighed in a way that struck Laura as odd. Daniel didn't notice and this wasn't the first time he'd proved to be lacking in much sensitivity. Instead he scowled at Laura as if frowning enough would change her into a doctor.

With ruthless efficiency, Grace began stacking plates. There was no need to scrape them, not a sliver of food remained.

Daniel said, "I'm taking Zeb with me." He slung the child under his arm and the little boy giggled wildly as Daniel left the house.

Because she wasn't even sure what she was here for, Laura shed her coat and hung it up along with her woolen bonnet and her gloves. Then she started clearing the table.

Grace filled a basin with hot water from her kitchen stove. She had a water pump coming up between her sink and the wall. Indoor running water.

The Reeves had a nice home, though nothing breakable was to be seen.

A small mountain of plates piled were up and Grace began washing. Laura grabbed a towel and dried. "I'm sorry Beth or Alex couldn't come out. But why did you want them? Surely you're not worried about the birth."

Grace stopped scrubbing for a time. She stood absolutely still. Laura narrowed her eyes at Grace trying to figure out what was wrong. Then as suddenly as she'd gone still, she was back to wiping.

"It's for Daniel. I thought he'd gotten over worrying about me birthing babies but then a woman died in childbirth last summer and he's been near frantic ever since. I've done my best to have all my babies without him noticing."

"What? How could he not notice?"

"Well, they come fast and if he's out of the house or asleep I can usually just get the baby birthed and then tell him about it afterward. He's known three times of my seven babies and he's been absolutely worse than no help at all."

Laura laughed then clapped one hand over her mouth. "I'm sorry. That's not something to laugh at."

"Do you know anything about delivering babies, Laura?"

"I do honestly. I helped bring the last two of Ma's babies into the world. She had them after the big girls moved away — except for Beth of course. Beth did most everything but I was allowed to stay in the room and lend a hand."

Nodding, Grace said, "Well, you may get

another chance because this baby is coming very soon."

"No, I doubt I'll come out with Beth when she comes. I don't usually ride out to see patients. Mostly I stay in at the doctor's office in town and help there."

"I don't mean you'll get a chance by coming again."

The tone more than anything caught Laura's full attention and she looked at Grace and realized the woman, though outwardly calm was almost vibrating.

"I mean —"

"I don't want to know what you mean." Laura was dead certain about that.

Grace turned and gave Laura a rather wild-eyed stare. "That's a shame because I see no way to avoid telling you that I'm going to have this baby now. Probably in the next hour."

"You mean you're in labor right now?" Laura knew she'd yelled because her own ears were ringing.

Grace opened her mouth, then fell silent and turned to face forward. Breathing slowly in and out.

Laura found herself breathing along. Knowing exactly what was happening. When the labor pain ended, Laura said, "You just had a contraction about five minutes ago. They're coming fast."

"All my babies come fast, thank the Good

Lord. It helps me sneak the labor past Daniel."

It seemed to Laura that Grace was worrying overly about her husband when she ought to be worrying about herself.

"If you don't mind, I think I'll go lie down. That last pang was hard enough I don't want to be standing for the rest of them."

Laura whipped an arm around Grace's middle and, even though it was probably completely unnecessary given Grace's calm, she supported the laboring woman to her bedroom door.

Grace whirled and pressed her hand flat on Laura's chest. "Stay out. I'll change into a nightgown myself."

"Wh–what should I do?" Laura had seen her ma have two babies. There'd been considerable yelling and fuss. Nothing like Grace's calm.

"Just pray as you've never prayed before."

With a gasp, Laura said, "Are you feeling like the birth is going to be difficult? Are you afraid?"

"No, heavens, nothing to be afraid of. I didn't mean you should pray for me."

"I shouldn't?" And anyway, Laura realized she was already praying. Mostly for herself.

"No, pray for Daniel."

"Why in the world would I pray for him?"

"Pray he doesn't come back. You don't want to have anything to do with that man while

377

I'm in labor. It's quite a sight."

Laura squeaked. Suddenly scared to death Daniel would return.

"And while you're at it, would you mind finishing the dinner dishes?" Grace slammed the door in Laura's face.

She turned back, beyond much clear thinking, so she washed dishes and prayed just as she was told. That was about the limit of her skill at delivering babies anyway. She decided she'd also pray that Grace kept up the good work of giving orders.

Another door slammed, this time open.

She whirled around to see Daniel coming in.

"Grace get out here." Daniel was a man who talked too loud in the normal course of things. Now he seemed happy and that turned him into deafening.

And behind him came a man Laura had hoped to never see again as long as she lived.

"Howdy, Ike."

Isaac Reeves. He seemed different. Harder. He was wearing a gun slung low, tied down. His eyes were blood shot. He had dark circles under his eyes and he was filthy as if he had ridden all the way from Chicago in a dust storm without stopping to wash.

"Laura." He just said the one word and gave her a tight nod, nothing more.

"We've got company. Ike's home for Christmas. And he's planning to stay. He's going to set up a doctor's office in Mosqueros."

Then Daniel looked around and finally his eyes landed on Laura. "Where's my wife?"

Isaac, her childhood nemesis more than any of the other Reeves boys, (and that was saying something) locked his blue eyes right on hers. Then he looked past her at the closed bedroom door.

Silence reined. Then Ike ran his hands through his hair and knocked his Stetson off in the process.

Finally, sounding exhausted, he asked, "How close are her contractions?"

CHAPTER 2

Ike tried to bar Pa from the bedroom but he failed, a useless effort anyway.

"Grace, are you all right?" Pa dropped to his knees beside Ma's bed and clutched her hand.

Laura came up beside Ike, where he stood in Grace's bedroom door. She whispered, "I'll just be going now. You're a doctor, no one needs me."

Ike's hand came out like a striking rattler and latched onto her wrist. "You're not going anywhere."

He dragged her into the room and shut the door with his back against it. If anyone was leaving it was him. He didn't want to deliver his mother's child.

That just wasn't right.

Ma looked at Pa for a second then her eyes slid to Isaac's. "I had hoped to finish with this before your pa found out."

"That's the best way." Ike nodded. "Howdy, Ma. Sorry I came home unexpectedly."

"It's bad timing but it's nice to see you."

"Grace, stop talking. You need to rest. You need to —"

Pa was a mighty good man in nearly every way. Ike had a lot of respect for him. But when it came to birthing babies he was just plumb loco.

"Laura," Ike talked over top of Pa — who was pleading with Ma to not die. "I'm going to need a basin of boiling hot water. It's okay to let it cool after it boils, though I'd like it to still be warm. You'll have to stoke the fire to get it hot enough to bring the water to a boil."

"I know how to boil water, Ike."

As he hung up his gun belt for the first time in weeks, he was surprised by the urge to grin. He hadn't done much smiling for a long time.

Laura had always been the sassiest of the McClellen sisters — and that was saying something with that sassy bunch. She was littlest of the girls and it was said that she had her pa wrapped tight around her little finger. Ike had seen it and knew it was true.

"Of course you do. I'm sorry." He sort of wanted to just go mess her up a little. Her hair was always perfect. Her dress pretty, tidy blue with too many ruffles for Texas. Her blue eyes wide and sweet, which Ike knew was a complete lie.

Her lips just as pink and pretty as he remembered. "Once the water's on, there's a doctor's bag on my horse. I'd ask Pa to get it but —" Ike jerked his head at his father, "he ain't up to it."

Laura rolled her eyes and walked toward where he blocked the door. When she was close enough, he whispered, "Don't you dare think of running off."

She hesitated, which he respected. It was clear she wanted to promise she wouldn't go, then ride off the minute she was out of his reach. But she was a woman who didn't like lying.

"I'll stay. But you don't need me."

"I might. No telling how hard this is gonna be."

"On your ma? She's always had babies with no trouble."

"No, on Pa. I may need help with him."

Laura turned and looked at Daniel, who had hoisted Grace into his arms and was laying her on the bed as if she was made of spun sugar. Grace was patting him on the back and trying to calm him down.

"I'll stay."

Ike handled everything mighty well, in his own opinion. His father's panic. His sassy nurse. His calm Ma who honestly didn't want his help with the birthing any more than he wanted to see . . . so much . . . of . . . his mother. But he knew he had to stay and help as the only person here with any doctoring skill.

Laura McClellen had been sent out by the doctor but after asking her a few questions, Ike could see her baby delivering skills came down to watching a couple of births.

He had her beat there.

And Ma probably would have been fine alone. She'd had most of the babies by herself with no fuss. The only fuss came the times Pa had caught her.

Yep, Ike handled it mighty well and things were going great, Pa's hysterics notwithstanding. Until the baby was squawling in his hands and a crisis came. And along with it, the shock.

"I can't believe this." Ike's turn to shout.

Ma sat up.

Ike held the squirming infant. "It can't be. What will we do?"

"Is your ma dying, Son?" Pa always went to the worst place in a situation like this.

"Is the baby all right?" Ma was much more sensible, but he could see he'd scared her. Darned right she oughta be scared.

"Ike what's wrong?" Laura rushed over, gasped and nearly fell over backward. "No!"

"Isaac Reeves you tell me right now what's the matter." Grace did have a mother voice that could wring obedience out of her sons. And that included Ike even though he was only seven years younger than her.

"It's . . . it's . . . it's . . ." Ike swallowed hard and forced the words past his throat.

"The baby's fine, Ma, but it's . . . it's . . . it's . . ."

He held the baby up, unable to say the stunning words. So Ma could see plain as day that —

"It's a girl?" Ma, calm and dependable as the rising sun, held her breath and stared and stared and stared. Then she broke into sobs.

"A girl?" Pa said it like it was a foreign word, like maybe Ma had said something in Apache and he was trying to translate it.

"Yes." Laura seemed to take the whole thing in stride after the first moment. Which was good. Someone had to switch on their brain and let it run. Ike wasn't having much luck with his.

"You've got a daughter, Grace." Laura swept the little wriggling tyke out of Ike's hands, swaddled it with a blanket she had at the ready and took it close to Ma, on the side Pa wasn't on, and turned the baby to rest in Ma's arms.

"A girl." Laura smiled. "A precious baby girl. Congratulations."

"But . . . but . . . but . . ." Ma could hardly speak through her tears. "I can't have girls."

She ripped her hand out of Pa's iron grasp and clutched the baby until Laura looked poised to wrestle it away from her for the child's own safety.

"Twelve boys in a row for you, Daniel," Laura said. "And now you've got yourself a daughter." There was something in her voice, almost like she was gloating.

Like Daniel had been denied a thirteenth son and she was gleeful about it.

Well, it was no surprise that the McClellens were fond of their girls, even though Sophie had turned to birthing boys after having four daughters — of whom Laura was the fourth.

Ike's head was spinning with what it all meant. Ma was going to make them all settle down so her daughter would be safe from the rampaging horde of boys.

Then and there Ike started planning.

He'd take the boys and run.

Let them live with him.

Do whatever it took to save them.

It'd also serve to save Ma from murdering them. It was an awful thing to see a mother hang.

Except taking them wouldn't work. Pa needed them to run the ranch.

Maybe Pa could build his sons their own house. Or build Ma a house for her and the little g-g-g-girl.

He needed to focus on the positive.

Something to keep things under control.

He had to look at the bright side.

Well, they'd been running the boys through the twelve tribes of Israel, "All the good tribe names are taken. Except Dan but that might prove confusing since it's your name, Pa. At least you won't have to name a baby Issachar or worse yet Gad."

Pa, still on his knees and looking like he planned to stay that way for a while since his daze was apparently bone deep, whispered, "We thought Asher wasn't too bad."

Ike immediately thought of a way to make it mighty bad. Nicknames could be cruel.

"I liked Judah," Ma said. "But your pa was afraid the other boys would call him Judy."

With a little spark of glee at the potential for torment, Ike knew he would have.

"So what are you going to name your little girl, Grace?"

Grace's eyes went wide and her arms went slack.

Laura dove and snagged the baby before it could roll onto the floor.

Laura knelt by the bed, holding the baby close. Ma didn't seem to notice. She definitely needed time to recover from this birth, though she never had before.

"A girl's name?" Ma looked at Pa. Pa's answer was to just drop his face straight down on the bed. Ike hoped he didn't smother. If he did, Ike could probably save him after he passed out and maybe a little nap wouldn't be all bad. It might help restore his senses.

"Not Dinah, she had a hard time of it." Laura stood. *Her* legs seemed to be working just fine.

"Who's Dinah?" Ike had managed to throw a modest cover over his ma and he'd not done much else.

Laura snorted as she cradled the baby and cooed at it. Her. She. A girl. God have mercy on their souls, none of them knew anything about raising a girl.

"Dinah is Jacob's daughter."

"Jacob had a daughter?" Ike asked.

"Yes, but her story is rather sad. Let's name her something happy. Something feminine and joyful and sweet." Laura looked at Ma. "Grace is such a name. Very pretty and girly. Maybe Joy or Hope or Faith. Those are good names for a miracle baby."

She was right about the miracle. Many was the time they'd talked of how Pa and Ma could only have boys. And Ike figure it went double for Pa who'd had five sons with his first wife.

But while Pa had pretty much collapsed, Ma — though clearly shocked — seemed to be handling it fine . . . except for almost dropping the baby, but she'd get over that.

Sooner or later.

Then Ma's eyes turned on Ike and he saw that those eyes weren't exactly shocked. That wasn't the word. And though she'd gotten quiet, he couldn't say she was exactly calm.

Or rather she was calm — insanely calm.

Then those eyes suddenly flashed with a blue fire he'd never ever seen before from his mother. A woman mighty good at handling chaos and rolling with the punches.

She made a sudden move and snatched her little baby girl back from Laura, then she said, maybe to the ceiling — maybe to the baby, though she wasn't looking at her. Maybe she was talking to herself.

Nope, Ike had a feeling she was talking to God. The blaze in her eyes said whatever words boiled out of her carried the power of an oath spoken directly to her Heavenly Father.

"Daniel Reeves." She almost growled with the kind of passionate fervor Ike had only before heard from a fire and brimstone preacher.

"What honey?" Pa raised his head,

Ma's voice even got through to him.

She spoke in a voice Ike had never heard before.

A voice that vibrated fit to set off an avalanche in the canyon.

A voice Ike imagined Jesus using when he told Lazarus to come out of the tomb.

A voice that made Ike want to grab his little brothers and run.

"Things are going to change around here."

CHAPTER 3

Laura wasn't sure but she might now be a hostage.

They just wouldn't let her go home.

Daniel acted like he needed her as a human shield.

Grace acted like Laura was part of some mysterious puzzle that involved making her hoyden sons behave.

Ike acted like she was handy to cook and clean and that was part of being a nurse . . . which it most certainly was not.

"Why doesn't Ma come out?" The littlest boy was named Zeb. And he seemed to need a mother's care. But then Laura had pulled him out of the fireplace twice now — he didn't need a mother's care so much as he needed to be surrounded by a cavalry division.

Climbing up the chimney was a mighty poor idea even when there wasn't a fire. And there was a fire tonight.

The rest of the boys, well, it was hard to

explain what they were doing. They seemed to be testing each and every inch of the house looking for something to break — and that included each other's bones. Fortunately there wasn't a piece of glass in the whole house. And though Daniel appeared to be a madman when it came to his wife having babies, Laura had to hand it to him, the man knew how to build things sturdy.

"She just had a baby, Zeb. She needs to rest." Laura patted him on the back and a small puff of dirt rose up. Laura didn't mention it, afraid Ike would decide part of being a nurse was doing laundry and giving baths. And she didn't mind doing laundry and giving baths, but it sure enough wasn't a nursing duty and she really wanted to go home. Tomorrow night was Christmas Eve and she wasn't spending the holiday in the Reeves' Lunatic Asylum.

She was planning to have a long, hard talk with Beth about sending her out here.

"She's never rested before," the next biggest boy said.

"Nope," this was the biggest one — not counting Ike. He was taller than Laura and old enough he might well know how Grace behaved after giving birth. "She just pops out those babies and gets right back to feeding us."

"But that's not good for her." Laura remembered Ma staying in bed for about a day, maybe two. Then she'd gotten back to work, though she'd tended the baby and left more to Laura when she had a newborn. "A woman should rest after she's had a child, she should stay in bed for a week."

Might as well set the number high in hopes of getting a day or two for poor Grace.

"And did you say it's a girl?" One of the middle boys asked that — possibly for the one hundredth time. Apparently, the truth was just unbelievable.

Laura herself was tempted to go in and change the little one's diapers just to make sure.

Twelve sons in a row. Six of them rampaging through the house — well, five. Ike wasn't exactly rampaging. At least not much of the time.

Daniel had gone outside for quite a while. Laura hoped the man didn't stagger into a creek and drown. He wasn't thinking clearly, a female child was too much for him.

The boys came and went a dozen times through the afternoon, and right now they came.

Laura had never finished the dinner dishes, she did that and immediately started supper. She'd washed an alarmingly big pot that was scraped so clean Laura could only guess it had contained stew.

"And you're sure you ate this whole pot of stew for one meal?"

"No offense, but we only like our ma's cooking." The oldest boy Benjamin said.

"Well, I am offended so don't say that again. You'll eat what I cook or starve." Laura had learned that phrase in that exact tone from her mother. As if these boys were one bit particular about what they ate. The littlest one had been gnawing on the kitchen table leg. "Don't you boys have chores to do?"

They all exchanged strange looks. Possibly guilty looks.

"Get out." Laura's first brothers had been born when she was three. Twins. There'd been more after that. She had no trouble working with boys, bossing boys around and just generally abusing them, at least verbally, for her own entertainment.

The boys all ran except Ike. She wished he'd go, too. "Don't you have chores?"

One shoulder shrugged and he grinned at her. She'd always been able to tell Ike and Abe apart. The triplets Mark, Luke and John had been tougher. But there was something about Ike. He'd liked healing and that had been a good fit for talking to Beth. Maybe that's why Laura had learned which one he was, not by the look of him but by his actions.

He'd been so nice and smart and caring, except for when he threw in with his brothers and nearly turned the school upside down.

"I've just returned home after being gone

for about six years. So I reckon I don't have any chores."

Laura didn't know why he'd picked now. "Where have you been?"

She found a hank of beef in an ice box. Nine people in the house . . . ten counting the baby. And every one of them looked like a carnivore. Thank heavens the little girl hadn't grown in teeth yet.

"Can you cut this meat into steaks?"

"Sure." He came and started in with decent skill.

She found a bucket of potatoes and began paring. She expected to be at this for some time. Her experience with brothers . . . added to the sight of that huge empty stew pot, told her to plan on each boy eating his weight in food.

Ike got done ahead of her. He stoked the fire on the big square cook stove and left the steaks beside it. Then he helped finish the potatoes and they got them on to boil.

It turned out he could make biscuits, too.

By way of celebrating the new baby, Laura found the makings for an Apple Brown Betty and got it shoved into the oven. The steaks and biscuits would only need a short time to cook so they quit that and began setting the table.

They were just finishing up when the bedroom door swung open and Grace came out. Fully dressed, her hair neat, babe in arms, fire in her eyes.

CHAPTER 4

"You didn't exactly show a courageous side of yourself, Ike."

Ike wasn't proud but he kept riding. "You ran just as fast as I did."

"She's your mother. And those are your little brothers back there."

"Who was I supposed to save, the boys or Ma?"

"You think your brothers have a chance?"

"She did seem determined." Insanely determined, Ike thought. He feared for his brothers and father. "Well, I didn't see any reason to stay there and get caught in the crossfire. There's no escape for the rest of my family — although Ben is sixteen, he could move out. But I don't even live there anymore. Why should I have to listen to Ma laying down the law?"

"Those are the words of a coward, Mr. Reeves."

Ike smiled at her snippy tone. A normal man might be offended by being called a coward, and Ike considered himself normal. But these weren't normal circumstances and he thought running for the hills was appropriate, cowardly but appropriate.

"Tomorrow is Christmas Eve. I promise to find my backbone and go back." Maybe not for Christmas Eve, he decided, but Christmas Day for sure. Maybe things would calm down by then.

"I should hope so." Laura turned up her cute little nose at him.

Watching that McClellen woman sass him reminded him that for a few years, when he was real young, he'd been sweet on Laura's big sister, Mandy. Nothing had come of it though. Clay McClellen had gotten wind of his interest, probably from the way Ike looked at Mandy in church, and scared Ike into reconsidering his youthful adoration.

Now that had been Ike at his most cowardly.

"Well, you're the one who got sent out by the doctor. You're the one who's abandoning her job. Haven't you ever heard of the Hippocratic Oath?"

"No, but it sounds terrible and you shouldn't use that kind of rough language in the presence of a lady."

Ike chuckled.

"And anyway, you're the doctor. I can only be described as a nurse by someone who doesn't know me. You, on the other hand, went to college. If you're going to be swearing oaths at hypocrites, then start with yourself."

"Hippocratic Oath."

"I told you to stop that."

Ike laughed again. He hadn't had this much fun in a long time.

"Here's that awful canyon entrance." Laura shuddered visibly and pulled her coat tighter. "How can you stand living in here?"

"It was the best place to live in the whole world." Ike shivered too, but it was from the thrill. What if a rock slide started? What if a blizzard hit hard while he was in the middle? What if a bull had gotten out and came rampaging back? This narrow slit in the rocks set his imagination to running wild and he loved it. "Some winters we got snowed in and couldn't go to school. Even when the weather warmed up there was something about the way the wind hit this canyon and no sun could shine down and it would just fill up and stay till spring.

"And even if the snows didn't block the entrance we could stir Pa up thinking it might happen, so he wouldn't go out in the winter for fear he couldn't get back." At least not easily, there was a high trail that worked. Had to be managed on foot. "We got to run wild in here. Pa never even watched us. I reckon he figured we couldn't get into too bad a scrape." Which was absolutely not true.

They'd defied death at every turn. "We all loved it."

Oddly enough they'd all left as soon as they were old enough, even Abe who stayed to ranch, had gotten out of the canyon and put some space between him and Pa. Or maybe he put space between himself and mayhem. Maybe it wasn't all that much fun.

The wind howled like a tormented soul through the tight canyon. Laura pulled her collar up to her ears as she rode ahead of him. Night had fallen in the short days of December and the shadows swallowed them up even though there was a full moon and an army of stars. It was a long ride to town and it was only decent that Ike ride along with Laura. If he led his family to believe he was coming back, well, they hadn't listened to him very closely had they? He did tell them not to wait up, he might sleep in Mosqueros. They wouldn't worry about him overly. Maybe by tomorrow his back bone would grow in and he could go back to see how Ma had set about changing everyone into polite gentlemen. He wished her all the luck in the world.

He also said a quick prayer for his little brothers who, up until now, had managed to avoid anything remotely resembling good manners.

As they rode out into the open, a cloud covered the moon and what had been a chilly but nice night for a ride, was suddenly sharply cold. The first flakes of snow sifted down.

"The wind's coming up." Ike rode closer to Laura. "Stay close. Without the starlight, I can barely see the trail."

Laura looked sideways at him. "I know the way to town, you don't need to even come with me."

Which reminded Ike of something he'd always wondered about. "You never liked me as a kid. It seems to me you were worse to me than all my brothers. Why is that?"

Laura was silent. He wondered if she'd answer. He could see her mainly because her skin was fair and her hair so blond.

"It was just childishness. You were a reckless boy and I was a fussy little girl." That was all she seemed prepared to say and they had a long ride ahead.

"But you picked me out of all my brothers. Plenty of Reeves boys younger than me by the time you were in school and they were wilder than I was." That probably wasn't true, they were all equally wild. "You won't hurt my feelings, I just thought we could talk about it."

"Well, I suppose I —"

Ike reached out, grabbed her arm and hissed, "Shh."

The intensity of the almost silent hiss made Laura instantly fall silent. He heard the clink of metal. Like maybe a horse shaking its head and making its bridle rattle.

No one came out here but the Reeves' and certainly not in a snow storm.

He knew.

It was everything he'd been running from.

Ma's blessed event had driven it from his mind but now it all came rushing back. He slapped his gun only to realize he'd left his holster hanging on the wall in Ma and Pa's bedroom.

He dismounted and dragged Laura from her saddle. With both horses' reins and Laura's hand in his, he moved fast, angling away from the trail. He noticed Laura had pulled a rifle from a scabbard in her saddle and he almost asked for it. A suspicion flickered through his head, from the confident way she'd taken hold of that long gun.

The lady might be better with a gun than he was. And he figured himself to be mighty good. Especially lately.

He had to admire Laura for coming along quietly. No questions asked. In the darkness he could see her head up, looking all around. Alert, trail savvy. Ready to fight but moving fast to avoid it.

The girl, for all her prissy ways and frilly dresses was a tough Texas cowgirl to the bone.

Ike knew exactly where they were. This was his home territory and he knew every inch of it. The riders kept moving, cutting him off from going back into the canyon.

Snow began filtering down. Darkness would have covered Ike's trail — but if the snow was heavy enough tracks would shine like lantern light.

He whispered, "We've got to get under cover and stop moving before the snow covers the ground."

She nodded and said nothing, just stuck by his side and let him lead.

This part of the land right outside his canyon was as familiar as his own face, which was saying something since, being an identical twin, he'd looked at his own face all day every day of his life when he looked at Abe. At least he had until he'd moved away from Mosqueros.

Abe wasn't far but he had three young sons and a wife to care for. Ike wasn't bringing angry gunmen to Abe's door. The canyon with his little brothers and newborn sister was out of the question, even more so because he'd have to get past the gunmen to get to it.

Mosqueros . . . he needed to get to town, but not on the main trail. Now, with snow coming down faster every minute, when the two-legged wolves turned back, as they would soon, they'd see prints and come riding hard.

If they took the trail to town, it could turn into a running gun battle with Laura in the line of fire. He thought of her parent's place. Clay McClellen was a tough man with a bunkhouse full of tough cowhands. If he could get to McClellen's they'd be safe. But that was miles and miles in the pitch dark and there was no trail from where they were to McClellens. He'd need to get most of the way to Mosqueros before he could turn and head east toward Laura's home. It was the same danger as just riding straight to town.

Then he knew.

The perfect place.

A hideout only a bunch of rambunctious kids could find . . . and he and his brothers had found it. There was even room to hide the horses and it was close enough they could hole up there quick before the snow got deep enough they were leaving tracks right straight toward them. There was no time to think of somewhere else.

He heard another hoof beat. The men had followed the trail as far as the canyon entrance and there, like everyone else save the Reeves, they'd found an impassable wall of rock.

And they'd turned back.

Laura's hand clenched on his and he turned, looked at her and knew she understood the danger.

Out of time and out of choices, Ike turned toward the rugged land that formed the canyon. He found a windswept stretch of stone where no man could find a trail, and began to climb.

CHAPTER 5

Laura prided herself on being a lady.

That didn't stop her from jerking her gun out of its scabbard when she dismounted. Reaching for it at the first sign of trouble was a reflex any smart girl learned growing up on the Texas frontier. She kept her finger only inches from the trigger.

She held onto Ike's hand so they wouldn't get separated in the pitch dark night, but she'd like to let go of him and swing a fist. She held the idea in reserve for later.

And she wanted to punch Ike because, as always, when there was trouble her mind started working with almost painful clarity, examining everything she knew with ruthless logic. It came to her mighty fast that Ike knew exactly what kind of trouble they were in.

He knew those men.

She remembered her first sight of him. He'd looked so tired and saddle weary. He'd worn that gun slung low and tied down.

A man ready for trouble. She'd assumed he

was just a sensible man who knew to always be alert.

But trouble was following him and he knew it.

As the wind buffeted them and the snow came harder, she considered that he might be lying about his medical training. Maybe he was an outlaw on the run. She hadn't seen him for years. Heaven knows what he could have gotten up to in all this time.

He'd certainly shown some doctoring skill with his ma, but he'd worn that gun like it was an old habit.

He'd always been a strange mix. Gentle and intelligent one minute, ready for mayhem the next. It was no trouble at all to imagine Ike in big trouble through some reckless act.

Oh, mercy did she ever have some questions to put to Ike Reeves but this was no time for chatter. She could tell by the way he moved he had somewhere in mind to hide and it was his territory so she let him lead.

Listening hard, though the icy wind was putting up a low moan, she didn't think those men had picked up their trail.

Sound could travel far if words were blown the right direction so she didn't even whisper. They didn't move at a run so the horses made little noise.

Any trail they left would be covered soon if this snow kept up. But who could count on that? Texas weather could be mighty unpredictable.

Ike leaned so close for a shocking moment Laura thought he meant to kiss her. Then he whispered, "It gets real steep."

They twisted sideways on the slope they'd been on and suddenly Laura could nearly touch the ground in front of her. Any trail there was had been covered by snow or disguised by the black night. Ike held onto her hand when she expected him to let go and tell her to drop back so they'd move single-file.

Instead, they stayed together and they kept moving.

The snow got thicker.

They reached a level spot and Ike whispered, "We're almost there."

A black, gaping mouth appeared out of the swirling snow and Ike led her right past it.

"Aren't we going in that cave?"

"Nope, too easy to find." Ike trudged along. Snow was beginning to layer the ground. It was still thin but from this step on, in any spot sheltered from the wind, they'd leave a clear trail. They had to stop. Not another footprint.

Then the trail took a sharp turn and headed steeply downward, and Ike turned again to walk along the side of the slope. Walls grew up on both sides and as suddenly as a blinking eye, the snow was gone.

A sigh of relief from beside her told her

they were where Ike had aimed.

"Drop back. There's a tunnel that leads to a bigger cave on back. But it's narrow. We'll have to go single file. Once we're through, I'm hoping we'll find some supplies, at least a lantern. We used to always keep one in here and a bedroll and even some food. I hope there's something left.

It was utterly dark. Her eyes didn't adjust. Water dripped. The *clip-clop* of the horses' iron-shod hooves echoed off walls. She could hear the horse Ike was leading well enough to not run into its rump.

Reaching out, she touched the tunnel on both sides without fully extending her arms. It was like walking into her own grave. Her breathing sped up and sounded loud in her ears.

"Just a little farther." Ike was mostly silent but in the pitch black his voice was like a life line thrown to a drowning woman.

Laura could do nothing but follow and breathe in and out, fighting back the smothering darkness.

Walking with her hand running along the stone wall, suddenly she reached an end to the tunnel and the hooves ahead of her had a different sound. An echo that bounced off walls that sounded farther away.

"Stop. Let me see if anything is left." Ike's words made no sense . . . except for 'stop.' She obeyed that.

A few seconds passed. The horse ahead of her got farther away and she wanted to shout at Ike not to leave her. Not abandon her in here.

A scratching sound — like rats working in the blackness — sent a shudder through her. Then a sudden pop and light flared. It almost startled a squeak out of her but remaining silent in danger was a well learned habit.

Then a lantern flared. More scratching as Ike adjusted the wick and replaced the glass lantern over the flame. It spread light in what was a decent sized cave — maybe twenty feet across in an irregularly circular shape with a slightly domed roof overhead that wasn't much more than eight feet high.

She looked behind her at the tunnel they'd just emerged from, then she saw another tunnel at the far end of this room.

A bit more time passed as her eyes adjusted to the dim light. Ike had crouched next to the wall and was rustling around with something. She decided to wait just a bit more to pepper him with questions.

Then a larger light flared. A fire. In the shadows, Ike had found firewood. And kindling. All of that had to be in here already. He'd said 'let me see if anything is left'. This must be a place he knew from his childhood. And since he hadn't lived with his parents in years, Laura considered it very good luck that things had been kept at the ready.

Finally the fire grew. He tossed more wood on and Laura saw a tidy stack of slender logs. Ike rose and gathered something in his arms and came to her, carrying the lantern.

"Warm up by the fire and wrap up in this if you're cold. Let me get the horses settled in the next room, then we'll talk." He handed over a scratchy wool blanket, took her horse and vanished into the tunnel across the cave. Before long she saw a faint glow from that tunnel and realized he must be lighting a fire in there, too. She saw the smoke from the fire following Ike, so the tunnel vented some-where ahead.

By the light of the fire she could see crates and stacks of supplies. A quick inspection revealed cans of food, pans, more blankets, all manner of things. This was most likely a little boy's hideaway and they'd turned it into quite the well-supplied home.

She was hungry, having left the Reeves's before dinner. She didn't want to watch them eat — she'd seen the Reeves boys eat before. Add in the militant gleam in Grace's eyes and Laura had run, Ike right along with her.

Now here she stood, her stomach growling. It was especially galling because she'd cooked their supper. She was disgusted with the whole Reeves brood . . . even Grace. Even that precious baby girl aggravated her.

Then Ike was back and she decided to aim her hunger and anger and fear right where it belonged.

"Who were those men?"

"Listen, let me build up the fire and see if
—"

"Ike Reeves you tell me what's going on
right now or I'll —"

A hand clapped over her mouth and Laura
considered punching him. It wasn't her way
to put up with much from a man. She arched
her brows and glared. If he wanted quiet,
he'd better start talking.

"Six men have been after me since Dodge
City, Kansas." He let go of her mouth and
rubbed his hand on the front of his shirt.

"You knew they were after you?"

"I hoped I'd lost them."

"Hoped? You'd hoped but you weren't
sure?"

"I *had* given them the slip a couple of times
before and they'd caught up with me. But
this time I really thought I'd gotten away."

"So you knew they were good trackers, and
they were serious."

"Good and very serious. I think that's a fair
way to describe them."

"So then why were you riding around in
the dark?"

"Well —"

"And why didn't you have a gun?"

"That's because —"

"And why in the name of heaven," her
temper grew hot and her voice grew loud,

"didn't you warn me," and yes she thought she still might punch him, "so I could stay a hundred miles away from you?"

He clamped his hand over her mouth again. "Shhhhhh!"

They'd come in to the cave too far for those men to hear her. Ike just didn't want to hear her either. She did her best to incinerate him with her eyes.

He shook his head and threw in a little shrug. "I did all of that because I've got a baby sister."

"You what?" She didn't her best to speak from behind his hand.

"I was so muddled by it I — I — I guess I forgot."

"You forgot six men were hunting for you?"

"Yep."

She clenched her fist. It really was time now to punch him. "And why exactly are these men hunting you?"

"Because I am the only witness to a bank robbery they committed. I was all set to swear I'd seen them in court and they broke jail and tried to kill me. They've nearly caught up with me twice since. And if you're with me, there's a good chance they'll try to kill you, too."

Her fist went slack and so did her knees.

CHAPTER 6

Ike caught her before she hit the ground.

Laura McClellen, passed out in his arms. And it was all his fault.

He looked at that pretty face. The blond hair a mess after the day she'd had dealing with his little brothers . . . and his little sister. He paused to try and come to grips with that.

In the flickering firelight he saw the smooth curve of her cheeks and the pink lips, closed now instead of yapping at him.

He'd have smiled at this moment if he wasn't responsible for putting them both in deadly danger.

But he'd get them out. They'd be fine here for however long they had to wait until his pursuers gave up and moved on.

He hesitated over that. Those outlaws where skilled trackers. He had no idea how they'd traced him all the way here. Could they find this cave?

No one ever had except him and his brothers. And even that wasn't purely true. Mark had found it and showed it to them. Mark was always a step ahead of the rest of them.

Ike regretted letting her go, but he lay her on the hard rock floor and made up a pallet of blankets. The cave was as well supplied as ever and nothing was coated in dirt. His little brothers must still come here and probably Abe and his young'uns along with them.

When the blanket was spread out, he lifted Laura again and moved her onto it. "Wake up, now."

She breathed steadily. She was probably overwrought from having killers after her, which had sent her into a faint. But besides that she was hungry, he'd noticed she didn't eat. He was mighty hungry himself. He decided not to fuss too much at her, just give her time to get over her swoon.

He found the little spring in the back of the cave and rinsed out a bucket and found a tin cup. He drank deeply himself, then found a tightly sealed glass jar, a row of them actually, full of jerky. They could live here for weeks. He found another pile of blankets and spread one over Laura to keep her warm. Then he ate and drank, built up the fire to take the edge off this chilly cave. He checked the horses. There was even a small stack of hay in one corner so they could eat.

This place was better supplied than some of the houses he'd gone to during his medical schooling.

A murmur from Laura brought him back to kneel at her side. The cave, with the firelight and lantern was bright enough to see as her blue eyes flickered open.

"You have killers after you." Her words were faint but Ike heard them clear as day.

"I'm sorry, it's just that with Ma having a girl and all —"

"Stop talking, Ike. I don't think it's Christian to want to punch you as badly as I do. Stop making it worse."

Ike just nodded. Then, blast it, he started talking again. "I'm glad you woke up. I want to go outside and scout around. The rocks up here are usually swept clean of snow by the wind so I should be able to go out and not leave a trail. I don't dare go down to low ground though. But maybe I can see a fire. Figure out where they've camped for the night. It's possible I can get us past them so we won't be stranded here overnight. There's food and water set up by the fire. I won't be long." He stood and got yanked right back down on his knees.

Laura had grabbed the front of his shirt. She sat up, glaring at him. "You are not leaving me down here alone, Ike Reeves. Give me a few minutes to eat and clear my head and I'll come with you."

"No, it's not safe. I know this land, and I won't get caught."

She jerked on his shirt and dragged him

toward her until their noses almost bumped. "I am better at slipping around in the woods than you any day of the week."

Ike had to admit she might be right. "The thing I'm worried about is leaving tracks in the snow. No amount of skill in the woods will stop that."

"I'll be careful. I don't want to spend the night stuck here with you if I can possibly avoid it."

That hurt his feelings just a little. "You never did tell me why you'd always disliked me so much."

"When we have some spare time, we can talk about it. Now let me grab a piece of jerky and we'll get moving."

Ike considered arguing more. He didn't want to put her in danger. But he thought she might be right. For a fussy, frilly woman, Laura was proving to be mighty tough.

She was ready in seconds, right down to her slinging her rifle over her shoulder from some strap she had on it. He'd never seen that before.

He picked up the lantern and headed into the tunnel.

"I can't keep this lit for long. I know the exact curve in this tunnel where from that point on, light can be seen from outside. So be ready to move on in the dark. I want you to hang onto me once we put out the light."

"I'm ready."

Ike's voice dropped to a whisper. "And now we stop talking."

She moved so quietly he glanced back. She wasn't letting even a footstep make a sound.

He came up on the bend in the tunnel he and his brothers had experimented with so many times. No more light from this point on. He looked back at Laura, caught her gaze and nodded and pointed at the lantern.

She nodded back. He turned the lantern down but didn't let it go out completely, then he hung it from a hook they'd rigged in the stone wall and reached out his hand to Laura. She took hold and, with her walking behind him, they rounded the curve and the light faded until they were swallowed up in the dark. He heard the faintest sound and knew Laura was running her finger tips along the wall to orient herself. He had just done the same.

He walked on until he felt the first gust of cold, clean wind. The entrance was just ahead. He drew Laura up to his side and eased forward.

They reached the entrance and he peeked out and jerked his head right back. Gripping her arm, he towed her all the way back to where they'd left the barely flickering lantern. Only then was it safe to talk.

"Do you remember that big cave we walked past coming down here?"

"Yes, that's where I thought we were

headed."

"This cave is very hard to find, you couldn't see that in the dark but trust me, the entrance is very well hidden, but that big obvious cave is where they set up."

"Right between us and any chance of getting out of here." Laura spoke in such a grim tone he was sure she never unclenched her jaw.

"I just had to make sure you knew that. I'm sure we can't get past them with the horses, but I want to get close enough I can see them, hear what they're saying."

"You're not going to leave me here."

"No I'm not. I need your help. Just stick with me and let's go. We'll need to stay low when we go out and stay close enough together I can touch you because we don't dare speak and it's so dark you won't be able to see so much as a hand gesture"

Ike took her arm and turned but she jerked him to a halt. "Wait."

"What?" Ike turned back hoping she'd say, 'I'm staying here. I'm scared.'

"I think we can catch them and turn them over to the sheriff."

Somehow he wasn't surprised by that. Disappointed but not surprised. The McClellen girls had always had a streak of desperato. "The two of us can't take six men into custody."

"I have an idea." She sketched it out and

blast it, it just might work. "And don't forget we can stop at any time."

She was right about that part, too.

"We can do it, but before we go I need you to lift up your skirts."

He ducked the blow just as he realized what that sounded like. He explained himself before she could take another poke at him. They were ready in minutes.

"Let's go." Ike took her hand and they headed for the cave entrance again, this time with a risky plan but one Ike decided was a lot better than his, peeking, hiding, listening and waiting.

Laura was a woman of action. He found that while it scared him to death, he also really liked it.

CHAPTER 7

Laura liked pretty dresses. She liked having her hair tidy and her nails neatly trimmed and clean. She loved to dance and flirt and most of all she liked all the feminine wiles she'd learned from a lifetime of wrapping her pa around her little finger.

But that didn't mean she couldn't take on six men, using all the sneaking she'd learned from a lifetime of working alongside her ma and her three big sisters.

It wasn't in her to cower. And it didn't suit her to let outlaws drive her into a hole in the ground like they were a pack of wolves and she was a scared rabbit.

Not when she had another choice.

And that choice was simple.

Divide and conquer.

She walked quickly and silently along with Ike until they reached the entrance. This time Ike dropped to his hands and knees and kept going. She was right behind him.

Laura still couldn't really see much about

418

the cave Ike said was so well hidden, but she could tell they were crawling along some kind of trench, walls on either side of her, but open overhead.

She crawled right into Ike, the first she'd realized he'd stopped. He turned and she could see him, just barely, a black shape in the black night. He reached back and towed her forward, there was room now for them to crawl side by side. She came up by him and he leaned close. Oh so close, she was so focused on him she didn't realize for a second he was pointing. Forward.

She quit looking at Ike and looked in the direction he was pointing.

And saw the man.

They'd posted a watch. Just as she'd expected them to. It was all part of her plan. She adjusted her rifle so it was centered across her back and they started forward.

They had to close about fifty feet. The man was leaning against a tree, his arms crossed, his head up, alert. Laura remembered Ike saying they were good and this was proof.

But he was watching down the valley and probably, considering the black night, overcast, snow still swirling down, he was looking for light. The guard was thinking he'd catch a glimpse of Ike's campfire in the distance.

The wide mouth of that cave was lit up with a fire burning inside. That's what Ike had seen when he'd first come out. The light was casting a bright enough glow it lit the sentry up or they'd have never seen him. Now, with his back to them, they could knock him cold and drag him silently away, disarm him . . . and by doing so arm themselves better . . . then wait for the next man to take his shift. If the others were sleeping they might be able to thin the herd enough to have an even chance of catching the rest of them and turning them all over to the sheriff.

Inching forward, silent as ghosts, Laura felt Ike tense beside her, ready to lunge and silence the man. He'd said if it went wrong they'd run for the cave. He was sure no one could find the entrance.

Then a snap from inside the cave froze them in place. Another man emerged and nodded at the sentry, who tugged at his hat.

Laura waited, barely breathing, for the man now on guard to go in while the newcomer took over.

But to her dismay both men stayed out. The second man took up a position near the first and they both still looked down the valley but one faced to the south and the other to the north.

Ike's hand closed over Laura's wrist and he leaned close enough she could see his face. They stared at each other, he pointed at himself and the man facing north and her and the man facing south. She knew exactly what he wanted.

He wanted her to take one and he'd take the other. In the cave she'd told him she wanted to do it. One butt stroke and she could take a man down.

He'd insisted the job was his to do, but she could be there to gag the man, or use her rifle butt if necessary.

Now he needed her help and they needed to attack at the same moment. Nodding, they both moved again, this time separating.

The air was chilly and the wind whistled through the skeletal fingers of the leafless, winter aspen, making them rattle together like bones.

It was a nasty business ahead of them. She gave one longing thought to her family. She would have spent tomorrow at home. Ma had always made a very special time of faith out of Christmas Eve. All day long they cooked and decorated the house, worked on last minute gifts while the boys went turkey hunting with Pa for Christmas dinner. Then they'd have a supper of oyster stew and a meaty chili con carne Ma had learned to make from one of the Mexicans who worked at the McClellen Ranch.

Then after their Christmas Eve feast Pa would read from the Bible about the birth of Jesus and they'd sing every Christmas carol they could think of. It was a wonderful tradition.

She turned back to the man she was responsible for and prayed. Hitting a man was a mean business, but she'd grown up in a hard land and she'd learned to do what needed doing.

She veered farther and farther from Ike and felt the loss of a partner close at hand.

She was only a couple of feet from the man she was after. The dull glow of the fire made it possible to see Ike slowly rise to his feet. He had no gun, he couldn't strike a blow like she planned to. But she trusted him to handle his part of this.

Standing in time with Ike, she silently swung her rifle off her back and in one hard sure blow she brought her sentry down like a felled ox. He crumpled silently at her feet. With one glance she saw Ike had his man down.

She grabbed the strips she'd sliced off her petticoat at Ike's suggestion. Grinning at the thought of how close she'd come to giving him a black eye when he'd said 'lift your skirts', she bound the man as quick and sure as a calf at branding time. She gagged him and then turned to see Ike finishing.

Then Ike came to her side and they dragged the man down to the cave.

Quickly, lest anyone emerge from the cave, they got the other man under cover.

Whispering, Laura asked, "Shouldn't we take them in by the fire?"

"This front part of the cave is far enough.

I'm not carrying these two lugs all the way through the tunnel."

"Won't they freeze?"

"Nah, it's not a bitter cold night. They'll be fine. Maybe if we can clear them all out we can bring their blankets down here."

They stripped both men of their weapons. Ike took the best gun for himself, checking to see if it was fully loaded. Then he collected two more pistols, a rifle, five knives and a length of iron pipe. They double checked the strips of petticoat binding, then headed out of the cave hopefully to fetch two more.

Laura might make it home to get ready for Christmas after all.

Ike wished they'd waited longer inside. It stood to reason the men were taking shifts that were a couple of hours long, there'd been no reason to hurry and yet they'd had to get in place and be ready when a new guard came out. They'd look for the men they were replacing and send up an alarm.

They only chance they had to make their plan work was if they silenced them before all the other men came out.

And if it worked, there were still two men to go.

It was getting to be the blackest hour of the night. The wind blustered and whined. The trees bobbed and clattered. Snow blew down into his collar.

Where he lay was fairly sheltered, close to where the first man had stood guard. But it was still miserably cold.

He hoped Laura had found a decent place to hide. The fire in the cave had burned low and it cast very little light. An hour had passed and he hadn't seen her since she'd ducked behind a rock. Had she fallen asleep? Was she so chilled she'd have trouble knocking out whoever took over as sentry?

Ike was building up a list of worries long enough he decided to crawl over there and make sure she was okay just as a shower of sparks came shooting upward from the big cave entrance. Someone building up the fire. He felt like a low down skunk making Laura help him with this fight, but he stayed put. Maybe just one man would come out. Maybe —

He quit guessing what might happen so he wouldn't drive himself mad.

Two men. And they headed straight for the spot the earlier guards had staked out.

When they separated the one closing in on Ike said, "Cash, my turn. Head on in."

It was dark enough the man didn't realize yet that his friend wasn't there.

He reached the spot where Ike hoped he settled and turned his back. The perfect time to take him but the other man was slower, muttering. Ike couldn't hear what he was saying, but he was grumbling and wandering a bit, looking for the other member of their band of robbers.

Ike drew his gun, rose up and coshed the man over the head. He quickly tied him up and gagged him, afraid even an unconscious man could groan. He turned, gun still ready, to see Laura hogtie her man.

Ike could really start to love that woman.

They had the two men dragged inside within minutes, disarmed and thrown in a heap next to the others in their gang.

One of the outlaws stared at them with mean eyes.

"He's conscious." Laura pointed. She whipped out another strip of cotton. "I'm going to blindfold him."

She bend toward the man. "I don't like you staring at me."

Ike double checked the bonds. "I don't want them to be able to untie each other."

When the men were secure, Ike said, "Let's go warm up for a few minutes." Ike remembered how long they'd waited for these two.

"Nope, we don't dare. It's close to dawn. There may not be another watch posted. The men left in the cave may just get going on the day."

"Do you really think the night is almost over?"

"I sure hope so." Laura dragged in a long breath. "Let's get in place."

CHAPTER 8

They had all six men taken prisoner just as dawn changed the black sky to gray. Laura was quietly smug. She'd been right to get back out there. The other men had stirred for the day after less than an hour.

The snow quit falling and the wind picked up as it often did when night turned to day. "Let's get them all on horseback and take them into Mosqueros."

She could almost smell the pies baking in Ma's kitchen. She'd be there in time to help.

"Leave these two tied up out here. Let's get the rest of them out of the cave." The men they'd taken prisoner were unconscious but still, Ike leaned close to her and a shiver that had nothing to do with cold rushed down her backbone. He whispered, "I want to do it before full light. It's a good hideout and I don't want anyone else to know about it."

Turning, they hurried for the other outlaws. As they walked, she whispered, "We can blindfold them before we bring them out so they can't see a thing." He smiled and she couldn't quite stop herself from glancing at his smile. "You are a good partner for a man, Laura." He settled one hand low on her back and she stopped at his touch.

"You're a good partner, too, Ike."

"Since we have them caught and we don't need to get them out of the cave before daylight, maybe it's time you told me exactly what it is about me that you've never liked." His strong, doctoring hand seemed to open and close right at her waist as if he were holding on to her dress maybe. She felt like he was holding onto a moment instead. "We never did get to that talk."

Laura thought of the night that had just passed and how dependable Ike had been. He was no longer that unruly boy. It was right that she tell him what had bothered her. And it wouldn't take long.

"All of you Reeves boys were smart. John was the best student and the nicest of a bad lot."

Ike smiled. "I reckon that's a fair description of us."

"Mark was always the ringleader. Abe took charge, after Mark devised some scheme. Luke was the mean one. That was one tough little guy."

"I always admired Luke's grit." Ike stood waiting patiently.

"You remember how you used to talk to

Beth about doctoring things? Even then she had a heart for wounded animals and people. And I could see you did, too. And here you are a doctor."

"That's why you didn't like me?" Ike's brow furrowed.

"No." Laura realized just how well she could see. Dawn was upon them and the sun would soon be up. She hurried on with her explanation. "What it came down to was, of all the Reeves brothers, you were the one that couldn't be trusted."

"What does that mean?"

Shrugging one shoulder, Laura went on, "John was the nice one, like I said, but he seemed to always be ashamed of that which made him dependably naughty. And the rest of your brothers were just as solid in their antics — including the one in my grade. But, well, do you remember I found a cat that'd been caught in a rat trap?"

Ike said, "I remember that."

"I had to run to the General Store to buy a pencil before school and I went in just as Mr. Steen, the owner was getting his gun to shoot the cat. He had tears in his eyes, the poor man. I begged him to let me tend the cat. Mr. Steen said it was cruel when the cat was in so much pain. But I talked him into letting me try. To me, trying meant taking the cat to Beth, who'd gone on ahead of me to school. So I wrapped it up and brought it with me.

The teacher excused Beth and you from studying so you could try and help the poor animal. And because I brought it in, I got to help."

Smiling, Ike said, "We did help him. We saved him. And the teacher let us keep him at school and we tended him at school for weeks." Ike touched her cheek with one finger and drew it down her cheek. "It was good what we did and you helped a lot. Why do you tell me that story when I ask why you don't like me?"

"You'd be kind and friendly and smart one minute and the next you'd be laughing when one of your little brothers put a worm in my lunch pail. I expected it from them but from you it really hurt. It was humiliating that you laughed while I was being tormented. You weren't to be trusted. And nothing you ever did up until today changed my mind."

Ike closed his eyes for a second. "I'd defend myself except that seems like exactly something I'd do." Then his eyes opened again. It was light enough now she could see the pure blue of them, rimmed with dark blond lashes.

A bird cried in the woods signaling dawn. The snow had stopped and the strength of the sun promised warmer weather.

Ike leaned forward and rested his lips on hers, gentle as a morning breeze. He lifted them and said, "I'm sorry I acted like that. I'm sorry I was the kind of boy you couldn't

429

trust. I'm not that boy anymore."

Then he kissed her again.

There was nothing boyish about him. His strong, callused right hand rested on her cheek and the other tightened around her waist and drew her close.

Then his hand slid from her face into her hair until he cradled the back of her head and tilted it to the side.

The kiss became more than sweet, more than warm. It turned passionate and deep.

The world faded around them until all she knew, all there was in the whole world, was Ike Reeves.

She was lost, so lost in the kiss, in the wonder of his arms.

She heard the metallic crack of a cocking gun. "Get your hands where I can see 'em." A deep voice cracked as loud as the gun.

Laura staggered back. She dragged Ike along because her arms were wrapped tight around his neck. He helped her let go then whirled to face that voice, backing up so she was pressed against rock. He was shielding her with his body. Offering to take the bullets that might come from that cracking gun.

Suddenly Ike relaxed. Laura was able to slip sideways and quickly step in front of him.

"You don't have to protect me," Ike sounded a bit doubtful.

"Oh, I think maybe I do." She looked up from the trench they'd been standing in and up to the man standing over them, looking down, gun aimed.

Though when she moved to the front the gun lowered and instead he seemed determined to glare her to death.

But she didn't have to see him. She already knew that voice.

"Hi, Pa."

"Pa, say something."

"You don't want to hear what I have to say, girl." Pa had all six men draped over their saddles.

Ike had helped.

In fact he'd helped so much Laura was pretty sure he was afraid to do one single thing to annoy the famously over-protective Clay McClellen.

A man who'd just spent the night with his daughter and then was caught kissing her — had better be afraid.

"Clay, I'd like to speak with you about what you saw . . . that is . . . speak about what was happening . . . not that anything was happening."

"Plenty was happening, Reeves. Which one are you, anyhow?"

Laura didn't blame Pa for that. He'd have probably known Abe, because Abe lived nearby. And all the younger Reeves boys, except those still at home, had left the area. When they were youngsters you could narrow down the possible identities by size. Abe and Ike, twins and the oldest. Mark, Luke and John, triplets, five years younger and next in line. After that they came one at a time, stair steps but otherwise alike as peas in a pod. Twelve peas loaded in a mighty big pod.

"I'm Ike."

Those eyes swung around and almost drove a nail through his hide. "I remember you. You had your eyes set on Mandy at one time."

"You did?" Laura was annoyed.

"It was a long time ago and it never was nuthin'. We were too young for it to be anything." He turned back to Clay. "I'm a doctor now, home from my studies. I'm planning to open a doctor's office in Mosqueros. And what I meant by nothing was happening is —"

"Mount up." Pa cut him off. He had a picket line of horses ready to move out. Ike had fetched their horses out of the cave and they all swung up on horseback and headed down the slope.

It was single-file down to level ground, then Pa snapped, "Reeves you ride by me. Laura, drop back and keep an eye on the prisoners."

Every one of them was tied up tight as a Christmas turkey. And they didn't need one bit of watching.

Laura considered kicking up a fuss but it would only delay what was going to happen. Pa would have his say. To Ike — and no doubt

432

later to Laura. There was no getting around it so Ike might as well get it over with.

Poor man.

CHAPTER 9

"Clay, uh . . . Mr. McClellen, sir." Ike swallowed hard. He'd spent the night with Clay McClellen's daughter who was not his wife. He wondered if a man had ever done that before. Let alone done it and lived to tell the tale.

And Ike had no intention of letting Laura be dishonored.

"With your permission, sir, I'd like to ask for your daughter's hand in marriage."

The sun was fully up now and when Clay turned his cold blue eyes on Ike they seemed to glow with an inner fire. "She's not marrying you. I thought nothing happened, beyond you spending the night together."

"Nothing did happen. And we didn't exactly spend the night together. From quite early on we had the outlaws."

"As chaperones?" Clay's voice rose. "Do you really dare try and use such an excuse?"

"No, sir. And anyway, they were all tied up and gagged. They'd've been poor chaperones

434

in that condition. But my point is, sir, you can see we were mighty busy. And that's not what I want to talk about."

Clay turned and glared at Ike until he thought holes might be burning right into his skin.

Swallowing hard, Ike forced the words from his mouth. "I want to ask for Laura's hand in marriage, Clay."

The eyes didn't quit burning.

"Uh . . . I mean Mr. McClellen. Uh . . . sir," Ike added with another quick swallow.

After way too long, Clay said, "Nope."

That shook Ike out of his near terror. "You can't say nope. I just spent the night with your daughter."

Ike saw Clay's hand twitch and for a moment it looked like the man might go for his gun. Clay McClellen was a tough man. He had a few tough sons and a bunkhouse full of tough cowhands.

No one crossed him.

But proposing to his daughter wasn't crossing him, except maybe Ike shouldn't have said —"

"If I ever hear words like that come out of your mouth again they'll be the last you say."

Ike flinched. His future father-in-law was threatening to kill him. This wasn't going as well as he had hoped. "I thought you were upset about us being together. I'm trying to make it right."

"No one knows you were alone together but me. And you don't suit me for a son."

"Why not?" Ike tried to sound calm but this was insulting. "I'm a doctor. I'm going to make good money. I'm a hard worker, and I'll treat Laura right."

And besides he'd just kissed the living daylights out of her and he wanted to do it again soon and often and for the rest of his life.

He didn't say a word of that out loud, thanks to Clay's twitchy fingers.

And then he was disgusted with himself. He was no kid and neither was Laura. Which goaded him into growing a backbone. "Laura is an adult woman. I'm going to propose to her and, if I can convince her to say yes, we'll be married. We'd like your blessing but we don't need it."

Clay's eyes narrowed to slits and a mean smile appeared on his face. "I'm going to let you talk to her ma."

Ike quit talking because fear swelled his throat shut. If Clay was a tough and feared man, then Sophie was fit to strike terror into the heart of anyone who met with her wrath. There were plenty of men in prison who would swear to it that they'd have rather faced Clay than Sophie.

Ike faced forward hoping Clay wouldn't read the abject terror.

"I'm going to pick up the pace, Laura."

Clay shouted. "I'm looking forward to getting home."

Clay glanced at Ike and said more quietly, "Come on out for Christmas Eve dinner."

Clay had the picket line of horses tied onto his so when he kicked his horse it was a minute dragging all six horses, each bearing an unconscious man, to a higher speed.

Ike decided not to distract him. He didn't want to hear what else Clay had to say anyway.

"Pa invited you to Christmas Eve Dinner?" Laura's wide blue eyes were hard to read. It was surprise not excitement or happiness. But maybe it was a happy surprise.

He didn't ask. He was afraid he might not want to know.

They stood on the Mosqueros sidewalk while Clay talked to the sheriff. Ike was amazed Clay gave them this much time together. But it would take a while to lock those men up. Ike had his chance to propose to Laura. He had to do it now, get her on his side before Sophie got to vote.

"Laura, when we, I mean when I — that is we had a moment —"

"Hi, what happened out at Reeves' yesterday?" Beth Buchanan came out of the doctor's office.

He had to fight the urge to tell her to go away. And since he wanted to live in Mosqueros for the rest of his life and work with Beth and Alex, and support the wife he was planning to take, he needed to be civil.

Beth's brow furrowed. "Are you Ike?" Beth always had known him better than the rest of them.

"Yep." He tugged on his Stetson. "And I'm back to stay."

He wanted to run her off and get back to talking to Laura but he had a feeling Beth didn't run off all that easy.

"Grace had her baby while I was there and Ike showed up in time to deliver it." Then Laura added, "She had a girl."

Beth, still walking toward him, tripped on a perfectly smooth board sidewalk. She pitched forward and Ike caught her before she landed flat on her face. He stood her on her feet.

"A-a-a girl?"

"I know exactly what you mean." Ike had kinda forgotten about the little sister now living at his home. How was Ma doing by now? Had his little brothers survived the night?

He shook his head to get back to the subject he wanted to discuss with Beth, no chance right now to get to the subject he wanted to discuss with Laura.

"I finished college and have been working with a doctor in Chicago all these years. I got tired of being so far away from family and came home. I hope there's room in town for another doctor, do you think —"

Beth threw her arms around him and squeezed him near to death. There was some squealing, too.

A door right behind him opened and he heard the crack of a gun being cocked. He knew by the cold chill rushing up his back exactly who it was.

"Get your hands where I can see 'em."

CHAPTER 10

Ike turned around slowly, hands in the air. It wasn't as hard to get away from Beth as it had been from Laura.

He faced Clay and thought maybe the man might just be looking for a reason to shoot him.

Another door opened. Ike didn't take his eyes off Clay. Honestly, the man looked more disgusted than angry.

"Alex, there's a new doctor in town." That squeal again.

"Really, where?"

"Right there."

Ike wasn't watching but he suspected Alex Buchanan had joined them and Beth was pointing at Ike's back. Better than her pa aiming at Ike's front.

"The man your pa is threating to shoot? Are you sure he'll make a good doctor?"

"If Pa doesn't shoot him, he'll be a decent doctor." Laura had decided to speak.

Last time she'd stepped between Ike and

her father's fire iron. Did this mean she didn't care if he got shot? Or did she not think Clay was serious?

Clay lowered the gun, looking a little frustrated. Probably decided he didn't have an excuse to pull the trigger.

Being his son-in-law was going to be a trial.

Ike hoped he was going to live through yet another encounter with Clay and turned to face the two Doctor Buchanans. And a little girl. Alex had a three year old in his arms.

"I want to open a practice in Mosqueros, that's right." Ike lowered his hands and reached toward Alex. "I don't want to step on any toes but —"

"No, you won't." Alex grabbed his hand. "We just found out Beth is expecting another baby and with two older ones in school and a third who's a toddler we were a little over-whelmed. You're the answer to prayers, uh . . . what was your name?"

"I'm Ike Reeves. My parents are Daniel and Grace Reeves."

"Oh, sure." Alex blanched a bit and added, "Some of your little brothers are in school with our children."

Ike laughed, "I can tell by your expression that you do know my little brothers. I promise I've settled way down."

Alex laughed, Beth joined in and slid her arm around her husband's waist but spoke to Ike. "Remember that cat with the broken leg we nursed back to health, Ike?"

"Yep, Laura and I were talking about it." Ike wanted to say he was going to join the family soon, but it was probably best to talk with Laura first.

Clay interrupted. "The sheriff said he's sure there are wanted posters on all six of these men. Some hefty money coming to you, Reeves."

Ike glanced at Laura and grinned. "Laura and I will need to share it. She helped catch those varmints every bit as much as I did."

Laura who had been kept far from him ever since Clay interrupted their kiss smiled and even blushed just a bit. Ike knew spending the night with her was as improper as all get out and a good enough reason for a wedding. In fact, that's how his own folks had come to be married.

But that wasn't why he wanted to marry her. He wanted permission before God, man and the laws of Texas to kiss her anytime he wanted. He wanted permission to spend every night with her. In fact, he didn't want to spend one more night without her.

And to manage that was going to take some fast talking to Laura, not to mention Sophie McClellen.

Clay was going to have to rest that rifle, too.

"We can talk more later," Ike said to Beth and Alex. "I'm invited to the McClellen house for Christmas Eve Dinner."

"You are?" Beth's brow rose and her eyes shifted from Ike to Laura and back again.

"He is." Laura's eyes shifted between Ike and Clay.

Clay's eyes didn't shift anywhere. They stayed locked on Ike cold as a Chicago blizzard.

"Are you just getting back to town now?" Beth asked as if she was thinking — finally — about something besides getting a doctor to help out. Like maybe where her little sister spent the night, and with whom. "Pa, you rode to the Reeves' last night didn't you? I just figured you went straight home with Laura. And here you are just getting home from the Reeves' with six wanted men?"

"And Laura and Ike caught all six of them?" Alex added.

"It's a story we can't tell while we're ridin'." Clay shucked his rifle into the scabbard on his saddle.

Beth gave her head a small shake. "Well, all right then, that's fine. We're heading out there in just a few minutes."

Pa said. "We'll wait so we can all ride together."

It was like a death knell. Ike wasn't going to be allowed a minute alone with Laura. He'd hoped if he was just riding with Clay and Laura maybe he could drop back. Maybe there'd be a narrow spot in the trail and somehow he'd get a chance to —

"Let us help you gather the little ones," Clay interrupted his thoughts which were foolish anyway, Clay wasn't going to leave off his vigilance over Laura for a single second. "Are you hitching up the wagon?"

"No, the children are determined to ride horseback and Alex can carry Melinda on his lap. It'll be much faster."

"I've got the horses saddled," Alex added. "In fact they should be —"

Four saddled horses rounded the building on the end of Main Street, led by an older girl and a younger boy. "Here they come now."

Alex and Beth smiled so fondly at their children it stirred Ike up. He hadn't been to Abe's yet but he knew they had young'uns. And Mark was married to Emma, a woman in Montana Ike had never met but he knew they'd started a family.

He was overdue.

The horses Clay, Laura and Ike rode to town were tied to the hitching post. The sheriff had sent his deputy to deal with the six horses the outlaws had.

They were on the trail to the McClellen's in minutes and Clay set such a brisk pace there wasn't time to talk.

CHAPTER 11

Sophie McClellen heard the door open. It was just coming on midday and Clay hadn't returned yet. He'd gone out last night to ride home with Laura. Word had come from town that he had to ride to the Reeves' to get her and he might be hours riding to that canyon and back.

That was the last she'd heard of them and she'd been worried, not overly because Clay handled trouble well. Laura, too.

Still, it was a relief. She whirled to smile at them and saw Laura, then right behind her, one of those bothersome Reeves boys.

"It's Ike, Ma'am." He doffed his hat. His twin brother Abe hadn't left the area but Ike had been gone for years. Though she'd heard of a trip home or two, but Sophie had never seen him.

"Howdy, Ike." Every thought that filled her head was some version of 'what are you doing here?' which was just plain rude. So she waited until maybe someone would offer an explanation without her demanding one.

Beth's young ones raced past Ike. "Your uncles are in the corral practicing their roping."

All three children ran straight out the back door.

"Pa and Alex are putting up the horses," Beth said. "We rode home like we were chased by the Grim Reaper. Now, maybe, Laura and Ike, you'd like to tell me how you came to be riding into Mosqueros early in the morning. And why Pa was holding a gun on you, Ike."

Laura shrugged and said, rather weakly Sophie thought, "Grace Reeves had a baby girl yesterday."

Sophie's mind was boggled. "A girl? Are you sure?"

Laura exchanged a look with Ike. "I'm mighty sure. Are you?"

Ike nodded. "Yep, it don't seem likely but it was a girl sure enough. Twelve sons and now —"

Beth cut him off. "I want to know why Pa seems to want to shoot you."

"Well, your pa wants to shoot me for spending the night alone with Laura."

"You what?" Sophie's eyes went to her butcher knife.

"We were *not* alone. Ma, nothing happened." Laura's reassurance didn't stop Sophie from picking up the knife.

"Oh, I'd say something happened," Ike glared at Laura.

Considering the knife in her hand, Sophie couldn't decide if that made him very brave or very stupid.

"I know it did. Your pa sure as certain knows it did, Beth seems to understand it did, and look at your ma now holding a knife. Why does everyone think something happened but you?"

"What happened?" Sophie's voice cut through the room as surely as this knife was going to slit Ike Reeves's gullet if he'd mistreated Laura.

"I asked your husband for Laura's hand in marriage."

"You did?" Laura sounded shocked.

"You did?" Sophie echoed Laura. Then she added, "What did he say?"

Ike turned to look hard into Laura's eyes and didn't answer Sophie. "I most certainly did. And I've been waiting for a chance to speak to you in private but it is clear that isn't going to be allowed, so I will speak my piece in front of your ma and Beth."

Sophie decided on brave.

Then he looked back at Sophie. "And nothing beyond the pale happened, Ma'am. I in no way dishonored your daughter. But we did find ourselves drawn to each other and I'm in —"

"Ike Reeves," Laura cut him off, "don't you

dare say another word."

Ike fell silent.

Sophie wondered for the first time if Laura and Ike might suit. He seemed to obey well.

And then he quit obeying. "I'm in need of a wife and I think your daughter would make a fine one. I'm surprised and honestly offended," Ike turned and faced Laura, "that after what passed between us you don't agree with me that marriage is in our future." He completely ignored the knife.

Sophie decided on stupid.

She was so focused on Ike that she didn't notice Laura coming over until she wrested the knife from her hands.

"Ike, you stop talking and Ma, stop threatening to kill him. We were kept out together, overnight, through no fault of our own. And nothing improper happened and besides we were busy capturing six armed bank robbers. Pa came along and caught Ike kissing me, that is the first and last thing that passed between us, and it's certainly not reason enough for a marriage."

"Kissing you?" Sophie was shocked. Laura, nearly famous for how ruthlessly she rejected men, had driven Sophie and Clay to near despair. The girl would never settle on a husband.

Then Sophie thought of what else he'd said. "You caught six armed robbers?"

She set aside the kiss for a while. "How did

you do it? I want to hear every detail."

She'd taught her daughters to protect themselves so it was not surprising that Laura handled it. Ike probably helped some, too.

Laura was nearly done explaining when Clay came in with Alex behind him.

It was good she was nearly done because Sophie figured Clay wasn't going to want to talk about anything but Ike and that stolen kiss.

Ike listened to the women talk about capturing bad men when they should be talking about a wedding.

Now finally a man came into the house. Ike had already talked to him, that was true, but someone reasonable needed to make a decision.

He paused for a moment of guilt while he thought about his ma, she was by far the most reasonable one in the family — or at least she had been until yesterday.

Well, this was men's business and Ike needed to make Clay see that.

"Clay, Laura and I should be married at once."

Laura whirled away from her mother and her story to narrow her eyes at Ike. She strode right up to him so they were nearly nose to nose.

"You are making it seem that we misbehaved. I won't have my ma and pa think such a thing."

They hadn't misbehaved, well, not much anyway. What they'd done is find each other, discovered a powerful attraction to each other. Come to respect and care for each other — or so Ike had thought.

"But what about your reputation, Laura?" Ike leaned close. He couldn't hope for actual privacy but he wanted Laura at least to know he was only talking to her.

With a dismissive wave of the hand, Laura said, "Bother my reputation. That's nonsense."

"You reputation isn't nonsense, Laura. I won't leave you without the protection of my name."

"No one is going to force a marriage onto my daughter and that's that." Sophie plunked her hands on her hips.

"But we spent the night together. When word of that gets out —"

"It won't," Clay said it like he was repeating a law written down in a book.

"But what if it does? Then Laura will have to marry me." If it came to that Ike would at least get this pretty woman for himself but he'd sure like it better if she'd cooperate. "And we will be rushing to get ahead of rumors that would already be in circulation.

If he could just get her away from them, talk to her, remind her how nice it'd felt to hold each other, kiss each other, be —

"No one would dare to say a word against my daughter." Clay had that cold look in his eyes. He settled his hand on his gun. Ready to fight anyone who dared speak ill of Laura.

"You can't shoot everyone who gossips, Clay." Ike probably should be calling him Mr. McClellen. On the rare occasion he'd spoken to the McClellens as a child, he'd always called them Mister and Missus. But Ike was no child and he hadn't been for a long time.

"I won't have to shoot everyone," Clay said with grim satisfaction. "Probably only one or two, then the rest of 'em will stop."

"Anyway, who knows outside of family and the sheriff?" Laura said with a nervous glance at her pa. She probably didn't want to be responsible for making him start firing that gun.

The door to the cabin slammed open and Abe stepped in. Ike's twin brother. Ike smiled, glad to see the other half of himself. He took a long stride to give Abe a hug.

Abe stopped him. "It's all over town that you and Laura McClellen are —" Abe slid his eyes between Clay, hand on his gun, and Sophie who'd picked her knife back up. "Uh — that you're — uh — c-carrying on."

"What?" Ike said it but he heard mostly everyone else in the room say it, too.

Sophie gasped. Clay growled. Laura put her hand to her mouth. Alex went to Beth's side and slid an arm around her.

"Who said such a thing about Laura?" Clay spoke through gritted teeth.

Abe dragged his Stetson off his head and proceeded to wring it into a knot. "All six of the men you arrested. Someone taunted them through the jail house window and they started in. A crowd gathered. Folks are mostly defending you and Laura but everyone's heard it. They've said — said — well — scandalous, terrible things. No one believes it's true. And I know Ike and Laura would never behave so sinfully. But the word is out, lies or not."

Abe's cheeks were flushed pink with embarrassment for having to tell this tale and Ike felt his own heat up. They'd always been as alike as two peas in a pod. Right now they were still a surprisingly close match. Ike usually kept his hair short but he'd been weeks traveling home so it was overly long. His clothes were disheveled. Abe should have been burned darker from the sun but it was December.

"I rode over to Pa's canyon today and heard you were back and gone into town. I went in to see you and heard all of this. I knew you'd ridden from the canyon to Mosqueros with Laura yesterday but the rest of it — I had no idea of what had happened. I told them —" Abe wrung his hat harder, and Abe was a tough man who didn't let much upset him. "I couldn't think of a way to stop it and the sheriff knew you'd ridden out here with Laura and Clay so I came as fast as I could."

Ike turned away from Abe and looked at Laura. "Now, we've got no choice."

He reached out and took her hand. "And I want to marry you, Laura. I think we'll suit. Would you do me the honor of marrying me?"

"Yes," Clay McClellen answered, not Laura.

Ike turned and glared at his future father-in-law, "Will you please let Laura answer me."

Turning back to her he said, "In private, please. Could we talk?"

Laura's eyes brimmed with tears. She dashed her hand across her eyes and nodded. Ike sure hoped she was crying because she was embarrassed not because she was facing marriage to him.

He took her hand and led her right out the door Abe had just come in. He heaved a sigh of relief when none of Laura's overly vigilant family followed them.

CHAPTER 12

Ike turned Laura to face him and took both her hands.

She felt his strong grip and it held her from pure panic. The thoughts jumping around in her head about the whole of Mosqueros, Texas with her name on their lips sent her stomach to churning.

And her pa and ma looked so hurt. Pa was angry and she couldn't bear to think of him fighting for her good name.

"How did this happen? I just rode out to your place to visit your ma? I didn't do anything wrong." She looked at Ike and blinked her burning eyes. Tears cascaded down her cheeks.

"Laura, honey, don't cry." Ike pulled her close and she was so frantic to think of what was happening she didn't protest when he hugged her tight.

She buried her face against his broad chest and wept. He let it go on plenty long before the worst of her storm of tears passed.

He bent his head to her ear and whispered, "I would be honored if you'd agree to be my wife, Laura. You were the best partner a man could have yesterday delivering the baby, then helping with my family, then fighting those outlaws. All of that made my thoughts turn to what a fine woman you are. And then I kissed you." He stopped talked and eased back enough to kiss her again.

She should have shoved him away. Instead her arms crept up his chest, so slowly, so surely.

He ended the kiss with noticeable reluctance. "I'd already decided I'd do my best to convince you to let me come calling before all this happened. And I had a notion that it'd take some talking because you were set against me. But with that kiss, I'd hoped your feelings had changed."

Laura lifted her head. "They had. I could see you'd grown into a good man."

Ike rested a hand on her cheek. It was just past mid-day and his blue eyes, awash in kindness, reflected the Texas sky. "Your pa catching us, and now this gossip forces us to act fast but the end is the same. If you say yes, I get to spend the rest of my life with the prettiest woman I've ever seen. A woman I don't want to spend my life without. Will you marry me, Laura?"

Sniffling, Laura nodded her head, the smallest possible movement, but a smile bloomed on Ike's face and he swept her up in his arms and twirled her around.

It wrung a small laugh out of her. He kissed her again, enthusiastically. "Let's send Abe to town for the parson. We can get married right now, today. It'll quiet all the talk and —" Ike learned close and whispered again, "— it'll mean I don't have to spend another night without you."

That sent a shiver through her that had nothing to do with the cold.

"Tomorrow is Christmas Day and its Sunday. We can go into church together as a married couple." She stepped back.

Ike let her but he took her hand as if he didn't want to let her go. It warmed her heart.

He jerked his head at the cabin door. "Let's go tell your folks and Abe. I can get my brother to stand up with me. My family won't come, not with a new baby. So we don't have to worry about them."

"That will make for a much more peaceful ceremony," Laura said. Then she squeezed his hand so hard it got his attention.

"In case you think differently, any sons we have are going to behave. I'll see to it."

Ike's brows rose in surprise, then his face bloomed into a smile. "I'd appreciate it very much if you'd see to it. Why do you think all my brothers move away the first chance they get? It's a madhouse in that canyon, no one past the age of about sixteen can stand it. My brother Ben should be moving out any day."

Laura grinned then she laughed and Ike dragged her into his arms and tasted that beautiful laugh.

"Let's go tell your folks, then send Abe running for the parson."

They went into the McClellen cabin hand in hand.

CHAPTER 13

Laura tingled with pleasure as she rode to town on Christmas morning with her family, Ike, her brand-new husband, at her side. They'd gotten a slow start and heard the peal of the church bells as they rode into town.

Laura was surprised when Ike came to help her down off her horse. She'd been dismounting by herself since she was about four.

But she enjoyed his strong hands on her waist and the sparkle in his eyes told her he was just looking for an excuse to touch her.

Last night, their wedding night, there'd been no such opportunity. Pa, Alex and Ike all slept in the barn.

Ike didn't like it but Laura wasn't going to sleep with him in a room that shared a wall with her parents and that was that.

They walked into the church hand in hand.

Laura headed for the front. The McClellens always sat in front.

Ike headed sideways. The Reeves always sat in the back.

They tugged against each other and stopped. Turned to look at each other.

Smiled.

Then the smile melted off Ike's face like candle wax in a prairie fire. Laura followed the direction of his gaze to the front of the church. Three pews.

Full of Reeves.

Each boy sitting absolutely still.

Like stair steps. Completely silent stair steps.

Ma and Pa had gone ahead, not watching Ike and Laura, they took up their usual seats on the right side of the small church. The Reeves were on the left. The rest of the church was full, or nearly so.

Parson Radcliff was already speaking. Laura yanked on Ike's hand and he followed her. There was room on the McClellen side so they squeezed in.

Ike kept looking at his little brothers and Laura had to admit she couldn't stop from studying them either. Though the service ran long, not a one of them wiggled. No one crawled out of the pew on his hands and knees. No one yelped as if someone had bitten them. (Someone most often usually had.)

She's never seen them sit so still.

Come to that, she'd never seen them in church in the winter.

What in the world had Grace done to them?

"Now, please rise and join me in singing,

'Silent Night'."

Parson Radcliffe gave Laura a fond smile.

When the hymn died down Ike leaned over to Laura and said, "What did Ma do to them?"

Laura shrugged. "Whatever it was, they probably deserved."

Then the service was over and everyone headed for the back of the church. Not a single Reeves boy went dashing down the aisle. The politely waited their turn and filed out. Ike watched them go past. Each of his brothers gave him a friendly greeting but not boisterous, no shoving or shouting.

When at last Daniel and Grace stepped out, Ma went to Grace and the two women fussed over the baby girl. Then Grace's eyes lifted to look at Ike.

She beamed at him and came to his side. "Abe rode in late last night and told us your news. We had to risk leaving the canyon so we could see you and say how happy we are."

Grace pulled first Ike, then Laura into a hug without ever letting loose of her daughter, who lay sleeping in her arms.

"What did you end up naming her?" Laura asked.

Grace looked down at her sleeping child. "Hope. I named her Hope."

Daniel came up beside Grace and congratulated them. "Welcome to the family, Laura. I thought I'd get all my daughters this way."

Daniel spoke more quietly than Laura had ever heard before. He looked over his wife's shoulder at the baby. "Hope is a pretty name. For a little girl as pretty as her ma."

Grace and Daniel shared a long, happy look then wished everyone a merry Christmas and headed up the aisle together.

Hope. The perfect name for a baby born at Christmas time.

Laura thought maybe there was hope for the changes in the Reeves family. And it described how she felt about her own marriage. The rest of her family had already headed out so for one brief moment she and Ike were alone together.

"I think we're going to deal well together, Ike."

He smiled and leaned in for a kiss. "We're going to do more than deal well together, Mrs. Reeves. We are going to share a love that lasts a lifetime."

Laura thought so too, but she hadn't expected Ike to figure it out so soon. She smiled and returned his kiss with interest. "Let's go before Pa comes hunting us."

Ike closed his eyes briefly. "Now that we're married don't you think he'd let us be alone together?"

Laura laughed. "We'll give him the slip after Christmas dinner."

Sounding forlorn, Ike said, "Something else to hope for."

They walked out of church arm in arm.

Laura tried to imagine a finer thing than the gift of hope for Christmas.

■ ■ ■ ■

THE SWEETWATER
BRIDE

■ ■ ■ ■

CHAPTER 1

Montana
July 1897

Despite the worry about drought rabbiting around in his head, Tanner Harden's chest expanded as he rode around his property. He hadn't explored it all yet, and he *would* find water.

Nothing could stop him from making a home in this beautiful place.

Yes, it was in one of the meanest stretches of mountain the world had to offer — not that Tanner knew much about the world beyond his home — but it was hard to imagine anything more rugged than this. And he loved it. It was his.

But it wasn't just. *mean.* What he and his family knew, that nobody else did, was that between all these stretches of jagged rock and treacherous trails, the crumbling cliffs and the soaring peaks, were pockets of sweeping green meadows, lush, belly deep. Tall grass that'd fatten a cow and make a man prosper.

Pa had helped him scout this land, and then he'd left him to run it . . . unless Tanner needed help. He couldn't help but smile when he thought of how much his folks had done to help already.

Silas and Belle Harden were the best parents a family of nine kids ever had. They'd been generous to him when he struck out on his own. They'd said he'd worked for it and deserved it. And he'd worked mighty hard all his growing-up years — that was the plain truth.

They'd helped set his big sisters up when they married, too, so this seemed fair. But still, he knew he was starting out much easier than a lot of men.

This stretch was up where the eagles soared. It was between his folks' property and near his sisters Emma and Sarah and Betsy. And on past them was Lindsay. He closed a gap that might one day, if all his brothers did as he did and claimed stretches along the spine of the Rockies, connect Harden land all the way to Helena, Montana.

He'd bought his land, and Pa had cut some good young stock out of his herd. Then his family had come up here and helped him build a tight little cabin.

Just two days ago, he'd hugged his ma and shook his pa's hand, and they'd left him alone . . . at home. His chest expanded some more. His own home. His own land. And yes, he was worried because it was a dry summer, and he was out today scouting for springs. A couple that he'd thought he could depend on had dried up. But he'd find water. It was all part of building something in a wild, unsettled land.

He smiled as wide as his face would allow.

A scream ripped through the thin air and wiped the smile away.

Gunfire followed. A rifle. One shot.

Another scream so sharp it seemed to rip into his bones.

That was a woman's scream. There were no women up here. But when a man's common sense told him one thing and his ears told him something else, a man was apt to believe his ears.

Tanner turned his horse, trying to find the source.

The peaks and tumbled boulders, many taller than a man, echoed with gunfire, bouncing and surrounding him until he couldn't tell what direction it came from, but he had a notion and he was a man to trust his instincts.

Except his instincts told him the sound came from a pile of rocks that he saw no way to cross, a pile that seemed to lead straight to a wall of solid rock that reached overhead fifty feet. His black stallion, a descendant of Tom Linscott's prize thoroughbreds, might well break a leg crossing the rock — and this young giant was to be the foundation of a herd of horses Tanner planned to raise. He hated taking it onto the rock-strewn path, and if it got any more treacherous, he would leave the horse behind rather than risk its safety.

But the black moved forward with surprising speed, picking his way between scattered rocks. Tanner, who considered himself a mighty savvy tracker, finally realized this was a barely visible trail. Each step was taken carefully, and he was glad to trust his horse.

Another shot rang out. No scream this time. His horse responded to tension in Tanner's grip on the reins and picked up speed. They walked forward, approaching the sheer rock wall. He had no idea what he was supposed to do when he got there.

And then, only a dozen feet before he had to stop or run his stallion's nose into granite, the trail twisted right — Tanner wouldn't have seen it, but his horse did — then it turned left, and he looked straight into the heart of the mountain. A crack in stone that was only a bit wider than his shoulders. Yet the black kept going without pause.

His horse twisted through pure stone, open overhead. And then he saw green.

A thrill of discovery urged him onward. He entered a mountain valley that perched on top of the world.

Before he could study the valley, he heard a

voice again, shouting this time, not screaming. And now inside this vast expanse of open ground, he could tell exactly where it came from. The ground was easy to ride now and he urged his horse to a trot.

The land rose gently then crested. He reached the top. Grass spread wide in front of him, a vast land, a thousand acres or more. The expanse was dotted with maybe a hundred longhorn cattle. At the far end of the meadow a small house stood, nearly swallowed up by a beautiful stand of majestic Douglas fir trees. Two smaller buildings were spread out beyond the house, also right against the woods that seemed to climb the edges of the mountain that created a bowl to conceal this beautiful land.

And in front of one of those buildings stood a woman.

A woman who looked nearly as wild as this hidden land. She wore leather, and her shining red hair was long and wild as if it had never seen scissors or a comb. She had a shotgun in one hand that she wielded ably. It was an old one that reminded him of a Sharps his ma kept hanging over the door, though it wasn't her preferred weapon.

He'd been in this area many times hunting a place to settle, and he'd never seen hide nor hair of a woman, nor a cattle herd, and he'd had no idea this rich valley existed.

She faced the woods near her house, gun in

one hand, the other arm full of . . . Tanner wasn't sure what. It looked like a bundle of something brown.

Wary of the gun she held, he stopped at the top of the crest. "Howdy, miss."

The woman spun around, leveled her rifle, then froze. She stared at him as if he were a ghost. Something beyond her understanding. Her eyes got round, her tanned skin went pale as milk.

"Don't shoot, miss. I just came to see if you were all right." He braced to dive off his horse. He had no idea what she was thinking, nor what she'd do.

She dropped the rifle and the brown thing, which flapped its wings, went running . . . but not far. She covered her face with both hands, including her eyes, and some sound he didn't quite recognize came from her, a song maybe? No, not a song. No reason for a body to start singin' right now.

She was acting mighty crazy, which was bad. On the good side, she was disarmed.

"Are you all right? Was that you I heard yellin' and shootin'?"

She didn't move. Not sure what came next, Tanner pressed his heels to his horse's side and they descended the gentle slope.

He rode right up to her and she drew her hands down to uncover her eyes and stare. Her hands lowered farther until she clutched them together on her chest, maybe in prayer.

Her throat worked as if it'd gone bone dry beneath the collar of her strange leather outfit. He wasn't sure quite how to describe it. Leather, and very clearly made by hand. It wasn't an Indian dress, and she definitely wasn't a native woman with her bright red curls that hung nearly to her knees.

Then she said, "Wh–who?" her voice was like a rusty gear. He'd heard her scream then later shout. She'd sounded nothing like this.

"Name's Tanner Harden." He tugged the brim of his Stetson. "I'm getting down now. I mean you no harm."

He moved smooth and slow, no sudden moves. Her rifle was within grabbing distance, and he didn't want a nervous woman like this to decide she was in danger.

He ground-hitched his stallion and came face-to-face with her. She had eyes a shade of blue the Montana sky would envy. She licked her lips.

"Are you all right, miss?" He paused over the word, wishing she'd supply a name. Nothing, just staring. "I heard you scream and there was gunfire. Were you in danger?"

The woman glanced away at the bird she'd dropped. Tanner realized it was a grouse. Tanner had hunted them many times. But he'd never seen one that scratched and pecked at the ground ten feet from a man. They were always wild, flapping and running away. This one seemed to be her pet.

He looked back at her and saw her looking past the bird, past her house. Tanner looked at what must be a chicken coop, except a flock of grouse were inside a fence made of woven saplings.

Right near the pen lay a full-grown wolverine.

Dead.

Tanner had only seen a couple of them in his life. They were night creatures. Vicious killers who fought shy of people. He'd seen the damage they could do to a pen full of chickens. The time he'd seen their handiwork, a wolverine had killed the whole flock and only eaten a few.

That was what made her scream and shoot. He couldn't say he blamed her.

Finally a strange scratchy noise drew his eyes back to the woman. Who asked, "Where did y–you come from?"

The way she said it made Tanner doubt she'd ever had a visitor before. As suddenly as he thought it, he decided it might well be true. After all, the entrance to this place was about as hidden as could be.

She was probably about one thousand times more surprised to see him than she'd been to see that wolverine.

Tanner really didn't know where to start.

"I'm your new neighbor."

Those beautiful blue eyes widened until he could see right into a mind full of pure terror. "You are moving in here? Into my valley?" She glanced at her rifle.

"No!" He'd started out all wrong. But maybe there was no right. "I'm going to live outside your valley. I've built a cabin and brought in my herd. I didn't know anyone lived near." He tried a friendly, neighborly smile. "I reckon we'll get to know each other well."

She just watched, her brow furrowed.

"Do you need any help? Did the critter hurt more of your animals?"

The woman opened her mouth, closed it, then as if forcing the words out, she said, "He was getting to my chicken house."

Tanner glanced at the tame grouse. "This is your . . . chicken?"

The girl smiled. "I know it's not a chicken, but I raised them. I gathered up hatchlings and brought them home and gentled them. I've got a nice little flock, and they provide eggs and —" Suddenly her eyes were filled with tears. She took a swipe at them and fell silent.

He decided he needed to ask simpler questions. "What's your name?"

There was a long moment of hesitation, as if she had to think the answer over. "Debba McClain."

"Debba. It's nice to meet you. I welcome company up here."

"No one should get in here. And I never go out."

"Never?"

"Why would I? I have everything I need."

Why indeed? Tanner could think of a lot of reasons. "You never go to the general store?"

She shook her head. "I went as a child. But I have nothing to buy."

Tanner had four big sisters and a ma. Women always needed to buy something. Why, they took the long ride to Divide at least twice a year. And of course once a year they made the cattle drive to Helena.

"Do you live here alone?"

Nodding, she said, "Since my pa and mama died."

"How long ago was that?"

"I don't keep track of such things. I think it's been four or five winters."

"You've lived here alone, completely alone, for four or five winters? And you've never gone out? Never seen anyone or gone to town?"

Those tears were back. She shrugged, the smallest motion possible. Her voice dropped nearly to a whisper. "I don't know where a town is."

Something odd and painful snapped in Tanner. Such sympathy for her swept through him he could hardly breathe.

He had to take her out of here. Take her to his mother. Ma would know what to do. She was something when it came to raising up girls. Boys, too, for that matter, but Tanner loved all his feisty big sisters, and Debba could use some kindness and attention from Belle Harden.

Of course, here she stood with a tame grouse and handmade clothes and a wolverine pestering her that had died for its trouble.

Add to that, she said she'd been here alone for maybe five years and she still had bullets left. This was a woman who knew how to take care of herself. Ma would love her.

"Can we talk?"

"We *are* talking."

At her confused look, he smiled. "I mean sit down and talk for a while, get to know each other."

Her nodding was as tiny a motion as her shrug. Tanner realized she was out of practice making gestures, the little clues people used to communicate. Maybe she yelled at wild animals all the time, but most likely, she spent more time in silence than any human alive.

"I don't have time."

Tanner fought back a smile. "You have an appointment somewhere?"

"Nope, I will skin that skunk bear before the smell sticks to the fur. And get my hen locked up before something else gets her."

Tanner had heard a wolverine called a skunk bear before, but mostly he had little experience with the critters. "I'll help you."

"Have you skinned a skunk bear before?"

He had to admit he had not.

"We must be mindful of the scent glands — the fur is unusable if they are punctured, and I shot it very carefully to avoid that."

She was a good enough shot she avoided glands inside a wolverine? Tanner was so full of admiration he felt a little dizzy.

"I'll catch the grouse for you, then, while you get on with the skinnin'."

She picked up the grouse and held it out to him. He wondered if she was realizing right now, having caught the bird herself, that he was not of much use.

He carried the placid grouse to the chicken yard while she headed for the wolverine.

As he looked at the pen, Tanner, who'd been trained by his pa in the way of building, realized it had been built without a single nail. It was a log structure, but the logs were saplings so it wasn't a heavy coop. And the fence was made by twisting and braiding branches no thicker than his thumb.

It stirred something in him to see the skill that went with this fence.

What's more, there were sections he could tell were new. His first notion was that her father had built this before he died. And maybe he had, but she'd learned enough to carry on.

Having spent all of two minutes returning the grouse to her little fenced yard, he went to watch Debba skin her catch.

Her knife must have been razor sharp, and each motion was swift and sure. She might be shy of visitors, but there was no denying how skilled she was with that knife.

"You are really good at that."

"Thank you." She looked up from her work and smiled as she hadn't before. A full smile with true happiness lighting up her eyes.

It was a smile so pretty, Tanner followed her without looking left or right until just before he stepped inside. Then he did notice what he should have seen right from the first.

A stream, a good-sized one, flowing full and fast right along the far south edge of the valley.

Plentiful sweet water.

In a dry year.

When springs he'd counted on to water his cattle had gone dry.

She was already acting mighty friendly. He hoped that continued after he asked her to let him water his herd.

Chapter 2

Debba's fingers itched to touch the man.

Tanner. Tanner Harden. The sound of his name was like music. Another person. The shock of it was almost too much to bear. He was tall and slim, with dark brown hair and eyes a startling color. Brown and green and golden all at once. She'd never seen the like. He had the sleeves of a blue shirt turned up to his elbows, and she saw the corded muscles in his forearms.

He wore thick brown leather chaps and brown jeans with rivets here and there. The clothes looked like some she remembered Pa wearing long ago.

She forced her attention back to her work, and he crouched beside her and watched in a way that made her clumsy.

It was almost impossible to speak, but it was even more impossible to remain silent.

"Where did you come from?"

"In through that keyhole pass on the northeast corner of the valley."

She nodded. She knew that pass well, but she'd never gone through it — not since Pa had died. He'd warned strongly against it. Talked of the dangers. Talked about how Mama had died. That had happened so long ago. Debba only had mixed-up memories of Mama.

"Are you alone, too?" The notion twisted through her that they might be the only two people in the world.

"I live in my own home a few miles away. Downhill from here. This is about the top of the world."

She was silent. She didn't know much about the world and if it had a top, bottom, or sides.

He added, "But I have a big family, and they live on a ways. I'd like to take you to meet my ma."

Her heart started pounding. He had a mama? The longing was wild. But she didn't dare leave her mountain meadow. Her pa's dying words, the last words he'd spoken, were too strong. And she'd heard no other words for all these years, which gave what Pa had said more and more weight.

"I — I can't go."

Tanner rested a hand on her shoulder, and she quit her skinning and turned to him. He looked at her, really looked hard, like he was memorizing her eyes or something. Then he said, "Well, all right. Maybe I'll bring them to meet you sometime."

That would probably be safe. She nodded, scared to tell him how much she'd like that. Wondering if Pa's warnings about the outside world included letting them in.

"You've lived alone here for years?" Tanner asked.

She nodded and got back to work, glad for something to do so she could force herself not to stare at this man.

"Don't you get lonely?"

"I'm used to it." She got so lonely she talked to her animals and the walls and sometimes she imagined her parents were at meals with her. She'd asked herself often enough if that made her a lunatic.

"Your meadow is nice. The house and coop and barn are well built." Tanner looked around. "Did you do it, or did you have family when you first came here?"

"I lived here with my mama and pa, but Mama died so long ago I can barely remember her. The house and barn were built when Mama was alive, but I was too young to help. Pa wanted a bigger chicken coop when I was older, and I helped with that. And I learned to build chairs and such with his help. And it's good that I learned because I've had to go on alone."

"I've never seen anyone skin a pelt this fast." Tanner's voice was quiet, like he really meant it. She looked and he was watching

480

her hands whip along, doing the job.

"Th–thank you." She had a vague memory of proper manners.

"Did you build the chicken coop fence?"

"Yes." She stood and took the hide to the coop fence to hang it up.

"I've never seen anything like it before."

Debba felt her cheeks heat up. He'd embarrassed her. It was overpraise. Such a strange feeling. She didn't want to pursue his flattery. "A skunk bear, what did you call it?"

"Wolverine is the word I've learned."

She scowled a bit. "I prefer wolves to skunk bears. For that matter I prefer bears to skunk bears. Wolverine is a good name."

"I agree."

"A couple of years ago a wolverine killed every chicken I had. That greedy varmint ripped a board out of my coop and crawled in and killed them all. He didn't eat them either, just killed for sport. And this one was up to the same thing."

"So catching and taming grouse was something you did on your own?"

"Yep, they lay a decent-sized egg, so I trailed a grouse hen and found her nest, when it was still full of eggs. I waited for them to hatch and grow just a bit so they weren't too fragile, then I caught them, about eight chicks, and brought them home and raised them up. They are as tame as my chickens were."

"It's a good-sized flock."

Debba finished with the hide. "They've hatched out new babies every spring. They give me plenty of eggs as good as any chicken."

"Do you want me to bury the carcass or cut it up and feed it to the grouse?"

"Bury it. They'll probably peck at it until they find the scent glands, then it'll smell too strong to interest my flock, and then I'll need to bury the reeking thing."

"Do you have a shovel?"

"I'll get it for you. It's in the barn."

Tanner walked along with her to fetch it. Honestly, as fascinated as she was to have company, the way he tagged after her made him seem almost as lonely as she was.

When that chore was done, Tanner said, "Can we walk around the meadow? You've got a stream running, and I'd like to see where it goes. Maybe I can find where it leaves this canyon and use the water."

She shrugged again. It was so easy not to talk, to make silent gestures. She had talked easily while she'd worked — to the grouse and her horse and herself. Maybe the chore had distracted her from fretting over how exactly a woman talked to a man.

They strolled together toward the far end of the pasture. She checked her cattle as they passed, looking for any sign of sickness or injury.

"Debba, what would you think of me bringing my ma or my sisters here to visit?"

The fear and excitement clashed until she
couldn't speak. Whether that was because she
had nothing to say, or too much, she wasn't
sure.

He touched her elbow, and through the
doeskin arms of her tunic his touch seemed
warm.

When he tugged, she stopped walking and
turned. He faced her, looking worried. "Does
the idea bother you? I think you'd like Ma,
but I don't want to do anything that will
bother you."

"I — I think I would l–like to meet your
mama."

"And you won't come with me?"

She shook her head frantically. "I can't."

"What makes you say that? Are you worried for your animals? I reckon another
wolverine could come."

"No, or um . . . yes, the skunk bear could
come, but no, that's not why I won't leave."

"Can you tell me why not then?"

"My pa said I mustn't ever leave this
meadow."

Tanner frowned and studied her for far too
long. "Why did he say that to you?"

"He always said it. Long before he died,
but on his deathbed he made me swear I'd
never go through that keyhole pass."

"But he was condemning you to a life of

483

terrible loneliness. Why would he do that?"

"Because" — she wove her fingers together and stared at them — "the world outside this meadow killed my mama. And he said it would kill me, too, if I went out there. It's a dreadful, dangerous place."

Tanner opened his mouth and closed it about five times. Finally he said, "I live out there and it's not all that dangerous, Debba. I can't figure what your pa could be talking about. How did your ma die?"

She wavered, then, from her fear to confusion. "I'm not sure. I don't remember. She died when I was young, eight years old, I think."

"Was it sickness or an accident?"

Debba looked through him into the past. "I don't remember an accident. We'd been out, one of the few times we went to town. Pa liked keeping to ourselves. She wasn't hurt while we were there because I remember riding home together. Pa wasn't happy we'd gone. He always fussed, but Ma was in high spirits, teasing and laughing about how nice it was to get out and see others. Then one morning a few days later, I woke up and she'd taken to her bed. After she died, he rarely talked of her except to tell me it was dangerous outside of this canyon."

"So she must have caught something, a sickness, while she was outside. I can see how your pa would blame the trip. And he probably didn't plan on dying until you were full grown."

Nodding, slowly Tanner reached out and took both her shoulders. "But he can't have wanted you to spend the rest of your life, maybe forty or fifty years, completely alone. He just can't have wanted that. It sounds awful, cruel. Was your pa a cruel man?"

"No." She shuddered at the feel of his hands. It was deep inside so she didn't think he could tell, but to be touched!

She had no idea how wonderful it would feel. She lost all control of herself and threw her arms around him and hung on.

Tanner gasped and his hands came off her shoulders. She shouldn't have done this. She had to let go and step back. But just another second. Just one more second of contact.

Then Tanner's arms came around her and held her tight and close. It was like hearing him speak. It filled a desperately empty place inside her.

Until now she hadn't seen it, but it had been cruel of her father to make her swear to live this completely lonely life.

Was her pa a cruel man? She'd never thought of him as such.

Tanner released her, and she was going to let go of him in just one more moment.

His hands settled firmly on her shoulders, as they had when this started, and he eased her back far enough their eyes met.

Chapter 3

"Come out with me. Come and meet my ma." Tanner now felt an almost overwhelming need to take her away from this canyon.

It was so strong he was determined to throw her over his shoulder and kidnap her out of here if he had to.

He hoped it didn't come to that. "We'll feed your grouse and hope that's the only wolverine that comes by for the year." He tried to sort out all she needed to do before she left. What chores did he see to before riding to his folks' place?

"Your cattle will be fine for a few days while I introduce you to my ma and my sisters, their husbands, and my little brothers — who are near grown-up men these days."

"You have a huge family."

Tanner smiled. "My sisters all have little ones, so it's even bigger than it sounds."

A bellow sounded from behind him and he whirled around to face the biggest longhorn bull he'd ever seen. Standing not twenty feet away, its head down, pawing the dirt. It was the color of midnight, with a spread of black-tipped horns that had to be more than eight feet. He lowered those massive sharp horns and kicked dirt onto his belly with his front legs. Tanner reached back to grab Debba and run.

"Shadow, you sweetie." She'd run all right. Right around him and right up to a bull that looked like a killer.

"Debba!" He drew his gun, knowing a single bullet would never kill this thing, not in time.

She didn't even notice his warning or his gun because she was busy hugging the monster. She wrapped her arms around his neck. Arms that had just been around him. The bellowing stopped, the pawing stopped. She pressed her cheek against his massive forehead and crooned. Then, with a pat on his massive black nose, she stood up and took one of his horns and led the critter right up to Tanner.

Well, he'd seen a lot of things in his life. Seen his skinny squirt of a ma throw a thousand-pound bull. Seen every one of his big sisters rope and brand a spring crop of jumping, running calves. Seen a neighbor, Mandy Linscott, shoot a running wolf from five hundred yards out. So Tanner didn't underestimate women, ever.

But this moment, right now. He looked old

Shadow in the eye and saw his own death. That bull was as good as speaking to him, telling him no outsiders were welcome.

"Scratch him between his horns. He loves that."

Tanner could swear the bull's eyes narrowed, daring him to do it, daring him not to. Tanner figured either way, unless Debba could save him, he was bull fodder.

And, since there was no way to save himself, what the heck? He reached out and scratched the old beast. The bull lowered his head and tilted it as if he had an itchy spot Tanner wasn't reaching.

"C–can . . . uh . . . do you pet all your longhorns?" His ma had once told him that a longhorn was little more than a wolf that was good to eat. They were mean and wild and not to be fooled with, and especially not to be approached unless they were tied up or you were on horseback. And even the ones that'd been gentled for milking could turn on you and be deadly. It was one of the reasons the Harden family had switched away from longhorns. It'd taken years and there'd been plenty of mixed breeding, but these days the Circle H brand was slapped onto Angus or Hereford or a cross between the two.

"Well, of course. What's the use of them if I can't play with them?"

Tanner didn't mention food. He didn't think Debba would like that, and he was sure ol' Shadow wouldn't.

He stood there scratching a one-ton monster that had been gentled into a house cat. He sure hoped Shadow didn't take exception when the scratching stopped.

What would Ma and Pa make of this moment? One thing was for sure, Debba needed to get out of here. This life was nothing Tanner considered good or normal, and he was a man who prided himself on letting people live as they pleased.

He decided he'd make an exception to that outlook in this case.

Dear God, let me figure out a way to get this woman to come along with me. And let me live long enough to do it.

And then he had a thought, which, considering the praying he'd been doing, he took to be inspired straight from God. "I have some supplies in my saddlebags." He'd been planning to scout all day and maybe even be out overnight and sleep by a campfire. And cook by one, too. He wondered how long it'd been since there'd been any cornmeal, flour, or sugar in this place. He had a small pouch that had cookies in it — his ma had left them when she headed home. Maybe he could entice her with food. Give her a couple of bites of sweets then lure her out with a trail of cookie crumbs.

If the bull didn't kill him, that's just what he'd do.

A movement on past Shadow drew his gaze, and he had to admit it wasn't easy to take his eyes off the big beast. A whole herd of longhorns was wandering toward them. Based on their horn spread and the moss growing on them, some might be ten or twenty years old. Calves frolicked among them. Several horses came along, two of them ancient draught horses. Belgians, maybe. He'd seen a couple of them in his life. At least three mustangs and some that looked like a cross between the two. He counted ten horses, three of them colts. All as tame as dogs.

He wondered if she ever rode. Then again, why would she? That would suggest she had somewhere to go.

"Debba, the sun is high in the sky. It's time for a noon meal."

She stood, done with her hugging at last, and turned to him. "I have food in the house. Come and eat with me." Her voice rose with every word as if the idea was too exciting to bear.

Shadow bunted her in the back and knocked her right into him. She clasped his shoulders to keep from falling. His arms went around her waist.

Maybe the bull was annoyed the scratching had stopped, but Tanner decided to believe the old boy was matchmaking.

His eyes went to that stream. He planned

to find a way to work with Debba because he needed her water. But to drive his black and red cattle in here with this strange valley full of gentle giants was hard to imagine.

Tanner slid one arm around her waist and turned her. Not making any sudden moves. He glanced back to see he led a parade. "Is Shadow going to follow us all the way to the house?"

Debba glanced back and patted the black head. "If he wants to."

Tanner decided if she wasn't afraid, neither was he. But he kept up a steady pace, not letting go of her, for fear she'd go back to her pets. Or that her pets would keep parading. So if Tanner and Debba stopped, the parade would walk right over the top of them.

They never got to the stream because having that bull on his heels made him head straight for Debba's cabin.

He let go of Debba and detoured to his horse. He puffed out a sigh of relief when the bull followed her. He didn't think that made him a coward; the bull was really fond of her.

Because his feisty stallion most likely wasn't a good fit for the friendly animal kingdom here, he took the black into the tight log barn near the house, stripped the leather off him, gave him a bait of oats, and left him in a stall.

The barn had several stalls, all empty, and the split log floor was clean enough that if he dropped one of his ma's sugar cookies on it, he'd pick it up and eat it without a second thought.

He peeked out the door and saw that the cattle had started grazing and were wandering off. With a sigh of relief he tossed his saddlebags, full of food he hoped to use on Debba, and hurried to the house before he had to shake hands with one of the Belgians.

He was back!

She'd almost refused to let him care for his horse she was so afraid he'd vanish as mysteriously as he'd appeared. After years of having no one around, the few minutes he'd spent in the barn left her with loneliness flowing over her like the winter wind.

Tanner stepped inside, smiled, and swung the door shut. Those golden brown eyes flashed so friendly it was hard to look away. She was building up the fire to make him eggs and the rooted vegetables she always ate. Ma had called them potatoes, but Pa had said they weren't exactly that.

He set something on the table with a thump and started pulling things out, spreading them around. The fire needed to heat a bit so, fascinated, she went to his side.

"What do you have here?"

"Have one of my ma's sugar cookies."

Debba remembered sugar. Oh, she had honey, she'd found a hive she could rob. But sugar, it lay over the cookie in white drifts.

She reached for it so eagerly she should have been embarrassed.

Tanner got another packet out and a small tin pan. "I'll make coffee."

"Coffee?"

"It's a drink. You boil the coffee" — he held up some black crumbs — "in hot water and have a drink to go with the cookies. It warms a man on a cool mountain morning or a bitter cold winter day."

"I've never had such a thing." She thought she'd heard of it but not for a long time. Her pa hadn't kept it in the house. How could he when he rarely went to town? They went without anything he couldn't raise himself or find in the forest.

Without asking for help or permission, Tanner made quick work of putting his pan into the fireplace, with the water and what looked like black dirt mixed together.

She looked at the cookie, practically crying out to her with its prettiness, round and thin and the sugar so appealing.

"My ma made those."

"Your ma." The words did something to her heart. A mother. What a wonderful thing.

"Ma is the best cook in the world." Tanner came and guided her into her chair, touching her again. Then he picked up a chair — from where she'd shoved it against the wall about four years ago — and dragged it to the table. He picked up a cookie and said, "I have a pack of them. We can eat one while we wait for the coffee and then have more."

He took a bite and then watched her take one. Her eyes went wide and she chewed slowly, like she wanted to live a lifetime in each bite.

She took her second bite and was chewing when he added, "And then we can talk about how fast you can get packed up and ready to come with me."

Chapter 4

That'd gone badly.

Tanner ducked when she threw her head back. She almost smashed him in the face with the back of her head.

A muffled scolding kept up a steady rumble as he rode his black stallion out of the canyon. He didn't like gagging her, this was not a kidnapping, after all. It'd be a kidnapping if he wanted to get money for her. Taking her to meet Ma didn't count as kidnapping. Exactly.

It struck him that he'd never had call to hog-tie a woman before, and it wasn't something that suited him. And the gag would come off as soon as they were past shouting distance of her pet longhorn. He wouldn't put it past her to be able to summon that soft-hearted monster to come to her rescue.

"I swear I'll bring you back. But right now I have to go, and I can't stand the thought of leaving you behind. I don't know why you have to fight with me this way. Now settle down and I'll untie your hands and feet and take the gag out." She tried to head butt him again.

"Fine, Debba. Stay tied up. It's a long ride to my folks'. A long old day's ride, and we didn't get started until after noon. But we're going the whole way. And my stallion is strong enough to carry double and still set a good pace."

It was a good thing she was a little mite of a woman.

They threaded their way out of the canyon, and his horse picked its way through the jagged rocks, finding the nearly invisible trail like he had before. They finally reached open ground, and Tanner urged his horse into a long-legged gallop. It'd be long after dark when they got home, but he wouldn't sleep. It was wrong to keep a woman out alone with a man through the night. Even if the night was edging toward morning, he'd go until he got home.

He had to do that because he was an honorable man . . . for a kidnapper.

He rode a long way down the mountain before he took off her gag.

She yelled for a while. He probably oughta listen to her, but he had a fair idea what she was saying, and he was busy watching a tricky stretch of the trail. By the time he was on safer ground she'd calmed down.

He said, "We've been riding for over an

hour. I'm sure as certain that if you jumped off my horse right now and headed home you'd never find your way back. Do you agree?"

She finally shut up.

The silence was nice so he figured if she didn't answer him, he'd just enjoy the quiet.

Finally, long after he'd given up, she said, "It's so big."

Since they'd come a long way down what had to be one of the biggest mountains in the Rockies, he figured that's what she meant. "Yep."

There wasn't a lot of fight left in her, so he untied her wrists from the pommel and handed her his canteen. She didn't try to brain him; instead she took a good long drink and passed it back.

Maybe they were becoming friends. If she kept this up he might just give her another cookie.

He started telling yarns. About how his ma had married three times to three worthless men, then she'd married a fourth time to his pa.

He told all about his four big sisters and his four little brothers. Then he told about buying land not that far from her and building a cabin up near hers without knowing she was there and how many cows he had and plans for the future.

He found himself to be a talkin' fool, but

she either wasn't speaking to him or she was so interested in the scenery that she was struck dumb, which amounted to . . . she wasn't speaking to him. And when he lapsed into silence, his kidnapping crime wore on him, so he kept telling tales.

When he thought his horse was about all in, he found a bubbling spring and pulled the black to a halt.

He swung off the stallion and lifted Debba down. She seemed unsteady, so he hung on to her while he tied his horse to a scrub bush.

He helped her kneel by the spring and drink.

"Sit here for a while and I'll fetch you something to eat." He eased her onto a flat-topped boulder that was about knee high and fished around in his saddlebags for the last of his cookies, figuring to sweeten her up.

"Debba." He sat next to her on the huge rock. "I am sorry about dragging you out of that canyon. I hope you know I will never hurt you."

Hoping she understood that he was sincere, he studied her as she ate her cookie. She finished it in several quick bites. No denying it, the woman liked sugar.

When the cookie was gone, crumbs clung to the corner of her lips, and he smiled and reached up to brush them away. As he touched her, something tugged deep in his gut. His fingers stopped then swept slowly along her bottom lip. Unable to resist, he leaned down and replaced his fingers with his lips.

A gasp stopped him. He drew back, shocked at what he'd done. Then she reached both hands for him, rested them on his cheeks and pulled him back.

He shouldn't kiss her. He knew it. He was innocent of women, but nothing compared to how defenseless she was.

Pulling back, he looked at those bottomless blue eyes full of loneliness and wonder. All he could feel was a powerful sense of confused longing.

"We mustn't do this." He kissed her again in direct contradiction to his statement. But he ended it and pulled her to her feet.

"We've lingered long enough."

The afternoon worked its way into evening. Tanner had to give his horse one more break, but this time he behaved himself, though he didn't want to, not one speck.

The break was short, and he pressed on as hard as the black would allow.

Finally, the sun fully set and Debba's head lolled back to rest on his shoulder. He leaned forward to see those pretty blue eyes closed in sleep. At last he was able to hold her as close as he wanted.

Debba woke up being shaken around, no idea what was going on or where she was. The stars were blazing and the night was cool. A thudding sound brought her more fully awake.

"Ma, Pa, it's Tanner."

Tanner Harden, that kidnapping skunk bear. The thief of kisses.

He'd acted so friendly, and then it was over and she felt certain it was something she'd done. She knew nothing about men, and somehow she'd given him a disgust for her.

It made her fear this dangerous outside world and long for her home until the pain nearly cut her in half.

She had gotten tired of trying to fight him, especially since she had no luck, but she clenched a fist to take one more good shot at him just as the door swung open. A man stood there holding a lantern.

"Is she hurt?" The lantern man's eyes locked with hers. She blinked against the bright light.

"Nope, just tired. I'll tell you all about it after I put my horse up."

"Get in here. I'll see to your horse, you look all in." The man reached.

Debba thought he was going to grab her. She drew in a breath to scream.

The arm went past her and dragged Tanner inside. Then the man went out with the lantern and for a second things were dark. Then a light flared and another lantern lit up . . . this one hanging on the wall.

"You said she's not hurt?" A woman spoke. In the dim light, and with her eyes still blurry with sleep, Debba couldn't see her face.

"Nope, but I found her alone, Ma, stranded. Her pa died and left her alone in a high valley. It's a long story."

"I wasn't stranded," Debba mostly croaked. Her throat was dry and her temper was worn thin. This was his ma. Tanner had talked about her more than anyone else. This is who he wanted her to meet.

Tanner set her down, and when he let her go she ached at the loss of his touch. Before she could decide what to do with her first moment of freedom in hours, the woman spoke again.

"You poor thing." Another lantern lit, this one from behind. Tanner must've lit it. It cast light on the woman's face and finally Debba saw her.

"I'm Belle, Tanner's ma." The woman came and rested two callused hands on her cheeks. Debba looked into brownish, greenish, golden eyes, a perfect match for Tanner's, full of kindness and strength.

With absolutely no idea how to act, she stood there, aching. Another woman. The longing from being near was so overwhelming she was incapable of moving or speaking.

Then Belle pulled her into her arms and hugged her. The second person to touch her in just one day. These arms were different.

501

The coddling. The strength of them, matched with a mothering concern . . . Debba felt like she was breaking apart inside. When tears came flooding there was no stopping them.

She wrapped her arms around Tanner's ma as tight as she could hold on and wept. Tears came from so deeply inside they might well be tears for her own mama. And tears for Pa who'd stayed to himself completely after Ma died. And tears for all the years she'd been alone. At first she'd been terrified, in fact she'd barely cried because fear was so much stronger of a reaction.

Tears that had turned to stone from all their years of being stored away.

And now they broke free from where they'd been waiting, until it was safe. Until now.

Tanner hated tears about as much as Pa did.

Not quite, but close.

He was mighty tempted to go help Pa strip the leather off his stallion — which was a one-man job and probably already done. Not a good enough reason to stay here. And while he was out there he'd warn Pa not to come inside anytime soon.

He even backed up and fumbled behind him for the doorknob when Ma noticed and about burned him to death with her eyes.

She was hugging Debba, crooning to her, patting her on the back and reading Tanner's mind all at the same time.

502

Not much got past Ma.

So Tanner hunted around in his head and decided he could feed himself. It was closer to morning than night, and much as he was near asleep on his feet, it didn't look like he was going to find a bed anytime soon. Since he was mighty hungry and his folks probably weren't going to get back to bed and his little brothers would be rising soon — in fact he was surprised they hadn't gotten up already what with all the ruckus of sobbing — he figured he might as well cook.

So he headed for the kitchen and stoked the fire, put coffee on, then started heating up skillets for breakfast.

Ma might not want him to leave the house, but he didn't have to stand right there watching, did he?

Debba was bound to quit crying and be hungry, too, in a minute.

He found his mind straying to that kiss they'd shared. He was about to crack an egg right into the top of the cookstove with no skillet when his pa came in the back door.

Which reminded him of the crying.

Pa was a smart man. He'd probably heard the sobbing and come around back.

They were out of the line of sight of the women and probably, considering Debba's caterwauling, out of earshot, too.

"So, where'd you find the woman, son?" Pa heard the crying, but for some reason he wasn't running for the hills, and that just wasn't like him. In fact, he looked amused. Almost like he considered this crying woman someone else's problem, maybe Tanner's.

Tanner explained, and Pa listened and asked questions. He'd helped scout the land Tanner claimed.

"That mountain grows up on the west side of your property. And I remember the jagged rocks all around the base of it. I can't believe you found a trail across 'em."

"Debba screamed and there was a gunshot. The black followed the sound, and he found the way in. Even while he walked on it I had to use my imagination to see it." He thought the crying from the front of the house was fading a little. He hoped Ma was pulling Debba out of her doldrums.

"And a keyhole pass into an inner canyon." Pa had a spark about him in wild land. The Hardens lived a long way out, and though the town of Divide had grown and the train had come through, theirs was still a solitary life and it suited the whole family.

Tanner proved that by moving even farther from town. But to think a meadow like that existed . . .

"Don't you wonder what's left in these mountains to be discovered? Are there more meadows like that, in the heart of a mountain? I wonder if the Indians knew about it. Or if maybe her family stepped on land that no human had ever touched." Pa made that sound like the finest thing that could happen to a man.

"And I've been in there. Maybe the fourth person to ever see it." Tanner loved the thought of it. "It's a beautiful place, Pa, hundreds of acres of lush grass, with a fast-movin' stream, and she's got longhorns in there that may be twenty years old." He told about Shadow while they cracked eggs and sliced bacon.

Pa laughed and looked befuddled at the same time. "I don't suppose she's thinking that a hundred head of longhorn oughta be culled. Wonder how she'd act if I told her she needs a cattle drive?"

"I've got a feeling that if she got wind of a cattle drive having the end result of turning a cow into beefsteak, she'd be fully opposed to it." Tanner poured the eggs into the skillet, hot now on their rectangular cookstove. A luxury Pa had brought home for Ma a few years back. The livin' was getting mighty easy on the Circle H these days.

"It don't matter what Debba thinks; no one's gonna drive those cows anywhere." Tanner pictured himself trying to ramrod that big friendly bull out that narrow pass and across that rugged trail, just the first stretch on the long route to Helena.

"Maybe they'd come along if you lured them with buckets of wheat." Not unlike

Tanner's plan to lure Debba with sugar cookies. Considering she ended up hog-tied, he might as well stop all his planning right now. He showed no talent for it.

Murmuring came from the other room. He heard Debba's voice break and Ma's soothing response, but he couldn't make out the words.

Then he heard Ma say, "He gagged you?" in a voice that wasn't one lick soothing.

"I've got to see this place," Pa said, "and see a one-ton longhorn that acts as tame as a house cat."

"I half expected her to weave him a necklace of dandelions and then ride him around the meadow."

Pa laughed and shook his head.

Which didn't distract Tanner from wondering what exactly Ma was going to have to say about his tactics. He decided to hurry with his cooking since he'd long ago noticed that Ma really appreciated help around the house.

He got real busy breaking eggs.

Ma came into the kitchen, her arm around her newest chick.

Tanner said, "Breakfast will be ready in just a few minutes."

At the falsely hardy tone, Pa gave him a strange look, arched a brow at him, then flipped the slices of bacon.

Ma settled Debba at the table and got her a glass of milk. They had glasses made of real glass these days, though Ma rarely let the boys touch one. She'd learned that in a hard school.

But Debba rated a glass. Then Ma set a pitcher of milk on the table, came over to get plates, and while she was close to hand, slapped Tanner on the back of the head.

"Hey!" He didn't say more. He figured he deserved it.

"A gag, Tanner?"

He shrugged helplessly. "I thought about leaving her there, but she really didn't want me to leave, did you, Debba?"

He looked at the poor, soggy little red-eyed filly. He wanted to pull her into his arms and help her get through her upset.

She shrugged then shook her head. She really needed a haircut.

"But she wouldn't come with me. Her pa has filled her head with a lot of nonsense about never leaving that canyon."

"Don't you say a bad word about my pa!" She was angry, but he could see she was exhausted. The long night and the crying jag had about done her in.

"But I couldn't stay, and I — I — well . . . I just couldn't stand to leave her . . . but she wouldn't come." Tanner shrugged to match Debba. "I just thought no one could talk to her better than you, Ma."

"You thought you knew best, so you did what you wanted without regard to her feelings, is that right?"

He reckoned that summed it up nicely. "Yep."

Ma closed her eyes as if the very sight of him caused her pain.

"I'll take you right back, Debba." There was no possible way on God's green earth that he was taking her back. "We'll head out as soon as we eat." Except he'd think of a reason to delay it. Maybe if she slept for a while she'd come to her senses.

"I'm sorry." And that was purely true. He really had hated manhandling her. "I did *not* want to do that to you, but I was at my wit's end." Tanner gave her a weak smile that could hardly have been more unnatural. "Did it help at all to talk to Ma?"

Debba gave him such a forlorn look he half expected to get slapped in the head again. He was tempted to slap himself.

He scraped the cooked eggs onto a platter. Pa was taking up the bacon. Ma saw to the plates and such, along with bread, butter, and jelly. Tanner noticed he got a tin cup. He was probably lucky she didn't dump hot coffee over his head.

Ma urged Debba to her feet and settled her in a chair between the table and wall, with Ma and Pa at the ends of the rectangular table with the red-and-white gingham table-cloth. Tanner sat right across from her so he could read every expression in her bright blue eyes.

The smell must have done the work all the noise wouldn't do, because about the time Tanner swallowed the last of his breakfast he heard a stampede that'd impress old Shadow.

The noise made Debba clutch her hands together at her throat, her eyes wide as she turned to face . . . the dangerous outside world? Had she been waiting for trouble like this?

"It's two of Tanner's little brothers," Ma said.

"Two, there are more?"

Tanner was sure he'd told her about there being five boys, but maybe he'd mentioned that after she'd fallen asleep. Or maybe she was nervous enough she couldn't make sense out of anything.

"Mark came riding in and asked if he could have some help digging a spreader dam. We sent him your two littlest brothers. Emma can feed them for a while."

That left Si and Cade to come storming down the stairs, like a pack of hungry wolves on the scent.

They skidded into the kitchen, shoving at each other to get to the food first. Then Si's gaze lit on Debba, and he stopped short. Cade plowed into him and they both about tumbled to the floor, but Si held his ground and finally Cade noticed. He turned and looked, too, looked hard. Tanner was surprised to feel his temper rise up.

And he really didn't like it when he noticed Debba looking back, although he thought that might be fear. The house was filling with people, and for a woman too long alone it might be overwhelming. Which made Tanner want to toss his brothers outside and lock them out for good — or at least until he took Debba home — which he didn't see how he could ever do.

His little brothers were destined to live permanently in the barn.

"Howdy." Si was the image of Pa. He was twenty-three, only a year younger than Tanner, who figured all five of the brothers looked like Pa, except he alone had Ma's eyes. The rest of them had blue eyes like Pa's.

Si had Tanner's full six feet of height. Cade two inches taller. They'd finally had to leave off calling him Shorty.

Luckily Jake and Will were at Emma's.

Ma spoke, and it was a good thing because Tanner didn't want these two to know who Debba was — which was rude and mighty stupid.

"Debba, these are two of my five sons. Si is the oldest save for Tanner, and Cade is my third born. The next two, Jake and Will, are away." Ma rested a hand on Debba's arm to draw her attention. "I have four daughters who are older, but they are all married and moved to their own ranches."

With a sweet smile, Debba looked at the two knot-heads who'd come in. "Hello, Si. Cade."

They both came straight for her. Of course the food was right in front of her on the table, so Tanner wasn't sure what exactly they were aiming for. Tanner grabbed his plate and made a quick move to sit beside Debba. He didn't think she'd like sitting next to two strange men. And his brothers were mighty strange.

"Debba, that's a pretty name. Is your name Debra?" Si asked. "My real name is Silas, but with it being Pa's name I get called Si."

With a·nervous blinking of her eyes, Debba seemed to be searching around the inside of her head. "I th–think my name is Debra."

"You don't know?" Cade asked, sitting square in front of her.

Si slapped him on the shoulder to make him scoot down and leave room for another chair.

"No one has called me that for a long time. Not since before my ma died." She rested one hand on her mouth then said, "We have a family Bible. I am sure my name is written in it, but I haven't opened it to those pages for years. I could find out for sure."

Si and Cade settled in and started loading their plates with food, and loading Debba with questions at the same time.

About the time Tanner was ready to tell them to both shut up and let Debba eat, Pa's hand landed hard on his shoulder and lifted him out of his chair. He had no good reason to refuse to mind his father, though he wanted to. He resisted fussing and let himself get dragged to his feet and pulled out of the kitchen into the front room. He did his best to make it look like he wanted to go. He hated to look like a child in trouble in front of Debba.

The minute they were out of the room, Pa asked, "What should we do, son?"

"Can't we keep her, Pa?" Tanner flinched when he heard a little kid coming out of his own mouth.

"She's not an orphaned pup who showed up at our back door."

"Honest, she sort of puts me in mind of one."

Pa nodded.

"All I can think of is, can we find someone to go home with her?"

"Like hired hands? You think she needs hired hands? Or a housekeeper? To tidy a house for one that she tends just fine for herself?"

"Don't start arguing with me, Pa. It's a waste of time. I know all the troubles, none of 'em bigger than what to do with a two-thousand-pound house cat with an eight-foot spread of horns. But she can't go back in there and live out her life alone. I wondered if she could live here with you and Ma. She needs parents."

"She's a grown woman, Tanner. I'd say she's twenty years old at least. She doesn't seem real sure. The normal way for an adult woman to add to her home is to" — Pa's eyes sparked with mischief — "take a husband and have some children."

Tanner spun around and leaned sideways to look in the kitchen, where both of his worthless brothers were talking to Debba, and she was turning back and forth between the two of them and smiling to beat all.

"Who's she gonna marry? She don't know anyone."

There was such a long silence that Tanner finally tore his eyes away from Debba and his two flirting brothers.

He looked at Pa, who said, "How about if she marries you?"

CHAPTER 5

"That's the dumbest thing I've ever heard, Pa." Tanner sounded horrified.

"Nor will I marry you." Debba rushed into the room, looking widly between the two of them. Then she found the door and raced out.

She heard the door open and shut behind her and thudding footsteps closing in on her. Tanner grabbed her around the waist and swung her up in his arms.

"I want to go home!" She wanted to start crying again, but she'd done so much of it she really couldn't stand the thought. Being angry held more appeal honestly.

"You took me so far from home I have no way to return. I couldn't find my canyon if I searched for a lifetime." She balled up her fist and considered swinging it, though she'd never struck anyone in her life. That gave her pause. She might have swung a fist or two at Tanner earlier, and kicked him. And tried to smash him in the face with her skull. But she'd never hit anyone in her life, except him.

This was obviously Tanner's fault.

"Listen, what Pa said, Debba, we don't know each other nearly at all. We can't think of getting married. I'm sorry you heard that and it upset you. But you can't go back and live out your life in that canyon all alone." He dropped her legs so they swung down, and he stood her firmly in front of him, his hands on her shoulders.

She noticed the sun had come up. Somehow she'd passed an entire day and night with Tanner. Kidnapping was very time-consuming.

The sights around her stopped her from punching Tanner. She probably wouldn't have done it anyway. The house she'd been in was beautiful. Large and tightly built with spindles lining a porch. There were two huge barns and a corral with grazing horses that connected them. Cattle, black and red cattle of all things, spread out beyond the buildings. No horns anywhere. There was a low-slung shed with one side open, and parked in there were a wagon, a buckboard, and a buggy. She only even knew what a buggy was because it was referenced in one of the books she had in her house. Books she'd read over and over until they were nearly memorized.

There was so much life here. It over-whelmed her to the point of silence; at the same time she wanted to ask a thousand questions. There was so much she wanted to know she couldn't collect her thoughts to begin. Which made her realize how exhausted she was. Her anger and embarrassment drained away. She was simply too tired to do anything more right now. Her shoulders slumped. Tanner was holding her up anyway — in addition to arranging her life. Why bother doing anything herself?

Lifting her chin took all her energy, and she looked into those unusual golden eyes. She didn't know quite what to say, but he took over, as he'd been doing since they met.

"You need some rest. Let's go back inside. Ma will find you a place to sleep. We can talk more later."

"Tanner, what are we going to do?"

She said *we*. That was wrong. What was *she* going to do? Tanner had caused this problem, but it was her life. Her problem to solve. Pa had always told her an adult had to stand on her own.

Tanner touched her cheek, drawing her back from her worry.

"I think, Debba, that . . . you can't go home. Not for good. Not alone. So when you ask what we're going to do, you need to spend time admitting you can't live walled off from the rest of the world, not anymore. So decide what you're going to do instead of what you've always done. It's your only possible choice."

516

■ ■ ■ ■

Tanner watched Debba walk back to the house. Ma reached out an arm to wrap around her shoulders.

Pa left them to the house and strode toward Tanner with a glint in his eyes. "Let's go for a walk, son." If that didn't make a man nervous, nothing did. Tanner figured Debba's upset was mostly Pa's fault for his crazy notion about marriage. But there was no sign of remorse on Pa's face. Which most likely meant Pa was of a different mind.

Si and Cade picked that moment to come riding in, and Pa waited for them. It was something in the way he stood but his brothers slowed way down, like a person might when they were facing their own doom.

"Howdy, Pa." Si swallowed hard. "Uh, is something wrong?"

"I want you boys to ride out to the line shack."

They exchanged a glance. Cade said, "But we want to get to know Debba better. She's the prettiest woman we've ever seen."

She was about the only woman they'd ever seen. Ma and Pa didn't go to town much, and when they did, they rarely took their children along. And even in these modern times, Divide, Montana was a small town, mainly full of western men. The few respectable women were all married.

The boys all went along on the yearly cattle drives to Helena so they caught a glimpse of a woman on those trips, but they didn't linger in town after the cattle sold.

"The line shack, now. Do a head count while you're there. See how the spring calf crop is faring, and see if there's any trouble with wolves."

The line shack was right near a trail that went up and over a mountain, leading to the most treacherous trail known to man . . . well . . . that is, the most treacherous known to Tanner. They drove the cattle that way to Helena.

"Can we go up to the high country while we're over there?" They both had a rifle in a boot on their saddle and a holster with a six-gun and extra bullets. A man didn't ride out without being ready for trouble in the West. Besides, the line shack was well stocked with ammunition and food — even a few changes of clothes.

"Don't be pestering critters that aren't pestering you. But yep, you can go up in the high country. Stay together. Use your heads. Don't come back until I come and get you."

Si shrugged then flashed Cade a smile. "I reckon Pa wants Debba to spend time with only Tanner. Two good lookin' men like us around and it might confuse the little woman."

518

Tanner clenched a fist, and Si and Cade whirled their horses and rode off laughing.

Then Pa turned to Tanner. "I've been meaning to build a bigger chicken coop. Help me chop down some trees."

With a shudder, because he knew what was coming, Tanner followed Pa and shouldered an ax. Pa's own personal solution to every child that gave him any trouble was to put the problem child on the business end of the heaviest tool he could find. If it wasn't the ax, Tanner would be pitching the straw out of the barn all day and night, or swinging a hammer on the longest stretch of fence west of the Missouri.

"I don't know why you're upset at me." Tanner flinched. He was pretty sure he'd just said something that would have sounded better coming out of a five-year-old.

Pa sighed. "Maybe it's the kidnapping."

"I don't see how I could have avoided that, Pa."

"Maybe it's the gag."

"I thought her yelling might set off her cattle. I didn't put it past them to fight me for her." She'd tried to bite him, too, but he didn't mention that. He figured that was fair, considering the kidnapping.

"Or maybe it's that when I suggested you marry her, you said something so rude you should be ashamed of yourself. I made a mistake to suggest marriage where she could overhear."

Which didn't mean Pa thought it was a mistake to suggest it, he'd just needed to pick a better place and time.

"But you were downright unkind. What you said really hurt her feelings." Pa glared at Tanner. "She might've started crying again."

And that was where Tanner had really messed up. Pa's dislike of tears was legendary.

They walked on in silence for a long time. Tanner noticed Pa didn't bring an ax, which didn't bode well for who was going to be doing most of the work.

Then Pa pointed at a stand of slender aspens, the closest stand to the house. "You get busy chopping. I'll talk."

It's was Pa's very own version of a slap on the back of the head.

CHAPTER 6

Ma came into the kitchen late that afternoon with her hand on Debba's back.

Tanner couldn't quite decide if she was just giving the poor confused girl support or was she shoving her into the room?

Probably, considering how Debba was and . . . how Ma was, it was shoving — as gently as possible of course.

Then Tanner forgot all about shoving because Ma had combed Debba's hair and cut off about two feet of it, but it still hung past her shoulder blades. Washed her up and given her a new dress that Tanner recognized as one of Ma's own. Debba was shorter than Ma, but Ma was quick with a needle and the dress fit just exactly right.

Tanner had to admit it, Debba cleaned up real good.

Then Ma sat her down at the table in the same place she'd sat before, between the table and the wall, and gave her a long hug before she stepped back.

While he was really glad he'd brought her to Ma, the hug gave him a little jab that he suspected might be jealousy. Tanner kind of wanted a hug, too.

And it wasn't just the hugging that made him jealous. Debba got a nap, too.

At the rate Pa worked him today, Tanner probably could have added a room onto her cabin and just kept Debba up there and stayed with her. Which was all kinds of improper, but still the idea occurred to him.

Instead Pa got a bigger chicken coop out of the deal, and Tanner got some sore muscles.

And he shouldn't have said marrying Debba was the dumbest thing he'd ever heard. He knew that before he'd caught up with her outside. Chopping down all those trees would sure enough help him remember not to do it again.

Tanner was busy putting plates on the table. Ma had always expected inside chores from her sons as well as her daughters. And since Tanner's big sisters worked hard outside every day, that'd been fair. He'd been nearly an adult man before he'd heard such a thing as men's work and women's work.

Pa dished up steaming chicken stew. Ma put a plate of biscuits on the table and a bowl of mashed potatoes.

"Put the milk pitcher out, Tanner, and get the pie."

It was apple pie. Tanner had been smelling

it ever since he'd come in. Ma always bought a bushel or two of apples in Helena after the cattle drive in the fall. They feasted on them, and when they began to wither, Ma diced what was left for pie and applesauce. There weren't many to put up, and the apples were hard to find and costly. She must really want Debba to like being here.

It lifted Tanner's spirits. Despite his ham-handed tactics hauling Debba here, Ma was on his side.

Tanner took the chair straight across from Debba. Pa sat on Tanner's right at the head of the table, and Ma on his left at the foot and closest to the stove, so she could refill the serving dishes.

"Let's ask the blessing." Pa did a nice job. His prayers were always sincere but brief. But today he mentioned Debba, and it felt right and good to pray for the lonely woman.

Figuring a hard talk was coming, Tanner dug into his food and so did everyone else. He couldn't figure out if they were just dreading what had to be said or if the food was better eaten warm. Maybe some of both.

Tanner had his pie half eaten when Ma said, "Debba, have you thought about what you want to do?"

Debba stopped chewing and fixed her eyes on her dessert like she thought it held the meaning of life. Silence hung thick in the room. Tanner regretted it. He didn't want her upset. Ma was trying to let her make her own decisions. None of her daughters had ever had much trouble taking charge of their own lives. Ma was a whole lot nicer than he'd been.

Finally Debba lifted her chin as if her head weighed fifty pounds. Her skin was pale as milk. She looked at Tanner until she'd chewed and swallowed her bite of pie. "You asked me if my pa was a cruel man."

Ma reached across the table and slapped him in the back of the head. He'd be building fence in the moonlight if Debba didn't mind her words.

"I have never considered him cruel, but compared to whom?" Debba bit her bottom lip, and her eyes lost focus. Tanner thought she was looking into the past.

"I think we might have gone to town a couple of times a year when I was really little. But once Ma died, we probably went to town three times in my memory."

"Were you born in that canyon?" Ma asked.

"No. We moved there before Ma died, though. Pa told me we found that canyon when I was four."

"Do you know where you came from? Do you have aunts and uncles who might take you in?"

"No one." Debba answered slowly, and Tanner wondered if she was even sure of that.

"My birth is recorded in our family Bible,

and Ma's death is, too. If there is other family, I might find names in there, but I don't know them and I've never met them."

There was silence for a time, and then Tanner spoke up with a notion. Chopping wood had a way of clearing a man's thoughts. "Did you see Luther when we were in Divide last spring?"

Pa nodded. "He had to be eighty years old."

"He's not as old as we think," Ma said. "That long gray beard puts years on a man. Mandy Linscott told me Tom built a cabin for him on their land and told him he'd earned some easy years."

"And did Mandy tell you that Buff and Wise Sister were coming to stay, too?"

Frowning, Pa said, "I didn't hear that."

Ma shook her head.

"Well, I talked with Luther for a while and he said he don't like it. He's been put out to pasture. His knees ache and he has to sit for longer between jobs, but he hates the thought of a rocking chair gettin' him in his old age. And he said Buff and Wise Sister have always roamed. They like the high-up hills, but it's a hard life, and coming down to live near Luther is what's ahead of them. They don't like it, either."

"This is all interesting, Tanner, but —"

"I wonder," Tanner cut Ma off, which was always dangerous, "if Luther, Buff, and Wise

Sister would consider living in Debba's canyon."

With a little gasp, Debba said, "You want to give someone else my home?"

"No, I mean they could live there with you."

Debba blinked her eyes, as if stunned by the idea. As if shocked to think her choices might include going home.

"The thing is, Debba, I think you do need to consider coming out of there. And I think . . ." Tanner hesitated to say this in front of Pa and Ma, but he doubted they were going to give him much choice. "I think there is something between us."

Debba was watching every breath and word.

"I'd like to get to know you better, since we haven't known each other long." Tanner had worked hard all day and been slapped twice. He thought he'd learned his lessons well. It wasn't wise to say one of his misgivings about her was that she was furiously mad. He liked her, but before he proposed, he oughta make sure she wasn't a lunatic. That'd get old fast in a wife.

"We can ask them. I think they might like the idea of living up there. They'll have the wilderness, but they might need some taking care of. I'm not sure if they're up to much hunting anymore. And there might be days when keeping enough wood chopped will be too big a job. We'll lay up a good supply, but I'm not sure if I can get in and out through that narrow pass when the snow gets deep. I'll do everything to help I can, and I'll be in during the spring, summer, and fall."

He was surprised at the pang he got from thinking he might not see her for months. "If the idea suits you, you can go home. And since I live close, we can get to know each other and see if we'll suit."

"I — I don't know if I want three strangers in my canyon."

No one responded for a time. It was up to her.

She seemed incapable of deciding.

Finally Ma said, "Would you like to meet them? Talk with them? They are fine people, and you'd be much safer with them around. Of course, they may object to the idea."

Tanner doubted it. Linscotts' ranch was two hours out of town, and on an earlier visit, Tanner'd heard Buff claim he could smell people. Luther fussed that the whole Rockies had been hunted out. Wise Sister, a Shoshone woman, had gotten quiet . . . even for her. She rarely left the cabin, and she sure as certain didn't come into Divide.

Debba smiled her quiet smile. "I appreciate this. I'm worried about it, but all afternoon I've been thinking I had no choice. Now maybe I do. Thank you."

Tanner nodded in satisfaction. "Good. Tomorrow we'll go find them and see what they say."

"Do you mean we're going to see more people?" She looked terrified.

"We'll skirt around town," Ma said. "You'll see the Linscotts but few other people. We'll have to hit the trail early. On a fast horse it's a five-hour ride — and just as far back. We can make it in one day, but it'll be as long a day as one of our cattle drives."

With a sigh, Debba shrugged and said, "I'll meet them."

Tanner sighed with relief, and then, his dessert gone, he said, "Debba, as for getting to know you better, would you like to step outside and take a walk with me?"

He glanced left and right at his parents and asked, "Is that all right with you?"

It was more than all right, they practically shoved the two of them out the kitchen door.

They walked a few steps, and, feeling like the world's clumsiest oaf, Tanner took Debba's hand. She smiled and hung on. Not acting crazy at all.

"You know, it's a funny thing, my folks fought it every time one of my sisters got married."

"Fought it, you mean they didn't like their husbands?"

"Well, no they never have met a man they thought was good enough for one of the girls. There was always a fuss. And my brothers-in-law are fine men and all live close around. But they don't seem to have much concern about you."

The smile melted off her face, and Tanner felt his eyes go wide. He could almost feel Ma slapping the back of his head.

"No, I don't mean to be insulting. I'm just stupid around women. I've never been around a woman."

"Well, I've never been around a man, either."

"Then you know what I mean? You don't know what to say or how to act when you're trying to get to know a man better. How could you? You've never gotten to know anyone at all."

The hurt look faded off her face, but it wasn't exactly a cheerful expression.

"What I'm talking about has nothing to do with you."

"It doesn't?"

"Of course it does." Tanner covered his eyes with his free hand and sort of hoped he stepped into an open well. "I mean my folks are just treating me real different than they treated my sisters."

Then he got a bright idea. "Or maybe you're just so nice that they don't have any worries." He squeezed Debba's hand. "That must be it."

She smiled again, and Tanner considered shutting his mouth and never opening it again so he wouldn't say anything that hurt her feelings.

And then he realized they'd come a fair distance from the house, way outside of Ma's range of vision. He pulled Debba to a stop, turned her, and kissed her.

No talking now.

Finally he felt brave enough to say just about anything and believed she'd like to hear it.

"Debba, I —" A rush of something moving fast in the dark spun him around. He couldn't see what it was, but something was coming fast and quiet.

He'd come out without a gun, no way to protect them.

"Run!" He grabbed Debba's hand and ran toward the house as whatever came at them gained, running twice as fast as he could. He wasn't going to make it. He veered to the side and sprinted toward the barn, much closer. It was all motion and silence beyond thudding hooves. No shout for them to stop.

"What is it, Tanner? What's going on?"

"Someone's after us." He couldn't talk and run at the same time, so he just dug in deep, getting every ounce of speed he was capable of. Debba kept up and he was grateful; he'd hate to drag her, and if he pulled her off her feet, whoever was out there would be on them.

They got close enough to the house that Pa was within earshot. "Pa, come quick!"

The pounding hooves closed on them. *A*

horse, he thought. There was something eerie about it, but he didn't know what. It had to be someone on horseback. He braced himself for the sound of gunfire and prepared to grab Debba and throw her to the ground, shield her with his own body. Then they reached the barn and he wrenched the door open, hauled Debba in, and slammed it shut.

The hooves kept pounding for long minutes. Finally the sound stopped. Dead silence. He had the fleeting thought that Debba had been right. The outside world was dangerous.

Tanner pressed all his weight against the barn door. There was a heavy latch on the outside of it, but that did them no good.

From the house, Pa shouted, "Tanner, what is it?"

"Pa, look out. Someone's out there chasing us. We barely made it to the barn."

The silence lasted too long. Had the riders run off when Pa came out? Had they turned their attention to Pa? Tanner's stomach twisted to think he'd put Pa in danger. Taking a walk with Debba had appealed to him so strongly that he hadn't armed himself. He hadn't shown a lick of caution.

Then Pa shouted in fear, and the door to the house slammed.

Whoever it was scared Pa.

"Debba, my pa isn't scared of nothin'."

Which really set him to thinking. He edged along the barn wall, keeping hold of Debba's

531

wrist. He reached a window with a tight shutter, but not so tight he couldn't see out into the yard.

Nothing showed in the small crack. Then a rectangle of light appeared. The house. Pa stood, rifle in hand. He saw Ma behind him. They both just stood there. Not acting scared at all now.

"Pa, what's going on?"

Just then, Tanner heard a loud moo.

"Uh . . . there is a huge longhorn bull in our yard. Black. And he's just standing there. He came toward me earlier, but now he's standing right outside the barn door, staring. Uh . . . he has friends."

Debba slipped away and got to the barn door and flung it open.

"Shadow!" She rushed outside.

Tanner stepped out, and there wasn't just a tame-as-a-house cat, two-thousand-pound bull in the yard. No, that would be too simple.

There was a whole herd of longhorns. They'd all missed their mama. Who had wrapped her arms around Shadow's neck and was kissing him on the cheek.

The yard was full of cattle, the whole herd came. They were really dangerous animals, all acting like they'd taken part in a parade from their mountain canyon to the Hardens'.

If Debba ever let them take her pets on a cattle drive, it'd be mighty simple. She'd just ride to Helena and they'd all follow.

Tanner would probably follow, too.

He gave them a wide berth as he walked to the house. He'd told his folks about the canyon. But honestly, how could a person believe it until they saw it?

"Is she hugging a longhorn bull, Tanner?" Ma asked, sounding confused to a point that could only be described as reasonable.

"Yep."

"That bull could turn on her and stomp her into the ground," Pa said. "You can't trust longhorns."

"Look, there's one of her Belgian horses. She said he's as old as her memory. Her folks had them already when they moved into the canyon." Tanner kept watch. "Just be glad her grouse didn't join the parade."

"Grouse?" Ma asked.

"Yep, she caught them and tamed them for their eggs. Leastways, I suspect they're just for eggs. She talks to them like they are family, so I'm not sure if she's up to eating one of them. But she shot a wolverine, and I watched her skin it. As fast as anyone I've ever seen with a skinning knife."

Ma whispered, "I like this girl more every minute."

"What are we going to do with that herd of cattle?" Pa scratched his head with the hand not holding his rifle. The yard was still filling.

"Not much you can do. They like Debba. They tracked her all the way here."

"That's the truth," Ma said, sounding like she wanted to laugh.

"That's the biggest longhorn I've ever seen. I wonder how old it is?" Pa was a cattleman to his bones. "I saw the ridges on Shadow's horns and the length."

"He's twenty years old at least, I'm guessing." Some of Debba's mustangs were here now. They mingled with the longhorns like a reunion of old friends. Pa usually kept the horses and cattle separate because the horses had some instinct to start herding and the cows didn't like it.

"I had one born on my place when I first started out that lived to be twenty-seven years old." Ma took the rifle from Pa, who gave it up without a fight. "An old cow who had a baby every year."

Ma stepped inside to return the rifle to the hooks over the door.

"I'm gonna bet this one don't drive worth a hoot." Pa stared, and then finally he made a decision. "I think I'll ride out right now and get Si and Cade home."

Tanner had to agree with that decision. Reinforcements were definitely in order.

CHAPTER 7

It took some wrangling, but they finally came up with a plan to get the cattle to go home.

Debba felt like she was lying to her cattle, but they really were inconvenient milling around the Hardens' ranch yard. She started out riding for her canyon, along with Si and Cade and Tanner. Si and Cade carried the clothes that Debba had worn down the mountain the first day and rode two of Debba's mustangs.

They got ahead far enough they were out of sight of her herd, her best friends, so when they reached a stream, instead of crossing, Tanner and Debba turned into the water and rode fast — hopefully out of smelling range since they hadn't had to see Debba to follow her.

Si and Cade rode on up toward her place. Tanner had given them careful directions to the canyon. He was hoping the horses knew the way and would take the trail with good spirits. If not, they'd just go to Tanner's house and let the cattle congregate there for now.

Debba listened carefully, in case she needed to get herself home later.

Tanner rode on, and Debba followed him. They eventually got back to his parents' house, and then they all headed out for the Linscott place.

Belle had promised to avoid Divide because Debba wanted no part of a town. Belle seemed to agree, so that was a promise easily made.

Silas had a gate across the trail they were taking to Divide. He'd spent some time reinforcing it in case the longhorns figured out they'd been tricked and came hunting Debba. She hoped it held.

"I hope that gate holds." Silas sounded glum. Like he doubted it.

Since Debba doubted it, too, it gave her a friendly feeling toward Silas.

"We could go tomorrow." Debba was pretty sure her heart was going to pound out of her chest — due to fear — which would kill her. Meeting new people was a terrible idea. Inviting them to live with her even worse. Thanks to her cattle and horses, they'd already put the trip off two days.

"Do you think Si and Cade will remember to feed my grouse?"

"You reminded them fifteen times, Debba." Tanner sounded tired and it wasn't even noon yet. "And besides, they know ranch life.

They'd've thought of it on their own."

Putting this trip off a day wouldn't be so bad. Tanner had taken a walk with her both nights since the cattle had come. Shadow kept them company. The bull seemed to blame Tanner for taking her away, as well he should. And now he was guarding Debba so close she was afraid he might end up in the house with them.

The Hardens were good builders, though. The cabin door was sturdy and withstood all attempts by Shadow to breech it.

"Nope, no sense delaying." Belle seemed to be in charge in this family.

Debba had been in charge in her canyon for years. She was certainly no such thing now. She found herself surrounded by people with much stronger wills than her own.

She sort of missed being in charge. Then she thought of Shadow and wondered who'd really been in charge at her place.

Belle had wanted to start out before daylight, hoping to make the trip in one day. But she was afraid to wait for fear the cattle would come back, so they left just before noon and pushed hard.

Silas and Tanner had saddled eight horses, and they'd cut time by switching saddles and pressing on. The horses needed to shed the weight of a rider in order to keep moving fast, but it appeared that, with the saddle switched and the rider gone, the horses could rest while they galloped flat out.

Debba couldn't quite believe that was true — sure, a saddle and a person weighed a fair amount, but, well, it seemed like the running would be tiring regardless of the weight. But the horses — and the Hardens — kept going, so she did, too.

It was late in the afternoon when Debba saw evidence that they were nearing someone's property. The trails were widened, and there were magnificent black cattle grazing in herds. They were much rounder than her long-horns. And no horns anywhere. She'd seen a few of the Hardens' cattle, red and black, and black with white faces, but these were all shining black.

Shadow would fit in here well, except of course for the horns.

About the time the trail became hard packed, they veered away into a faint trail that led into the woods. Debba was relieved because she thought that wide trail probably led to more people than she wanted to see.

They rode deep into a densely crowded forest, and when Silas, who led the way, reined back his horse, Debba took awhile figuring out why.

They were only a few feet away when she finally saw a house. It was almost a door in the woods, then behind the wall of trees, she saw a real house.

The door swung open and a woman with

white hair stepped out. Debba knew she was an Indian by her clothing and old stories she'd heard of native folks. She wore two long braids and a brownish dress with fringe and leather decorations. This had to be Wise Sister, and the look in her eyes made Debba wonder if that wasn't the perfect name.

Right behind her an older man stepped out. Probably her husband, Buff. He had long hair around a bald head, with a full beard, more white than gray. He wore brown pants and a light-colored cotton shirt buttoned up the front.

Both of them nodded without speaking.

Silas said, "Buff, Wise Sister, howdy. Is Luther around? We'd like to talk to the three of you."

Another man came out of the woods just then, dressed much like Buff.

"Howdy Silas, Belle." His eyes shifted from Tanner to Debba.

"This is Tanner."

"Knew it was your boy, but I wasn't sure which one."

"And Debba is a young woman who lives in the high-up hills, and I'd like to talk with you about her."

"Light and set." Luther must do all the talking for the three.

They dismounted and headed inside, and Debba wondered where Luther's house was.

Debba was shocked to see a huge painting

on one wall that didn't seem to fit with the otherwise simple but pretty house. The house was small, but there were benches along the table and they almost fit. Debba ended up next to Tanner, and it was a tight squeeze. They sat across from Belle and Silas. Wise Sister stood at the stove, leaning back, arms crossed, and when Silas offered her his chair she waved a hand and Silas didn't push it.

Belle said, "Debba lives in a canyon so high up we didn't even know it existed, and Tanner lives close. We'd never seen the keyhole pass that leads into it. She's lived there alone since her father died several years ago. Tanner found her and brought her to our place. She loves her canyon and wants to go back, but not alone. I've heard you speak of not liking to be so near people, and I wondered if . . ." She looked from one to the other, studying all three of them. "If you'd consider living up there."

She stopped talking.

Debba wondered if they'd even speak enough to say no.

"I'll help you get a cabin built, two cabins like you've got here," Silas added.

"Buff," Wise Sister surprised Debba by having a voice, "I am going."

Buff nodded. "Yep, we'll go."

Luther said, "Me, too. No decent fur to trap. No hunting. People everywhere."

Debba hadn't seen a single person, but she

could feel them. She knew just how he felt. Of course, maybe she'd like them if she met them, but they all seemed so dangerous. And yet she felt no danger in inviting these three into her canyon. They looked like about the most dependable people in the world. And they wouldn't fill her ears with talk.

"Give us an hour to pack." Luther rose from the table.

"Hour?" Buff gave Luther a confused look. "I can go now."

"So can I, but I'd better ride over and tell Mandy we're leaving."

"She won't be surprised." Wise Sister stopped leaning and grabbed a pack and started loading it. Then she stopped and frowned at the huge painting. "We can come and visit that."

"Tell Mandy bye for me." Buff started filling his own pack. "We'll come for the picture."

"Shouldn't we tell them about the cattle?" Tanner asked.

"What's there to tell?" Debba couldn't imagine.

"No matter. Whatever you tell, I am going." Wise Sister didn't even pause in her packing. Neither did Buff.

"I'll pack your food." Belle headed for the cupboards and the icebox.

"I'll saddle the horses. Tanner, help me." Pa left and Tanner, too.

Debba hated to see him go. She'd have followed if Belle wasn't still in the house.

Buff seemed to be finished because he slung a pack over his shoulder, grabbed a rifle, and followed the men.

Once there were only the three of them, Belle started talking and working at the same time. Debba was the last up from the table and did her best to help.

There were details about what Debba's life was like. Wise Sister stopped packing and looked over her shoulder during the part about Shadow.

Then Belle talked about how fast Debba could skin a wolverine, and Wise Sister's black eyes flashed and she gave her chin one hard nod of approval.

"I will teach you to sew a dress in a different way. There are many things I could teach you. There are things you can teach me, too."

Which was about the nicest thing a wise old woman could have said. Debba decided she liked Wise Sister very much.

Suddenly going home wasn't quite so upsetting.

She decided it was time for her to talk. "My pa always taught me that the world outside my canyon was dangerous."

"It is." Wise Sister dropped a pack by the front door and began filling another.

Belle was nearly done with the kitchen cupboards. She was leaving most things

542

behind, and Debba had no idea how she was choosing.

"There is danger inside the canyon, too. And danger in being completely alone. You have been lucky to never fall and break a leg. With no help you might lie there until you died. There are bad men outside the canyon, but being alone can make you forget the joy of love and friendship."

This from a woman who was packing as fast as she could to leave a cabin that seemed very remote.

"We will talk of those dangers, and you can consider if a trip outside once in a while would suit you. Yes, there is danger to be faced, but you are strong enough to do it."

"You think I'm strong?"

Wise Sister quit packing. Belle, too. They both looked at her as if she surprised them.

Finally Belle said, "Debba, to have lived alone, cared for yourself in every way, all these years, is an act of strength. You may be the strongest woman, no, strongest *person,* I have ever known."

And all Debba could see was that she was scared.

Belle and Wise Sister went back to work. Debba noticed Wise Sister take rolled-up tubes of paper from a shelf and pack them with great care. She was taking only the minimum things. Debba wondered what those tubes of paper were.

Luther was wrong about it taking an hour. They were on the trail in forty-five minutes, and Wise Sister had been tapping her moccasined toe for fifteen minutes before Luther was ready to go.

She muttered about men who talk too much.

CHAPTER 8

Ma had been fretting about being gone overnight, but as Tanner had expected, they got home. It was full dark, but they slept in their own beds.

The next morning they all set out. Si and Cade were most likely at Debba's canyon already. If not they'd find the herd on the way there and lead them home.

The long days in the saddle were wearing on Tanner, mostly because he hadn't had a chance to take a walk with Debba or hardly even talk to her. They'd set a blistering pace yesterday, and today was little better. The land they were riding into was so rugged they made far slower time, and Pa had five pack horses with all the tools he needed to build a house. But slow didn't mean Tanner could ride side by side with Debba and talk to her.

Everyone was too busy making sure they didn't tumble off the steep, rocky trail.

As they neared that wall of rocks, Tanner didn't have to worry for one minute about finding his way in. They were following the footsteps, out and back, of a herd of cattle. That hidden trail wasn't so hidden now. A herd of cattle couldn't walk through a trail and not leave plenty of evidence that they'd come this way.

Tanner couldn't wait to see how Si and Cade had handled those critters.

"I hope my grouse are all right." Debba hadn't done much talking. Most likely she was weary to the bone.

They rounded the curve to that keyhole pass, and Pa said with wonder in his voice, "I never suspected this was here."

They went straight on in, and Tanner smiled to see that his brothers had already chopped down a stack of trees. They were good men.

Debba visited her grouse and satisfied herself as to their survival.

Luther and Buff did some hiking around with Pa to hunt for a place to build cabins. Si and Cade went along.

Wise Sister looked around, almost glowing at the beautiful meadow surrounded by high walls. She didn't seem like a woman who wanted to be walled in, but apparently it satisfied her to wall the rest of the world out.

In a few minutes, Buff came back and said to his wife, "Come see if this suits."

Wise Sister followed him into the woods.

"I thought they would be living right next

546

door to me." Debba wove her fingers together, almost as if she were praying.

"Did you want them to?"

With a weak smile, she shrugged and said, "I like that they are here with me."

She gave Tanner a wide-eyed stare that he was sure meant she wanted him here, too. But he might be wrong. And it was too soon to propose.

She went on, "But I was wondering if we'd get to bothering each other. I like that we have a bit of space between us."

Pa came out and showed them where the first cabin went so they could get on with building. Then he left to explore some more.

"How deep does the snow get in winter?" Ma and Tanner, along with Debba, who followed orders with a sweet spirit, began dragging logs to the building site by hooking a chain to each log then to their saddles and hauling them along.

As they worked, Ma and Debba talked quietly. Tanner wanted to hear every word Debba said, but there was no time now, just like he hadn't had time to talk to her since they'd ridden out to fetch Buff and Luther.

The ring of an ax echoed out of the woods. Tanner's brothers were back at work.

The cattle and horses had spread to the far end of the canyon, some of them over the rise so they couldn't be seen. A few had watched the newcomers with placid curiosity for a time, but now they went back to crunching grass.

Tanner couldn't wait for Wise Sister to meet Shadow.

They'd gotten to the canyon with plenty of sunlight left. They burned it all and worked well into the dark. All the logs they needed were cut, and the first few feet of the walls of Buff's cabin were started before they quit for the night.

Ma and Wise Sister showed Debba a few cooking tricks. Tanner knew they used ingredients Debba hadn't worked with for years, like flour and sugar and coffee.

The next day went on at the same relentless pace, and the next. Finally on the fourth day, Si and Cade rode away. They needed to check the Harden place.

As he watched them go, Tanner decided he should do the same thing. He hadn't been to his place for nearly a week.

He asked Pa, who agreed he needed to check his cattle. Tanner rode for the pass out of the canyon, and as he neared it, he had a flashing memory of hauling Debba out of here against her will.

Somehow he felt like he was doing the same thing, only this time, with himself.

He slowed his black down, then down again. He drew closer and it echoed in his head, the way she'd protested. He pulled the stallion to a halt.

He couldn't make himself go. He turned his horse back and looked at the pristine beauty of this hidden meadow. A rise concealed Debba's cabin. Her cattle and horses weren't in sight. The new buildings were tucked back in the woods.

He thought of the dangerous longhorns as gentle as kittens. The wild grouse tamed into barnyard chickens. If he gave her half a chance, he wondered if Debba could make a lion lie down with a lamb.

It was as if he were the only man on earth and he was abandoning Eden. Even Adam was too smart to walk out on his own. God had to kick him out. The thought brought a smile to his face and helped clear up every confused thought in his head. He rode right back the way he'd come.

As he neared the top of the rise, Debba came running, her red hair loose and tangling in the wind. She saw him and stumbled to her knees. She was crying.

Swinging down, Tanner ran to her. "What's wrong? Are you hurt?" He caught her shoulders and lifted her to her feet.

She flung her arms around him and hung on like clinging vine. He held her just as tight.

Finally he was able to speak through his panic. "Did something happen?"

"Yes, something happened."

Tanner thought of Ma and Pa. Had there been an accident? Had —

"You left me." The grief in her words, the raining tears. They said to him exactly what he wanted to say to her.

But before he got to talking, he lowered his head and kissed her.

The moment stretched. The clouds overhead rolled by. A soaring eagle screamed on the wind. Babbling water and lowing cows, aspen leaves quaked and danced.

He was here, with her. The perfect woman in the perfect place.

At last he broke the kiss and looked at her, those deep-blue eyes that carried secrets and fears and loneliness, and a lifetime of hard-won knowledge of how to live in this harsh land.

The swollen lips that she so generously shared with him.

"Debba, I love you."

The fear faded. Her loneliness turned to hope.

"I love you, too, Tanner. That's why when your pa said you left —"

"I was leaving to go check my cattle. My land is low on water, and I might need to do some scouting. But only a bit today. I intended to only be gone an hour or two. I didn't think you'd even know."

Debba shook her head frantically. "The sun dimmed and the birds quit singing. The trees wept and the wind turned cold. I knew you'd gone out of my life."

He smiled and felt his heart fill — and he'd thought it was full before.

"I couldn't go. Not even for an hour. We've been together ever since we met. And Debba . . ." he kissed her again, long and hard. "I don't ever want to be away from you. Marry me. We can live here, or we can give the canyon to Wise Sister, Buff, and Luther and live at my place and come in here to care for your critters."

"Drive your cattle in here with mine and let them drink from my sweet-water creek. And I'll ride with you to scout for more, outside this place."

Nodding, Tanner said, "Thank you. Yes, I think I can go check my cattle now, if you'll ride along. I was thinking I couldn't leave this perfect place, but the truth is, I couldn't leave *you*. We'll live wherever you want, because my only wish in life is to find a way to make you the happiest woman who ever lived."

"Then marry me, soon. Because that would make me blissfully happy."

Tanner smiled and hugged her close. "We're going to have to hit the trail for a bunch more hours."

She pulled back just far enough to meet his gaze, her eyes wide and worried. "Why?"

"Because we need to find ourselves a parson."

Her furrowed forehead smoothed, and she

smiled. "And say some vows before God."

"That's right. We need to get married, and I don't want to wait another day."

This time she kissed him first. They were a long time thinking of anything else.

Tanner said, "Let's go tell my ma and pa they've got another long ride ahead of them."

Debba laughed, and they walked arm in arm back to tell everyone the good news.

EPILOGUE

They didn't manage to get married that day, nor the next.

And when they did ride away, Tanner had no trouble leaving the canyon, not with Debba along. Pa built a fence across the keyhole pass that was so sturdy it just might keep Debba's cattle in.

They didn't get married that day, either, because, before Ma set to cooking, she sent Si and Cade and Pa in different directions. Tanner, too. His job was to get Red Dawson to come and perform a ceremony.

The rest of them were gathering family.

They had about the biggest wedding any of them had ever seen. Especially when Tom and Mandy Linscott showed up. Red brought his wife, Cassie. Wade and Abby Sawyer came over, too. All of them brought their young'uns and a bunch of food.

All Tanner's brothers and sisters and his sisters' husbands rode in. They all brought a passel of children.

Red smiled as he held his prayer book and had them speak their marriage vows.

Ma managed to get a side of beef roasting while the family gathered, and they had a feast, though Debba was horrified that they'd cooked a cow.

Tanner would talk to her about that later.

Then they all split up to head home before Shadow arrived demanding to be a bridesmaid.

■ ■ ■ ■

TEXAS TEA

■ ■ ■ ■

CHAPTER 1

June 6, 1895

Luke Reeves stepped into the entry hall of the small school in Sour Springs, TX, wondering how to play this.

Then his cousin Libby Cooper, who was in no way *really* his cousin, started speaking.

He stayed out of sight in the entrance hall and listened. She sounded like a kind but no-nonsense woman who was in complete charge of her voice, her pupils, and her life.

She'd been that way ever since Luke had met her and it was one of the things he liked best about her.

"Class dismissed." She finally finished up. "Enjoy your summer vacation, children."

"Good afternoon, Miss Cooper." The children spoke as one voice, then stood in one snap of noise and almost instantly began filing out of the classroom. Books in their arms. They didn't whisper, they didn't whoop with joy and stumble over each other trying to get out the door first — the way he and his brother had always done — especially when there was a school break.

They walked straight out the door and headed for home. He noticed them form small groups and begin talking quietly.

Libby had them in perfect order even after they were beyond her grasp.

If she'd been his teacher, he'd have spent every ounce of his talent breaking her spirit. It was just what he did when he was in school.

Call it a hobby.

He wasn't proud of it, but why deny the truth?

Once the orderly little students were all gone, he went through the door that led to the school room and almost jumped back out.

Libby had grown up. A pretty blue dress sprinkled with white flowers. Her dark hair in a tidy bun pulled back from her pretty face. Those blue eyes as sparkling as ever.

She looked up and saw him for about one second before she said, "Luke!"

In direct contrast to her controlled voice and orderly children, she ran around her teacher's desk and raced for him.

He saw it coming and spread his arms wide. She flung hers around his neck, laughing. He lifted her right off her feet and whirled her around. "It's been a long time, little cousin."

"What brings you here?" She gave him a loud, smacking kiss on the cheek then swatted him in the shoulder, laughing. "Little cousin indeed. I'm older than you Luke Reeves."

"You're talking years, I'm talking inches. I can never believe how you can tell my brothers and I apart."

She tugged on his hair, overlong because he'd been too busy to get a haircut.

"Whitest hair I've ever seen on all you boys. And the same blue eyes and all the same height I'll admit. But beyond that," Libby rolled her eyes. "you look nothing alike."

"Just because everyone in the world says we do, and can never tell us apart, doesn't prove a thing." Luke amended that. A few could tell. Ma and Pa — most of the time, and of course his other brothers. Beyond that it was only Libby. And it had been years.

"It's been years." She pulled back a bit so she could see him. She gave him a look of completely false worry. "Are you sure you know who I am?"

Luke returned a lighthearted kiss. "You, Libby, are one of a kind. I can't believe you make these children go to school in the blazing Texas summer heat."

"They have a long break in the spring to help their families with roundup and all the spring work. Then we go back in May and quit a couple of weeks before the Independence Day festivities so they can all get involved in the planning." She smirked at him. "That sounds very patriotic, but the real reason we take a break is because it gets so awful hot. This is their last day until September."

"Do you have things to do today before you can head out?"

"Nothing that can't wait until my favorite cousin isn't here to talk to."

The grin she gave him lit something up inside. He wasn't sure what, it was like nothing he'd ever felt before. Strange. But he was so happy to see her that it was all he could do to step away . . . and then just a few inches.

Giving his head a mental shake to clear it, he said, "Then let's go. I've already got your horse from your brother at the blacksmith shop. You're saddled and ready to go."

"You saw Will?"

"Yep, first words out of his mouth, 'Which one are you?' "

"Will isn't sharp like me, of course."

Luke slung his arm around her shoulder just because he couldn't quite resist touching her, and they walked out together. "Joshua was there, too. It made me lonely to see your folks. You're kind of your mom's sister right?"

Libby poked him in the ribs as they walked down the school house steps and headed for the horses waiting patiently at the hitching post. "Kind of."

"Which means you're kind of *my* mom's sister. Which means you're my aunt."

Libby giggled. "I don't think I'll explain it

to you, Luke. You seem reasonably bright. Figure it out all on your own." She gave him an affectionate slap on the shoulder.

With a laugh, he caught her by the wrist and held her tight.

They stopped at the hitching post.

Something strange happened in the middle of their teasing and laughter and touches. That odd light inside him flared up. Their eyes caught. Her smile faded and her blue eyes sparkled with something very different from teasing.

"You're not a little girl anymore, Lib."

At a whisper, she replied, "I haven't been for a long time."

"No, you haven't been, have you? Instead, you're a full-grown, beautiful, warm woman."

Silence stretched as a breeze from the warm Texas summer ruffled strands loose from her tidy, chestnut-brown bun. Her blue eyes were so dark it was like looking at the night sky just before the last light faded.

He shook his head, but it didn't break the tie binding them. He kept hold of her wrist and felt his thumb massage a little circle right over her pulse.

He'd never been so aware of a woman in his life. With no plan to do such a thing, Luke leaned down and kissed her right on the lips. Not another silly peck on the cheek as he'd given her before.

He deepened the kiss and as he angled her

head so her lips were closer, the kiss caught fire. He drew her by the wrist and brought his other hand up to caress her cheek. She touched his chest with the flat of her free hand and clutched his shirt.

A buckboard rattled down the street and Luke jumped back. Libby turned away immediately without letting go of his shirt, which jerked her back. Then their eyes caught again. She let go, shook her head frantically, whirled away and strode for her chestnut mare. He touched his lips trying to figure out what had just happened. Then he rushed for his own black gelding and mounted up, wanting space between them.

When they were riding out of town. Libby said, "That shouldn't have happened. It was a disgraceful display right by the school house. I could get dismissed from my job for that."

Luke thought that if she got fired, she'd be free, nothing to hold her here. Which reminded him of her mixed-up relationship to the family.

"So then, Aunt Libby," Luke cleared his throat, trying to forget how much he'd enjoyed kissing her.

"If I'm your aunt," Libby cut him off with a trembling smile. "Then that gives me the right to discipline you, youngster. You have behaved badly. Shame on you. Now let's hurry home. Ma and Pa will be thrilled to see you."

She kicked her mare and the animal, after a day of idleness in Will's corral, was eager to run.

She raced off and Luke did his best to not quite catch up. Because there was no sense in riding close when they had nothing to talk about. Luke didn't have a single thought in his head that ought to be said out loud.

CHAPTER 2

As if she hadn't behaved badly, too.

Libby wasn't sure what had happened back there. She's been so glad to see him. He wore a light gray suit with a jacket that emphasized his broad shoulders. He had boots on in the same shade of gray and a Stetson that also matched. He wore a white shirt with an open collar when he should have had a matching tie, but even that, she suspected was a deliberate choice. He looked like he gave plenty of thought to presenting himself as a professional, well-dressed man. In all the gray with his blond hair curling out just a bit from below his hat, his blue eyes shone, bright, intelligent and kind.

There was no way to deny that he was the most handsome man she'd ever seen. And considering he was one of a set of identical triplets, she thought that was a high compliment.

But he was her cousin. She shouldn't be kissing her cousin. Except he was no more her cousin than this horse was such.

She counted her ma Hannah, and Luke's ma Grace, as family. Ma and Aunt Grace were orphans who'd met when they'd been adopted by a horribly abusive father in Chicago. They called themselves sisters. Then Grace had run off, luring their adoptive father on a wild chase to catch her. The moment he was gone, Hannah took all the other children in that home into hiding. One by one she'd found them good homes, but then there'd been other children on the streets and she'd taken care of them. Grace was to lose their father, Perish, get a job, and find a home for them all. Then Hannah would bring the children and join her wherever she was. Libby was one of those children Hannah had found after she'd escaped her father. Libby was so much younger than the nearly grown Hannah that she'd thought of Hannah as her ma from the first. Then she'd been adopted by Pa, and Hannah had married Pa. They'd been together for most of her life. Grace had landed a husband close to the time Hannah had. A man with five sons. Including Luke, age five, the youngest of identical triplets. So there was no blood shared between any of them.

Still, he had always been her cousin.

She shouldn't have been kissing him for heaven's sakes.

There oughta be something to say, and

Libby didn't want them to be awkward together when they reached Pa and Ma's ranch. Since she was used to plain speaking, she reined her horse a bit so Luke could catch up.

"Luke, that's never going to happen again."

"You're darned right it's not."

That pinched a bit. "I'm glad we're in agreement. Now," she decided some casual conversation was in order, "what brings you to Sour Springs?"

Luke gave her an odd look, uneasy. Awkward, as if he didn't want to speak of why he'd come. "Have you ever heard of the Corsicana Oil Field?"

Libby pulled her horse back so suddenly, Luke rode on and her horse reared and whinnied. She relaxed her hold, patted her horse's shoulder, sorry for upsetting it. On the other hand she had plans to upset Luke Reeves mightily.

Luke wheeled around, his brow furrowed. "I guess that means you have."

Fighting from the anger that wanted to erupt bigger than an oil gusher, Libby said through clenched teeth. "Do you think you're the first man to come down here sniffing for oil?"

Luke seemed genuinely confused. "So you're saying Uncle Grant has already sold his land?"

"Of course not. He wouldn't do business

with a low down, lying con man. And if you're after oil there's a good chance we'll be adding you to the list of varmints trying to steal our ranch."

"Libby, I wouldn't try to cheat your folks out of their land. And there's a very good chance Grant could end up very rich."

"We've got all we need." Her scorn might not be appropriate, but the oil men were a ruthless, sly lot. "If all you came for was to talk oil, you just head back for town right now."

"There's no cause for you to get angry like this. I'm sorry if someone has treated you badly."

Treated her badly? As if it could be labeled something so mild. She sniffed and turned toward home. "If you'd like to visit family, you're welcome to ride on with me."

She heard hoof beats behind her so he was coming, but he didn't try and catch up with her. Which gave her plenty of time to wonder if he really even wanted to kiss her, or if he wanted to charm her over to his side while he worked on Pa and Ma.

It wouldn't be the first time a man had done such a thing.

And that time she'd only been saved from his false courtship because she'd overheard her former fiancé laughing to other men about it.

CHAPTER 3

That'd gone badly.

Luke didn't bother to catch up to her because he had somehow stepped into a rattlesnake pit and now he'd messed up the calm talk he'd planned to have with Grant and Hannah.

Instead he spent the rest of the ride mulling over the things he wanted to say — wondering what Libby would think about it — smart enough not to ask.

He rode lost in thought until they reached the Rocking C.

Luke saw the large, pretty house, the tidy ranch yard. The big herd grazing in the distance. Grant had done well for himself. He'd raised himself a passel of orphan children back when Luke was growning up a short train ride away in Mosqueros. The number had gone mighty high but Luke had lost track. The Reeves would come to visit at least once a year and it'd always been so much fun.

Every couple of years the orphan train would come through and a couple more youngsters joined the family. Grant and Hannah birthed some of them, the rest were off the train. Grant had always had room in his house for a child in need.

The train had quit running through Sour Springs and Grant, though troubled when he felt so called to help children, accepted that he'd adopted and cared for the children God had put in his path and he was willing to accept that maybe being father to thirty or forty children was God's plan.

Grant stepped out of the barn with a big smile for Libby, then his smile faded, then bloomed again as they got close and dismounted.

"You're one of the Reeves boys. Welcome to the Rocking C."

Luke had always really liked Grant Cooper. He loved his own pa but Pa worked them hard and let them run wild. Luke and his brothers had long ago realized it was Pa's desperate method for getting them to sleep at night. Keep them exhausted. The truth was Pa loved them fiercely, but there was not much stern about him.

The other father he knew best around Mosqueros was Clay McClellen and for a family full of boys like the Reeves, and McClellen, who's four oldest children were four beautiful daughters close in age to Luke and his older brothers, had been just plain scary.

Grant was in the middle. He was what a real father should be. He showered his children with love and his speckled-hazel eyes always sparked with humor and concern. His kids worked hard, but Grant was the quickest man with a hug and a prayer or a laugh Luke had ever known.

Before he could ask the eternal question, 'Which one are you?' Libby said, "It's Luke. He's in the oil business now and he's come to try and trick you out of your ranch."

Grant looked between Libby and Luke, then said, "Now, Lib, Luke wouldn't do that."

Then with a gaze that contained not one speck of the usual laughter and no sign of a hug nor a prayer, Grant asked Luke, "Would you?"

It was a nice tone. Letting both of them know that he took his daughter's side in everything, and he took Libby's words very seriously.

Luke glared at Libby a second, then spoke directly to Grant. "I don't know what's happened before, but I have no intention of tricking anyone. But I *am* in the oil business, and I remembered the oil seep on your land. I want to make you an honest offer. And, if we find oil, a chance for you to make a lot of money."

Feeling a little sly, Luke added, "I can see you're a prosperous man, Uncle Grant. But what if I find oil here and you can earn a percentage of what we find? You'd be in a position to leave each and every one of your children a nice inheritance."

"My children are all hard workers who are making their way in life very well. A big chunk of money from me might well turn 'em lazy and be the ruin of them." Then Grant softened again. "Doubt I'm interested, son, but come on in and say your piece, then join us for supper. Hannah always makes plenty."

After digging around for another reason Grant might want money, he came up with a really good one. "So all your children are grown and gone but Libby? It must be mighty quiet around here."

Before he could build up to his idea, Grant slapped him on the back in a friendly way. "Let's go put the horses up and go in. Hannah will have my hide if we linger out here talking without her getting to hear every word."

The three of them made short work of unsaddling and turning the horses out to graze, then walked to the house together.

Luke looked across Grant — who was between Luke and Libby — and saw her upset. Not anger so much as hurt. Someone had caused her pain. Someone involved in oil. Luke determined then and there to present his case to Grant and Hannah and put no pressure on them at all. Family was more important than money.

He realized with a jolt of surprise that it was the first time in years he'd thought anything was more important than money. That stabbed at him all the way to his soul.

They entered the house. Grant said, "Look who's stopped to visit, Hannah, Luke Reeves."

Aunt Hannah saw him and smiled then rushed forward and threw her arms around his neck. "My little nephew Luke."

He laughed, being about eight inches taller than her.

She laughed, too. "Can you stay a while? Are you heading home? I know your ma is lonely for you. Have you been home since your baby sister was born?"

"Hope is eight years old now. And no, I've yet to meet her and there's a brother or two a little older than Hope that I haven't met. And I left when Abe had two sons. I understand there's a couple more little ones there. And Ike and Laura had two babies. Ma writes real regular."

"Shame on you for not coming home more often, Luke."

It was odd to enjoy being scolded. He really had stayed away too long. "Trains are better than they used to be, Aunt Hannah. Getting home has finally gotten so it doesn't make a man miss an entire season to visit. My boss has a real low opinion of a man taking three months off. Sort of figures if I can be gone three months, I can be gone forever."

"Do you still live in Chicago? Do you —"

Grant cut her off with a laugh. "Give the boy a chance to speak, Hannah."

Her smile didn't even dim. "I am dying to hear you speak. So I'd best hush up. At least until you've answered all the questions I've asked so far. Now, wash up while I set the food on the table. We have fried chicken, mashed potatoes, gravy, and apple pie from the last of our dried apples from the fall."

Luke washed his hands. "That sounds like a meal to put heart into a man, thank you for sharing it with me."

He began taking platters and serving bowls from Hannah as quickly as she dished things up. A glance at Libby warned him that his helpfulness wasn't making inroads with her. In fact, if anything it was deepening her suspicions. Like a man wasn't allowed to help his aunt out once in a while?

Grant asked God to bless their food. Then they passed dishes and filled plates.

Luke had just taken his first bite of chicken when Grant said, "Now tell us about this oil drilling business, Luke."

Libby stopped chewing to listen with grim intensity.

Hannah's wonderful smile faded from her face, replaced with suspicion.

"What happened here?" Luke knew he had

no chance of making any kind of deal with Grant when every one of them threw up fortress walls at the very mention of oil. "I can tell it was bad. Did someone threaten you in an effort to scare you off your land?"

Grant looked at Hannah, who looked at Libby.

"I don't mind telling him." Libby sat straight across the table from Luke while Hannah and Grant were at the head and foot. She added, "I know Ma and Pa would never speak of it if I didn't want them to.

"Speak of what?" Luke was dreading whatever she said because it had to be bad.

No one at the table was eating now. A big old shame because Hannah was a fine cook.

Libby's cheeks flushed a bit and she looked down at her plate as if she found a chicken leg fascinating. Finally she lifted her chin and spoke, her voice even and strong. "The last man who came near to talking us out of our land and oil took a very different approach."

"What did he do?" Luke knew well enough there were some unscrupulous men in the oil business.

"He convinced me that he was in love with me. He proposed marriage and I said yes. This was two years ago that he came to town and he courted me and brought me flowers and finally proposed after he'd stayed nearly six months. Then one day I was walking toward Will's shop to get my horse after school, when I heard my fiancé laughing about getting the oil for free if he didn't count being saddled with a lame, old maid. He was talking with a crowd of oil men. They were all in town to pester Pa. And there they stood, laughing uproariously — about me."

With a fond smile, Libby said, "I'd like to think I scared them away on my own, but I reckon they could see that if Pa was going to be angry at all of them on my account, then they'd never talk him out of his oil." Her eyes flashed and he saw the strength in her.

"What fierce thing did you say?" Luke had trouble imagining being very scared of Libby.

"I waded right into the middle of that group of awful men, and found my fiancé at the center. I told him the engagement was off. His chance at owning Pa's oil was off, and he was lucky I didn't have my gun or parts of his mangy hide might've been shot off. I called him a liar and a cheat and a few other names. Then I turned to the rest of the group and said I was going to tell Pa about each and every one of them laughing about me, mocking the fact I had a limp and that I was an old maid. None of them would be allowed to set foot on the Rocking C again."

Luke jerked his chin in satisfaction. "Good for you."

"Libby has a fierce streak." Grant's voice echoed with pride. "They'd started coming around shortly after the Corsicana Oil Strike because word of the oil seep on my land got out. After Libby confronted them, they all left town — they didn't even sleep in Sour Springs one more night. A few oil men have been back — not those who were involved in that nonsense — but others, one at a time. All with offers. I'm inclined to consider them all untrustworthy and it grieves me to put you in that category. But it also grieves me to see you in that business."

Luke nodded. "The oil business is in chaos, and that attracts a lot of the wrong sorts of folks. But I have business interests in Chicago who are looking to challenge the Standard Oil monopoly and we aim to make a stand right here in Texas. We have done some good, honest work with landowners, Grant. I'll give you my word that I'll do you no harm, but more than that, I'll insist you get a lawyer to read over every word of any contract I'd ask you to sign."

"I'm a long way from lawyers, Luke, and a long way from even considering saying yes. But I'll give you your say and listen with an open mind."

"That's all a man can ask for, Grant. Thank you."

"No more of it tonight though. Tonight let's eat Hannah's good cooking and talk about your folks and how they're doing. We may know more than you, so we can catch you up. But you get regular letters, so who knows, you might be able to tell us a few things."

Grant gave Hannah a look so fond it awakened a quiet ache in Luke's chest. He'd never had much use for the idea of marriage but once in a while he felt an urge to have someone all his own. And seeing folks as contented and in love as Grant and Hannah made him realize it could be good.

CHAPTER 4

Libby entered the kitchen late the next morning. The sun was already up.

And there sat a large blond man at her kitchen table. He was disheveled and dirty. A match for Pa, so they'd already done morning chores and were in for breakfast. Ma was at the stove cooking.

It made her feel like a lay-about.

It also made her suspicious. Pa respected hard work. Libby figured Luke was trying to buy his way into Pa's oil by milking cows and cleaning out stalls. The bad thing was, it was the kind of tactic that just might work.

"Morning, Lib." Luke got up and for a treacherously tempting second, she thought he was going to greet her in a more friendly way. But he went to the stove instead and grabbed the coffee pot and poured another cup for Pa and himself, then one for her. The steam curled up from the cups. Pa took a long sip while Luke returned the pot, then he grabbed a plate of biscuits and put it on the table, already set with plates and utensils. He added butter.

"What else goes on the breakfast table, Aunt Libby?" He reminded Libby of his teasing from yesterday.

Helping again. Being charming and funny. Working his way into their lives, the big, handsome sneak.

"Jelly, milk," Ma ignored the 'Aunt Libby' and listed a few more things. She was laying bacon directly on the cast iron stove. Libby grabbed an apron, dropped butter into a hot skillet, and went to work breaking eggs. These two men most likely had already worked for a couple of hours and they'd be hungry.

She broke a dozen eggs that sizzled as they dropped onto the skillet, a noise that matched Ma's bacon. The kitchen was rich with the smell of frying food and coffee.

They took up the warm eggs and bacon and carried it to the table. When they were all settled in, Pa said grace then began to talk of their day. "Luke wants to ride out and look at the oil seep after breakfast. He helped so much with chores I have plenty of time for it. Hannah, I think you should come along with me. Libby, too."

Libby smiled. Not much in the world could keep her from coming. Ma and Pa were too friendly. Someone needed to keep them safe from Luke and his sharp business dealings.

"I haven't been out there in years." Ma

smiled at Luke. "We keep the cattle away from that area so we never have cause to go that way."

Then Ma's smile faded. "We don't know much about oil companies but we've heard stories of work done to the land that uses up many acres and leaves the ground foul. Men coming in who are sometimes rough characters."

"That may be true of many oil workers, but my company pays top wages and as a result attracts the best men. They will need places to live, Aunt Hannah. At first we'll put up bunkhouses but soon enough there will be houses built, groceries and clothes bought. They'll bring their own horses but they'll want to rent land to graze them or buy oats, have them shod, jobs that will make money for Will and Joshua." He named her two brothers who owned the livery and blacksmith business in town.

"We have to see if we can find a good supply of oil but, if we do, this town could really prosper."

"By prosper do you mean a dozen new saloons?" Pa asked. "Will we need to hire a bunch of deputies to break up fights? Will our women and children be accosted on the streets?"

Libby had heard many stories of things like this at oil digging sites.

"There was a time, right at the beginning,

when too much of the business was rough, but now those men have either settled in and are decent, hardworking fellows or they've gone on to cause their trouble elsewhere. My men are family men who will want their wives and children near them. The school will need new rooms and more teachers than just Libby. Businesses will grow and new ones will open to supply the needs newcomers have. Those families will steady the area, not disrupt it."

There was a long pause and Libby could tell Luke was ready to make a big sales pitch. She braced herself.

"Grant, I like what you said last night about your children being hard workers who care for their families themselves, but that reminded me of something. You haven't taken any new orphans in for years, have you?"

A somber expression came over Pa's face. "Nope, the orphan trains quit coming to Sour Springs. I accepted it but it wasn't easy. If God puts orphans in my path Hannah and I have agreed to take them in. But I don't ride away and search for them."

"How about if you had a sudden windfall of money? Maybe you could use it to help orphans. I know of several good orphanages in Chicago but they always struggle for money." Luke's eyes shifted to Hannah, "That's where you grew up, and escaped your cruel father, right?"

Then he looked at Libby. "And Hannah and Grace found you there, living in an alley, your ankle broken."

Libby remembered too much about Chicago. The cold, hunger, fear and pain. Oh, how she'd like to help children living on scraps, hurt in alleyways.

Next he turned to Grant. "And you came from New York City. They still run orphan trains but just not to Sour Springs anymore."

"I know. I've looked around trying to find the end of the line but it's not even in Texas anymore."

Libby knew how it cut at Pa to think of those orphans who were left over at the end of the line, that no one wanted, that had to go back to New York.

"Maybe you could donate money to the trains." Luke went on. "Or start your own orphanage, run it the way you think it ought to be run. Make an orphanage that children don't want to run away from. Pay high enough wages that you attract the finest people. Set it in the town where the train turns around and take all the left over orphans."

Pa's eyes sharpened and he exchanged a look with Ma. "Or hire someone at the end of the line to claim those children and bring them here to me."

Luke leaned forward, probably with enthusiasm, but to Libby it looked like a hungry wildcat sensing weakness, ready to go in for the kill.

"I don't know Texas well, but Houston is getting to be a big town. If there are kids on the streets, maybe you could help. You say you don't want or need money, but there are things you can do that will help others. And I'll make sure the terms are fair for you, Grant. I won't let anyone cheat you."

Instead of the casual 'no' Pa had been giving right along, he was silent. He looked at Libby and his concern was so deep it was like a cloud surrounded him. She knew he was thinking about how she'd looked stepping off that train as a child. She was cold, and so hungry. Terrified of the man who became her beloved Pa, because he made a poor first impression in his rugged western clothes. Heartsick to think she had to get back on that awful train and ride on. Pa had been so kind. And Charlie, another orphan boy who'd been adopted by Pa at the same time, had told her he'd stay with her.

Pa, with Ma's whole-hearted support, wanted to save every child in need in the whole world.

"Let's ride out there," Pa said, standing from the table. "All four of us. You haven't even seen the place have you, Luke?"

Looking a bit sheepish, Luke said, "My brothers and I went to that seep every time we came to visit."

"I told you to stay away from there."

Libby remembered Pa telling them all.

"Your young'uns went with us, but only because we begged 'em."

Libby raised her hand and smiled sheepishly. "I went every time."

Pa just looked tired. "Let's clear up the kitchen, and then we'll go."

CHAPTER 5

Pa's pistol was drawn before any of them could react. Luke was only a second behind.

"What are you doing on my land?" Pa's voice cracked until it was almost as shocking as if he'd fired a shot.

"I know them, Uncle Grant."

The whole family gave him an angry look.

Libby said, "So you sent your men out here to start work before we even agreed to sell?"

"No, I did not. And I can't believe you'd accuse me of that. We're family. I said I know them because I've met them before, and I'll tell you straight to ride in easy and keep your gun cocked and ready. That's what I'd have said next if you'd trusted me for even a second."

Luke turned forward. He wanted to yell at the whole Cooper family that he was hurt by their constant suspicions, but he had some men to run off first.

Just as Luke believed the men were going to stand fast and talk, a shot rang out from overhead on a high hill beside the seep.

Libby felt a blow and for an addled minute thought she'd been shot. Then she slammed into the ground and realized Luke was on top of her. She landed with such a thud it knocked the wind out of her. Then they rolled up against a boulder with a hard thud, that tucked them right at the base of that hill. Five shots fired, kicking up dust just a pace behind each move they made.

They knocked up against the boulder as one bullet pinged off it. They crouched low and ran around the back of the boulder. There was only a small space between it and the mountain. A half step later, Pa and Ma were behind the boulder, too. Luke whirled to face the two men standing in the open.

One fired and Luke's gun exploded a second later. He emptied it at the men before Pa could even get his gun in play. Both men staggered back, diving to the ground. Blood bloomed on one man's chest. Crimson streaked down the leg of the other. Shots rained down from overhead. But they were sheltered from that dry-gulching varmint. Pa ducked to the far side of the boulder, so close to the bluff, the man overhead wouldn't be able to draw a bead on him.

Turning back, Luke looked at where Pa had gone, waited for a break in the shooting, then went away from the boulder the other direction. Libby leaned forward to watch Luke spring toward the shelter of the hill. He hugged up against the side of it just as bullets rained down again. A rifle. Libby could tell it held multiple bullets.

She looked at the men who had fallen. They lay still but she couldn't tell if they were dead. If they weren't, then they could still present a danger. She itched to race across the open space and get their guns.

"We should never have come out here unarmed," Libby whispered to Ma. Relieved that their men always carried guns.

Ma looked back, furious and helpless at the same time. "I have never needed to carry a gun in my life. No man in Texas would harm a woman. Or at least they are few and far between. The fact that they opened up on the four of us, with two women clearly along, tells me these are the worst kind of low down filth there is."

The gunman must have emptied his rifle because the shooting stopped. Libby counted, to see how long it took him to reload. That's how many seconds she had to dash over to those guns, grab them both and get back to Ma.

The shooting started up again. "It took him twenty-five seconds to reload, Ma." Libby looked hard at her mother. "I think the next time he runs out of ammunition, I can get across to those wounded men and take their weapons."

"You'll do no such thing, Libby Cooper."

Libby counted shots and then silence again.

"Start counting off seconds. See how long it takes."

She and Ma watched each other in silence.

When the shooting resumed, Ma said, "Twenty-seven seconds, but I might have been counting overly fast just because of nerves."

"What do you think? Can I make it? If we could shoot from down here, safe behind cover, aren't Pa and Luke in less danger?"

Ma's jaw was a grim tight line. "I don't want to shoot up because we don't know where our bullets will fly and our men are up there. But these men down here could come around and get back in the fight."

Then Ma looked at her hard. "Which of us is faster?"

Ma was referring to the fact that Libby limped and for the first time ever she hated her damaged foot because, if she wasn't very careful, Ma would take this run, and Libby's reckless idea could get her mother killed.

CHAPTER 6

Luke kept his belly pressed tight to the rock wall he planned to scale. He eased along to the left, knowing there was a trail up. But was the trail too exposed? He'd climbed this hill, with its sheer drops and steep trails, many times as a child. Mainly because Uncle Grant had forbidden it. But he'd never climbed it while someone shot at him.

Grant hissed and drew Luke's attention. He was sliding to the right. He pointed at a rugged side of the bluff that almost formed stair steps. Definitely almost, because the 'steps' were narrow and far apart. Climbing them would be the toughest kind of climbing a man could do this side of the Rocky Mountains.

Grant started up. The man overhead aimed at the boulder where Libby and Aunt Hannah hid. Did the shooter still think all four of them were behind it?

Then a ricochet shot bounced off the boulder and missed Luke's leg by inches. It sent him scrambling for that trail. The man either knew where they were or he was trying to bounce a bullet off the rocks and behind that boulder. Either way their situation just got urgent because he could hit the women.

Grant was already ten feet up that cliff. They needed to come at this varmint from two directions.

Luke took a long hard look at the two men he'd shot. One was almost for sure dead. A chest shot was fatal unless something very unexpected happened. Luke swallowed hard. He'd done plenty of rugged things in his life, but he'd never killed a man.

He hadn't done much talking to God in a long time. But this called for time spent on his knees. Time spent making his peace. And while he was asking for forgiveness he had a whole lot of other things to ask for.

He edged along. Then the bullets stopped, as Luke had noticed they did with regularity. It sounded like a Winchester, one of the newer ones. They could hold a lot of lead. But it took a man a while to reload. Of course he didn't have to fill the gun. If he was in the middle of reloading and he saw something that needed shooting, he could just close the gun and start firing.

Luke moved fast while the gun was silent. The dry-gulcher had already emptied that gun three times. How many bullets could he carry?

Reaching the base of the trail, Luke saw a good-sized boulder for shelter about twenty feet up. He rushed for it. If the man couldn't see him he'd be safe. If he could see him, he'd use the boulder for safety and maybe draw the man's fire away from the women.

No sign of anyone up there. Luke did see curls of gunsmoke rising from behind a jumbled pile of stone, pinpointing the man's location exactly. He pressed on, climbing fast, keeping low. He couldn't see where Grant had gone, but he didn't want one of his favorite people on the earth to face this man without backup.

"I'm going." The gunfire stopped and Libby tensed to jump into the open and run.

A hard hand clamped on her arm and jerked her over backward. Ma glared at her.

"We wait until the next time. Look where your pa is, on the right."

Libby looked.

"Up higher."

Her eyes widened as she saw Pa halfway up the bluff. Clinging by his fingernails.

"He'll be nearly to the top by the time the shooter reloads and empties his gun again. We wait until then to run. Our movements then will draw that outlaw's attention and give Pa a chance to find cover up there. But if you go now, Pa might see you, and be so distracted he falls right off that cliff. I don't know where Luke went, but I reckon he's climbing somewhere, too."

"Ma, I could have been there and back by now. Whether that man's distracted now or a few minutes from now, what's the difference?"

"The difference is, Pa and Luke might be ready to charge him the next time he's reloading, especially if he sees you and isn't paying attention to someone coming up behind him."

It made enough sense that Libby relaxed. It was too late this time anyway.

"Let me just poke my head up. Even that keeps his attention on us."

Ma nodded. "Quick, it's been almost long enough."

Libby raised her head above the top of the boulder. She wasn't keeping it there long but it was probably ten seconds until he'd be ready to fire.

A bullet slashed into her arm and she fell hard, right beside Ma. Who surged to her side, keeping low, as the lead rained down on them.

"My sweet Libby." Ma ripped the arm of her dress away. "It passed through just below your shoulder. It's bleeding fast."

She was too shocked to hurt for the first few seconds,

Ma finished tearing the sleeve off, wrapped it around her arm and knotted it securely.

And all of a sudden the pain was white-hot. She fought to not let a single moan of pain escape.

"There's an entrance and exit wound high on your upper arm. I have to press it to stop the bleeding. It'll hurt. I'm sorry."

Ma's firm hand on the gunshot wound hurt so badly Libby's vision went dark and the whole world swirled around.

The pain didn't lessen but the shock of it did, a bit. Ma leaned close. "He started right in shooting, did you notice that?"

The gunfire died and the silence stretched again. Libby and Ma counted. Thirty seconds this time.

"Of course if he sees anything he doesn't have to finish loading." Ma lay her forehead against Libby's. "I didn't even think of that. If you'd dashed out from the shelter of this rock he'd have started firing within seconds. You'd be dead, Libby." Ma's voice broke.

Libby would have comforted her and told her not to spend time worrying about something that didn't happen, but the terror of the mistake she'd almost made was too overwhelming to allow speech.

Grimly, Luke realized the man hadn't fully reloaded because he'd seen something to shoot at. Either Libby or Aunt Hannah must have shown themselves behind the boulder because that's where all his bullets went.

Since Luke was out of the line of sight of the women, he prayed through near panic.

"God get them under cover. Keep them safe."

He climbed faster, determined to be ready to strike the next time the man quit shooting. How many bullets had this sidewinder carried with him anyway?

He watched for the curl of gunpowder smoke and judged if he'd be visible to this man once he reached the top. He didn't think so, the man was hunkered down behind a jumble of rocks and firing out through a gap in the pile. Luke couldn't see him and he doubted the man could see Luke, at least not for a few paces.

He moved faster, fighting to keep quiet, worried about Libby and Hannah. He reached the top and crawled on his belly toward those rocks.

He got to the base of the rocks and looked around to see Grant coming from the far side. Their eyes met. The gunfire stopped, they both launched themselves around the back of the boulder pile and Luke tackled the burly man crouching there.

The gun flew, and Grant snatched it in mid-air. Luke hammered a fist into the back-shooter's nose. The outlaw roared like a wild animal and went for his throat. Luke tumbled sideways under the choking grip. Just as the man rolled fully on top of him a dull thud stopped the roaring. The outlaw's hands flexed hard, once on Luke's neck, then the clutching fingers went limp and the outlaw slid sideways, landing on his back.

"We've got him, Hannah," Grant yelled as he stripped a pistol and two knives from their prisoner. "Are those men still unconscious down there?"

"Yes." There was a stretch of silence and Luke heard pounding footsteps, then Hannah shouted again. "I've got their guns. But come fast, Grant. Libby's been shot."

Luke surged to his feet.

Grant clamped a hand on his shoulders. "I'm going. Bring this scoundrel down and be quick about it. We don't dare to let any of them come around and ride off, not unless Libby's in such grave condition we have no choice and have to run —"

The words stopped. Luke looked up to see Grant sprinting for the path Luke had come up. Luke wasn't in any mood to take his time so he latched onto the back of the man's collar and headed down that trail almost as fast as his uncle.

By the time he got down, Grant had pulled the outlaws' wagon around, tossed out the barrels of oil, and was throwing the men into the wagon.

"How is she?"

Hannah said, "Shot in the arm. Not bad but she's bleeding. She needs a doctor."

Luke picked up speed and heaved his man

into the wagon right after Grant's second one. Then Luke ran for Libby and swept her up in his arms. She was pale but alert. Her arm a bloody mess.

"Libby will ride with me," Grant ordered.

Luke lifted her to the high wagon seat and Grant took her and held her against him.

"You and Hannah bring our horses." Grant leapt up on the wagon seat and slapped the reins.

Luke looked at Libby's bandaged arm as they drove away and jogged to keep up with them.

Brave Libby saw him and said, "It's not serious, Luke."

"I brought you out here. I let you walk into this."

Libby didn't answer, she just rested her head on her pa's shoulder as if it was too much effort to make her neck do the work.

"Are you able to sit on the seat by your pa? Otherwise you can ride on the saddle with me. You're not going in the wagon box with those men."

Grant had a supporting arm around her as they drove.

Not satisfied, because he wanted to hold her himself, Luke fought to keep his mouth shut, stepped back and let them ride away. Hannah had their four horses and brought them over to Luke.

He mounted up and they rode right behind

the wagon all the way to town, watching the unconscious, possibly dead, men in the wagon for signs of consciousness.

He also paid close attention to Libby in case she showed signs of falling off the high seat.

He looked at Hannah, feeling terrible, feeling responsible. "I never considered there were men out here who might be dangerous. I'm so sorry. I was careless with your safety."

She edged her horse close and rested a hand on his arm. "The west is a dangerous place, and Libby is going to be fine. We've captured three men who need to be in jail so they will harm no one else. I don't hold you to blame and neither will Grant and Libby."

Considering Libby had a bullet hole in her arm, Hannah might want to let Libby speak for herself.

"This is why Uncle Grant needs to sign over his mineral rights and sell outright. So he starts earning money from people who know how to protect the oil and drive off outlaws. More men, all scoundrels, will try and steal it. Grant says he never comes over to this part of his property. After this he'll have to hire hands, post guards. And those guards will face more armed outlaws. And all while your family earns nothing on something that could be very valuable."

"Now's not the time to talk of this, Luke. Please, I just need to focus on getting Libby to a doctor."

Luke nodded. "You're right. This isn't the time. But the time is coming, very soon. After today, you'll have to believe it's not safe to handle this on your own. You need to let me and my men worry about security. I'll explain it better once we're sure Libby is all right."

From then on he and Hannah didn't talk. It made it much easier to keep his gaze riveted on Libby. He held back, riding behind the wagon, when he wanted to be at Libby's side. But he didn't take his eyes off her.

A good thing because suddenly she slumped forward.

Luke spurred his horse forward. Grant grabbed her before she pitched right down between the wagon and the team. Luke got to her and lifted her into his arms. She didn't even react to being handled. Her eyes were closed and her face was pale as milk.

Luke had to tear his eyes away from Libby to look at Grant. "I'm taking her to the doctor."

Grant seemed to be ready to start shouting and demand to take her himself. He didn't want anyone else taking care of his daughter. But Grant was a sensible man. With a nod, he said, "Go, then. Get her to town. You can make better time on your horse."

Luke gave his chin a firm nod of agreement, then shouted to his mount, slapped the reins and the horse leapt into a full gallop from its first step. He pushed as fast as he could while Libby lay limp and bleeding in his arms.

CHAPTER 7

Luke found the doctor's office before he could shout a question at the people who turned to watch him race down the main street.

He swung off with Libby in his arms, whipped the reins over the hitching post, and rushed inside, his boots thundering on the wooden sidewalk that fronted the doctor's office.

"Doc! I need help." Luke hollered as he rushed for the only door that led deeper into the building and nearly plowed over the doctor running out in response to his shouts.

He took one look at the blood soaked bandage on her arm and gasped, "Libby's hurt?"

"Yes, she's been shot."

"Bring her in here." The gray-haired man led Luke into a room with a high, narrow bed. Luke laid Libby down.

"I'm Doctor Ellis." Ellis bulled Luke out of the way. "Is her arm the only injury?"

"Yes, she was shot once."

"It shouldn't be a fatal wound." The doctor quickly pulled the bandage away and studied her arm. He heaved a sigh of relieve. "She's lost a lot of blood and gunshots are always painful and shocking. But this isn't a mortal wound. She'll be fine, but we need to tend this."

Doc Ellis gave the bullet wound another close look. "It's through and through and it's going to hurt for a long time. Watch her so she doesn't roll off the bed. I need soap and water and I need to make sure the wound is clean. The bullet when through her sleeve and if there are threads embedded in the wound it's more likely to get an infection." He whirled away and was gone.

Luke hovered over Libby. She lay unmoving for what seemed too long.

Doc returned with a steaming basin of water and a stack of clothes under his arm. "Grab my doctor bag, it's on the counter right behind you. Open it and hand me what I need."

Luke was suddenly a nurse. He wanted desperately to help so he got the bag open fast.

"Tweezers. They're in one of the side pockets."

Luke hunted and found it.

"I need a magnifying glass, too. It's in a black cloth bag all the way in the bottom."

He had it slapped in the man's hand within seconds.

Hannah rushed into the room. "I left Grant behind, poor man. He'll be another ten or fifteen minutes, then he has to stop at the jail. Can I help, Doc?"

"I just need quiet and some time. I want to get this done while she's unconscious because it's going to hurt." He held the glass close to the wound and pressed on the injury with his tweezers.

"I'm keeping her from falling off the table." Luke felt useless. He stepped sideways to make room for Hannah. She could help him do nothing. The two obeyed the doctor's order of silence.

A long time passed then at last Doc Ellis said, "It looks clean. Get me that brown bottle, Luke. I want to pack the wound so it won't suppurate. I'm leaving it open. Stitches would minimize the scar but a stitched up puncture wound like this is more likely to get infected than one left open."

The doctor carefully medicated, then bandaged the wound.

Luke heard the jingle of traces outside. It sounded like the wagon they'd driven but more time passed before Uncle Grant entered.

"Is she all right?"

"Pa?" Libby's eyes flickered open and they looked straight at Luke. Her brow furrowed.

"I'm here, Libby." Uncle Grant came up to stand beside the doctor. "I had to drop those men off at the jailhouse."

"Yes, she's all right," Dr. Ellis answered for Libby. Then he jabbed a finger right at her nose in a way that told Luke he'd known Libby for a long time. "But you need to lie still a while longer. I'm going to get you some water. When I say you're ready, you will sit up and sip it slowly, with your pa and —" the doctor paused and looked at Luke, "— and whichever one of the Reeves boys this is, right at your side in case you faint."

"I'm Luke, sir." There was no denying Luke and his brothers had made themselves notorious on their visits to see Grant and Hannah.

"Well, you and your brothers were trouble-makers and you look like peas in a pod."

Libby glanced at Luke and rolled her eyes.

The doctor went back to his very kind-hearted scolding. "Once I've decided you have sufficiently gathered your strength, with plenty of support right by your side, I will let you sit up. Then if you don't fall on your face —"

"I'm tougher than that, Doc."

"You already fainted once today, Lib," Luke reminded her.

She looked annoyed like it was rude of him to mention that.

The doctor snorted. "When I'm sure you're up to being moved, I'll let you go home if you promise me you'll take things slowly. Is that all very clear?"

Libby nodded sheepishly. Luke had never seen her this obedient before. She even sassed her parents a little.

"I'll get the water." Hannah rushed out. It was clear that she wanted to do something to help take care of Libby.

Luke knew just how she felt.

Libby looked from Luke to Pa, to Ma rushing away.

Her parents. The best people she'd ever known. And Luke. What was he up to and why did he have to look so sweet and concerned and handsome?"

Ma came back with water. Libby's head was propped up and Ma helped her sip water. She felt stronger for it and was finally allowed to sit all the way up. Her vision spun and turned dark but with Pa holding her from one side and Luke from the other, things cleared gradually and she thought she was up to going home.

A door slammed open and the doctor, who had left them alone, came back. "The whole, massive Cooper family is here."

"Libby was shot? What is going on here?" Will charged in. A few steps later came Megan, his wife. Then Sadie, with her shining black skin and her flashing smile, the big sister Libby'd met when she first came to

Sour Springs, entered. Then Pa and Ma's son, the one born first after they'd married. Libby had been old enough to help care for him and she loved him as if he were her own child. He was taller than her now of course, and a married man with three children, so he didn't allow much babying.

The room kept filling. Everyone clamored for an explanation of how in the world Libby had ended up shot.

The story was retold as more brothers and sisters — Pa and Ma's adult adopted children — flooded into the doctor's office.

It was chaos for a time, exhausting but a wonderful reminder of all the people in the world who loved her. And through it all as they crowded in, Luke never let himself be dislodged from her side.

The doctor finally let her stand and, when she didn't collapse, he allowed her to ride home in the back of the wagon. Luke walked beside her, resting a hand on the small of her back for support. One glance at his intense concern, made her fight to keep each step steady. One wobble and he'd be carrying her — and not home. He'd be carrying her back into the doctor's office.

She got outside to find a fine bed had been made in the back of the wagon. Her family at work.

Hands reached to support her, but it was Luke who gathered her in his arms and settled her into the wagon box. Then he tied his horse on the tail gate and jumped in to sit beside her.

Pa swung up on the wagon. It occurred to Libby that this was Will's wagon. She noticed that the one they'd found out by the oil seep was parked in front of the sheriff's office. Two horses still hitched to it.

So they must have captured the outlaws and brought them to jail. Her thoughts were muddled ever since the shooting. Pa had said that but until now it hadn't quite registered. And she'd caught so many snatches of the story that she'd heard most of it, though not in order.

Perhaps she shouldn't say 'they' captured them. After all 'they' included her and she hadn't been much help. She'd managed to sleep through too much of this adventure.

Through all this the family kept chattering, they mostly all knew Luke, or at least they knew some of the Reeves boys, though it was hard to tell them apart.

Luke was talking with them and sharing news, all while his attention never wavered from her.

"He wants to buy Pa's ranch to run an oil well?" Libby wasn't sure who'd said that but it dropped into the mix of voices and suddenly all was silent.

"Luke you're one of those no-account oil men?" That was Will.

"If your pa had gone out to that oil seep alone, or with Aunt Hannah and Libby, they might very well be dead right now." Luke's voice sounded strong and honest. "The men we captured *are* no-account oil men. And there are plenty more where they came from. I have a plan that will make Uncle Grant a lot of money and keep varmints like those we arrested away from his property and his family."

It was probably that she'd been shot and was generally emotional, but the tone made tears burn in her eyes for some reason. She felt safe. But then, until today, it had never occurred to her that she might be in danger.

Unless she went way, way back. Some ugly memories from before she'd found Hannah, who was living on the streets of Chicago, just as Libby was. But Hannah was a mostly grown girl, Libby had been about three — she had no idea of her real age.

And the ugliness that had put her on the street had traumatized her so badly she hadn't spoken a word for a long time. Then Pa had found her and taken her into his tiny home, she made his sixth child — that was to say his sixth child living with him at the time. She was his twenty-seventh child. Many of them were grown and already married and had children.

Shortly after he'd adopted Libby, Pa and Hannah had married, and Libby came to think of Hannah as 'Ma'.

Libby eventually found the courage to speak again. But the memories locked inside — memories that closed her throat, still stayed locked away. That time of her life, before Hannah and Grant became her Ma and Pa, was the last time she'd felt danger.

Until today.

And she wasn't letting anyone blame any of today on Luke.

"Luke protected us. If he was a man we couldn't trust he'd have sided with those outlaws. Or come sneaking in like they did. We are going to talk with him and hear what he has to say. He's been trying to explain and something's stopped him every time. But we are *not* having that talk now. I hurt like the dickens and I need to get home. It's Pa and Ma's ranch and they can do whatever they want with it. But right now, the way I'm feeling, I'd support them if they decided they needed help dealing with that awful oil."

Libby lifted her head to see Pa watching her. "Can we go home now? My arm hurts something fierce."

"I'll follow you home, Libby." She had children older than Libby. "I've got fried chicken at home."

"I made a pot of stew, enough to last Joshua and the kids four meals, plenty to share." Libby had been at Pa's with Sadie and Joshua, another of Pa's adopted children. But they'd married and moved to their own place mighty soon after Libby had come.

Another voice piped up. "I just baked bread. I'll bring a couple of loaves and —"

"Stop!" Libby hadn't been a teacher all these years for nothing. She could quiet a crowd down in short order.

It worked now.

"I swear the first one who tries to turn my gunshot into a pot luck dinner is going to have all their children expelled from school."

Since Libby threatened this about once a week, no one took her seriously, not even her massive brood of school age nieces and nephews. The threat was all the more empty because school was on vacation for the summer. But just because they didn't believe her, didn't mean they missed her point. She was in no mood for a party.

"I started a roast this morning." Hannah was always far nicer than Libby. "It's been in the oven all morning. We'll be mighty late for a noon meal but we have plenty of food."

Someone reached over the edge of the wagon box and patted her head. She turned to see Joshua, Sadie's husband. He grinned at her. "I'm glad you're okay, baby sister. Are you sure we can't all come out? We'd like to listen to Luke try and steal Pa's land."

He stepped well away. Which was good because she'd have bit him on the wrist given half a chance, just for the head pat.

"I'm not stealing anybody's land." Luke growled from where he'd settled into the straw beside her bed, leaning against the wagon box.

"A couple of you go over to the jail." Pa interrupted Joshua's teasing. "I talked to the sheriff when I dropped those three men off, but you've heard the story now in detail, go make sure the sheriff hangs onto them."

Libby didn't bother trying to sit up and watch, though she was curious. She sure hoped the whole family didn't invade the sheriff's office. He might let his prisoners go just to make a point about overcrowding.

Pa backed the wagon away from the hitching post, then slapped the reins; they headed for home under a chorus of goodbyes.

Libby'd seen some Fourth of July parades that didn't draw a crowd like that. At least no band had started playing.

CHAPTER 8

Luke wasn't having much luck managing a calm, reasonable visit with his aunt and uncle.

He'd been thwarted last night by talk of family. Although he admitted that'd been fun.

Then this morning, well, for heaven's sake getting shot at was a big old distraction, and having Libby hurt, no one could even think of talking business when you were busy running for the doctor and your cousin was bleeding in your arms, and there were three men to haul to jail.

He'd been here now nearly a full day and he'd yet to get to his point. And he was a man who always got right to his point.

Of course he'd never tried to get land away from someone he loved before. He was finding that to be a badger hole in his trail toward an oil well.

Now the evening chores were done. The meal was eaten and he'd helped clean up. He didn't mind behaving in a way that would endear him to Grant and Hannah, but that

611

wasn't his only reason for helping. He just wanted to have a bit of their undivided attention before they all decided it was bedtime.

Luke saw Libby looking heavy-lidded. He didn't want her to fall asleep at the table. And, tempting as it was to try and have this talk without his overly-suspicious cousin, he was pretty sure anything he settled tonight with Uncle Grant might all come unsettled in the morning once Libby was awake again.

"Now, let me tell you at least the basics of what I want to do with your land."

"Luke, I don't —"

"Libby, please I'll be very brief. You've got some really wrong ideas about what I'm hoping to accomplish here. I'll tell you all quick what I'd like to arrange then we can all go to bed and end this long day. I hope you'll feel better in the morning, Libby, then we can talk more details, but at least take my idea to bed with you. Give it some thought."

Grant hesitated but then he nodded.

Hannah said, "Let's pour another cup of coffee."

Libby, well, he expected Libby to squawk but she'd been quiet all day. A long nap in the afternoon had helped her regain her strength and pinked up her cheeks but it hadn't started her talking.

All through the evening meal, she'd had a different expression on her face. Not exactly what he'd call friendly but the suspicion seemed to be gone. Maybe she saw him being shot at right along with her and decided he wasn't the villain here.

Hannah had coffee in front of them so fast, Luke couldn't offer to help. She put a platter of sugar cookies on the table between them and sat.

Luke was afraid to hesitate for even a second. It seemed like every time he hesitated, someone started shooting at them, or Libby started scolding.

"There are two main ways we strike a deal with landowners." Luke looked at each of them, including them in this discussion. Which didn't mean he wanted them to actually talk.

"First, the simplest choice. You can sell me the land around the oil seep outright. We'd pay you well for it, far above what an acre of land would cost." Luke saw Uncle Grant's eyes narrow. "The reason I don't recommend that is because we have no idea what the oil on your property is worth. If it's worth little or nothing then you'd be ahead to sell, but if we find a substantial oil field — well, that brings me to choice number two."

Luke took a long drink of his coffee just to break up this discussion enough so they'd remember the different choices.

"Choice number two is a contract between you and my company that says you get a little bit of each gallon of oil they dig out of your land. If there is a lot of oil, this can be worth a lot. Not at first maybe, but if the oil keeps coming you can have an income off that land for as long as it lasts, the rest of your life if the wells last. And you can leave that contract to your heirs — they'll inherit the contract just like they would a house or land or money. The contract will last for as long as they're pumping oil."

Grant tilted his head a bit as if he was really considering that. "And if I'd sign this contract, and you don't find oil, will I get my land back at some point?"

"We can write the contract that way. We can say if the income on that land drops to some set amount, the rights will return to you. But Uncle Grant, that isn't going to happen. I've done some work hunting for oil and they are going to find plenty of it out there."

"So the first choice is a nice, one-time payment of a guaranteed amount." Libby said.

"That's right, and the second is pure potential."

"When would men come in? How many?" Grant asked. "Will they live in Sour Springs? Because there aren't any empty houses, or none I know of and there's one boarding house. When that first crowd of men came in here — a couple of years back — they were sleeping on the ground under wagons. Around campfires just outside of town. It wasn't a bunch of men I liked having around.

We had one quiet little saloon before they came. Two more opened mighty fast once the men were here. One was a —" Uncle Grant glanced at Libby, then his wife. He said, ". . . one had dance hall girls that . . . that entertained men. The men were drinkers and fist fights broke out in the bars and spilled out onto the streets."

Libby hadn't forgotten that. "I had to be very careful of my children at school. There were sometimes men sleeping on the playground. Drunkards loitering around in the middle of the day using foul language. I didn't dare let the children walk home alone. Is this what your men will be like?"

Luke leaned forward and spoke urgently. "This is the best part of letting me make this deal with you. I work for a company that has a new branch interested in finding oil. I helped found this piece of the company and have ownership in it. I pick the men who will come here. We pay decent wages and we attract decent men. There won't be a horde of crude men flooding into town. Instead, if oil comes through like I think it will, you'll have families. The men will want houses. If you've got builders in this town, there will be work for them.

"Uncle Grant, you've got beef. I'm sure you ship most of it but now you'll have a market right here in town. You raise horses and families will want to buy them. Will and

Joshua at the livery will be building wagons and carriages and renting and selling horses, shoeing them, doing iron work. The General Store will double its income. When you have families the churches grow. New stores open. New jobs so the kids that go through Libby's school will stay in town and raise their own families here."

"So many of the children head on west." Libby thought of her brother Charlie. She hadn't seen him in years. "If there isn't room for them on their father's ranch or his store, then they're left with no choice. So many of my brothers and sisters have moved far away."

"Think of that, Grant and Hannah." Luke looked between them. "Imagine the potential not just for you if you work with me, but for this whole town to prosper." Luke could feel himself getting enthused. He knew he could overwhelm people once he started selling something he believed in. He needed to calm down and let them think.

"I'll stop now and you can ponder this overnight. You'll have questions after you consider it. But remember this while you think. I love you." He held each of their gazes for a moment. "Even if I was the lowest kind of worm and cheated people every day, I would never cheat you. I hope you believe that. If you don't want to do this, I won't pressure you. But if we do work together, I'll have men around that oil seep within days.

There'll be no more intruders. My men will make this area safer."

He studied Libby's bandaged arm for a moment and it made his stomach twist to think how close that bullet came.

"Nothing like what happened today will ever happen again." He managed a genuine smile, not easy when he remembered Libby getting caught in a gunfight. "If I fail to protect you, my ma will come out here and stomp me into the Texas dirt."

Libby smiled at that. "And you haven't seen her since Hope was born. She's a truly dangerous woman these days."

Luke shuddered to think of it. "We'll talk more in the morning, now I'm going to get to bed before you're sick of the sound of my voice and decide against working with me just to shut me up."

CHAPTER 9

Too Late.

Too late to avoid being affected by the sound of his voice. But instead of getting sick of it, she'd been coaxed and swayed. Blast it all, she was really starting to like the man. He'd taken such good care of her today.

She lay awake in her bed, hearing gunfire and feeling the impact of that bullet. Her arm ached. She was weak and jumpy. She wished she could go find him and make him talk some more. Tell her more about how he would protect them.

Despite the fact that she'd liked Luke as a child, she well remembered that Luke was the toughest of the Reeves boys. He was the youngest of the triplets, Mark, John and Luke, and they had twin brothers five years older, Abe and Ike.

Back then, maybe to make up for being youngest, Luke had become the boy who made everyone sorry if they messed up some prank his brothers were planning. He was the one who stayed last, made sure the damage was done — made sure everyone was too scared to carry tales to someone who might punish them.

It might be fair to call him ruthless.

And then he'd gone off and made a lot of money. He'd never come home again, though he wrote occasionally and sent his ma nice gifts. Grace was always talking with pure love about all her boys and she loved bragging on Luke and his big success. Libby'd always thought it was a bit forced. To her way of thinking spending money was a poor substitute for spending time. Grace was hurt by Luke's absence, though missing Luke Reeves was something Libby found difficult to believe.

Until now.

He didn't strike her as ruthless, only very smart and willing to do whatever it took to get his way which — now that she thought about it — was pretty much the definition of ruthless.

But when men are shooting at you, having someone ruthless fighting beside you was a fine thing.

As she tossed and turned, the gunfire running through her head over and over, her arm aching with every move, she tried to find fault with Luke, tried to put his convincing ideas down to greed and lies.

He'd just sounded too sincere. If he was a

liar he was the best one she'd ever heard, and considering her former fiancé, she'd heard her share.

His promise to protect them, his promise to hire decent men with families, it sounded so good. The town would grow. Her whole family would prosper. The school would grow, maybe they'd build on and the school board would hire a second teacher.

Her mind flipped back to those awful men at the oil seep, shooting.

Frustrated to near screaming, she threw her blanket aside and got up. Her arm hurt so bad she wanted to stay still but her mind was going round and round.

She wanted to pace, but she'd wake Ma and Pa, and she wasn't sure she was up to pacing anyway. Instead, she slipped on her robe, tiptoed down the stairs and turned up the lamp in the living room. She needed to find the Bible, and read until it soothed her.

She wanted to stir up the fire but the June heat made that a ridiculous idea. She sat in a rocking chair in the living room, flipped her Bible open at random, and read the words, 'a woman leave her home,' just as a creak sounded on the stairs.

Luke came down the steps and looked at her, his brow furrowed with worry. He'd looked at her this same way earlier.

"Can't sleep?"

Libby hated to admit that. But here she sat

in the middle of the night. Not much chance he'd suspect anything else.

She noticed he'd dressed. Whereas she was in her nightclothes. It was a stern reminder that Luke was not, in any way, shape, manner or form, her cousin.

He flipped the rocking chair beside hers around so he faced her, then asked, frowning, "Is it the pain or did my request that you think about my offer keep you up?"

A shrug was no proper answer. She managed to say, "A bit of both. The memory of all that gunfire mostly."

Libby braced herself for him to say, 'I can protect you. Sign this contract.' Instead he just rocked quietly. Finally, he said, "That's why I'm awake, too. I keep seeing you bleeding, then fainting. I keep feeling you limp in my arms. I keep seeing a bullet strike you somewhere worse, deadly. It won't stop running over and over through my head."

Then with a grin he added, "And I keep hearing you holler at your family not to turn your wound into an excuse for a pot luck dinner."

They smiled at each other as they rocked.

When the silence had stretched too long, he added in a quiet voice, "And I keep thinking about kissing you. I know you have a special disgust of oil men after what that fool did to you. And now that you know I am one,

621

I don't reckon I'll get another chance at a kiss."

His voice dropped to a whisper, "But I'd like to Libby, and it'd have nothing to do with that sour spring on Uncle Grant's land."

In the lantern light, both of them relaxed, the dark of night wrapped around their little circle of golden light.

Libby was brave enough to say, "I'd like that, too. But not tonight with me dressed improperly and weak from blood loss and exhausted. I'd like to wait until I have my strength back and see if I still feel the same way."

Nodding, Luke said, "Then I'll go on outside and listen to the coyotes howl because here in this little golden glow from the lantern, I can't think about much else." He said it but he didn't go anywhere.

It was impossible not to smile at him. He didn't even try to resist smiling back. They rocked on for far too long without speaking, without touching and most certainly without kissing.

Finally, with a sigh that sounded like pure regret, a sigh Libby found very flattering, he hoisted himself out of his chair and walked for the door. Once there, he turned and looked at her. She couldn't look away. Her hands tightened on her chair to keep her from launching herself at him.

With a weak smile that seemed to reflect

back exactly what she felt, he turned and rushed outside, careful to close the door silently.

Libby sat there rocking a while longer, pondering their talk, and that unlikely Bible verse that had been all she'd read before he came.

Yes, she was stirred up again, but in a slightly different way that didn't seem to overpower the heaviness of her eyelids. She rose and headed up the stairs, hoping, finally she might sleep.

CHAPTER 10

"So did you and my daughter have a nice chat in the middle of the night last night?"

Luke was snapped out of one of the most inappropriate day dreams a man could have in front of a young lady's father.

With absolutely no proof, he had a terrible feeling Uncle Grant was reading his mind. He sure hoped not because that would mean Luke had a good chance of being shot.

They were standing in the barn brushing horses after riding out to check the cattle. Luke had found he could do all that and still think about Libby nearly full time.

He shaped his mind up and then did what a truly honorable man would do. He told the truth, well, most of it. Foolish to repeat their talk about kissing.

"If you know that much, you know I went outside mighty quick. I heard her go downstairs and when she didn't come back I was worried she might be in too much pain to sleep, and too kindhearted to interrupt your sleep with complaints. I found her downstairs in her rocking chair. She was being tormented by memories of the day. We visited a short time. It wasn't proper for me to sit with her in just a nightgown, but I honestly didn't think of that at first. I thought only to hear what she was fretting about. I figured I knew, but I thought talking it over with her might help her shed it enough she could sleep."

Grant stopped brushing to listen to him. So far no hollering, and no gun which Luke appreciated.

"Uncle Grant, I find I have strong feelings for Libby."

Uncle Grant's hand tightened on his horse brush until his knuckles went white.

Stumbling on, Luke said, "Considering her distrust of oil men, I don't know if I dare ask her to accompany me to the diner for a meal or go with me for a ride, but I would like to. Would you allow such a thing? Can you think of me as a decent man or is my involvement with oil too much of a barrier?"

And then another thing needed to be said, and quick before Grant threw the brush at his head. "Would you trust me to have only her best interests in mind and not have our talks about your oil seep be any part of my interest in her?"

There was a silence so long, Luke leaned close to his horse until he heard it breathing, just to rule out sudden deafness.

"Libby is a woman in her thirties. A very smart, self-supporting woman. The teacher at Sour Springs school gets paid enough Libby could live on her own if she wished, but we've always wanted her here and she stays because she wishes too not because I force her. She doesn't need my permission to go riding with a man."

That sounded like Grant was saying yes. Luke was surprised to feel his heart speed up with excitement.

"I will tell you, though, son, despite her tough treatment of that man who abused her trust, I saw the pain in her eyes. His gossip about her was devastating. She kept her chin up and went on with her life.

"And she had a serious beau early in life, in her school days, but he changed his mind and chose a different girl to marry. She has spent time with other men, but it never lasted. Through all that, it never occurred to me that my beautiful, bright Libby might never marry, never find a home of her own. It hurts my heart because I know when she was younger, she wanted those things.

"But this broken engagement was years ago, and she's never shown a bit of interest in any man again."

"I thought she broke off with that varmint more recently than that."

"I'm talking about the first beau, back when she was a youngster."

Grant fell silent and Luke let him think. Finally he went on. "I guess what I'm saying is, I think you'll find her reluctant to trust a man but that is between the two of you. I give you leave to try. And my second point is that if my Libby ends up hurt again like she was before — if I have to see that tormented, humiliated pain in her eyes again . . ." Grant shook his head and ran one hand deep in his hair. "I don't know if I can be stopped from doing you serious harm. I don't know if you can run far enough and hide deep enough to protect yourself from me. And that's true no matter how rich you are and how powerful. I will make you sorry your ma didn't smother you in the cradle and that's a promise."

Grant wasn't quite done. "So you think long and hard about whether your intentions are serious before you start something that engages Libby's heart." He nodded hard. "Is that clear enough?"

"It's not just clear, it's terrifying."

"Good then our talk is over." It might be over, but Grant still sounded mighty grim. "It's near enough to lunch time we can go in now."

Luke loitered just a bit. It gave him chills, even in the Texas heat, to think of Uncle Grant walking behind him.

What's worse, he had a feeling that talking with Libby was going to be even more frightening than talking to her pa. Luke decided maybe he'd better just think about how serious his intentions were before he asked Libby to go for this life-and-death horse ride.

Libby noticed that Luke helped with dinner with more energy than any man alive.

He seemed downright nervous. And Luke was never nervous.

Was it possible he was thinking of the next oil talk they'd have?

Libby hadn't spoken of oil with them all day but she knew Ma and Pa had gone on a long walk after lunch and, though she hoped they'd include her in their discussion, she wasn't surprised they decided between themselves first. And Libby had ridden into Sour Springs to attend a meeting of the church to plan the dinner that would be right in the middle of the Fourth of July Festival. There hadn't been time to discuss things with Pa and Ma.

Luke poured them all coffee and they sat at the table. Libby wished she wasn't learning about it at the same time Luke did. That didn't seem quite right. Still, it was Pa and Ma's ranch to do with as they chose, and she would abide by whatever her parents decided.

"I know you two went off walking today," Luke began. "I hope you came to a decision."

Ma and Pa exchanged a long look.

Pa asked, "Are you going back to Chicago once this is begun? Or do you stay here? Do you make sure promises you made are kept by the people left here?"

Libby hadn't even thought of that. She'd just assumed all his talk of protecting them included his presence. But why would it? He'd hire guards and head back north.

"The man I work for in Chicago has far flung business interests. I'm his man in Texas now. When his company got involved in oil exploration in Texas, I told him I was ready to go home and settle near my family. So I got the job of running things down here permanently and part of that is an ownership stake in what oil we find.

"I will be here as long as my company is working here. I suspect it will take years to develop. Texas had its first oil strike in 1866 in Nacogdoches County. Since the first oil found at the Corsicana Oil Field they found oil in two more wells and they have hopes of more. They've been digging in a place called Spindletop Hill since 1892 without finding a bit of oil yet. It's a long, drawn out process, Uncle Grant. And I'd be here for the duration. I might live here in Sour Springs for the rest of my life. Even if the job goes elsewhere I don't intend to follow it, not if it's far from family. My days of chasing after money in Chicago are over. I want to be home."

"Why not Mosqueros then? Right near your folks?"

"This is close enough I can run over there

and back with only a few days off work. That's close enough." Then he gave a chagrined smile. "And the oil is here."

There was an extended silence. Libby spent it thinking and she was pretty sure her parents did, too.

Finally, Pa looked directly at Ma and she nodded. Pa said to Libby. "Ma and I made a decision today, but we wanted to hear what Luke had to say to our questions first."

Then he turned to Luke. "We are willing to sign the contract to get a share of whatever you find. But we'd like you to move fast on bringing in some sentries so nothing like what happened to Libby ever happens again."

Libby's stomach swooped. Not because she was all that upset with Ma and Pa's decision but because she knew they made it because they were worried for her.

"It's not just for you, Lib." Ma was reading her mind, she was good at that.

"I don't want you to do something you're opposed to, to keep me safe."

"What about keeping Ma safe?" Pa asked. "What about me? Joshua used to climb that hill, the very one that man was shooting from, to get a good look at the land. Some of the grandkids still do. We're not only thinking of you. If it was only you in danger we'd just tell you to not ride out that way and we'd be fine, but if more men come like those shooting yesterday, none of us will be safe. Ma and

I decided we needed some help from trained men."

Ma reached across the corner of the table and rested her hand on Luke's. "If it had been anyone else we'd have sent them down the road. But we trust you, Luke. Trust you to keep your word about paying us our share of the oil that's found, and trust you to bring in honorable men to tend to the exploring. You're the right man, which goes a long way to making this the right time."

With a quiet nod, Luke said, "Thank you Aunt Hannah. I've got a contract in my suitcase. I don't want you to sign it until you've read it and understand every word. I'll be glad to spend as much time talking the details over with you as you want. And if you want to, you can bring someone else in to read through it, some of the language is a bit technical. And taking my word for it isn't a good idea when I'm profiting by you signing it."

"Thank you, Luke. Yes, we'd like to see it."

Luke stood, jogged up the stairs, and seconds later came jogging back down.

Libby noticed that the day was wearing down. It'd been a long one, at a time of the year when daylight stretched on until ten in the evening. They'd eaten late then lingered to talk, but it surprised her to think it might be near nine o'clock at night.

Luke slid the contract toward Grant.

"And now," Luke's gaze swung to Libby, "I'd like to ask Libby if she'd be willing to come with me for a short walk."

Libby felt her cheeks turn hot. She felt more than saw her parents' attention focus hard on her.

Did she want to go for a walk with Luke? Well, there was just no way to deny that she absolutely did. In fact, she had been hoping for something like this.

"Yes, I'd like that very much." She didn't smile. She couldn't quite manage that right in front of her parents. But she scooted a chair back and Luke rose quickly.

"We won't be long," Luke came around the table and took her arm.

"We'll know exactly how long you are," Pa said in a cold voice. "Because we'll be waiting up for you."

That almost wrangled a smile out of her. She walked out the back door, holding Luke's arm.

CHAPTER 11

"I have a feeling your pa is standing at the window holding a spy glass on me."

"And Ma's right next to him with a shotgun." Libby smiled and squeezed his arm where she held on at his elbow. "They've always protected their children. It's a big part of what makes them great parents."

They walked on the road toward town. "Are you all right for this, Libby? We could find a patch of grass under a shade tree and sit a spell."

"June in Texas does make a body wonder where they can find shade. It's late in the day though, the sun's lost some of its strength. I think we can walk a while."

"I'm not talking about the heat. I'm worried about your arm and all the blood you lost." Luke slowed down and she turned to him. "And are you strong enough? You were just shot, you know?"

"Let's go on a ways. I feel strong enough, but I will admit to wondering if there are any other evil men lingering around here, men who may be upset because there are guards posted around the seep."

"Are you interested in getting to know each other better, Lib?" He felt her whole body raise and lower on a long sigh.

"I've given up on marriage."

Luke rested one hand on hers and said, "I don't blame you for that considering the way that man treated you. And you are a smart woman with a good job and a nice home. I can see why it would feel like a risk to change everything."

"My parents are wonderful people, and I think they will be lonely without me. They've never acted for one moment like they wish I'd get on with growing up and moving out. But they don't know something about me, and I've never told anyone else, not even the man I was engaged, too. But I think it's best I tell you."

Luke stopped and pulled her gently to face him. "What is it?"

"Yes, I was terribly hurt and humiliated when my engagement ended in such a harsh way. But I wasn't exactly broken-hearted. It didn't take me long to realize I didn't love the man I planned to marry. In fact I think I felt safer marrying someone I didn't love. I was protecting my heart."

"From love?" Luke felt his brow furrow and his heart beat harder. She didn't want love from a man. That meant she didn't want it from him.

"I spent time with a boy I went to school with and thought he was the one God had chosen for me. It was the same time young men and women get married. I was headed in the direction that was normal. And then, about the time I expected to hear a proposal, he told me he wanted to part ways."

"Why, did he have a reason?"

Nodding silently for a while, she finally spoke words that were torn out of her deepest heart. "You know I spent several years living on the streets in Chicago. A cold, brutal place to survive without shelter. I was thrown out in the street after my leg was broken working in a textile mill."

"I've seen those. There are organizations right now fighting to end the use of very young children in factories and make working conditions better for everyone."

"I was about three years old but I remember the job well. They like very small children who can run under the presses and pick up bits of lint. But the presses are all machines. They go up and down at the same pace regardless of what the children are doing. We'd dash under the press, grab the scraps, lint, threads, anything that didn't belong, then we'd dash out. But that heavy press came down with no regard for a child who fell or was in some way delayed. The press came down on me and broke my ankle. Because I was no longer good for work the people who were letting me live in their overcrowded home with many other adopted children, threw me out on the street. They weren't about to feed me if I couldn't earn my way."

Luke gasped and his hand tightened on hers. He could picture it. He had known Libby from a very young age, since shortly after she'd moved in with Uncle Grant and Aunt Hannah. "They just threw you out? How could anyone be so heartless? Those people should be in prison."

Libby went on. "Hannah found me, living in an alley, on scraps of food I found in garbage cans. She said I didn't speak a word and I could barely hobble along because I'd had no medical care for my ankle and it had healed crooked. She took me to a doctor. I know now that your ma, Aunt Grace, was working at the school in Mosqueros and sending nearly every penny she made back to Hannah. Hannah was to save it up and come to Texas as soon as she had enough money. But Hannah spent every penny of it, *every penny,* on doctors who . . . who . . . rebroke my ankle and set it as best they could and put it in a cast. She didn't hold back money for food even, so we were eating scraps out of garbage cans or food we could beg."

"Your leg must have been so painful." Luke

slipped his arm around her shoulders and pulled her close.

"There were other children living with us in a shed Hannah had found. Just as Hannah paid off the last of the doctor bill, the money stopped coming." Libby gave him a narrow-eyed look. "I believe that's when Grace was fired because she couldn't control the school with you and your brothers there."

Luke flinched. He well remembered taunting Ma into swatting him with a ruler. She hadn't done it even though he goaded her, because he knew Pa was watching. He and his brothers had been terrors. "We've always known we got her fired, but she ended up married to Pa and we all fell in love with her. We thought it was God's plan. I didn't know she was sending her money to someone."

"And we were starving in a little shed in Chicago. Hannah managed to find homes for the other children. But no one wanted a little girl who limped. We hid on a train without paying the fare, heading for Texas. We got to Omaha and were found and thrown off. We waited a few days and then jumped a train again. This one carried a group of orphans. Hannah slipped into their group by helping care for the children. The lady in charge of them thought she was being helpful. The conductor thought she was part of their group. I was hiding in the baggage car and Hannah sneaked food for me. I was found and again Hannah worked things so I was included with the orphans. I was herded out over and over as we passed through towns, to stand before couples who wanted a child. None of them wanted me. Finally, we reached Sour Springs. The end of the line. I was going to be sent back to New York City, which is funny because I'd never been there. Then Grant . . . Pa —"

Libby's voice broke. It was a few seconds before she went on. "He saved me. He adopted me. I couldn't speak, I limped. No one wanted a child with so many troubles. But Pa never hesitated for a second to take me in. Not for one second. And Hannah was there, she had hoped to slip me away from the group and we'd hide until we saw a chance to get on our way to where Grace lived. But Hannah lost me to Grant and then finally they ended up married."

"Why are you telling me this now?"

"Because in an effort to be honest, I told that first young man. I wanted him to know everything about me. He was new in town and the trains weren't running to Sour Springs anymore. Grant's children had mostly grown up. My young man had never heard about the huge family of orphans.

"We were on a walk. After I told him, he said something about keeping that a secret. Like my past was shameful. I didn't take him seriously. In fact I laughed and told him that half the young adults in Sour Springs had grown up on The Rocking C. An exaggeration of course but close enough to true. There was no keeping it secret. I told him he might be the only person in town who *didn't* know. Then he looked at my leg as if that was shameful, too."

"You don't even limp, how can that be shameful?"

Libby shook her head. "There was no sense to it. But even so, there was no proposal. Our walk ended quickly, which I realized later was his way of breaking things off with me. But at the time I didn't see that he was upset. It took me a bit to understand he was finding excuses not to talk to me. I caught up to him once and asked what was wrong. He made stumbling excuses that made no sense. I finally knew the truth. He quit caring for me when I told him about myself. For no exact reason except he — he felt I wasn't good enough to bring into his family. Then I saw him taking another girl for a buggy ride. They were married before the end of summer."

Luke rubbed one hand up and down her arm. The warmth of it steadied her.

"You're well rid of him, you know that. Cruelty from a fool like that shouldn't make a beautiful woman like you give up on home and family, a husband and children."

"I didn't give up, exactly." Libby spoke to the tips of her boots. "But I never quite trusted a man again. I was always ready to be rejected. It wasn't a good way to carry on a courtship and things always ended. I think one of the reasons I got engaged to the oil man, was because I didn't care that much for him. Oh, he was a charming man and I found him very likable, but I felt no deep, strong love. I knew he couldn't hurt me because I never gave him my heart."

Luke gripped her shoulders and raised her onto her tiptoes until she met his gaze. "Well, Miss Libby Cooper. I'm very interested in you giving me your heart."

"You can't be, not after just a few days."

"You're right. We need to get to know each other. Spend time in each other's company. I'm going to scout your pa's oil seep, the land around it, do some testing, get the sentries in place and my crew here to start work. That's my daytime schedule.

"With my evenings, I'd like to spend time with you, get to know you better. But we don't need a long time, Libby. We've know each other for years. I've always felt like we were special friends, even as children. Now that we're adults, all that childish friendship has caught fire for me. It started for me the first day when somehow you ended up in my arms. You felt it, too. I want to spend time with you, and my intentions are very serious."

"Luke, for heaven's sakes."

"I know it's too soon, but I can see you're already thinking of how things end. Well, they're not going to end."

Luke drew her into his arms. "Libby, when you were shot, I knew how much you meant to me. It broke my heart to see you bleeding . like that, and the fear." He rested a hand on the back of her head and pressed her face close to his neck. "The terror I might lose you. I'm telling you that I'm not going to let you get away. I'll give you some time, but I'm not going anywhere, not when I think you're about the most wonderful woman I've ever known."

He held her for a long time, finally he eased his hold enough their eyes met. He lowered his head, watching her, giving her plenty of time to escape.

And she didn't. Instead, she raised her lips to meet his.

CHAPTER 12

Libby and Luke came into the house holding hands and smiling.

Her parents were right there, obviously counting the minutes until they returned.

With the happiest voice she'd ever heard, Luke said, "Libby has agreed to let me court her."

Ma gasped.

"You said you wanted to go for a walk." Pa stood up slowly. "That's a long way from courting."

"That's right it is, but I want Libby to know my intentions are honorable and very serious. I'm moving to Sour Springs permanently as of now. I have things packed and ready to ship from Chicago. I'll sell my Chicago house. Then I'll find a place in town. One of our first projects will be to build some kind of temporary quarters near the oil seep, a bunkhouse of some kind, and once it's done, I'll live there. You can plan on me coming over here nearly every evening *after* dinner.

Aunt Hannah, I don't expect you and Libby to feed me."

"We don't mind feeding you, Luke." Hannah reached over and patted his hand.

"And then each evening, I'll take Libby for a walk or a horse ride."

Pa looked disgusted. "That's the part I mind."

"Some evenings we'll sit, all of us, on your front porch and visit. I'll tell you all that's going on with the oil, and we'll get to know each other better."

Libby had never seen a man who'd come courting — and there'd been a few over the years — who was so comfortable with her parents. So completely adult in his dealings with them. She knew Pa and Ma had always been very protective of her, because of her struggles when she'd started out. Those she'd had as an adult only made things worse.

Luke tugged on the brim of his Stetson and said, "And now I think I'd best head to town and get a room at the boardinghouse."

"No need of that," Ma said, too nice to toss Luke out.

"I think there is a need. It's not proper for me to be sleeping under the same roof with the woman I'm courting." Luke looked at Libby and smiled in a way that warmed her heart. Past warm really.

She didn't want him to go at all, and maybe that was the reason he should.

"There's a room we used for the occasional hired man out in the barn." Pa could talk tough but honestly, under his gruff way of protecting Libby, he was more soft-hearted than Ma. "It's decently clean and comfortable. You can sleep there, starting tonight, and share our meals. You're welcome to that room until you get the bunkhouse done over at the seep."

"It's getting late. I'd be glad not to have the long ride back to town. Thank you, Uncle Grant. I surely appreciate it."

CHAPTER 13

Libby could feel her heart growing more and more vulnerable to Luke.

It was just plain frightening.

They walked or rode or sat on the porch every evening.

Men were now guarding the oil seep day and night. A group of about ten men, besides the sentries, were working for Luke and a bunkhouse was going up fast. They seemed like honorable, decent men. It pinched to think that Luke would be moving out soon.

As they walked that evening, hand in hand, Luke asked, "Will you ride into the Independence Day Festival with me tomorrow?"

She smiled. "I have to help with the church dinner from eleven o'clock to one. Beyond that, I am planning to enjoy all the activities. We aren't having fireworks because the one year we did a fire started in the dry grass around town and almost burned down Main Street."

Luke smiled. "Good reason to quit."

Libby nodded. "But there is a horse race and several foot races planned for the morning. The mayor is reading the Declaration of Independence after the meal is done. There are games. Tug of War and three-legged races, egg tosses and even a baseball game. The ladies have set up a lemonade stand and there is a bake sale. Ma's taking four pies.

"There will be a church service after an evening meal to raise money for local Civil War veterans, they are getting older and some of them still struggle with injuries from the war. Then we'll close the day with a singing."

"That sounds perfect." Luke swung their hands between them. Then he turned to her so suddenly it was shocking, and dropped to one knee.

"Luke!" She tugged at his hand. "This isn't the time or place."

He looked up at her and smiled. "It's the perfect place and to my way of thinking, it's past time."

He took her other hand and pressed them both to his lips, then to his forehead. "I'm in love with you Libby. Every minute I spend with you just makes it more solid, more wonderful. Please tell me that you share my feelings. I don't want to move away and share a bunkhouse and be separated from you. I want to spend every possible moment with you."

He stood and pulled her into his arms. And

she knew she was lost. Or maybe found.

"Marry me, Libby. I hope and pray every day that you're feeling safe enough to trust me." Luke reached into his trouser pocket and pulled out a little box.

Libby's heart, already pounding, sped up.

Luke opened the box and showed her the prettiest gold ring she'd ever seen.

"Oh, Luke." She looked at the ring, then raised her head to study his shining blue eyes. "Can we get married right away, before you find a reason to escape?"

He looked startled, then his expression switched to kindness and compassion. He rested one strong hand on her cheek. "We can get married tomorrow night at the singing if you'd like. That will add to the fun. Then we'll come home and you can move into the barn with me."

Libby laughed. "Pa might let you back in the house if you married me."

"Not if, Libby. We're getting married. Say yes, please." Luke kissed her long and hard.

When the kiss ended, even though her willing kiss probably made it unnecessary, she said, "Yes, I will marry you, Luke."

He caught her around the waist and lifted her right off her feet. He spun her around in circles until they were both laughing.

"Honestly, Lib, I found a house in town to rent until I can build one of my own. I haven't moved their yet but my things are here at last — shipped from Chicago — I've been waiting until I could offer you a real home. Now, finally, the house is ready for me to move in."

He lowered his head again and when the kiss ended, he whispered, "Or for us to move in."

A shiver of longing nearly shook her body. It must have because Luke pulled her tight against him and wiped away all the hurt from her past. All the distrust men had taught her.

Luke murmured against her lips, "I think we need to get married in the worst way, sweetheart. Waiting until tomorrow is a poor idea."

She stepped back and took his hand. "Let's go tell Ma and Pa, and thanks to the long Texas days of summer, we can ride into town tonight."

Then she grinned and said, "We can put the word out and see how many of my brothers and sisters show up. And this is short enough notice, no one will try to turn it into a pot luck."

"They're welcome to come, but were not waiting for them." He laughed and slung one arm around her waist. "Let's go talk to your folks, then head for town."

EPILOGUE

Libby and Luke were waiting at the station on a pretty October day when Daniel and Grace — and four stair step children — climbed off the train. The youngest one a girl.

Luke was shocked into immobility for a moment when he saw the children standing so straight, so calm. But they were definitely a row of little Reeves. He accepted it, rushed forward and drew his ma into his arms, then added a hug for Pa. Who bore the hug with surprising patience.

And all four children, three little brothers who looked just like Luke (only smaller) and one little sister who looked just like Luke (only female).

None of them had ever met him. A couple had grown and moved away without him ever seeing them. That was shameful.

As he went down the line introducing himself, to his own brothers and sister for heaven's sakes, he marveled at their perfect behavior.

He'd heard Ma had shaped them up and he could see it was true.

"Grace!" Libby threw her arms around Luke's ma and then Hannah came right beside her and Grace and Hannah squealed like little girls.

"Pa, I'm sorry we couldn't get over to Mosqueros. We got married and then I had to move fast to get things started at the oil well, but I never intended it to take three months. I —"

Pa slapped him on the shoulder. "We're mighty glad to see you, Son. We were happy to come, and when things settle down, you can come see us."

Because Hannah and Grace were caught up, yammering, Pa took a turn hugging Libby. "Welcome to the family, Lib. You always were my favorite of Grant's young'uns."

Uncle Grant came up and reached a hand out. He shook with Daniel and Luke couldn't resist having a word with his baby sister. Pa had twelve sons in a row before Hope was born.

The merriment of the reunion went on throughout the day. A mighty big share of the Cooper family showed up and this time it *was* a pot luck.

The fun got even better when Libby announced to the crowd that she was going to have a baby. And then he told them they'd

650

found one small gusher of oil on Grant's land with hopes of finding many more. Luke had taken to calling Grant's oil Texas Tea.

Uncle Grant talked about the orphanage he was planning in Houston, where the orphan train turned around these days. There was a decent chance Grant and Hannah might end up adopting more children. And when Libby expressed interest in adoption, Luke knew he'd go along with anything she wanted.

She had agreed to let their first baby be born so they could get some practice first.

It was always a big party when the Coopers and Reeves got together and this was no exception.

Luke rode back to town with Libby long after dark, to sleep in their own newly built house, with plans for another family gathering at their place tomorrow.

He held her hand as they walked into the house, smiling at her. "You glow, Libby. Your dark hair and blue eyes glow in the moonlight. I've always thought you were beautiful, but since the baby has come along, you're even more lovely than I ever imagined."

Libby leaned against Luke's arm and said, "I thank God every day for bringing you into my life. I was happy before, teaching, but to have a fine man's love and the joy of this child," she rested one hand on her flat stomach, "it's made all my old memories fade away and replaced them with happiness."

"God sent me into your life, Lib. All I did was work before, I had no time for family, nor for love, nor for children. You've made me a better man."

They entered their darkened front hall and Libby turned and kissed him gently. Luke returned her kiss enthusiastically.

"You were a wonderful man when I met you. And you just keep getting better."

They turned and headed up the stairs. After years not knowing they searched, they had found each other at last.

■ ■ ■ ■

HOPE FOR
CHRISTMAS

■ ■ ■ ■

CHAPTER 1

December 1, 2014

"Just admit it, you're lost!" Kelsey Blake slammed the side of her fist into the steering wheel.

Punching something made her feel a little bit less frantic. Yelling at herself was almost like having company, in a split personality kind of way.

Somewhere, back a long time ago, she'd made a mistake — and that didn't count her lousy marriage though that'd been a mistake, too.

Staying on side roads, and paying with cash was part of the plan but wow, talk about 'the road less traveled!'

Her car bucked through a small drift.

How long before she hit a drift she couldn't drive through? Praying she'd come upon a town soon, she let go of the steering wheel with one hand. Her knuckles ached from how tightly they'd been clenched. She swiped at the fogged over windshield of her temperamental, rusted out Chevy Cavalier. Her heater had quit working and the snow was blinding and getting heavier with every passing minute. Her wipers were caked with snow and her headlights didn't help much in the howling wind.

She was freezing and visibility was near zero. She had to find a place to stop. Darkness had fallen. The narrow, climbing mountain road was treacherous and there was no sign of a town or even a home along the rugged stretch. Boulders lined the road between trees. Wind buffeted her car and she fought to keep driving forward.

Glancing at the gas gauge her stomach twisted. A red light had appeared by it. Not much more gas. She'd filled up this morning and had one opportunity hours ago to fill up again in little Divide, Montana, but she'd decided to wait. With no idea how long it would be between towns. How far could a car go after the low fuel light came on? Nerves stretched so tight they made her muscles ache, she kept going forward because there was nothing behind her to go back to.

She hit another drift and clenched her teeth, leaning forward, trying to see past the driving snow.

"God just get me somewhere safe. Somewhere safe." Kelsey wasn't sure there was such a place, considering all she had behind her.

A sudden dark blur appeared in the road in front of her. Something, a deer maybe, dead center. She had one flash of glittering wild eyes. Then she slammed on the brakes and the car went into a skid. Whatever it was, leapt away. Kelsey skidded sideways and the rear of her car clipped something and swung her back. The nose slewed around and suddenly, instead of constant, unbroken trees and rocks, a gaping black expanse opened in front of her and she saw railing.

A bridge.

Dead ahead.

Clawing at the door handle she swung it open and leapt. She didn't get away! Her seat belt!

She frantically pushed on the button to free herself. The stubborn, sticky thing fought her then suddenly it gave. Terrified of jumping, but with no choice, she threw herself out and twisted madly to land on her back. She slammed into the hard ground. The Cavalier plunged over the side of the road.

The car's inertia tumbled her along in its wake right toward the smashed, missing railing. She scrambled for a hold on the ground. Her fingernails tore on icy dirt and gravel and stone. Her head cracked into the side of something solid and spun her around. The solid, whatever it was, she caught. Her arms jerked nearly out of their sockets and her feet dangled over emptiness. Her car crashed far below. The horn blared, somehow set off by the impact.

Her grip was slipping but she hung on just as she'd hung on to life all these months. She found a toe hold that supported her enough she could wrap her arms around what she now realized was a post along the bridge railing. The ground crumbled under her foot. For one sickening moment she swung free, held only by her weary, battered arms.

Then a solid rock held under one foot. She heaved herself upward, found another ledge to hold her other foot and finally rolled onto the road. Flat on her back, trembling from every limb and her head ringing from the blow, she gasped for breath and thanked God she'd survived.

It was long minutes before she felt cold seeping into her bones. How would she get out of here? She heard the horn mocking her from far below on her left. Carless, freezing, battered. She'd finally hit bottom.

A snarl from the right whipped her eyes around hard.

A wolf, its teeth bared, inched out of the woods. The beast was black as pitch and it showed against the white snow. This is what had sent her into the skid. Not a deer.

She sat up and scooted away until her back hit the railing. Her choices were to jump away, over the edge or let a wolf sink its teeth into her.

"God, get her somewhere safe."

Reaching behind her she caught the railing and dragged herself to her feet.

The wolf laid its ears back, crouched low, preparing to spring.

She shouted at it and waved her hands. It inched toward her and gathered its muscles. She glanced down and saw a rock. Picking it up, she hurled it at the beast. The animal ducked, then came at her again.

Over the railing. She saw no other possible choice. She's heard how far the car had fallen.

A blinding light hit her. Tires ground against gravel and slid to a stop. The wolf's head turned just as Kelsey's did. A sharp metallic crack sounded as a door opened and an overhead light revealed a man wearing a Stetson. A shot rang out and the wolf whirled and vanished into the woods.

Kelsey's knees wobbled and she slid bonelessly to the ground.

Sitting, shaking from cold and terror, she rested her hand on her belly.

The vehicle came on across the bridge and stopped just feet from her.

The driver's side door swung open and a heavy boot landed hard on the ground. It set off an earthquake. Or maybe that was just her shaking from all the shocks of the last few minutes.

Blinded by the headlights, she could barely make out that it was a pick-up truck. The man, his cowboy hat pulled low over his eyes, came toward her, swept her high in his arms and hurried around to the passenger side of the truck.

"You're freezing, Miss." The cab light came on for a second but she couldn't see him under his hat.

He set her on the seat, tucked in her coat and made sure her arm was away from the frame, slammed the door, then came back around to climb in behind the wheel.

Once he was inside he fiddled with the heater to turn it high, then he took time to aim the blowing air at her.

It was warmer than outside but not by much. "I haven't had the truck running long enough for it to warm up. Let's get you in the cabin."

He threw the truck into reverse and backed across the bridge. He got on solid ground, turned the wheel and headed down a lane. She would never have seen it if she'd been driving. And if she had seen it, she'd have never taken it. It was barely a trail cut through the woods.

"Are you all right? Do you need a doctor?"

It took every ounce of energy she had to say, "I don't think so."

"It's a good thing because I can't get you to one in this blizzard."

"Wh—where are we going?"

"My house is a mile down this way. I heard

your car horn and came out to see what had happened. What were you doing on this road? No one comes up here."

"I was lost."

He nodded his head silently. Finally he said, "We do get the occasional person who is lost."

Then he looked at her and tilted his hat back. Overly long brown hair, square jaw, it was too dark to see much more in the dashboard light.

"What's your name, Miss?"

And that was the one thing she wasn't going to talk about. Not her whole name. "K– Kelsey."

He seemed to realize exactly what she wasn't saying. With a grim smile he tilted his head forward, as if to point, and she saw lights in a house just ahead. "Let's get you warmed up then Kelsey and make sure you're okay. By the way, I don't mind admitting my name. It's Tanner Harden."

He drove the truck into a big steel building near the house. He shut the rig down, swung the door open and she saw that his eyes were hazel. They glittered until they reminded her too much of the wolf.

When she'd prayed for God to keep her safe, she should have been more specific.

CHAPTER 2

Tanner spent about two seconds assessing the situation. Kelsey No Name claimed to be all right but he was sure asking her to walk was too much, so just how 'all right' could she be?

He rounded the truck, swept her into his arms and hauled her into the house like a feed sack.

Well, he might've been a little more careful than that, but he treated his feed sacks well, so maybe not. She was a little heavier than he'd expected based on her height and her fine bones.

Maybe she was a tub of lard under her thick plaid coat. Her hair, dark and tangled, hung long over his arm.

He'd heard the crash and the horn and ran. He was a little surprised to see he'd closed the door behind him, but a man got into that habit in a Montana winter.

Once through the door, which he closed, he carried her to the living room and set her on the couch right in front of the fire he had let drop to embers.

Only as he slid his hands out from under her did he realize just how badly she was trembling. "Let me get this coat off you and build up the fire."

"Th–thank y–you." Every word shook

He dropped to his knees beside her as he slid her coat off her shoulders. It was cold all through. "I heard the crash. You weren't out there that long? How did you get this chilled?"

"M–y car's heater quit."

The coat he noticed was fancy. He didn't know much about fancy but he could feel the weight of it and saw a brass tag on the collar. He'd heard the word Burberry somewhere before and knew it was nothing that grew on a bush.

He had the coat shucked off her and tossed aside. Pivoting on his knees, he grabbed a thick, fur blanket off the back of his side chair, turned to cover her and froze.

Just as surely as she was near frozen, so was he. Because he knelt there face to face with her. No, not face to face. Face to belly. "You're pregnant?"

Her hand rested in a protective gesture over her middle. She was silent for far too long then finally she seemed to relax enough to speak. "I'm worse than pregnant, Mr. Harden."

"What could be worse than pregnant?" Which summed up how he felt about babies pretty well.

She gave him a strange long look, almost as if she pitied him. Or maybe she pitied herself for being stranded in a Rocky Mountain blizzard, with her car wrecked, and no way to escape a stranger.

"I can tell you what would be worse. I could be in labor. Which I am."

Since he was on his knees anyway, Tanner started to pray.

Tanner Harden looked like he might just fall over in a heap. She hoped he didn't land on her, she had enough trouble.

His eyes had the panicky look of a scared horse, those eyes locked right on her midsection. Well, who could blame him? He was trapped with a woman in labor.

"When I said I didn't need a doctor, I was wrong. I don't suppose there's a hospital anywhere near here?" She had to ask. But she already knew.

Tanner slapped his hand over his face. She had the distinct impression he was covering his eyes to stop them from being locked on her stomach. He hadn't quit looking at her pregnant belly in horror since he'd figured out what it meant, and that was before she'd mentioned labor.

"No — no — no." He slapped himself in

the face again and it got him to stop sounding like an old vinyl record that was skipping. "No, there's not. It's a two hour drive at least and the roads are closed — I don't know how you kept going as long as you did? I could barely get out of my driveway in my four-wheel drive truck. What's more, I couldn't call the life flight helicopter to come out in this blizzard, not even if it was life and death. They're all grounded." She saw his Adam's apple bob up and down on a hard swallow. "It's not life and death is it?"

Kelsey tried to remain calm. Someone had to. "Okay, well, no, not life and death." Probably. "Woman have had babies without doctors and hospitals through most of human history." Plenty of them died but Kelsey veered her thoughts away from that grim fact.

The contraction was about double as hard as any she'd had up until now. In fact, until just now, she'd been telling herself these were just the usual preterm contractions she'd had off and on for three months. She'd learned to not let them scare her. And the baby was at least three weeks away.

Unless she was wrong about her due date. She hadn't darkened the doorstep of a doctor's office since right before Derek died seven months ago, so who could be sure?

And all because of her dreadful mother-in-law, who her husband adored and conspired with against Kelsey. If her weak-willed husband hadn't already been dead, she swore she'd hunt him down and kill him. Thinking of what would happen if Mother Blake showed up, a sob tore loose and suddenly she was crying as if her best friend had died. Although, since she was friendless, she couldn't be sure how that felt.

The contraction went on and on until she curled her whole body around her stomach, knees drawn up, arms wrapped tight, head bent low. "God keep me safe. Protect me. Protect my precious baby."

"Let's get you to bed." Tanner picked her up. "I can't even phone anyone. My phone is connected through my satellite dish and it always goes out in a blizzard, sometimes just until the storm's over but a couple of times the dish has been ripped clean off the house."

She'd have slapped his hands away if she hadn't been trying to breathe through the wicked contraction.

Tanner carried her through a house she didn't notice, except it beat being outside with blizzards and wolves. He set her down on a bed and she touched a quilt. Her mind jack rabbited in a sudden unexpected direction.

"You need to get me off your nice bed-spread. Do you have any plastic sheets?" Like maybe he had drop cloths? Or maybe a plastic shower curtain?

Leaning over her, he met her eyes. "Don't

worry about my quilt. We're just going to — argh —"

She grabbed his shirt collar with both hands and twisted it hard enough to choke him, then used all her considerable weight to drag him down nose to nose with her — as if any of this was his fault. Still, she felt extreme satisfaction when he looked to be strangling.

"Get something to protect this bed." Her voice shocked her. The only time she'd heard something similar, a movie character's head had soon begun spinning around. Could green projectile vomit be far behind?

"Okay." He grabbed her hand. "I've got something. Let loose!" He ripped her fingers free and gasped for air.

Then he gave her one wild look, and ran. She hoped he came back.

Although him not coming back had its good points, too. Privacy for one. Because she was going to have this baby and if he was here, well, it didn't bear thinking about.

Of course being completely alone was its own nightmare.

The contraction ended, not the panic unfortunately. She gathered her strength, got out of bed and stripped off what she saw was a beautiful, old quilt. Having a baby on it was unthinkable.

Two thick blankets went next, then the sheets. She had the bed stripped bare by the time Tanner got back.

"I'd have done that." He went to the far side of the bed. He dropped what looked like sheets on the bedside table, with quick flicks of his wrists, spread some kind of plastic sheeting.

"These are old sheets but they're clean." He covered the bed with a second layer, then a third, then a fourth.

He'd finally gotten the idea that birthing a baby could be messy.

CHAPTER 3

"Here, get back in bed. Let me take care of everything."

Kelsey gasped and looked at him as if he'd asked if he could have her baby for a snack.

"What's the matter? What did I say?" Tanner was not a man to panic in a tight situation. He'd been attacked by a two thousand pound bull — in fact being a rancher, he practically did that for a living. He'd been thrown from a bucking bronco and one memorable night, been surrounded by a pack of wolves and forced to climb a tree and wait for help.

Through all of that, he'd never panicked.

With this situation, he'd apparently reached some kind of limit because he kept picturing himself running, and diving right out the bedroom window.

Of course this was probably the tightest spot he'd ever been in and panic was looking like the most reasonable reaction to it. Only a fool could remain calm.

"I don't want someone taking care of everything. That's like being a prisoner in my own home."

Shaking his head, he knew by the depth of her reaction that what she was saying was important. Maybe it was about women's liberty or something. But really did they have time to debate anything right now? "This is nothing like being a prisoner in your own home. I just want to help. Feel free to yell orders at me and I'll obey." Unless she ordered him to do something he wasn't going to do anyway, then they might have a problem.

He rounded the bed and, with insistent hands, guided her to the bed. She must have been about all in because she didn't fight him

"Lay down now and let me get you, a–a —" What came next? He'd been planning to offer her a blanket but the hard truth was he had to get her undressed and, for good or ill, this was something Tanner had absolutely zero experience with. "I have a long shirt that will cover you, but we had to get–get–get —"

A hammer to the head would have been easier. He swallowed hard. "We have to get you out of those pants."

The look she gave him was so horrified he almost laughed. "Well, we do."

Then she tore her gaze off him and clutched at her stomach again.

He admitted it, the window was looking

better every second. "I'll just go get that shirt."

Too bad it didn't take long. He got it and had no choice. He had to go back. The house his ancestor, Silas Harden, had built for his bride, Belle Tanner, wasn't big so even a woman in labor could probably hunt him down. Dragging his feet, he went back to find her fully dressed, laying curled up around her stomach.

He stood silently until she finally relaxed. He'd seen cows in labor, plenty of them. He knew how labor pains worked and as the birthing got close, the pangs hit faster. She'd had three since she'd come in the house. No way was she outlasting this blizzard so a helicopter could come and haul her away.

"Are these just the first pains?" He came up to her with the longest, biggest t-shirt he owned. He hoped it hid her well, but he had a bad feeling about all he was going to have to see, no matter if the shirt reached all the way to the Montana border.

"You're supposed to call them contractions."

"Uh . . . okay. Why?"

"I don't know why." She gave him a look so furious he took a step back. "Because it sounds nicer than pains, I guess."

"So whoever made up that rule was hoping you wouldn't notice that it hurt to have a baby?"

The pain must have finished because she uncurled and sat up, frowning. "Whoever made that rule is an idiot."

"Agreed." He held out the shirt. "Can you get changed on your own or do you need help?"

Snatching the shirt out of his hands, she hugged it to herself. Then she looked up, eyes brimming with tears. "I–I'm being so rude to you and you saved me."

Not more tears! They slowed everything way down.

She lurched to her feet, threw her arms around his neck and proceeded to soak his shirt with salt water.

Honestly, he wished she'd go back to being rude. It was looking mighty good by comparison.

A stab of compassion, much like what he felt for his cattle, goaded him to say, "Whatever helps you is okay with me. If you want to yell and kick a little, you just do it. I can only imagine what you're going through, the pains — uh, I mean the contractions. The car wreck, a hungry wolf, being stranded with a stranger, no hospital. Anything you need to say or do, you do it. I can handle it."

He tilted her chin up and her tear-drenched blue eyes looked at him. It probably wasn't wise but he said, "Where is your husband, or, uh . . . the baby's father?" These days, who could say husband with any confidence?

"Derek died about seven months ago. I've been — wandering for a while. I needed a clean break from my old life. We'd only known I was pregnant for a short time when he died in a car crash."

Resting one hand on her cheek, he finally understood the tears. "I'm so sorry. To have a loss like that and then have to deal with a baby on your own. Don't you have family?"

"I don't. Derek does and his wretched family is the reason I ran off. The reason I won't tell you my last name. They're who I needed to make a break from."

"I'm sorry there's no one to protect you from them." While he said it, he realized she did have someone, she had him. "And I'm so sorry for your loss."

"He wrecked his car while he was running off, leaving me for another woman."

Tanner flinched.

"Can you get changed by yourself? Because I'll help in any way and I promise I'll treat you as a doctor would a patient. I'll be respectful and–and — as doctor-ish as all get out."

"I can get changed. But modesty at this point is just delaying the inevitable."

He patted her on the shoulder. "True, but still, let's delay it, okay?"

She nodded.

He left the room. He should probably boil water, though he had no idea why. He went to the fireplace, sank down on his knees and tried to ponder helping a woman give birth. The last cow he'd helped had kicked him half to death. He had a feeling the experiences were going to be far too similar.

Chapter 4

Kelsey's choices were all bad. She didn't want him anywhere near her but more than that she couldn't stand being alone. She swung the door open and peeked out. "You can come back now."

She'd taken her time changing, trying to stave off the moment she invited him back in. Now, she'd just had another contraction so she had a few minutes. Stepping away from the door, she went to an old chair by the bed. It looked like it had been built by hand, slender branches twisted to create the frame, then a seat of thinner branches wove together. It was beautiful and as she sank into it she was amazed how comfortable it was.

Tanner came in, still looking scared to death. Seemed like that was just common sense so she didn't fault him for it.

There were two chairs so she waved him toward one. "I timed the contractions . . . which are definitely pains, by the way . . . and they're coming about ten minutes apart."

"They seemed faster than that to me." He sat without once taking his eyes from her.

"Me, too." She felt like an idiot sitting in his massive shirt, bare naked underneath. Keeping anything on was just pointless. Which reminded her. "Did my car land in a creek or river? Was that what the bridge was crossing?"

"No, it's just a deep gorge."

"All my worldly possessions are in it. A suitcase, my purse, other things." Not much honestly.

"I'll get it as soon as the weather clears enough for me to go down."

He really was a decent man. Not that she believed such a creature existed. She should talk about the impending birth of her child but she couldn't stand to, not yet. While she'd changed she'd looked around.

"This house looks ancient." She flinched and added, "That's not a criticism, it's beautiful. Was it built long ago or was it just a skilled architect who made it look old?"

"My great-great-great grandpa Silas Harden built this house for his new wife. The first Tanner Harden was born right in this room nearly one hundred and forty years ago."

"The first? And you're Tanner Harden? How many of you have there been?"

"I'm the fifth. Tanner Harden the Fifth." He made a V sign with his fingers, like vic-

tory. Like two. Like Roman number five."
Pride echoed as he said it. What would it be
like to have deep roots and a family to be
proud of?

"So your father and his father before him
passed this house on down to you when they
died?"

A sharp furrow appeared on Tanner's
brown. "My dad and grandpa aren't dead.
He and Mom built a house on the far side of
the ranch, near my brother Silas."

"Silas the Fifth, too?"

"Yep. And there are honestly more than
five, that name has been landed on a lot of
baby boys, second and third and fourth
cousins, but Tanner always goes to the first
born son of the first born son. We've settled a
strip of mountain's and run cattle pretty
much all the open valleys between here and
Helena. Mom wanted to be closer to a city
so they built to the north a ways."

"And your Grandpa Tanner?"

Tanner shook his head. "You don't want to
hear all this."

"Oh, yes. Believe me, I want something to
think about between these pains."

With a shrug, Tanner said, "Grandma and
Grandpa Harden live in town in Helena now.
His knees were giving him too much trouble
to stay out here and Grandma has convinced
him to spend a chunk of the winter in Arizona
nowadays."

"Your grandparents are both still . . . still . . . st—" She clutched her stomach and forgot about everything else.

Tanner rose slowly from his chair. His eyes locked on her. She was tempted to laugh but she was far too busy.

"Should you lie down?"

"No!" She hadn't meant to shout. But that one word summed up her life in many ways so she might as well be emphatic.

"Okay, I'm sorry." He raised his hands, not unlike a man surrendering to an armed gunman.

He approached her, and she focused on him out of a pure need to focus on something. She had found a book called, *Thank You, Dr. Lamaze* in a used bookstore as she drove across the country, with no idea where she was heading and or what her circumstances might be when the baby came. She's read through it a few times, probably God whispering in her ear that she needed to prepare for such a time as this. It was about all she'd done to prepare.

That book was at the bottom of a gorge or she'd have shoved it at Tanner and told him to study up. A shame she couldn't because, based on his terrorized expression, he could use some education.

He got close enough and she grabbed him. She definitely remembered she was supposed to relax but she couldn't remember how in the world the book had told her to do that. There were breathing techniques and she began short hard breaths that sounded to her, a little like a chugging train.

He'd made the mistake of rolling up his sleeves, which meant her fingernails sunk in and he gasped in pain.

It was a shame for him, but she wasn't quite capable of letting go.

Tanner gritted his teeth and stayed right there through the contraction.

Kelsey was making a strange sound when she breathed, like she was saying, "He, he, he."

Was that normal or was she saying 'he', maybe cursing her dead husband with every breath. Better Dead Derek than him.

He considered himself a tough man.

Fingernails shouldn't be too much for him. And they weren't, though he vowed to unroll his sleeves before the next pain.

Finally the tension eased out of her. He glanced at his watch. No way was she lasting ten minutes between these contractions. Of course considering her delicate condition, this was no time to tell her she was wrong.

Her claws retracted and he saw no blood, though there were definite dents in his right arm. He quickly covered both his arms, no sense waiting until the last minute. And next time he'd steer her toward his left arm. Just in case he ended up with nerve damage, he'd prefer that be in his non-dominant hand.

Finally, she blew out a long slow breath and seemed to wilt. Tanner decided he was done letting her make decisions. He scooped her up out of the chair and carried her to the bed.

How could that be a bad idea?

Once she was settled on the plastic-covered mattress, he pulled up the chair she'd been sitting in and turned it to sit by her side.

"Don't do it!" Her snapped order stopped him from making a single move further.

"Okay." Uncertain what she was talking about, he didn't do anything. "What don't you want me to do?"

"Sit down."

"Okay," he scooted the chair aside. "I'll stay on my feet as long as you want me to. What can I do for you, what do you need?"

"I don't need a thing, I just don't think you should sit down."

He'd heard women in labor were going through a hard time so he decided not to tell her that seemed a little selfish. Although curiosity got the better of him. "Why not?"

A blush crept up her face and she spent overly long smoothing out the t-shirt she had on. Finally, with a tiny jerk of one shoulder, she said, "Because the chair is soaked. During that last contraction, my water broke."

Tanner took one wild look at the chair and

sure enough.

He swapped out that chair for the one he'd been in and sat down. "Now, if your . . . if your," he cleared his throat so he could go on, "if your water broke then things might go fast. That always happens near the end with a cow."

A shaky hand reached out for him and he almost dodged her, in case there were more claws coming his way. But he stayed put. She patted him on the forearm, uncoordinated, but gentle.

"Please don't compare me to a cow ever again."

"I know that." Nodding, Tanner added, "Every man knows that. I guess I'm a little nervous."

"Me, too."

Which he'd bet was no more than the absolute truth.

Chapter 5

"I think the baby is coming."

"I–I'd better go catch him, right?"

Since Kelsey was way too busy to answer, Tanner worked up his nerve and went to check. He expected to be embarrassed and awkward and clumsy. The truth was, there just wasn't time. He was busier than a one-legged man in a butt kicking contest.

Up until now, he'd stayed beside her for hours. (His prediction that the baby would come soon proved to be overly optimistic.)

He'd fought down panic about a dozen times.

He'd wondered what to do if nature didn't take its course in a peaceful manner.

But he hadn't looked under that shirt.

He'd boiled water.

He'd sterilized a pair of sharp scissors in it.

He'd sterilized a long piece of mailing string in it. These last two were orders she'd given him and he'd obeyed, though he had no idea why he did it. Sterilize the scissors and string that is, he knew exactly why he obeyed her.

He'd fetched water and a damp cloth to ease her brow.

And, if she'd thrown any other orders at him — and God have mercy she had — he'd obeyed them right quick.

But now time was up. He could see no way out of catching this baby.

He got lucky because she was right, the baby was coming. And Tanner got very busy and didn't have one spare second to think on things like modesty.

A whirlwind took over. He eased a baby into the world. There was a cord to tie off and cut. *The scissors and string!* A few other intimate details to see to that he managed with almost medical calm. Then a soft towel (the closest he had to a baby blanket) to wrap around the squirming tyke.

"It's a girl." His eyes went from baby to mama.

"I wanted it to be a girl so badly." A lone tear streaked down her face, he had a feeling it was the first of many. He was tempted to shed a few himself.

Tanner flashed on a memory of the family lore where his great-great-great grandma Belle had prayed hard for a girl every time, until she'd met her beloved Silas Harden. Tanner came from that branch of the family.

"Why'd you want a girl so bad?"

Kelsey shrugged one shoulder. "It's not a

reason I'm proud of."

"Don't tell me if you don't want to."

The tiny smile on her face told him she did want to.

"I just couldn't stand my husband and I hoped the baby would be unlike him in every possible way."

That sounded like Belle.

"And his mother is a horror. I'm hoping and praying she won't be quite as determined to get her hands on a girl as she would a boy who'd carry on the family name. My husband was the last of his line."

Tanner nodded for a second. "Probably just as well, his line sounds like it's full of half-wits."

He handed the little girl to her mama.

The whole birth and now this little girl was an experience he'd carry with him forever. It was the most beautiful thing Tanner had ever seen.

The baby cried. Her little arms and legs waved in all directions and nearly kicked the towel off. Tanner settled the baby in Kelsey's arms and she hugged her. It turned out Tanner was right about her tears because they came flooding.

Tanner reached out to wipe away her tears, and before he could touch her, one of those tiny waving fists grabbed ahold of his little finger.

His finger filled her whole hand.

The wonder of it made it nearly impossible to speak. He finally tore his eyes away from that firm grasp and looked at Kelsey. She smiled at him through her tears and reached up, wiped her fingertips across his cheek, and pulled her hand away, wet. He realized he was crying just like her.

He couldn't even feel embarrassed about it, it was too important, bringing life into the world.

She went back to looking at her baby, who was still holding Tanner's finger. He felt like they were bound together, Kelsey holding the little one, the little one holding him. To make it a complete circle he rested one hand on the new mama's shoulder.

"What shall we name her?" He asked, then knew how much that 'we' didn't fit here. There was no 'we'.

Kelsey rested one hand on the little one's bald head as if she was baptizing her. Then Kelsey peeked up. "Maybe I should name her Tanner?"

"No!" Tanner shouted.

Kelsey jumped. The baby startled wildly and began wailing as if Tanner had scared her half way to old age. "That's fine. I won't. Why not?"

His reaction came from soul deep. He had to fight down the intense rejection of that idea. Trying to sound light hearted, he said, "I'm not hanging that name on a precious little girl."

As Tanner calmed down he was hit with the real reason he didn't want this girl named Tanner. It was because he was thinking of another child Kelsey might have, a son. Named Tanner. Harden.

It was like running into a brick wall to realize he was planning to have more children, him and Kelsey. Dear Lord God in Heaven he was losing his mind.

Still, he didn't want the name to be used up. "It's a manly name, Tanner is. You'd be doing wrong by the baby to choose it and you'd be insulting me."

Shocked, Kelsey gasped, "I don't want to insult you. You saved me. From the wreck and the cold, from the wolf and from having my baby die in the c–cold." Suddenly Kelsey was sobbing to beat all.

Tanner decided he was going to shut up permanently. He wrapped his arm tight around her and held her and the baby and maybe cried a little himself. When she finally calmed down, she said, "I think I'm going to name her Hope. You can't believe how badly I hope for things to change, hope for a safe life, hope everything straightens out. Hope, now that's exactly what her name should be."

"That's a beautiful name." It was also a sad name because of all that was happening in Kelsey's life and her 'hope' was all to make her chaotic life settle down. Tanner figured she'd start crying again so he didn't say that. Anyway, Hope was a nice name and Tanner had a few hopes of his own.

"I'm going to get you something to eat. I can heat up a can of soup. I'll find a new shirt for you and clean sheets and some other things to make you more comfortable." Personal things that he knew she'd need and didn't know how to discuss. "Then I'm going to throw the clothes you just took off in the washer. By the time you wake up in the morning, you can get dressed all proper."

She nodded. "Thank you. I'd appreciate all of that."

"We've done the hard part, your little Hope is here and fine. Now we just have to wait out the storm."

"I won't even need a hospital." Kelsey smiled.

"You'll have to go in and make sure her birth is registered."

"No!" Her voice was almost as forceful as his had been when he'd denied her the use of Tanner.

So he figured he'd better respect it, though it made no sense.

"Is this about why you're driving across the country in a blizzard while you're almost due to have a baby and you don't want to contact anyone to tell them?"

Nodding, she started talking. He figured she was so tired and emotionally stirred up she was forgetting it was a big secret.

He didn't remind her.

"Once word gets out, my baby's grand-mother will be coming for me with an army of lawyers and nothing to lose. She's gone to great lengths to find people who will swear I'm a bad woman who drove her poor son into the arms of another woman and that I'll be an unfit mother. She even told me her son had begun the paperwork for divorce and to fight for custody so she can say she's fighting for his wishes. My husband left me a note saying he was leaving me, but that news came as a surprise to his mother. She didn't even pretend to know of it when I told her. Then later, here she came with papers acting like her son had talked it all over with her. I suspect it's all forged."

Tanner nodded. "And I reckon driving across the country in a blizzard and having your baby away from a hospital isn't going to make you look any better in the eyes of the law."

Kelsey shuddered and clung to her new-born.

"You seem like a real devoted mother to me." He decided not to count reckless drive into the wilderness in a blizzard against her, though he was sorely tempted. Surely she'd learned her lesson.

"I have little money because I haven't used a credit card or debit card since I took off.

My husband had a very generous trust fund that we lived on and after I realized I had to run, I drew cash, slowly so as not to gain any interest in it, then hoarded it. It's about to run out. Derek was in line to inherit a fortune from his mother and now my daughter is the only living heir. What's more, Mother Blake can't change the will, it was set up by her husband so she can't alter it. Carlotta Blake has always hated me. I know her reasons for wanting my baby have do with money not love."

Tanner patted Kelsey on the shoulder, as he considered all she was saying. He wasn't a man who was used to delivering babies, but when it came to trouble, well, turns out this little lady had come to the right place.

"You sit and hold onto Hope."

A sudden smile broke over Kelsey's face. "Hold onto Hope. That sounds good."

"I'll bring you soup in a cup so you can drink it and hold her, then we'll get you settled for the night." Yep, the hard part was definitely over.

CHAPTER 6

About halfway through the night, Kelsey considered changing the baby's name to Blizzard, because she was a stormy little thing that was going to be the end of her mama.

"She's crying again?" Tanner came in, stumbling over the doorway, though there was no threshold. But he was as tired as she. He had to be, he'd gotten up every time little Blizzard had cried.

The tears she'd been fighting burst free. "I don't know how to take care of a baby."

Why didn't they make people take a class and get licensed before they got pregnant? She'd have never passed the class and her poor baby, already doomed by her idiot of a mother, would have been spared a life of misery.

"You're too tired. Go to sleep and let me care for her." Tanner plucked the baby out of Kelsey's arms and began walking and bouncing. The room was dark but light spilled in from the open door. Despite the house's age it had a good furnace and electric lights and all the modern conveniences, including a nice bathroom. It might be old but it had been updated to be very comfortable.

"I should be doing that."

"Give yourself a break and get some rest. I'll walk with her."

Kelsey would have protested more but she'd barely managed to get up a couple of times for trips to the bathroom. At that, she'd ended up leaning hard on Tanner until she closed the bathroom door in his face. She wasn't up to walking the floor at night.

"Is she nursing?"

Kelsey felt herself blush but why? Was nursing so personal, considering all that had passed between them?

"Yes, and she falls asleep fast when I do it, but she doesn't stay asleep."

Tanner walked and swayed in a way that told Kelsey he'd been around babies before.

"You're good at that."

He grinned. "I've got a lot of nieces and nephews, and a bunch of second and third cousins."

"I thought you were the first born? You're not old enough to have nieces and nephews."

That shook a laugh out of him. "Where'd you get the idea I was first born?"

"You said the name Tanner went to the first born."

"Oh, right. No, the first born son. *Son* being the important word. I've got three older sisters and they've got kids. I'm up to five nephews and two nieces already. Besides that I've got a seventeen first cousins that live within a hundred miles of me. And lots of little ones there. So I've been around babies all my life"

"Which explains why you're a lot better at this than I am." She started crying again. "H– honestly, I'm not much of a crier."

Tanner smiled as he walked and bounced. Little baby Blizzard had cheered up and possibly fallen asleep. Why wouldn't she do that for Kelsey?

Where was her maternal instinct? Would Carlotta Blake use this against her, too?

No instinct.

Custody denied.

"I'm naming her Blizzard."

"No you're not."

"Wolf then."

"If you're not naming her Hope I'm going to start calling her Belle. You're going to figure out how to be a mom before you know it. Learning to walk and bounce like this, well, it might not come naturally but I promise you Baby Belle will force you to do it constantly and anything you do constantly, you get good at it."

"Don't call her Baby Belle, it sounds like a mushroom. We might as well name her Portobello."

"Fine, we don't want to name her after a fungus. I'll just call her Hope. Admit it, Blizzard is no proper name and if you think so then right now you're not up to naming this baby."

"I'm not up to anything."

"True. But it's been a tough day. You'll be up to more tomorrow." Tanner smiled which, in the dimly lit room had an intimacy to it that made it hard for Kelsey to look away. It had definitely been a tough day, as she was clearly losing her mind.

"Hope is asleep, but I'm betting the minute I quit walking and bouncing she'll be right back awake. You go to sleep and I'm going to walk the floor in the other room."

"No, you don't have to —" The door shut with a dull thud and Kelsey had a moment of terror. Her baby had been kidnapped!

Then she thought of the blizzard and the wolves and knew Tanner and Little Blizzard couldn't go far.

She slumped down on the soft bed and drew the soft quilt up to her chin and exhaustion caught up with her almost instantly.

CHAPTER 7

Tanner heard footsteps in the bedroom. He fought down the urge to go in and let her lean on him. He wanted to go so badly he knew it was about more than needing to help, it was wanting to see her.

He'd walked for a while in the early hours before dawn, then decided to take a chance on letting the baby sleep. Hope had slept for two hours in a sock drawer Tanner had emptied out and set on the floor, lined with soft towels.

She'd just woken up again and Tanner was trying to let Kelsey get a few more minutes of sleep, but he knew the baby wasn't just being fussy this time. The little tyke was hungry and the only source of food in this house had to get up and get to work

But he'd hated to wake her.

Now that she was moving, he kept bouncing and cooing to the tiny girl. He was shocked how little she was, though he'd seen plenty of babies this small.

It was a while but finally Kelsey emerged from the bedroom. He'd set her folded clothes in the room and she'd gotten dressed. Rushing forward, Tanner slid an arm around her waist, handling Hope in the other with ease.

He got Kelsey seated in a rocking chair in front of the fire, and handed her the baby. He tried to be casual about adjusting Kelsey's grip but he couldn't just leave the little one without her neck properly supported. When he was satisfied, he stepped back.

"Hope needs to eat. I'll leave you to it and be in the kitchen getting breakfast, how do you like your eggs?"

"Uh, scrambled?"

"I can handle that." Tanner hurried out of the room.

Kelsey got treated like a queen all day. She rocked in the chair and food came to her. Tanner took the baby away to change her diaper, walked the floor with her when she fussed and tucked her into a drawer for naps. He'd pulled the drawer all the way out and set it on the floor, it wasn't like he put little Hope in the drawer like a pair of socks and closed her in.

He helped Kelsey out of her chair every time she needed to get up and, much as he babied her, he insisted she walk circles around his house a few times. He informed her he'd gone to the hospital when his sisters had given birth and he said he'd walked the halls with them many times. He had no idea why but it seemed to be encouraged by doctors.

The storm kept howling and it surprised her when Tanner turned on a small Christmas tree in the corner of his front room.

"What day is it?" She'd been driving aimlessly for weeks, trying to decide where to go, how to hide, when to stop, what to do about having her baby. There'd been so many worries since Derek had died . . . and plenty before, too . . . that she hadn't remembered what time of year it was.

"It's December second." He grinned boyishly, "Only twenty-three days until Christmas. Maybe I should hang a tiny stocking up on my fireplace for the baby. I'm pretty sure you'll still be here."

"You think I'll be here that long?"

Tanner shrugged. "I think your car will still be at the bottom of that ravine."

She couldn't exactly leave on foot.

Unable to figure out how to leave, she decided to think about it later.

She looked down at her baby Hope. "What time was she born? Before midnight?"

"Yep. I don't know the minute but I'd say around eleven at night. Her birthday is December first."

"She was due the middle of December.

She's nearly two weeks early."

"Well, she's a little thing, but she looks healthy enough."

"I've been on the road for — for —" Kelsey tried to do the math. When had she started this desperate journey? "Derek died in April. I'd just found out I was expecting. He ran away the same day I gave him the news."

"Sounds like a low down coyote." Tanner rubbed his face. "Way to pick 'em, Kels."

She'd have hit him for that if she was closer. On the other hand, he had a point. "It took me a few months to come out of the shock, not just of Derek's death but of finding out about his infidelity and being told he was dumping me because he didn't want children. He left a note. We were married two years, and he'd never mentioned not wanting a baby. About the time my head cleared, Carlotta Blake showed up at the house with papers demanding I sign away my parental rights. That was probably in August. I told her no, and she started making threats. The house we lived in was owned by Derek's trust fund. She claimed she could throw me out on the street with one phone call."

"You should have called a lawyer, seen what the situation really was before you ran."

"It wouldn't have helped. In fact it would have kicked off all the trouble Carlotta was threatening me with. She was dead serious. The only solution I could see was to run. I spent a while planning. I gathered together as much money as I could. She had people following me, I'm sure of it, and I had to really pick the moment to run. I paid cash for a car so she didn't know what I was driving. I knew she'd come after me. I think I took off around the end of October."

"For over a month you drove all over with no destination in mind?"

Kelsey looked at the window. The sun had set. They'd passed nearly the whole day, and he hadn't pushed for any information beyond what she'd told him last night. But as she heard the wind rage she thought of this man. She'd met him completely randomly. He couldn't possibly be on Carlotta Blake's payroll. Before she'd left Milwaukee she'd met several people she suspected were.

Why not tell him the nasty details? Maybe he needed help on his ranch. Maybe she could hide here permanently, or at least until Baby Blizzard turned eighteen.

"Carlotta hired an expensive lawyer and found people willing to take money to swear I've done things that make me an unfit mother. She showed me sworn statements that involved me in financial crimes to fund my drug habit. She promised to make those statements go away if I signed away parental rights. And she promised to put me in jail if I didn't, and then she'd get custody of my baby anyway."

"She's bribing them?"

"What are you implying?" Bristling, Kelsey asked, "Do you think her witnesses are telling the truth? You think I'm a druggie and a thief and an unfit mother?"

Tanner raised both hands to halt what she knew could become a tirade and probably more tears. "I can spend one day with you, your first day with the baby, and tell that you are sober and honest and you love that little girl and will take good care of her. I am not implying a single thing."

Nodding, Kelsey said, "I'm sorry. You've been nothing but kind." She looked at the snow scouring the windows. "How long will this last? How long until I can get to my car and . . . and . . . and." She fell silent for a time before she said, "Forget that. My car is toast. I don't know what to do. I can't drive on from here with my car wrecked. I've still got some money but not enough to buy another car."

Tears threatened again and it was possible this really was worth crying over. The money she had was at the bottom of a ravine along with her car and luggage and the few things she'd gathered for the baby.

Tanner came and stood behind her. It was dark enough outside that even with the blizzard lashing the window, she could see his reflection. He was nearly a head taller than her.

"I expect the snow will end in the night. I can't get any radio or TV stations in this weather but I listened before it started. Then I'll be a while scooping out the roads."

Kelsey turned to look at him, "You'll be a while? There's not a road crew to come out and clear the drifts?"

"They come to the top of my driveway, which is the road we took when we turned off, right after I picked you up."

"But we drove a long way."

"My driveway is about a mile long. No one clears it but me. But I've got a tractor with a blade. I'm used to it. And the cattle are all in sheltered canyons with water and enough hay to get along while the grass is covered deep. I'll need to go check them, but I've got a snow mobile so I can get around. Getting ready for blizzards is a way of life in the mountains of Montana.

He rested both hands on her shoulders. "There's no hurry for me to get myself out. And Kelsey, there's no hurry for you to get out either. You're safe and no one could possibly know you are here. Let's take one thing at a time and that thing is going to be getting through another night was Baby Hope."

Tanner smiled and the same swoopy emotions that made her want to cry for little reason had her fighting not to giggle. She blamed the mood swings on giving birth.

"Come and sit down, I've made supper."
Tanner reached around her and took Hope.

CHAPTER 8

December 8 — Hope is one week old

Tanner clawed his way up the side of the ravine for the third time carrying what he could find in her car. She'd really packed light, but then she'd said she had to slip away. You can't exactly back the car up to the front door and load the trunk. He'd brought up two duffle bags for her and her purse. A collection of white plastic shopping bags contained some baby clothes. He found a package of disposable diapers, too, and a baby car seat still in its original box. This last trip was the most difficult because the car seat was hard to manage. He shoved it ahead of him up that steep bank and nearly let it get away from him and go plunging back down.

He almost left it. Kelsey showed no interest in going anywhere. But it was over thirty degrees and no wind. He wasn't going to get a better day to scale this cliff. The contents of her car, which was mostly buried in snow, had to come up sometime.

His four wheel drive Silverado was parked on the road and he threw everything in, smiling at the fact that he'd left his rig right in the road for over an hour as he climbed up and down multiple times.

No one had come along.

It was mid-afternoon and the sun was almost set. He drove home and pulled his truck into his Morton Building and took a few minutes to fool with the car seat and get it settled into the truck. Then he hung duffle straps around his neck and looped shopping bags over his arms until he had it all loaded and could make only one trip wading through the remains of the blizzard. He'd trampled it down some but it was a fluffy, dry snow and it blew over the trail he'd broken, almost as fast as he'd broken it.

As he carried his load to the back door of the cabin, he smelled something good cooking. Mexican food. He hurried faster. She'd been with him a week now and he'd learned to look forward to getting home.

Kelsey showed no sign of moving out and, he had to admit, he wasn't in a hurry to send her on her way. Coming in from the cold after whatever chores he had to do, to a meal and a pretty smile and a cooing baby was just plain fun.

The best sign that she was recovering from all the shocks of the accident and the exhaustion from giving birth was that Kelsey had finally started calling the baby Hope instead of Blizzard.

He swung the door open and Kelsey's eyes went to all he carried. A smile bloomed on her face that made him feel like he'd slayed a dragon for her. She left the stove and rushed to him.

"Tanner, thank you!" She took the diapers and shut the door behind him. "There are even baby clothes. Hope has been living in flour sack diaper and blanket."

"Well, she looks mighty cute in them but I reckon it's time she had some real clothes on. Not to mention you can probably stand to have a change of clothes."

"I've been running your clothes washer constantly."

"That's fine." Tanner set everything he carried down in a heap right by the kitchen door. "And I think you look fetching in my shirts, so wearing your own clothes won't be as fun for me."

The glow of gratitude and thanks was so bright, Tanner oughta hunt up some sunglasses. "I brought everything from your car, even the contents of the glove compartment. I don't know what it'll take to get it back up, but there's a chance we won't be able to get to it until spring. And it'll be a wreck when we do drag it up. So I emptied it."

With a sheepish smile, Tanner reached in the front pocket of his jeans and dragged out her keys. Jingling them he held them out to her. "I locked the car behind me."

She grinned. "To thwart car thieves?"

"Something like that." He laughed. She took the keys and spotted her purse amid the stacks of bags and luggage and dropped the key inside.

One more look at him and he was transfixed. Her humor and those pretty eyes held him in place. She seemed to feel the same because they stood together, staring like a pair of fools.

Hope squawked from where she lay in her dresser drawer and interrupted the moment. "I looked for a bed for her but didn't see anything."

Kelsey rushed to the makeshift bed, and picked up the fussing baby. "I hadn't gotten that far, to buying a bed. Thank you."

"Dinner smells great." Tanner wanted those eyes on him again and he thought maybe flattery was the way to do it.

She looked and smiled, cradling Hope. It hit something hard in Tanner's gut. The perfect moment. His empty house seemed full and warm and welcoming. He'd never thought of his home as lonely, in fact he'd liked the quiet. He'd liked having his own place. But somehow Kelsey and Hope reminded him that sometimes he almost ached with loneliness.

"Go wash up. She's soaked. I'm going to

put a diaper and some real clothes on her and see if there are clothes for me, too. Then we'll eat."

Tanner nodded and jogged through the room to close the bathroom door before he did something stupid, like ask her if she'd stay forever.

CHAPTER 9

December 14 — Hope is two weeks old

"Tanner, wake up."

"What?" The urgent tone jerked him out of a deep sleep. "What is it?"

"Hope has a fever."

Kelsey flicked the light on and he was temporarily blinded. Sitting up, blinking, he saw Kelsey in the doorway holding a fussy baby. "She's sick?"

"Yes, and how could she be? She hasn't been around anyone but the two of us and neither of us has a cold or the flu."

Hope was two weeks old now, and Tanner was sorely afraid he knew how. "I've been to town though, for groceries and supplies." He'd bought diapers, too and endured some curious stares from Mr. Kroger at the grocery store. "I didn't notice anyone sick but I must've brought something home. Maybe I didn't wash my hands before I picked her up." Tanner swung out of bed, glad he was wearing sweatpants and a heavy, long-sleeved

707

t-shirt for pajamas. It kept him from shocking Kelsey. He hurried to her and pressed one hand on the baby's forehead. Lifting his eyes they met Kelsey's, tear-stained and frantic with worry.

"Do babies have to go to the hospital when they have a fever?" Kelsey was interrupted by a wail from the bundle in her arms. Hope, sounding unhappy in a quiet way that was like no cry Tanner had heard before.

"I have no idea." Tanner had never felt so helpless in his life. "It seems pretty high. The nearest emergency room is two hours away."

"I'm scared not to do something."

Tanner looked out the window, the sun was just beginning to push back the darkness. "It's almost morning. Let's take her to the doctor in Divide — he's my cousin, Jim Harden. We can get there in under an hour. He'll tell us if we have to go on to a hospital."

Nodding, Kelsey hugged the baby and rocked her but the crying went on. Kelsey's eyes were on Tanner as if he alone had the solution to all the problems in the world. It made him feel so heroic, so good, he fought down the pride he took in . . . coming up with a doctor he knew. Not that hard.

"Let me get dressed then I'll get the truck started and warmed up. You bundle her up and get your coat on. When we're ready to go, I'll drive a ways toward town before I call Jim. No sense waking him up before we need to. If he's cranky, he's liable to give out shots that aren't necessary."

Kelsey grabbed his arm when he reached to close the door and shut her out of the room so he could change. He needed to get his clothes on but he stopped, looked down. She looked up and kissed him full on the lips. His hand settled on the small of her back just long enough to feel the silk of her nightgown. The kiss didn't last long, but plenty long enough to get Tanner's attention.

"God bless you. You have protected us at every turn. God bless you." She turned and rushed for her room to dress. Or maybe she was just running away from the fact that she'd kissed him. And the fact that, if she had any sense at all, she couldn't fail to see how badly he wanted to kiss her back.

Her affectionate kiss of thanks wasn't near enough as far as kissing went. And he wanted to chase her down and tell her so, and kiss her again. But instead, he ducked back in his room and dressed faster than he ever had in his life.

"She's got an ear infection and a very red throat."

"But she wasn't even sick when I went to bed last night," Kelsey heard the wail in her voice and was embarrassed. "I'm sorry, what difference does last night make. Thank you, Doctor."

"Call me Jim." The doctor administered a liquid to reduce the baby's pain and fever.

They were at the medical clinic but it was before office hours so they had the place to themselves. Tanner and Doctor Harden had greeted each other like family not like a doctor and patient.

"I advise you to do nothing. These infections clear up on their own. I'll send you home with some of this." He held up the little bottle of red liquid. "The directions are on the bottle. She'll be fine."

Kelsey felt a sob catch in her throat.

"Isn't there an antibiotic you should give her?" Tanner asked. He sounded as upset as she was.

"No. Antibiotics are over-prescribed and in this case will mostly likely do no good. She'll heal up on her own as well without the medicine. But I do have to ask . . ." The doctor's voice faded and his eyes shifted between Kelsey, Tanner, and the baby.

"What is it?" The look was serious. Kelsey began to imagine what else might be happening to Hope. "Is something else wrong? Are you worried about her having some other illness?"

"No, what I'm worried about is that, Tanner, I need to ask . . . this is a nearly newborn infant. Where exactly did you find this baby?"

"She's mine. I didn't *find* her." Kelsey hugged Hope close to her breast.

"Hope was born out at my place. Kelsey was in a car wreck during that blizzard a couple of weeks ago."

"The baby was born at your house?"

"Yep."

"So you witnessed the birth, Tanner?"

"Yeah, sure."

"He delivered the baby, Doctor."

The doctor's brows arched nearly to his hairline and a smile broke over his face. "You delivered a baby?"

"Yes." Tanner's answer sounded as if he was in awe of the whole thing.

"Wow, really? Wait'll I tell mom."

"Just tell me what the problem is," Tanner kept trying to make the doctor get to the point.

"There just needs to be a witness to the birth." Doctor Harden's sharply intelligent eyes sparked with doubt. "But why haven't you brought the baby in to see me before this? The roads have been open. I've even seen you in town at least once in the last two weeks, Tanner. You need to do the paperwork to get a birth certificate."

"There's no hurry for that," Kelsey took a half a step back from the doctor. She could almost feel Carlotta Blake out there, scouring the earth, paying for information, searching for her grandchild.

Tanner's hand came up against her back. He made it look casual and friendly but his arm was like iron holding her in place. Her impulse to flee was strong but it was the wrong thing to do. She needed to remain calm and get away without doing any paperwork.

"You're not leaving here until you do the paperwork." The friendly, amiable, more family-than-doctor good old Cousin Jim was suddenly giving them a beady-eyed look that reminded Kelsey that he'd spent a quarter of a century in college to get where he'd gotten. "It might be different if you were from around here, Kelsey. Or if you were planning on staying here permanently. Then maybe this could be put off. But I'm wondering if you're not going to just head on down the road once you're at full strength. Tanner is the only witness to this birth. If you leave here without getting things in order I'd say a strong case could be made — at another place and time — for someone to accuse you of kidnapping."

"What?" Tanner shouted.

"Kidnapping?" Kelsey yelled right on top of Tanner.

Hope jerked in her blankets and began to cry that plaintive, sickly wail she'd had since her fever came up.

"Think how this looks? You have no roots around here. No ties to the only witness to this baby's birth. The next town you go through, what if the baby is sick again? You bring a newborn infant in to any doctor who's not a personal friend or family, and he's going to want insurance information, an address, a social security number for the baby and you. This is standard stuff when you're getting medical care. And it's clear you haven't taken a single step on any of this. You have to get this birth on record."

The doctor's jaw worked silently a minute as if he didn't want to go on, but finally he did. "I'm compelled by a lot of laws to gather that information from you right now and you look like you're about to make a run for it rather than give it to me. That makes me wonder if calling the police might not be the right thing to do."

Gasping, she tried to back away and again Tanner stopped her.

He said, "How do we do that, Jim? Do we need to go to a hospital or what?"

"I have a form here you need to fill out. I can help you with it, then both of you need to go to the courthouse and file it. The courthouse opens at eight and Suzie will know what to do."

"Suzie?"

"Another cousin." Tanner whispered.

"Then she'll notarize it for you and turn it into Aunt Madeline."

"Aunt Madeline?" Kelsey asked no one in particular.

"She's the county judge." Tanner patted her

on the back.

The doctor checked his watch. "And it's after eight now so Suzie will be in."

"Your cousin is the secretary for the county attorney who's your aunt? Isn't that nepotism?"

Jim shrugged one shoulder, "Not really, because Aunt Maddie is such an old bat no one wants the job. I don't think of Suzie as getting the job working for her mom through family connections so much as being stuck with the job because no one else can put up with Maddie. Someone had to beg on bended knee to persuade Suzie to fill out an application form."

"This town is overrun with Hardens."

Tanner said, "And even the ones without the last name of Harden mostly descended from a female branch of the family so watch who you gossip about."

As if she had the spare time to gossip — or anyone to gossip with. She grabbed Tanner's hand that he'd slid around her waist to tell him to shut up before she started screaming.

"You can go straight there after we're done."

Tanner nodded.

"And I'm going to go with you," Jim added after staring at Kelsey. She realized she was shaking her head no.

"Tanner, I'd trust you with my life, and I know your word is good. If you say you'll go over to the courthouse, you'll do it. But it's clear this woman has her hooks in you somehow."

"She does not." Tanner reached up and patted Kelsey's hand . . . which she just now realized was clinging to the arm he had around her waist. Her fingernails sunk in deep. She forced herself to relax her hooks.

"I either go with you, or I'm calling the police."

"You know Jim, it's hard to remember right now that we used to plot and plan to spend the night at each other's houses."

"You liked Billy better than me."

"He was my age, you were an old man."

Jim laughed.

"And we used to sneak around each other's house hunting for Christmas presents."

Shaking his head, Jim sounded dead serious when he said to Kelsey, "That was just last Christmas."

"It was not. And I played starting line as a freshman to your quarterback as a senior. I saved your life ten times every Friday night for a year."

"We lost every game so don't act like you were much help." All the humor left Jim's voice. "I've got laws I have to follow. Little Hope's life could get badly complicated if she doesn't have a birth certificate. Not having a birth certificate in order would make your standing as mother harder to prove, it'd take a blood test at the very least, and that still wouldn't get you a birth certificate. And besides that it makes you look negligent and irresponsible. Those are hard strikes against you in a time of trouble. Why, someone could come sweeping in and claim the baby as theirs and you'd have a terrible time getting her back."

Kelsey gasped as she thought of just how possible that was.

"You've got no choice but to do this." The doctor looked resolute.

Tanner looked at Kelsey. "You can't hide forever, Kels. And if trouble finds you, I promise I'll stand in the gap. I will protect you. My family will help and that's a tough bunch."

Her stomach twisted but she could see no alternative. Maybe Carlotta wouldn't have tentacles that spread so wide she could reach this remote corner of the world. "Give me the forms. I'll fill them out."

"I'm willing to listen, while you're doing the paperwork, if you want to tell me what's going on."

Tanner remained silent and Kelsey was grateful that he wasn't talking. "I've just got trouble following me, Doc. My husband is dead and his mother has made it clear she's a threat to me."

"If she's threatened you, then call the police and report her."

716

"And if the police take me seriously they go straight to her and start asking questions. And that will lead her right to my door. I know finding me is inevitable, but I wanted the baby born and to be fully settled with her somewhere before that day." And Kelsey didn't add she wanted to be acting responsible and sane and sober and honest. "But you're right. The baby has to have a birth certificate."

Jim dug through a file drawer and found the correct forms. While Kelsey filled them out, the doctor weighed, measured and footprinted the little one.

Then they all went to the courthouse together. Kelsey felt as if a rock pressed against her chest. Dread, the certainty of trouble coming. The doctor said Hope didn't even need to see him. It could have all been skipped.

She saw no choice but to put Derek's name down as father, knowing Carlotta had the means to notice if she spent enough, and there was little doubt Carlotta would spend.

They dropped Jim off at his office and Tanner convinced her to do a bit of shopping, including buying a packable crib and more diapers. Everyone in town who saw them stopped to say hi to Tanner and ask questions.

They had the back end of Tanner's truck half full before they were finished and Tanner paid for everything. And her existence was now known all over this small town.

The guilt she felt for being such a burden on Tanner was barely noticeable buried beneath the fear of Carlotta Blake.

They drove for home.

Kelsey was reminded of that first day, with the snarling wolf.

Carlotta had her own version of teeth and claws. And she was coming to eat Kelsey up. It was only a matter of time.

CHAPTER 10

December 21 — Hope is three weeks old
A ruckus at the back door jerked Kelsey's head up. That wasn't Tanner's voice.

She snatched a sleeping Hope out of the crib and raced into the bedroom, slamming the door loud enough that anyone looking for her would know exactly where she'd gone.

Frantically she looked around the room, wishing for a hiding place.

"Kelsey, come on out." Tanner, sounding cheerful and relaxed, not like a man bringing trouble. "My brother's here."

A shuddering breath escaped Kelsey's laboring lungs. Not Carlotta. Not yet. But a week had passed since Kelsey had filed that birth certificate. It felt like she'd waved a red cape at a bull.

His brother?
Another person in Tanner's house was jarring. Seeing the doctor had proved disastrous, but they'd driven away from the house. They'd gone looking for that trouble — none

had found them here.

Looking around the pretty room, she though what a sanctuary this house had been for her. She'd regained her strength after labor and delivery. She'd learned to walk and bounce in just the right way. Hope had settled into nursing.

A visitor felt like an invasion. Like there was a rip in the fabric of her quiet little universe and a Mongol Horde was riding in.

No offense to Tanner's brother, or Mongolians who had almost certainly moved on from their Horde phase.

Gathering her courage, she hugged Hope and left her room to face this intrusion into her sanctuary.

"Kelsey, this is my brother Silas. Silas Harden."

A man who looked like Tanner — only with brown eyes instead of Tanner's enthralling hazel, stared at Kelsey as if she had two heads. Or, probably more fair to say, he stared at her as if a woman he'd never met had moved into his brother's house and had a baby.

Then slowly a smile bloomed on Silas' face and he turned that almost blinding grin on Kelsey. "Can I hold her?"

Kelsey hoped he meant the baby.

It turned out Tanner's brother Silas Harden was in fact, very close to an invading horde. Especially because it seemed he was the first.

Somehow, Hope was snatched from Kelsey and the talk was all about cattle and a surprise baby and Christmas and a bunch of names Kelsey had never heard before while Tanner, who she'd never thought of as quiet, barely tossed in a comment now and then. Kelsey had been making dinner and so she went back to it without a baby to juggle and she'd made plenty. She heard Tanner invite Silas to stay and eat. Kelsey set a new place at the table, thinking how odd it looked with three rather than two. She focused completely on cooking and tuning out the invader. Then Tanner said her name rather loudly, as if he'd said it a few times already.

"So are you up to it, Kels? My family can be exhausting, and you're not fully recovered from having Hope. Still, I think we oughta do it. I'd rather have them on the road than us with Hope."

"What?" Kelsey was setting a pot of chili on the table and she heard what Tanner said, but she'd paid no attention to the rest of the conversation.

"Christmas Eve at our house. I told Silas the family should come here. It's not the big family gathering, we do that later, in the middle of January because everyone has their own get together on Christmas. But my immediate family will be here." Tanner looked around at the room. "It'll be so great, we haven't had it here in years. It's the twenty-first, so we've got four days. We need more chairs."

The kitchen table sat six. There was a bigger table in a room off the back that sat ten. They needed more chairs? "H–how many in your immediate family?"

Tanner looked at Silas, who of course started talking. "Grandma and Grandpa will be here. That blizzard scared Great-Grandma and Great-Grandpa off so they're staying in Arizona. And Holly, Ashley, and Amanda will bring the kids. Shorty's got a new girlfriend, not sure how serious it is. She may come or not."

As if one more person changed much when he'd just named off about ten. "Shorty?"

"Our youngest brother." Tanner rolled his eyes as he sat up to the steaming chili pot and began serving himself. "He's always got a new girlfriend."

"So that makes about twenty of us." Silas pulled a chair up and sat down.

"Twenty?"

"Yeah." Silas pulled the bowl away from Tanner and Tanner didn't fight over it, of course Silas still had Hope so maybe Tanner had planned to hand the bowl over to begin with. "I can seat sixteen but it'll be a squeeze. And I've got four folding chairs but I loaned them out to Mom for Thanksgiving. I'll call her and tell her to bring them back along with her folding table. If Shorty brings his girlfriend he should warn us because I might need more than four chairs."

Tanner nodded. "I'll write this down."

"Twenty people, in your immediate family?" Kelsey's mind was boggled.

"Yeah, my sisters are all married and have a herd of kids between them. And Aunt Maddie always comes, her kids are grown and moved away except for Suzie. Uncle Leon is dead and Suzie's husband's a long haul trucker. He's not going to get home until early Christmas Day, they haven't got any kids yet. So two more."

Silas gave her a worried frown. "Did you want to go home for Christmas, Kelsey? Tanner can help you get whereever you need to go."

Kelsey shook her head with almost violent motions. "No." Wow, she'd about yelled that.

She calmed down . . . outwardly, "That is, I mean," She cleared her throat, "Um . . . no." There that sounded calm "I have no one to go home to. I'm staying."

Somehow, though she'd tried to sound cheerful and calm, the last sentence had sounded like a vow said before the Lord. It occurred to her that Tanner might have too kind a heart to tell her to move along. What was he gonna do, serve her with an eviction notice? Call a cop?

She considered making him do that should he decide to get rid of her. She could just burrow in and make him force her out. Hopefully in a county this small they wouldn't have an available SWAT team.

"Okay, then," Silas gave her a weird look. Definitely noticing she'd overreacted. "Mom will be over here like a shot now that the road is cleared."

"They got snow plows over the high pass?"

"Yep, it's a pleasant surprise. I figured they'd leave it for the winter but I guess the drifts blew off in enough places they decided the county could afford to clear it. One of these snowstorms will close it up for the winter." Silas looked over at Kelsey, "Then it's about an hour drive from Mom and Dad's place here, that high road is a short cut, but it's a minimum maintenance road, no gravel, lots of ruts."

"Your mother is coming?" In her panic at having twenty people stop in somehow that hadn't registered. How could they talk about snow removal at a time like this? Kelsey needed to clean, and cook and dust and make curtains and —"

"Yep, she'll handle everything, Kels," Tanner grinned like he didn't have a single brain in his thick head.

"But she'll see the dust. She'll think I'm not taking care of the house properly."

"Uh, that's because you're not taking care of the house properly, and why would you? I'm the one who never cleans. And she knows that and expects to bring some order here. She lived here for years, and I think she enjoys dusting."

"No one enjoys dusting, Tanner. Are you insane?"

"You're acting like it's your house, Kelsey." Silas ran a hand through his dark hair, eliminating the dents left by his cowboy hat. "Any reason you've gotten to thinking of it as such?"

Silas grinned and waggled his eyebrows in such a suggestive way that Kelsey felt her face heat up. She was finding much to despise about Silas Harden.

And all while she was despising him he sat there holding Hope with more assurance and ease than she had.

She glared at him, and he just smiled bigger, the moron.

Chapter 11

December 24 — Christmas Eve

"They're here, Kels." Tanner loved Christmas. And he was looking forward to his family meeting Kelsey.

"Here? I thought they were coming for dinner, it's just past noon." Kelsey shouted from the bedroom where she was nursing the baby. "I'm not ready for company."

A grinned quirked his lips. Ever since Silas had left Kelsey had been in a panic. Cleaning, baking. She'd sent him out to cut greenery to decorate his house. He looked fondly at his little electric tree sitting on the end table beside his couch. It was two feet tall, it came pre-decorated and pre-lit. He'd opened the box, dragged the tree out, bent its branches a little, then set it on the table and plugged it in. It made the whole room cheerful and festive.

Kelsey seemed to think it wasn't enough. She'd tried to make him hike around to find a fresh tree but there were no decorations —

the only ones he had were permanently attached to his electric tree. She'd settled for pine boughs, which she'd laid on the fireplace mantle and over the doors and on top of the refrigerator.

Apparently the top of his refrigerator was a horror show all its own. She'd scrubbed a long time before she'd put pine branches up there.

Who knew?

Kelsey exploded from the bedroom and looked around, her eyes wide with fear, then she gave him a look of pure terror and darted back into her room, slamming the door. "Don't let anyone in here until I'm dressed."

He hoped she meant her room because there would be no keeping his mom and dad out of the house. He' grinned again. The woman only had two pairs of jeans and about four shirts. How much time could she possibly need?

Then his grin faded. He probably should have gone to town and bought her dressier clothes. It had never occurred to him and she'd never asked. She'd never asked for anything, and she'd yet to go three hours without thanking him for climbing down that slope for the few clothes she owned.

The front door banged open and his mother came in. "Merry Christmas, Tanner. Where's the baby?" She threw her arms wide and enveloped him with a hug. Tanner loved his mom and considered himself about the luckiest guy in the world to have his family.

Dad came in next. His brown eyes were like Silas's which always gave Tanner a twinge of being left out. The hazel color popped up now and then in the family. It was said that unusual eye color went all the way back to Belle Tanner. And Dad, Tanner Harden IV, didn't leave him out of anything. He was smiling, his arms full of gaily wrapped presents.

"Merry Christmas, Son."

Tanner heard another motor and caught a glimpse of a red truck. Shorty was here.

It had never crossed his mind to warn Kelsey his family would show up early and stay late. It was Christmas Eve, of course they'd want to make a day of it. He'd half expected Mom to show up at eight a.m.

"Where's that baby?" Mom quit strangling him.

"Kelsey's got her in the bedroom. She's changing. She'll be right out."

The bedroom door opened. Kelsey emerged, looking a lot like she'd looked before she spent time getting ready. She always looked terrific to Tanner. More than terrific. Beautiful. He saw her nervousness. She tilted her head in a way that reminded him of a shy child who wished she could hide behind her mom's skirts.

Poor woman, the crowd had just begun.

Shorty came in. Tanner rushed to Kelsey's side. Barely beat his mom there.

"Can I hold her?" Mom started in cooing. Tanner had heard it all before. Mom loved babies. "You named her Hope? That's so beautiful, such a pretty name for a pretty little girl."

"Mom, this is Kelsey Blake. Kelsey, my mom, Dorothy Harden."

"Just call me mom, it gets too complicated otherwise."

Tanner wasn't sure what was complicated about calling a woman by her name, but he let that go. Dad was coming in with a stack of Tupperware containers. Mom would have baked all Tanner's favorite cookies and she was a hand with the Christmas candy, too. And there would be the makings for oyster soup, plus the fixings for several kinds of sandwiches. Christmas Eve dinner Harden style.

"And this is my baby brother Shorty." Shorty came in, and Tanner marveled at how completely his 'little brother' had outgrown his name. Shorty was three inches taller than Tanner and the parson's collar was the finishing touch. Nothing Shorty-like about him. In fact the name probably hadn't qualified since Shorty had gotten past the Terrible Twos.

Shorty had his arms full. In the last two years since he'd finished Bible College and come back to Helena to preach, Shorty had taken charge of the Christmas Eve chili.

Shorty set it all on the table and approached just as Mom got the baby away from Kelsey.

Tanner quickly introduced his brother to keep her from fighting Mom for the baby. A tug of war would be unseemly and bad for Hope. Not to mention, Kelsey would surely lose.

"And this is my baby brother Todd. We call him Shorty."

Kelsey looked up, shaking her head. "Not a good nickname."

Grinning, Todd shook her hand with great warmth. "Thank you, Kelsey and only my two meathead big brothers call me Shorty. I'm Todd."

"And you're a minister, Todd?"

"Yes, I'm pastor of the Good Shepherd Church in Helena."

Kelsey smiled and shook Todd's hand for too long to suit Tanner. He's have kicked up a fuss if his front door hadn't been thrown open again.

"Aunt Maddie."

His aunt had a good heart but she was a tough old bird. They'd gotten used to her brusque ways, and Tanner loved her fiercely. Suzie was right behind, carrying a load. Tanner thanked God that the girl was stuck working for her mother so no one else had to do it.

Before he finished greeting Maddie and

Suzie, his sisters piled in the house with their rambunctious children.

He heard his mom chattering and all three of his sisters were angling for turns holding the baby, so he left Kelsey in their hands and helped haul in the food and gifts that his family had brought.

Todd started cooking. Mom dragged all the women into the kitchen and they set out all the delicious Christmas goodies, which Tanner, and everyone else, started sampling.

He caught a glimpse of Kelsey a few times and she was always smiling. It looked genuine and Tanner didn't know what he could do about it if it wasn't.

A laugh he hadn't heard before, carefree and joyful drew his attention and he realized it was Kelsey. He'd never heard her laugh, at least not like this. The sound of it tugged something so deep inside him, plans for Kelsey and Hope sprung to life in him. It was too soon to speak of them of course, but he decided then and there Kelsey and the baby weren't going anywhere.

He was too busy to think about how he could convince her of that, but her car was under a snow drift at the bottom of a ravine so he had plenty of time.

The whole day was a huge success. They opened presents and Tanner was delighted that Kelsey got a few and embarrassed he hadn't thought of such a thing.

731

Mom had, and all three of his sisters. Hope was given so many gifts it was practically a baby shower and having the party here, where the family roots went so deep, made him proud to carry on the family name.

Todd made a huge mess of his kitchen cooking chili but the boy was a good cook and there was a chair for everyone. Mom had even brought extra bowls and spoons.

They were easing away from the table, stuffed full. Everyone talking. Kelsey had even relaxed and was visiting with Todd as if they were old friends while his sisters cooed over the baby.

Everything was so perfect he felt a chill. Goosebumps rose on his arms. What was the expression? Like someone had walked over his grave? He'd never known exactly what that meant but it was bad, considering he had to be dead for it to mean anything.

And then his door slammed open and a woman stormed in, followed by two men in police uniforms.

"That's her officer!" Pink tipped fingernails long and sharp enough to slice salami jabbed right at Kelsey. "Arrest that woman. She kidnapped my grandchild."

"Carlotta!" Kelsey gasped and leapt to her feet. She held Hope in her arms and began backing away.

Where to hide? What to do?

Carlotta Blake was as fearsome as ever. Her white hair was chic and spiky. As tidy as if she had a personal hairdresser who traveled with her everywhere. Her make-up was flawless and accentuated her glinting eyes and sharp cheekbones. Stepping in from the cold she even blew a cloud of steam out of her nose . . . or maybe she'd finally learned how to breathe fire.

All she needed was a Dalmatian coat and a long cigarette holder and she'd be a dead ringer for Cruella DeVille.

Only not as nice.

"I am Carlotta Blake. I have legal custody of that baby. She's an unfit mother and a danger to her child. I demand you give the baby to me right now."

As suddenly as she'd seen Carlotta, she saw only Tanner's back.

Tanner stood between Kelsey and danger. Her own personal knight in shining armor. It hit hard and deep that she was in love with him. It was too fast, and they'd only known each other through traumatic circumstances, but the feeling was real and solid. What's more she knew she'd love this man for the rest of her life.

It made what she'd felt for Derek a pale imitation of love. A mockery of the sacrament that being married to Tanner would be. And she begged God in that moment to forgive her for not being wise. And asked to be so now.

He spoke loud and clear. "Kelsey is this child's mother. She's no kidnapper."

Kelsey peeked around Tanner's broad shoulders. Just having him there, standing between her and her worst nightmare helped her get her brain to work. Running, that's all she'd been able to think of. But there was nowhere to run and maybe, thanks to Tanner, she didn't have to.

"What's going on, Tanner?" One of the lawmen who stood on either side of Carlotta spoke.

"I'd ask you the same question, Hank. What are you doing out here on Christmas Eve accusing Kelsey of kidnapping? I helped deliver the baby and she's got a valid birth certificate, which I signed. There's no question of kidnapping."

"And you've left Bonnie home alone to come all the way out here?" Mom asked.

"Sorry, Aunt Dorothy."

Aunt Dorothy?

But Tanner had said they had family far and wide. And Kelsey could see that Hank looked so much like Tanner he must be family.

"We had no choice." Hank sounded helpless. "She has paperwork claiming custody of the baby."

"Did you check the date on it?" Tanner asked. "Because this woman is her mother-in-law and she's been chasing after Kelsey since before the baby was born, bribing judges, getting witnesses to make false accusations. Her behavior put Kelsey and the baby in danger. Instead of protecting and caring for Kelsey she's made Kelsey's life a torment. She drove halfway across the country, trying to escape these baseless accusations."

Aunt 'County Judge' Maddie stormed up to Hank. "Let's see this paperwork."

Hank smiled sheepishly and pointed at Carlotta. "She's got it, but we showed it to the county attorney and he said it was in order."

"Pete looked at this and said it was all right?"

Hank shrugged. "Yup."

"Well, Pete doesn't know his head from a hole in the ground." Maddie turned on Carlotta. "The papers." Maddie thrust out her hand. "Now."

"I'm not letting you touch them."

Maddie's face turned grim. "Fine, then get out. There'll be no arrest and this baby will not be handed over to anyone tonight of all nights. Christmas Eve for goodness sakes."

"Now see here." Mrs. Blake snapped. "You have no right to overrule a legal document."

"I have no right?" Maddie's tone made Kelsey hide behind Tanner again.

Tanner, glanced back and patted Kelsey, then whispered, "She shouldn't make Aunt Maddie mad."

"Who do you think you are?" Carlotta's voice was pure ice. Oh, yeah, she could wear a coat made of puppy fur. No problem.

"I am a judge," Maddie's voice sounded like the crack of doom. Kelsey had the nerve to look around Tanner again. Somehow the rather diminutive judge had grown taller and fiercer and just pure dangerous.

Hank took a step back. The other police officer grabbed hold of the door knob as if he was planning his escape. Carlotta of course, didn't retreat.

Maddie wasn't finished. "I am the person who has legal jurisdiction over this county. I am also a personal witness to this young woman applying for a birth certificate. And my nephew, whom I trust with my life, was a witness to the birth and the legal filing."

"She's homeless on top of everything else."

"No she's not," Tanner said. "She's got a home right here with me, and she and the baby are safe and sound."

"The birth certificate was in order, and I'll certainly not allow a stranger — especially one with no ties to the community — to abscond with a baby. We will settle this during court hours, not here and now. Now either leave here or show me those papers.".

Kelsey trembled at the thought that she almost didn't file the birth certificate . . . of course that's what brought Carlotta here.

Carlotta looked furious enough to explode,

but she fished papers out of her Prada handbag and slammed them at Aunt Maddie so hard Maddie stumbled back a step.

"Be careful how you behave, Mrs. Blake. Shoving me around is very close to assault, and I'm not afraid to order your arrest.

"So in addition to taking this child and running —"

"Not sure you can kidnap a child before it's born," Tanner interjected.

"— she is also living here with a man she's known for only weeks? And you expect the fact that you *trust him with your life,*" Carlotta sneered the words, "to convince the courts that my grandchild is in a decent situation when its mother is hooked up with a virtual stranger?"

"Hooked up?" Tanner shouted. "For Pete's sake she just had a baby. Nothing improper has gone on between us."

"A single man and woman cohabiting is common enough, but my lawyer will add it to everything else to call you unfit."

Maddie had been reading and flipping pages while everyone else fought. She slapped the document closed.

"I'm denying this action," Maddie handed the papers back. "I'm granting Kelsey custody of her child and issuing an injunction until we've had a day in court. Now, leave these premises, Mrs. Blake, unless you want to be charged with trespassing."

"I'm not leaving here without my grand-son."

"It's a baby girl, Mrs. Blake." Maddie crossed her arms and stood her ground. "You don't even know this child. Now go."

The regal tone in Carlotta's voice made Kelsey flinch. "A boy would have been much preferable of course, but regardless, the child's coming with me."

"Oh no she's not." Maddie seemed to grow taller if possible. Kelsey knew she'd obey the woman immediately if it was her.

Tanner whispered, "Uh oh, nobody ever pushes Aunt Maddie around. She enjoys pushing back too much."

"Come on, Mrs. Blake. We have to obey the judge." Hank touched her arm.

"Get your hands off of me." Carlotta snarled and slapped Hank's hand away. Then she tried to charge past Maddie and force her way to Kelsey.

Mom Harden gasped quietly and Todd came up to stand on one side of Tanner while Silas came to the other side. Kelsey was completely blocked from Carlotta. Kelsey found a gap to peek through.

Kelsey was reminded of that wolf that had wanted to tear her apart on the night Hope was born. Tanner had saved her then, too.

Both deputies grappled with Carlotta.

"I'm not leaving here without my grand-child." Carlotta elbowed Maddie but the judge didn't give an inch. "This woman is an unfit mother. She's a thief and a drug user, and I've got the force of law on my side."

The lawmen caught Carlotta to keep her from knocking Maddie over, though Kelsey doubted if that was possible.

Maddie looked at Hank, who stood up straighter even while hanging on doggedly to a squirming mother-in-law. Kelsey thought he might have saluted if his hands hadn't been full.

"Place this woman under arrest for assaulting a judge and a police officer."

Carlotta raged on.

"Add in resisting arrest. Lock her up in the county jail and keep her there until Monday morning. I won't be back in my office until then."

It was Wednesday. Carlotta would be spending five days in jail.

"And the only bail hearing won't be until Monday either, Mrs. Blake. You shouldn't have committed your crimes on a holiday weekend."

Carlotta screamed her outrage as poor Hank and his fellow officer dragged her out of the room.

Hank looked back at Maddie just as he left and grinned. "See you tomorrow for dinner."

Maddie waved cheerfully as Carlotta flailed at the two officers. Then she went to the door and called after them. "Write down every single time she strikes you. I'll find her guilty of every one of them. No one's going to count her as any kind of fit mother with felony assault on her record."

Then Maddie swung the door shut with a resounding thud.

She turned and smiled at the whole room. "If any of you aren't afraid of me already, then you should start." She looked past the row of men in front of Kelsey and caught her eye. "That was your mother-in-law?"

Kelsey nodded.

"I can't believe what you must have had to put up with. What an old bat."

Kelsey felt her knees wobble. "Tanner, help."

He whirled around and caught her as she collapsed.

CHAPTER 12

"Todd! The baby!"

Kelsey's arms went slack and Tanner's little brother made a snag that would've impressed Buster Posey.

Tanner swept Kelsey up in his arms and carried her to the couch. He laid her down and dropped to his knees beside her.

Reaching for her face, he brushed her dark hair back just as his mom came and bulled him aside.

He scrambled out of the way just before he tipped over.

Mom had a damp cloth and pressed it to Kelsey's forehead and cheeks. It reminded him of how kind she'd always been to him when he'd been sick. With six kids it sometimes seemed like the days he was sick were the only ones where he'd gotten much undivided attention. He'd bet big money Mom didn't remember it as fondly.

Tanner jumped to his feet and stood behind Mom, who'd sat on the couch beside Kelsey.

No response yet. Then Aunt Maddie came up beside him.

"Tanner, I'm afraid our Kelsey's got trouble on her hands."

Dad came up on Tanner's other side, then Todd, holding onto Hope. Silas and all three of his sisters stood in a line facing them from behind the couch.

"Trouble? How can such an obviously cruel woman think she can take the baby away from Kelsey?"

"The papers themselves wouldn't do it except for two things."

Tanner braced himself. Aunt Maddie was a brusque woman. She was used to pronouncing sentences on criminals and she had a tendency to make pronouncements with her family, too. But they all teased her about being a judge even off the bench and she would smile and apologize.

But right now she looked as dead serious as he'd ever seen her. She was in full judge mode and he didn't have one single urge to tease.

"What two things."

"One, Kelsey is homeless."

"No she's not!"

Maddie held up a hand so firmly it shut him up. "Yes, she is. This is not her home. She'd homeless and single, she has no visible means of support. Now, normally the solution to that is to apply for welfare benefits

742

and public housing. There are lots of programs available for an indigent woman and child."

"I'm not going to let her go on welfare, Aunt Maddie."

"Normally," Maddie ignored him and went on, "that alone wouldn't be enough to take a child away from his parents. But Kelsey isn't going to get any of that because, judging by what I read about a trust fund and fraud, Kelsey also has a decent amount of money. But rather than tap into it and use it, she'd out here with nothing. It will prevent her from taking advantage of the social safety net."

"Well, then we'll help her figure out how to use her trust fund."

"Fine, but it doesn't look quite . . . rational . . . that she hasn't done it before."

Tanner flinched. "And not being rational is a bad thing in child custody cases?"

"Very bad. And the second thing is Mrs. Blake's documents are all drawn up by some law firm back east with real fancy letter head and about ten partners. I could handle that. They may be a big deal back east but they've got no pull here in Montana. But she's also got a lawyer from in the state. She's got paperwork in that little stack with Moss Bertucci's name on it."

The whole family gasped. A man who'd run for State Attorney General five times. He'd never come close to winning but he'd made himself very famous. He was a ruthless lawyer with a reputation for defending the most disgusting criminals and getting them off. The Harden family had a few brushes with him. They'd never lost but Bertucci would enjoy causing trouble.

Bertucci was known far and wide for his cutthroat tactics. With Bertucci in her corner, Carlotta Blake could very well win and, even if she lost, she could make Kelsey's life miserable for a long time.

"What are we going to do?" Dad asked.

Tanner looked over at him, right into his eyes over Maddie's head.

"We can afford this fight, son, don't worry about that. We can get Jeremy to help."

Tanner's cousin was a good lawyer, and he would fight to the finish.

"The fact that she hired Bertucci is almost an admission that she's dishonest," Todd added, bouncing the baby.

"We all know that, Tanner," Maddie tapped her toe and looked at Kelsey, so still and pale. "But it doesn't mean he won't be hard to beat and make Kelsey's life a misery."

Tanner looked down at his formidable aunt, and repeated his dad's question. "What are we going to do?"

"Well, I've met Kelsey twice now, and I've seen you with her and that baby." Maddie looked at him. Her eyes burning right into his brain. "My advice is to solve the first problem and that will make the second problem mostly go away."

"The first problem?" Tanner didn't know what she was talking about, then he remembered Kelsey had two problems, the second was Bertucci, the first was — "Oh, okay, how do we fix the fact that she'd a homeless, single mother?"

Maddie was silent.

One by one every person in the room turned to look right at him. As if they knew something he didn't.

"There's only one way to solve that problem, Son." Mom looked up from where she knelt by Kelsey.

Tanner saw Kelsey's eyes flutter open and she looked right at him for just a second, so warm, so sweet, so persecuted. He vowed to himself he'd protect her no matter what it took.

"And what way is that?"

Mom said in a quiet voice that echoed thanks to the dead silence in the room. "You solve it by marrying her."

CHAPTER 13

Kelsey gasped and everyone in the room turned on her. She wished she'd remained silent.

"No, Tanner, no. You–you–you —"

Tanner set his mother aside then he dropped down on his knees beside her. "She's right, Kels. We need to get married."

"I can't ask it of you. You've already done so much. You've saved me, you've —"

Tanner scooped her up in his arms and said, "I'm going to talk to her alone. Go on with the Christmas party."

He carried her into her bedroom, and went to a chair in one corner and sat down with her still on his lap.

"Marry me, Kelsey."

"Tanner, I'll ruin your life. Now that Carlotta is here —"

The kiss cut off her refusal and it wasn't hard to let herself be cut off because the man she loved had just proposed. She couldn't let him marry her, not with all the problems she

746

brought with her, but it was so good, so sweet to be asked.

He deepened the kiss and slid his hands up to her face and when he finally came up for air, he rested his forehead against hers. "This is sudden, and your mother-in-law is forcing it, but Kelsey," he pulled back so he could look her in the eye, his hands cradling her face. "We were heading here anyway. Am I alone in being in love?"

She'd already opened her mouth to let this knight in shining armor off the hook . . . and then he'd mentioned love.

Because he must have thought she was going to turn him down again, he kissed her, more deeply, more passionately than he had before. Until she forgot most everything except being held in his arms.

This time when the kiss ended, he said, "This has been between us almost from the first, Kelsey. You know it has. I've thought you were a beautiful, brilliant, decent woman. I've felt so lucky you stumbled into my life. I've felt like God Himself blessed me by giving me a chance to save you and care for you and Hope. But we've been so busy with the baby and the storm and just . . . adjusting, that there's been no talk of feelings or romance. But it's there, at least for me. Tell me that it's there for you, too. Please."

Another kiss, this one nearly scorched her

brain. When it ended she said, "Stop kissing me."

Tanner looked shocked and hurt. Maybe even heartbroken. So she quickly added, "So I can say yes. I love you, too."

The hurt vanished and a smile broke out that was as blinding as summer sunshine.

"If you'd wanted to marry me just to save me, I couldn't have done it. Even though I've fallen completely in love with you." She ran a hand down his sculpted cheek. There was a bit of bristle because he hadn't shaved since morning. It made her fingers tingle all the way to her elbow. No, all the way to her heart. "But to hear you say you love me —."

He snuck in another kiss.

A tear trickled down her face. Tanner pulled away and used one thumb to wipe it away. "I do, Kelsey and I love Hope. I want you both more than I've ever wanted anything."

Another kiss, this one lingered. Finally, Tanner said, "Let's go tell my family, then we can watch Todd and Aunt Maddie argue over who gets to perform the ceremony. We can be married tomorrow, Maddie will open the courthouse and get the marriage certificate for us. And Suzie is a notary. I think she'll let Todd marry us though. We always like to have God bless the marriages in this family."

Then he leaned closer and said, "Hardens marry for life, Kelsey. And we're faithful. I'm planning to do this only once. I want to spend my life with you."

"That sounds wonderful." Kelsey laughed and stood, though her knees were wobbly. Not like when she'd fainted before. This wobble was directly connected to Tanner Harden's skill at kissing and his words of love.

"And then together, as a married couple and you with a good home and a big family to support you, we'll face Bertucci and Carlotta. We'll still have a fight on our hands, but we'll get through it together. I'll just bet when he sees us all facing him in court, he'll fold up his tent and go home. He's ruthless but he knows a lost cause when he sees it."

He held out one of his strong hands, and she took it.

"Tanner, you've seen me through some hard times and I am so thankful for it, but I've almost regained my strength from the birth. You're going to be surprised to find out you have a partner in this marriage, not some damsel in distress who needs to be rescued every few days."

With a smile, Tanner led her to the door and to their future, full of family and love and hope. "I wouldn't have it any other way. We like strong women in this family and you may think I've needed to rescue you, and I guess I have, but you've come through some hard things and you're still standing. I'm not going to be surprised at all."

They went to join his family together and

find their baby, the Hope that had come for
Christmas.

EPILOGUE

Tanner and Kelsey walked arm in arm into the courthouse on Monday morning. Tanner could feel Kelsey's fear and he admitted he was tense. But he had no fear about how this would end up.

Moss Bertucci sat at the front with Carlotta beside him. Tanner and Kelsey took their place beside Jeremy Harden, their lawyer. Bertucci glanced up when they came in, then he did a double take and stared hard.

"Harden? Tanner?" Moss sputtered. "What are you doing here?"

Tanner noticed his mom and dad come in and Silas behind them carrying Hope.

Mom was supposed to be babysitting, what was she doing here? He would have gone back to say hello but he figured Moss's question deserved his full attention. "I'm here to help prove my wife is a good mother to our baby. A great mother."

Bertucci's eyebrows arched nearly to his hair line. "She's your wife?"

Turning on Carlotta, Bertucci said, "You told me she was a single mother, homeless, a thief, and a drug user."

Carlotta sniffed. "She is."

Tanner took Kelsey's hand and extended to display her wedding ring. He'd brought the marriage license along, too and would produce it if necessary. "She's a married woman, we have a lovely home, and I'm willing to swear she's never gotten near any kind of drugs or alcohol."

Jeremy took over. "Your client has a huge financial reason for taking this child from her parents. The facts will show just that."

"Y–your word won't hold up." Bertucci picked up a stack of papers from his desk. "We've got blood tests. Hard evidence."

Jeremy said, "Aunt Maddie, uh . . . I mean, Her Honor, Judge Sawyer, saw the papers about Mrs. Harden failing drug tests and stealing money."

"She only looked at those papers for a few minutes," Carlotta snarled.

"Fortunately, Aunt Maddie has a near photographic memory. She noticed the most recent blood tests my client supposedly failed were taken in Milwaukee in late November. I can prove Mrs. Harden was a thousand miles away from there on the date in question. And once we prove one piece of your evidence is false, I think you'll find it hard to get anyone to believe the rest of it."

Jeremy pulled a sheet of paper out of his briefcase.

Bertucci looked at it. It was a picture of Kelsey on a surveillance tape taken in San Diego at a gas station. Bertucci looked at the time stamp and the sign behind the picture that clearly said Welcome to San Diego.

"Mrs. Harden has given me very clear details of the places she's been in the last month. I suspect some of the other reports your client has will be in conflict with the facts. In fact, from what I know of your client, I suspect all of them will."

"We're searching security tapes and matching receipts she had with her," Todd said, drawing all their attention. At which point Tanner looked behind him and saw the whole courtroom jammed with his family. Aunts, uncles, first, second, third cousins. More pushed into the room filling the aisle, every seat taken.

"Grandpa, Grandma, you drove all this way?" Tanner had just seen them for Christmas.

"Your sister came and got us," Tanner Harden III said, grinning.

Bertucci's eyes nearly bulged as he studied the crowd.

"The picture, Moss." Jeremy thrust it in his hands. "I suggest you take a good look."

Bertucci forced his eyes down and he studied the picture, then shoved papers aside until he got to the failed drug test. Finally, he shook his head and turned to Carlotta. "Everyone in this state knows the Hardens take care of family."

He swung his arm wide at the crowd. "Just look at them. We'll be laughed out of court if I try and persuade a jury Tanner Harden's wife is an unfit mother. I've got a reputation and being laughed at is no part of it."

"You'll do as you're told, Mr. Bertucci. I've paid good money for your representation."

Bertucci stared at Carlotta for a few long seconds then smirked and said, "I quit. Look for a refund check in the mail." He turned and stormed out of the courtroom.

Carlotta stared after her lawyer in shock, then she turned on Kelsey. "This isn't over."

Aunt Maddie said from the door to her chambers, "You're right, Mrs. Blake. You're under arrest for forgery and tampering with evidence and . . ." The judge gave Carlotta a cold smile. "I'm sure I'll think of more. Orderly?" Maddie's voice cracked like a whip. "Arrest that woman."

Carlotta started backing up, toward the exit door. But the aisle was blocked by Hardens and she was stopped cold.

"Fine!" Carlotta snapped. "I'll drop my claims on the child."

"Not good enough, Mrs. Blake. You don't break the law in my courtroom and then get out of it by saying, 'Never mind.' "

The orderly reached her and dragged her out of the room toward the cells to the sound of her squawking.

The whole room erupted into cheers.

Which woke Hope, who started crying. Kelsey rushed to get her as Maddie started banging on with her gavel. Tanner looked and saw a gleam of amusement in Aunt Maddie's eyes. She'd waited through quite a bit of ruckus before she called for order in the court.

Crime must have been slow over Christmas because she didn't seem upset to let the near riot carry on.

When things finally settled down, and Kelsey had been hugged by everyone in the place, Tanner said, "Maddie can you handle Carlotta or do you need us here to help?"

"Go on home. It will give me great pleasure to handle Carlotta Blake all by myself."

Everyone in the place laughed.

"Kelsey," Jeremy spoke during a break in the laughter, "I've begun the work to transfer your trust fund to Hope's name with you as executor. I'll call you when I need you to sign some papers."

"Thank you, Jeremy."

"Now, I want to take my pretty wife home and start teaching her about living in the great state of Montana." Tanner swept his wife away filled with excitement for the future, the joy of the Christmas season, and a love that would last a lifetime brought to him by this beautiful woman and the sweet birth of Hope.

ABOUT THE AUTHOR

Mary Connealy writes romantic comedy with cowboys. She is a Carol Award winner, and a RITA®, Christy, and Inspirational Reader's Choice finalist. She is the bestselling author of the *Wild at Heart* series, *Trouble in Texas* series, *Kincaid Bride* series, *Lassoed in Texas* trilogy, *Montana Marriages* trilogy, *Sophie's Daughters* trilogy, and many other books. Mary is married to a Nebraska cattleman, has four grown daughters, and a little bevy of spectacular grandchildren. Find Mary online at www.maryconnealy.com.

The employees of Thorndike Press hope you have enjoyed this Large Print book. All our Thorndike, Wheeler, and Kennebec Large Print titles are designed for easy reading, and all our books are made to last. Other Thorndike Press Large Print books are available at your library, through selected bookstores, or directly from us.

For information about titles, please call:
(800) 223-1244

or visit our website at:
gale.com/thorndike

To share your comments, please write:
Publisher
Thorndike Press
10 Water St., Suite 310
Waterville, ME 04901